Einstein's Theory of the Blues

Kathy Egbert

Copyright © 2020 Kathy Egbert
All rights reserved.
ISBN: 978-1-911249-51-1

First published 2020 by *AngelView Press*
(an imprint of Huge Jam Publishing)

Sometimes I feel like a motherless child

Sometimes I feel like a motherless child

Sometimes I feel like a motherless child

Long way from home

Long, long way from home...

— Traditional Spiritual

1

Everything is determined, the beginning as well as the end,
by forces over which we have no control.
Albert Einstein

Angels paced in heaven, unsure of their tidings.

And on Earth there was no peace.

Duermete, hija. Sleep, daughter. *Mi hija.* My daughter. *Mi hijita.* My little daughter. *Sh, sh, sh, sh.* The darkness rocked her and held her like a mother. But fear pulled her back from comfort. Fear and pain.

Outside the dark apartment, the city throbbed. Broken hearts begged for mercy, imagined love.

Fierce strobes of light sliced the tiny room into pieces, then abandoned it to darkness.

Teresa sat up, shivering with cold yet damp with sweat. She pushed a fist against her chest to still her racing heart.

"Who were you, baby?" she whispered to the darkness. "And where have you gone?"

Surely it was only a dream.

But no. Not a dream.

Get a grip, get a grip, she chanted to herself, forcing her jaws to unclench.

She carefully sat up and lowered her feet to the floor.

"Davy," she whispered

But Davy was not there. No one was there. She was totally alone in the world.

She held her abdomen and felt anew the waves of cramps that meant her baby was gone. It was not a dream. She had mistaken sex for love, and they had lifted the resulting burden from her.

The most shocking thing about the abortion was that no one was shocked. Kind and professional, calmly going about the grim business as if it were nothing. And, from the instant the baby had been swept from her, she had wanted it back.

Regret pressed down on Teresa's chest until her heart could barely beat.

"Baby, wait. Come back to me. You don't even have a name." Teresa curled up tighter against herself and cried until she could not feel the pain and the erratic loping of her broken heart.

"I will never forget you." Would never forget the bloody burden in the white gauze sock that she had not been meant to see. Would never forget that she, Teresa Chace, had lain down in a Dallas clinic not eight blocks from where a bullet had splattered President Kennedy's brains onto his horrified wife's pretty pink suit, and let them rip from her something she hadn't known she loved until it was gone. He. She. They wouldn't tell her if the fetus was a boy or a girl. They knew, but they wouldn't tell her.

Duermete, mi hija. Sleep my daughter...

Angel benignisimo de mi guarda... the childhood prayer to her guardian angel... Why in Spanish? Teresa Chace was certainly not an Hispanic name. Why did she dream in one language and speak in another? She had the faintest memory of an old man, stooped and white-haired. *Papi,* she called him, with a Spanish inflection. Was he someone who had loved her? Cared for her? Or only a little girl's idea of God the Father pieced together from years of Sunday School at the Avila Children's Home?

In her life she had only borrowed love. Or stolen it. Dad Morgan, the home's gentle founder and father figure, had fathered them as well as an ever-fluctuating census of a hundred orphans could be fathered. They had all loved Dad Morgan in their poignant orphan ways. They sang at his behest – duets, trios, groups – at the funerals of the town's prestigious but preacherless departed. Chased pigs for him at the rodeo fund-raiser. Gave testimonies at every drop of every hat. They hugged his paunch until it got so large that his health was endangered, then hid the ice cream bars from him while he dieted. He was easy to love, with his tall, slow manner and doleful basset hound eyes underlined with dark bags from years

2

of worry and work.

Then she had moved away and found it easy to steal love from other lonely people in the city. Only too easy. And, once stolen, to take it again because there was no longer any reason not to. But there was never enough love, and it never stayed, never healed the well of loneliness inside.

Only Davy's love was not borrowed or stolen. No, with Davy it was something else. *But you can't love a cripple; not in that way.* That's what everyone told her. In the years since their childhood she heard the words change — crippled, handicapped, disabled, differently-abled — but they always meant the same thing. That her beloved Davy was not like other boys. That it would not be right to burden him with her love or for him to expect hers. That they should be content with their sibling affection, fostered together there in the makeshift "family" of the children's home.

Teresa remembered the day at work. The day after the abortion. Determined to forget the pain, the loss. Remembered clicking into the cavernous exhibit hall, lined with artwork going up for a new exhibit, crates awaiting those coming down.

The *Einstein Papers* exhibit had been there for months. Posters and papers that put a very human face on the famous icon, the genius of physics and math. Teresa and her co-workers were there to re-crate it all then hang an art exhibition from England.

Vanessa, tall, big-boned and blonde, swayed on the ladder just above Teresa's reach. "Hand me the panel..." she grunted, trying to hold onto the drill and bracket and reach for the wood all at the same time, all in her usual no-nonsense, high self-concept manner. Teresa felt so puny by comparison. Small and dark and inadequate against Vanessa's Nordic confidence.

Teresa rested the large panel holding new paintings on the edge of the ladder and heaved it slowly up towards Vanessa's steady outstretched hand. She remembered that part. Remembered seeing the beautiful painting "Night with Her Trail of Stars" by E.H. Hughes... the angel carrying a baby close to its heart while so many other babies clung to her robes flying through the beautiful night sky. Why did it sing to her soul even while it broke her heart? Her own wounded heart trembling to think of the little girl that the great Einstein had lost. His daughter. Lieserl. Never to be found or known of again.

Some of the great icon's quotes were on the panels coming down to pack and send off.

"Life isn't worth living, unless it is lived for someone else."

She could feel her heart faltering within her, wanting her to die like the baby she had killed. She wavered, but kept working as Vanessa handed them down.

"The most beautiful thing we can experience is the mysterious.
It is the source of all true art and all science. He to whom this emotion is a stranger, who can no longer pause to wonder and stand rapt in awe, is as good as dead: his eyes are closed."

And then she'd come undone. She could not remember fainting, really, or Vanessa taking her home. She could only remember the explosion deep inside herself, the sparks of loss, loneliness, longing to be loved, the shower of unresolved grief, abandonment.

Teresa's soul wandered free, sniffing around her failing body. *Wake up and save yourself!*

She awoke from drowsing with a start and dialed Davy's number with trembling fingers, counting the three long rings before a voice finally broke the panic.

"Davy." She could already feel her body relaxing just to know that he was there. She loved Davy, even though she could not trust that love.

"Teresa..."

"You won't believe what I've done now...."

But it wasn't Davy. It was the 911 operator, asking her what the trouble was. And someone else, someone sensible but alien living inside her body, saying that she was sick. An angel, there to take care of the shivering animal body Teresa could no longer claim as her own.

Brisk strangers were at the door. At the door to take care of Teresa. The silent angel let them in because Teresa was too sick.

"We're going to admit you into the hospital overnight, dear. Just to be sure you're okay." They snapped the metal railings up and tucked the blankets in around her like a baby in a crib.

God doesn't give you more than you can bear, she remembered the promise.

Unless you die of something.

In the emergency room cubicle she mumbled the facts to the shining white figures, mistaking them for mercy.

Shakiness? Sweating? Heart pounding? Their questions were endless. Cold hands, dry mouth, dizziness, fainting spells?

Yes, yes, yes, to all of them, yes.

Name?

Teresa Chace.

Next of kin?

Good question.

No, she hadn't eaten today. Yesterday? Who knew?

She seemed to be getting the answers right; they nodded and scribbled and seemed satisfied.

It felt like she was a contestant on a quiz show and her category choice was "Things No Human Cares About" for a thousand.

Health problems?

Was the abortion a problem or a solution?

Medications?

Had she taken anything? No, she didn't think so. But she could use something for these cramps.

One doctor, too young for his jaded countenance, conferred with an older one. A group of three holding clipboards looked intently on. All big, strong, beefy boys who had never been sick a day in their lives.

"Any family history of…?" they began.

Of anything? They would never sit still for the long version.

"No."

Mother?

No.

Father?

No.

She only had questions of her own and no answers for them. Had she been placed at the orphanage doorstep by angels? Were they rescuing her or driving her away, their flaming swords hiding Eden? Strangers, remarkable for their kindness, had saved her. They may have even loved her; who could tell?

I said to my soul "Be Still," she whispered T.S. Eliot's poem to calm herself while she waited for their verdict. Memorized, like the Einstein quotes, from exhibit panels and displays at the gallery where she worked.

And wait without hope. Be willing to wait without hope for the love she had lost with that unborn tiny soul. Then wondered if she even knew what love was.

For hope would be hope for the wrong thing.

Yes.

Wait without love.

For love would be love of the wrong thing.

There is yet faith… The lyrical rhythm helped her stop shaking.

But the faith and the love and the hope are all in the waiting.

Wait without thought, for you are not ready for thought…

The older doctor, dressed in a business suit with a diamond tie tack, separated himself from the traffic of white.

"We'll put you in and observe you…" He never touched her.

Yes. Observe me. And then the tears came. The tears she had not dared shed for herself, the baby she had lost, the love she had wanted. Davy. More tears than they could understand, or she could explain.

They drugged her tears and let her fall into dull, cotton-mouthed complaisance, hope and despair rising against each other like waves on a storming sea. The white figures became vague, just as likely to be angels or devils.

She fell into hours of bottomless, dreamless sleep while an IV pumped drops of the nutrients she had ignored too long into her exhausted veins. She would just sleep until she disappeared.

When Teresa finally awoke and opened her swollen eyes, a round pair of luminous eyes stared back at her in the dim light of the room. Round shining orbs made larger by the thinnest ethereal face, the bones of the skull jutting around them.

"My name is Martha Ann," the voice belonging to the eyes whispered. "I will take care of you." She pulled the blanket up from the foot of the bed and straightened it, as if to assure Teresa of her sincerity and capability.

A nurse? No, she wore a patient gown identical to Teresa's.

Teresa lay still and studied the luminous orbs of covered-over sadness that were Martha Ann's solicitous eyes. Sadness so incurably deep and hopeless that a stone veneer of bovine peace capped it off forever. It would take more than a passing prince to wake whatever lay at the bottom of the pool of Martha Ann's eyes. The swollen bruise around one eye, her extreme thinness, and the misshapen bandage around her head made her look like a caricature of a person in a hospital. A TV cartoon.

"You want to sit up now?" Her eyes widened, the brows lifting over their swollen sockets, her hands flying from IV to nurse call button to blanket to guard rail to her own gown sleeve and back around with dizzying quickness.

Teresa's bladder, screaming in pain at being ignored through the hours of drugged sleep, finally gave her a reason to rise.

"Yes. Thank you." Her tongue was not her own, clumsy with dryness.

Martha Ann folded her blanket down gingerly, neatly, pushed the button in the guard rail to raise Teresa's head, then lowered the rail itself. Her motions were the studied, deliberate, jerky motions of the elderly or infirm or mentally impaired. But she knew everything there was to know. How to gather the IV tubing close to the pole and guard the wheels of the base from the bed legs and Teresa's toes. How to take Teresa to the minuscule bathroom and wait as discreetly as any nurse. How to raise the IV bag up high to flush the tiny tube of blood that appeared at Teresa's wrist back into her veins.

As the slow, foggy days unfolded, it turned out that Martha Ann was the badly beaten, most likely brain-damaged, wife of a wealthy councilman who, though not inclined to divorce her, nevertheless periodically beat her into silent submission. She wrote her name – Martha Ann, MARTHA ANN – on every scrap of paper in the room: magazines, nurses' notes, lined auxiliary stationery. The round, childish scrawl even appeared on the paper mat under Teresa's supper tray. By the third day, it no longer surprised Teresa to move her plate and see it there. And no longer surprised her to see Martha Ann – taller, bigger-boned than herself – pinch the skeletal thinness of her body and cluck to herself about her fat. Teresa's own tiny frame, not much bigger than a child's, seemed robust by comparison.

"Get over it, Martha Ann," she teased her. "You'll end up as a silhouette on 'Geraldo'."

But Martha Ann was not cheered; had, apparently, lost the ability to be cheered. But had clung to her gift of mercy. It was as if Gods' own mercy filled the center of her soul, leaving it tender and raw and innocent, subject to being pierced and scarred over and over again. As if it were nothing. As if it were what she expected.

When the flock of white-coated doctors made their rounds, Martha Ann fluttered away like a nervous little sparrow, robe flapping.

"Good morning ladies," the older doctor greeted them as Martha Ann skittered away, leaving Teresa to answer.

"Am I being discharged?" Teresa thought the group of six meant something momentous.

"Oh, no, honey, not yet," the nurse said. "You have several more tests scheduled."

When they left, Martha Ann appeared again as if by magic, her eyes solicitously searching Teresa's for reassurance.

"They had their chance, Martha Ann. I'm off to Lourdes."

Then Martha Ann went to the closet and returned with an iPad, handing it to Teresa like a prize.

"What? For me?" Teresa took it gently, waited for Martha Ann to tell her something.

"You can look things up," she whispered. Then turned and went out of their room and down the hall.

Teresa found herself wondering about the poet, William Ernest Henley, her last image of her job. Discovered his poem *Margaritae Sorori* was what inspired the gorgeous painting of the night angel with babies hanging on her robes and one in her arms. Death. The last word. And again, her heart ached with the baby she had sent away. Like Einstein's Lieserl, never heard from again. Like herself, abandoned. Lost.

She wondered what *margaritae sorori* meant. Then found a theory the poem was about Henley's daughter who died. And that *margarita* was Latin for pearl. And yes, that Henley's only child was a daughter, Margaret, who died. Teresa laid the tablet aside and cried tears for them all... for Lieserl, for Margaret, for her own nameless one. For all the lost and wounded children in the world, clinging like babies to that angel's gown. When her tears slowed, sleep overtook her. And dreams of her lost baby. Then a young girl reaching across a creek to her, smiling and full of joy and peace. Who? Teresa dreamt she leaned toward her and the girl handed her a pearl. She wrapped her hand around it.

Then awoke to realize the nurse was taking her oxygen level with a small instrument in her hand.

And Martha Ann behind her nodding and smiling as she crawled up into her own hospital bed.

So it was for Martha Ann that she finally ate. To Martha Ann that she confessed. By poor, damaged Martha Ann that she was absolved. Only the terrible innocence of Martha Ann that she would miss when she left the barren halls of Grace Community Hospital.

And, finally, it was Martha Ann who showed her where to find a phone with an outside line where you could make a collect call with some privacy.

"Davy?" she whispered. His deep, tender voice was real this time. Just like she remembered it.

"Teresa?"

"Yes, Davy. What's left of me, anyway."

"Are you all right? You sound different."

"Yes." And she began to cry. With relief for the concern in his voice.

"I dreamed I called you the other night…"

"I've had you on my mind so much. You haven't called in a long time…"

"But it wasn't you. I called 911. I was sick, Davy. And so scared. I wanted it to be you. But my guardian angel or someone called 911 and they came and took me to the hospital."

"You're still there?"

"Yes."

She listened to the pulsing hum of his breath caused by the palsy, pictured him considering this fact.

"I can be there by tomorrow, Teresa. I'll leave tonight."

"No, don't come. I just want to come home." She hadn't known she would say that. That she thought of him as home.

"Here?" His voice was breathless.

"But maybe you won't want me when you hear what I've done, Davy."

"Oh, Teresa. Don't you remember? We promised."

"Yes. But…"

"Forever."

"But…"

"No matter what."

She wanted to tell him everything. From the baby that was lost to the merciful luminosity of Martha Ann's eyes. But she could not. Not yet.

They murmured back and forth, sharing their lives. Davy's new internet company, his physical therapy. Teresa's artwork, the *Einstein Papers* exhibit. Their shared memories of their childhood at the Avila Children's Home.

"Davy… remember the baby animals? At the home. The orphaned kittens and crippled guineas we rescued? There was always a wounded animal that showed up that would have been easy prey for the coyotes and rats if you hadn't found a way for us to save them. They broke your heart, but provided an easy source of affection too, didn't they?"

She thought of the long nights with tiny doll baby bottles and mewling little hopeless, motherless babies, dangling light bulbs to warm the fuzzy chicks eagerly pecking at the food scattered around hopelessly crippled feet.

Davy's warm, pulsing laughter cheered her. "Yes. So many. You had a heart for that too, Teresa."

"And Rainbow?" Teresa's voice broke now, and she cried with fresh grief at all their losses, hers and Davy's. Rainbow – her own ironic name for a jet-black mutt, her only pet at the home. Surprised by a fast truck on the lonely dirt road by the home, Rainbow's little body had made an unmistakable soft mound with the earth. Another loss in the haven where they huddled like cattle hoping, praying against loss every day. As if any sorrow ever promised it would not return. As if God, like lightning, would not strike twice. But there she lay, mute and bloody, with Davy's trembling form hunched over her by the side of the road, tears, holy tears, falling from his eyes onto her furry loss. Only Davy had seen and cried, broken-hearted, over the stilled softness of Rainbow. Because she was Teresa's. She had seen then that Davy loved her.

"I'll be there tomorrow," Davy pressed.

"No. I can't. You can't..." She wanted to trust Davy's love, but could not. Wanted to tell him everything. How she had lost everything again. How the lost and motherless child she had been was now a grown woman with only grief and loneliness to show for the years. How no one cared for her soul. About Lieserl...

"I can, Teresa. Things are different for me now. Better. Let me help you. Come home. You can start over."

"Just say my name, Davy. Say my name a hundred times."

"Teresa," he whispered tenderly. "Come home."

Home? Only the children's home, where she had spent most of her twenty-five years, was home. "The Valley," the locals called it, the rich, flat delta of the Rio Grande. In the Hispanic tradition of subdivisions named Las Palmas, Los Lagos, Los Palos, the kids had called their rural enclave of cottages, church, and school "Los Boonies."

Before that? It was lost to her. Left at the Home at five, she could not really remember that other time. Her mother, her father, her connection to the world. All lost. There was no "home," for her, only *the* home. She did not think of her tiny apartment in Dallas as home, just a place to sleep and keep her few belongings while she worked at the museum in downtown Dallas and took painting classes at night.

But Davy was home. He, himself. Home in the way that mattered. And through him she maintained other connections, shared other memories with their common friends.

"Soon. You find me a job and I will come and stay a while with you. Do you have room?"

"Yes. Lots of room. I can come and get you. I have a car and driver. It's a ten-hour drive…"

"No. It is enough that you will be there waiting. And I have to stay a while longer. More tests. When I am stronger, I will come home."

"Okay." Reluctant, but he knew her, knew she would not relent.

Martha Ann fluttered back to her side looking worried and pointing to their room back down the hall. "I think the doctors have frightened my good friend Martha Ann again, so I'd better go, Davy. Thank you."

"Teresa. Everything I have is yours. You know that."

The tears came again. "Thank you, Davy."

She laid the phone carefully in its cradle, lifted the shoulder of her gown to wipe the tears from her face, and turned to Martha Ann who was dancing nervously around her. "Do you know who YOU are, Martha Ann?" she asked brightly, cheerfully.

Martha Ann looked at her hopefully, but confused.

"You're the good Queen Esther, from the Bible. Do you know her?"

Martha Ann blinked. "No."

"She took her chances with the king and did what she had to do to save her people. She became the queen. You take care of us all here, you know that?"

Martha Ann beamed. And straightened a little to be a queen.

The next day there was a new doctor to see, a kinder one. Dr. Santos, with answers to her questions, not just endless probings of his own. His office was a windowless, artless room strewn with stacks of magazines, books, charts and papers.

"Do you have any questions for me, Miss Chace?" he smiled, looking at her. His face was homely – thin and pale – but beautiful in its humanity.

"Well, yes." She was so surprised that nothing came to mind at first.

"Yes?" He folded his hands in his lap and waited.

"Well, am I sick or am I crazy?"

He looked at her harder for one second and then fed her soul with the one thing it was starving for in this place: he laughed. Tipped his homely, beautiful El Greco head back and laughed out loud.

And so they talked. As if they were human, as if it mattered, as if she were not all alone in the world.

"Who loves you, Miss Chace?" It was the first important question of the millions of questions. Who indeed?

"Only Davy."

"Brother?... Boyfriend?"

"All that... and more. But he's handicapped." Which word to use? How to explain Davy?

"So are we all." His smile was as tender as Martha Ann's.

"Yes."

"Do you love him?"

"Oh, yes."

"But he wasn't the father of your baby?"

A small shock ran through her. "Oh, no." The thought that Davy would even know about the baby... the abortion... turned her stomach over. She wanted to run to him, be with him. But she didn't want him to know what she had done.

"Still, it is something more than a platonic relationship, no?"

"I think Davy is one thing. The world thinks he is another. I know him for what he really is – like in Beauty and the Beast – because I read the book. Loving him is easy. I've always loved him. But complicated too. He has cerebral palsy. His life is hard enough without me in it."

"And he has always loved you?"

"Yes."

"But you don't talk about sharing your lives?"

"There is a lot unspoken between us, Dr. Santos. We are orphans who grew up like brother and sister and promised to always care for each other. More has never seemed right."

He chuckled as he wrote in the file for a minute, then looked up at her again. "Tell me, then, about your work. You're an artist?"

"Well, I don't know if I dare say I am. It's what I love; I have studied art as much as I could while working. I was working on the *Einstein Papers* exhibit at the museum when all this happened."

"The Einstein Papers," he repeated reverentially. "Yes. I've been meaning to go see the exhibition."

"It is closed now. A lot of surprises there. From the great man." She sagged a bit to remember hanging the huge panel, a black and white silhouette of the famous head with its wild shock of hair.

She looked directly at the doctor. "What's the verdict?"

"Well, Ms. Chace... Teresa," he said. "Physically you are quite recovered from the abortion..."

Yes. The problem of the abortion. Physically she was fine, but it was the bad thing she had always feared she might do. No, not do... WAS. A symbol for the bad thing she was afraid she was.

The kind doctor saw her tears and shaking shoulders and shook his head at her. "No, no, it is a hard thing, but you are certainly not the only one. A bit over 50,000 abortions last year," he consoled her, handing her a page with the statistic in bold type. "Just here in Texas."

"Imagine." Still, she heard her own baby's tiny cry. Being excused was not the same as being loved. Forgiven.

"And, then, there is the matter of your heart," he added, solemn.

"My heart?" A heart problem. Or a problem of heart?

"A slight wound to the soul," he offered, in his clipped Spanish accent. "And a slight wound to the heart."

Why?

"From your mama, perhaps. It is very often genetic, this defect..." He was murmuring to her as he wrote in the chart now.

"I don't have a mama."

He lifted his leonine head and smiled at her, tender, nearly teasing. "Everybody has a mama. I assure you, Miss Chace, even you. Maybe you might even want to look for your mama, eh, someday? Just to satisfy your curiosity?"

"Did you know, Dr. Santos, that Albert Einstein had a baby girl with his first wife and then lost her somehow, before she was two? No one knows what happened to her."

"Really," he murmured, contemplating it.

"Lieserl. She was never mentioned or heard from again. No one knew until these papers were released. He probably gave her away; just like that."

"Like someone gave you away?" He smiled tenderly at her, then dropped his hand and considered that fact, in its sudden starkness.

"Why do you suppose people give away their children, Dr. Santos?"

2

If S equals success, then the formula is: S = x + y + z
X is work; y is play; z is keep your mouth shut.
Albert Einstein

Leaning into the computer monitor required David Hurt's intense concentration. For him, on-screen work required two distinct but simultaneous efforts: the excruciating discipline necessary to coordinate his muscles to hit the keys and the abstraction necessary to forget it was actual money he was dealing with. Targeting the keyboard with his palsied fingers was not as difficult now that he had better medical help and an organized life. He thought of the charted graphs and fractions scrolling by as an advanced video game. It was better that way. Too many commands and subtleties rushing at his brain brought the whole effort down like a house of cards. Since he had the mental gifts but not the physical ones, he centered on computer things.

As a CPA, he had worked with many organizations and individuals, but now was using his computer background to run a fledgling internet company that provided services to Certified Public Accountants around the state. If it went over in Texas, his investors wanted him to take it public, listed on the NASDAQ. He didn't want to let them down.

CPA: Cerebral Palsied Accountant he sometimes joked, covering for the

14

lurches and groans as his body betrayed him.

He followed his own investments, too. EARNINGS PER SHARE, click, click, hum. PERCENTAGE CHANGE IN VOLUME, click, wait, wait, and click again. EARNINGS PER SHARE, tap, tap, wait again, and RANK. It was only a video game with money to him; with NASDAQ and AMEX chomping temporary little graphs of light instead of the 'Pac-Man' of his youth. Davy plugged in the daily numbers, compared the final numbers with what they would be if he altered a tiny detail. Draw the first line, then solve the problems it created... the way Teresa described painting.

But he would not think about that yet. No. That was too much; it would upset the careful orchestration of his muscles. Better not think about art, not think about artists. Not think about Teresa Chace.

RATIO OF PRICE PREMIUMS ON PUTS VS. PREMIUMS ON CALLS... yes, that he could do. Figure out what most folks are doing and put money on the opposite trend. Buy when the others are bailing. It seemed jaded and misanthropic, somehow, but it also made him money. Well, not money, he reminded himself. It only improved the current high score on his Nintendo for investments. It was, after all, only a game.

He realized that he had let his hand slide down to the side of the keyboard and now it clutched the edge of the desk. That was why he didn't allow himself distractions while he worked. Nearly impossible, though, to keep from tasting the delicious morsel of news: Teresa was coming. He ran his mind around her phone call, savored the words like candy that tempted but was too rich after all. Now his hand had lost its focused discipline and he gave up and backed away.

Just opening his jaw was enough to pull the overeager muscles into a smile. All was lost, now. His usual trouble separating his commands to his eyes from those to his head made the tiny dots of light on the computer screen jiggle and swim.

He had always loved Teresa and missed her so much since the move. He had sent her anonymous financial help and asked her closest friend Esmeralda to keep him advised, as he didn't want to bother Teresa. They had been close over the years, but he always knew he was never going to be normal enough to have her for his own. He understood her wounded soul and hard childhood but knew she wanted to make it out in the "real world."

He understood he was always loved... his mother did her best – wheelchair, crutches, help – but when he was ten she knew she was dying and put him in the children's home. He could always see the difference between his physical handicap and those wounded hearts in most of the other children who had worse childhoods, no safe love from parents. So he ignored their teasing and befriended the ones who needed his friendship.

Teresa was one of the first. When he arrived there at ten she was eight – and so lonely and prone to tears. He protected her and they became good friends. By the time she was thirteen and he was fifteen, they both were confused by their relationship and played with other kids, and she flirted with other boys. But he always protected her from the more damaged ones. Warned her what they said and did. Now he was overcome with joy to see her again. He pushed himself up and went to work to clear out the extra room for her to have when she arrived.

One of the odd ironies of his plodding life was his strength. And his health. In spite of the painful absurdities his body cast him into, he was very healthy and very strong. His stamina surpassed that of many of his friends. He could walk now without his crutches but couldn't drive. And could swim like an athlete. Swimming was freedom and delight; floating just above the gravitational realities of his disease. That was another of his happier memories with Teresa while they grew up. She loved it too. What had been "water therapy" when he was a child had turned into a lifetime delight. His chief reluctance in leaving the home had been the easy daily access to the huge Olympic pool and ever-available assistance. Now that he had his own driver he would be free to take them over to swim together. The new joy rose up in him.

Then he wondered… did she understand what the surgery on his legs had done for him? For short times he could walk unaided, barely swaying, almost normal. He knew he wasn't perfect – sometimes he gave up his goals in pure physical frustration. Failing sometimes, when seeing how the world sees disability and feeling the loneliness at the center of his generous soul.

But he still played board games with the younger disabled boys at the home. Taught them chess, rooted for them at tournaments, chastised those who made fun of them. To many he was a hero. But that lonely soul that longed for true love kept his days quiet and unfulfilled.

Now to think about Teresa coming back? After all these years? He was shaken in his very soul. In absence she had become like a sister he had lost or a lover he had only dreamed of. She had left five years before, barely on the brink of womanhood, trailing the sorrow of her wounded soul. He had never thought she would return to the cradle of that sorrow, hometown of the children's home she had shared with him for years. He had known she was in trouble sometimes, had grown used to the late-night phone calls. But also knew she didn't expect him to have any answers.

He had always known she needed a "normal" guy. Most girls didn't ever look at him in that way. That was one reason the desire of his heart became to help others. To help other wounded people who had not had his love and help in life. And to give those emotionally wounded by being rejected and sent to the children's home the help and support they needed. He did love his computer work in peace and solitude. But turning it all to give those things to others was the deepest satisfaction in his life.

But now she was coming back. Was she alright? What would he do? How could he help her? What were her needs? His mind whirled so much he couldn't work anymore. He must make preparations. Nothing was more important than keeping Teresa safe and somehow he, Davy, had been miraculously endowed with a part in that safety. She provided that to him with her need. Just as she had provided his only experience of love. She saw him as a person, saw his soul.

He would make no claims, ask for nothing she did not wish to give. He would give her everything, even her freedom to do what she chose with it. For him, it was enough that she was coming home. That she thought of him as home.

Might as well allow himself the luxury of looking out the room's one window. The last dripping dew drops shimmered on the heart shaped leaves of the Chinese tallow tree, hummingbirds tirelessly frisked the blooms on the young papaya trees. The beautiful scene right outside his window seemed intensified today. Teresa was coming back. "Davy," she had whispered. "I need you."

In his whole life, she had never said that.

"Davy," her voice quivering like his own. "I want to come home."

Had anyone, in his whole underworld life, ever asked him for help?

She was coming back. To live? Had he even asked? When she had gone off to seek her fortune she was, what, nineteen? Twenty? He himself, twenty-two and still dependent on the largess of the children's home where they had lived so long. Both of them older now; and wiser.

A sweet memory of when she did kiss him when they were young—fifteen and seventeen he thought. He had older boys making fun of him trying to walk across the basketball court. She ran across the court glaring at them and followed him into the hall behind the benches, calling "hey handsome" and leaning against the wall in her cheerleader outfit, acting like she was flirting with him. Then, when he leaned there to talk a bit, she stared him in his face, into his clear blue eyes. "You're so handsome, Davy." And brushed his cheek with a light kiss. He smiled then and he still smiled now, with the sweet memory.

DISTRIBUTION YIELD, the amber light blinked, and he tried to tell it 4.87%. But it was too late. Now he could only sit and nod his involuntary agreement. Soon his assistant would come for the day and Davy would be too embarrassed not to work. Until then, he decided, he would allow himself the rare luxury of sitting, dreaming over the inert glow of his computer screen, its tiny cursor gone begging.

This computer was one of life's myriad consolations; his central one, for sure. But no competition for the flesh and blood and railing inconsistencies of Teresa. The only person he had known in his whole lifetime who was brave enough to wait, simply wait, while he guided his muscles through their difficulties. Even his mother could never do that; no one else had ever tried. Helping, or hurting, or sighing, they filled the space. But not Teresa.

When Teresa first left for Dallas, she wrote. And called sometimes, asking about one then another of the teeming household. Then she never wrote, but still called sometimes, late at night, and asked for him. "Davy," she would whisper. He would know she had been crying but could only listen. What could he say? He knew when it turned bad for her. She never visited; not once. But sometimes, late at night, his own phone, private now, would ring and he would hear the whispered, "Davy." He knew how it was with her, somehow. What she wanted, how the men she attracted shamed her even though they may have loved her.

Teresa was coming back. She would touch him, as no one had in so long. Just lay her open hand on his pitching back without a thought, brush his hair back from his face like a mother... or a lover. Teresa wasn't afraid of him, didn't shy away from his lurching inaccuracies, didn't blush or look away when his voice could not be modulated in time. Teresa would stoop, without thinking, to tie the shoelace he could not manage, cover his teasing hand with her own to force a coin into a vending machine. She was funny and bitter and complicated and he loved her.

He rose, feeling the cool hard braces on his lower legs dig in as he reached for his arm crutches. He remembered that Teresa hadn't seen them; he had traded the pigeon-toed spastic dance for a series of three operations resulting in this louder but more dependable method of ambulation. The braces were awkward, the crutches loud, but it was better than the erratic lurches and constant sprawling debacles of his youth. Passing for a normal disabled man instead of a man with cerebral palsy was, for him, an important distinction. Almost a vindication of his big childhood lie: his insistence to his mother that the doctor assured him he would be "getting over" his condition someday.

Sometimes he could go a short while without the braces, and pretend. Finally, tiring, his weakened legs would bow and all pretense would be gone. But it was better, still, than the tip-toed prancing of his adolescence. Even the cumbersome arm crutches were a stabilizing improvement over the erratic, arm-waving, rocking freefall before. Teresa would be surprised.

Davy started out too quickly on the crutches and nearly toppled, then concentrated again. Focus, focus; forward only just so far then back, keep the range narrow; the margin for error narrow.

The apartment was sort of a duplex, he thought, as he cast a new eye over his meager belongings, tried to see it as Teresa would when she came. Too spartan, he could see now. He owned few things in the first place, and those few he kept carefully out of his general daily path to make his own erratic laps easier, reduce the potential for disaster. His bedroom and bath on one side, his office and another bath on the other, the kitchen, dining and living rooms in between.

It helped him divide his life into work and private space, even though it was an artificial division. In reality, his life and work were indistinguishable, here in his little "electronic cottage." He saw it now for the desperate and solemn stake of independence that it was. Other than the fifteen or twenty hours a week he hired Jesse to do some driving, shopping and general errands, he was totally on his own now. Looking at the bare floors, curtainless windows and cheerless but practical furniture, he worried what Teresa would think of his tidy, lonely life.

Then, looking harder, he wondered if his office side couldn't be made into separate living quarters.

No. It was too heady, it would be too much.

And yet...

By the time Jesse reported for work, Davy had disassembled the critical wires and components of his computer equipment, sorted the paperwork and worked the whole elaborate plan out in his mind.

"Mr. Hurt," Jesse called through the screen door, paused a moment, then entered. Davy had tried to have Jesse, barely five years his junior, call him David, but to no avail. Maybe Davy's condition lent him an expanded seniority. Mr. Hurt it had been for two years, and, he guessed now, it would always be.

"A busy day, Jesse," Davy stammered. "I'm moving."

"Away?" Jesse was genuinely alarmed.

"No, No. Moving my office things over to my bedroom. Half of an electronic cottage, I'll have now. I'm getting a roommate."

He stopped and indicated one of several different piles. "Take these papers over to the main office first. Then, when you get back, I want all this computer equipment set up just exactly like it is now, but in my bedroom. Do you think you can get it all in?"

Jesse did a quick lap of the two bedrooms. "Sure."

That was, after all, how he had started out. The same computer equipment, maybe only a little less paper, fewer filing cabinets, in his tiny room at the home. He could see that other life now, dimly, as in a dream, as if his own frail twin were living there still, the only physically challenged child in a house full of children who were 'challenged' in every other conceivable way. The trail from that tiny room at the home to where he stood this moment seemed pale, anemic: this room a poor reward for so much effort, so many operations, so much pain.

"Mr. Hurt?" Jesse's voice was timid.

Davy turned to him. "Yes?"

"I'll go now. To take the papers. I will be right back."

"Yes." It didn't seem to require an answer.

Still Jesse paused, as if unsure. He moved the big armchair back out of the way so Davy could pass more easily with the box of computer disks and printouts. Then rearranged the thick envelopes he was to deliver. "Mr. Hurt," he finally spoke.

Davy turned to him. "Yes?"

"Are you all right, Mr. Hurt?"

All right? What did Jesse mean? Why wouldn't he be all right? Then he followed the shy look of concern in Jesse's eyes to his own and became aware of the dampness clinging to his lashes, making his glasses slide down his nose. He steadied himself on his left crutch while his right arm flew out in an awkward gesture, then carried its hand to touch the tears that clung to his long lashes. "These?" he smiled at Jesse. "I guess I have a leak."

Long after Jesse was gone, Davy touched his own face from time to time to see if those miracle tears had returned. He could not remember crying since he was a small boy and his father left and he knew he himself had somehow doomed his own young mother to struggle on alone. As he pushed his own life resolutely to one side of the apartment, his half of a half of a house, he was happy. It did not matter that he had only a dim memory of any family life, never mind the painful struggle to cling tenaciously to the slim periphery of the life others leapt through without thinking, no thought for the cruel taunts of childhood still haunting him now into his twenty-seventh year.

He trembled under the weight of the unhappy years and then they were gone. Teresa was coming and she needed him.

He himself was a survivor. Life, when it was hard, made him more clever. But now he dared see it all. The void at the back of his life was filled with what he had not dared hope for. The tears, he knew, were for that. He remembered the great heavy door that had closed like lead on the parts of life he had seen would never be his and now he thought he could see it again, in some distant part of himself, swinging open wide again. He would take Teresa's troubles on himself, if he could, and then allow himself to weep with joy that the years of quiet without her might now be over.

3

Future medicine will be the medicine of frequencies.
Albert Einstein

The ward clerk stood by the bed table and pointed to the various lines where Teresa's signature was required. Soon a nurse joined them, tearing apart sets of papers and giving one lot of copies to Teresa while she herself reviewed her discharge prescriptions and appointments.

Martha Ann did not skitter off this time, but stood swaying by her bed watching the proceedings, her large luminous eyes filled with tears.

Goodbye, goodbye... it was easy with the uniformed attendants. And then a volunteer appeared with the obligatory wheelchair to escort her down to the lobby. Now the goodbye that was not so easy.

"This is it, Martha Ann. I've got to go." Teresa stood before her, taking her by the shoulders and waiting for her eyes to rise to meet her gaze. "I'll never forget you, Martha Ann. Thank you for everything."

Martha Ann brought her hands out from behind her back and held out a tiny plant to Teresa. "It's a present," she whispered, turning her back to the aide. It was a dark green English ivy with a red plastic heart that said *Congratulations*.

"It's beautiful. And I have one for you, too." Teresa opened a tablet in her bag and drew out a pastel drawing of Martha Ann's face, fuller and smiling, and with a small golden crown. "Don't ever forget – you are a queen. Don't let anybody hurt you. Promise?"

Martha Ann took the picture reverently and nodded. Then just stood and stared, tears streaming down her misshapen face, as Teresa gathered her few belongings and the plant. She opened her mouth and moved forward as if to say something to Teresa, some last thing that would prevent the loss, alleviate its permanence. But nothing came out. There were no words. Teresa's own eyes filled and she nodded as Martha Ann lifted her hand in a last weak salute.

Outside, the late afternoon sun was resplendent with the hope that is born when hopes are dashed. Honeyed, leaden, it dripped through the trees to the steamy earth. Teresa thanked the nurse who accompanied her and walked outside alone. She let go of the heavy glass door, listened to it hiss slowly back into the cold, bare hallway of Grace Community Hospital. The humidity felt good after the artificially dry cold of the hospital.

Teresa put her hand up to her chest. The poor thing is really loping along now that they've told me how puny it is. Do you think it's a good idea to tell someone with a bad heart that she's got a bad heart?

Teresa felt lightheaded, short of breath, but alive in the peculiar way a threat of death inspires. No heavy labor the cardiologists said. And no children. O.K., all right, she could do that. No problem. It was not the abortion. Not that she was a bad girl. Just that she had a bad heart. Broken. And just as well, they insisted, that she had not tried to carry her baby. Too dangerous. The very act she thought may have ruined her life had apparently saved it.

"Let not your heart be troubled..." These days memorized scriptures from her childhood filled her mind.

Cardiac Tamponade she had barely been able to make out on the diagnosis line of the release forms. Like some sort of French feminine hygiene product.

Each step was a heavy effort that she willed herself to make. One step, now another. Yes, yes that's it. That's how you go along. Let not your heart be troubled...

No children. How had they decided on that? But it did not seem sad now; only fair after what she had done. She would never have children; would spend the rest of her life mourning the one who was lost.

"If we had more of a medical history on you," one of them had offered weakly, by way of some dim hope. "It's hard to say if the fluid accumulation around the heart is due to some genetic type of progressive deterioration in the heart muscle or limited to the purely mechanical difficulty with the valve..."

"We can wait and see, of course," another offered. "Put you in for extensive testing and then follow you carefully."

Medical history. Yes. She could surely get a medical history. Somewhere in this world there had to be people who would know her medical history. And how, like Yuri Zhivago's daughter, she came to be lost. Her mother's name was Rose; that was a start. But was she dead or alive? Dr. Santos thought it would be a good idea to find out. Davy would help her.

Teresa stopped to rest, allowing the scant breeze to blow her dark hair back from her face. On the horizon, the Dallas skyline stood against the sky's fading blaze like a painted mural. The warmth felt so good; she was surprised at her pleasure. Maybe disaster was the very thing she'd needed.

She walked back to hold the door for an elderly woman who was struggling to maneuver her even more elderly husband in through the heavy glass doors in an uncooperative wheelchair.

"Oh, thank you, dear," the woman grunted.

"Sure." Teresa pressed back out of the way and helped redirect the big rubber wheel.

"Huh? What is it, Mama?" The elderly gentleman turned around to face his wife and Teresa, catching some part of their brief words.

"Nothing, dear, nothing. Everything's fine. This young lady is just giving us a hand here." The woman was plainly sweating with the effort now.

"This chair doesn't want to go in," Teresa gasped as she worked the wheel back around again. Louder this time, so the old man could hear.

"Me neither," he grumbled.

Then the chair was freed and on its way. The woman thanked Teresa and hurried off behind her unruly vehicle.

"At least you have your health," the old man called back.

"Yes."

A yellow cab pulled into the drive and Teresa stepped toward it. "1109 Ramsland, please."

Dizzy now, and short of breath, Teresa put her trembling fingers to her forehead, damp with the sudden exertion, and settled back into the hard rear seat of the taxi. Not crazy, Dr. Santos had assured her, and not in immediate danger with her heart. Tired of living, maybe, like the old song said, and scared of dyin'. Her bare thigh pressed against the metal ashtray filled with cigarette butts and a half-eaten candy.

She would just pack up her few belongings, make some phone calls, and try to get a good night's sleep. Tomorrow she would take the bus back to the Valley. Everything taken care of with money wired to her by Davy. She would just try to relax and let the closed windows and roaring air conditioner of the old taxi muffle the fear howling in the distance. Try to think of home and Davy.

Had she known him forever? She could not remember a time she hadn't known him. One of her earliest memories at the home was of sitting outside with him one evening on a red tile porch. She could almost feel the cool rust-red tile they called *saltillo* after the city in Mexico where it originated. Some of the tiles had paw prints from stray dogs that had run across them as they dried in the sun in the little neighborhood "factories" where they were made. No matter how much paint and polish glossed those rough clay tiles, they always smelled like sand when they were wet. Like the sand of the bleached dunes at the nearby shore of the Gulf of Mexico.

The whole Valley would have been a desert but for the seemingly endless grid of irrigation canals and pipes. Reclaimed, like a Middle Eastern oasis, the hot blowing dirt relented under the patient diligence of the people and the canals to give lush rows of palms and citrus and crops.

She had so wanted to get away from the Valley, go to the big city to try her wings. Now she could think of nothing but getting back. She missed her friends from the home, though they were hardly a comfort. You'd think orphans would be the most sympathetic to other orphans. But no. Those to whom mercy has been shown are seldom the most merciful. At the home they treated each other with a brisk challenge that seemed to say: "Get a grip. I did."

So much pain, they couldn't feel it anymore: Chaya's mother dead of cancer, father gone away to work up north; Jackie's father in prison for something he had done to her, something that had broken her mother. Davy, whose cerebral palsy required medical assistance that his divorced mother could not afford. Roberto and Luis dragged through six states to glean welfare and troll for church handouts by an uncle who was all they had. None of them cute little moppets likely to be taken in, even had they been free, conscious that they were somehow the crooked results of many mistakes. Misfits, all, wearing an ineffable sadness they could not name or touch; and not a source of mercy, but a bottomless receptacle for it.

Some had been so wild and rebellious that sometimes the quiet rural Baptist home was more like a reform school. Police scoured the countryside for those who "ran," trying to pick them up before they got into trouble or came home late, drunk and unruly, from the Mexican bars and clubs a mere five miles away.

A light burning late at night usually had something to do with the flamboyant ways wounded adolescents screw up their lives: alcohol, sex, drugs, crime, in more or less that order. Others, like herself, had only watched the daily drama from their own mute vantage points, too wounded to fight.

Still, she wanted to go back. Start over. Take different steps away from the beginning and try for a different result. Find her mother and maybe, with her, the missing pieces of her own soul. Maybe even the old man who comforted her in her dreams. *Shhh... shhh... Teresa... Hijita...* Why would the comfort, the prayers, come to her at night in Spanish? Was it only learned from her friends at the home or was there someone else, someone lost to her? Davy said he would help her.

Tears sprang to her eyes. She would run to Davy and be safe.

"Teresa, there's plenty of money for you to fly back..." Davy's voice shook with emotions that were always hard to manage.

"No, I'll take the bus." Teresa's voice was low, but firm.

"Then let me drive up and get you. Jesse is my driver and he says he can make it there by morning. Ten or eleven hours. I'll come with him."

"No." That was that. Teresa's voice was even firmer with both the certainty that she could not tolerate the claustrophobia of the airplane right now and the unwillingness to put Davy out any more than she already had. The bus was good enough for her. She thought again of the gauze sock they took away.

Teresa stared out the bus window, trying to let herself be hypnotized by the scenery sliding by behind her own ghostly reflection. She had to hold her breath and press in on her diaphragm to steady her heart the first roaring miles the bus slid away from the congested city. It was as if Davy held her there, though the magic comforting presence thinned in the stretches between towns, stretches that became longer and more desolate the further south she got.

She clutched Martha Ann's ivy like a talisman and imagined Davy waiting for her. His joy – clean and transparent as glass – gave her courage.

The lumbering bus glided past the rolling green hills and down, an endless ten hours down, down, south into the flat monochrome desert plain and finally into the revived desert fringes and flat delta of the Rio Grande river in the southernmost tip of Texas. "The Wild Horse Desert" the early Indian inhabitants had called it. The border, in more ways than one.

The graveyards were still dotted with the gaudy ribbons of coronas, and their more somber Anglo neighbors didn't seem to mind. The apples and peaches and pecans of the northern part of the state left off at the wall of humid heat and gave way to the tropical haven of papayas and oranges and crops that grew year-round.

An absurd hope rallied and rose within her. It was as if she had never left, had dreamed the intervening years in Dallas. They were behind her now: the rented apartment, rented furniture, rented lovers. Nothing of her own to bring with her but two suitcases of clothes and a box of art supplies. She was home.

The trickling streams of humanity ebbed and flowed as the bus found its way ever closer to her Valley destination. The muted chatter was predominantly Spanish now. And then, somewhere past exhaustion, it pulled into the Avila station and discharged its exhausted passengers.

Teresa waited for the first rush of people to exit; looking out the window she could see other passengers scooped up by loved ones and carried into the terminal. But no Davy. She sank back down into the empty seat and waited for the last of the passengers behind her to pass. The hot humid air from outside began to displace the drier air-conditioned coolness and Teresa felt as if her hair and clothes wilted all at once. She blotted the quick beads of perspiration on her lip and stole one more desperate look outside, scanning the crowd of people made dim by the tinted glass. Only one tall man, dark and watchful, two older women, and some children. Well, she couldn't stay on the bus.

She shoved her hand baggage out the doorway ahead of her and looked down to watch her feet on the steep steps of the bus. Her neck was so stiff that she almost cried out in pain. And then arms were around her and she was lifted very deliberately off the steps and brought down safely onto the ground. She felt the soft cotton shirt against her cheek before she could even look up and into Davy's familiar blue eyes.

"Teresa," he whispered.

"Davy? Oh my God, Davy..." Teresa cried out. It was Davy, and yet it wasn't. Not the Davy from her childhood, not the young, thin bespectacled boy she had left behind. "Davy, I didn't even know you. You're so... *solid*," she laughed as she ran her hands down the sides of his arms, rock hard with muscles that were impressive, though quaking with his ever-present palsy. His face seemed broader, heavier; his hair darker than she remembered. The faint aroma of his aftershave was not like the soapy boy-smell locked in her mind. He was strong and his arms were open to her. Like any man's.

"And you are beautiful," he said simply. "As always." His face shone with joy.

He stepped away from her, both to see her completely and to show her his new gait. No arm crutches or leg braces for this meeting; it was the most special occasion he was likely to ever have, and worth the extra effort and later exhaustion to meet Teresa as an equal. Not a "handicapped" boy, but a grown man, strong and sure of himself. He lifted her baggage from her and took her arm to lead her away from the crowded confusion and toward the street.

"My car is just across the street. Jesse can come back for your other bags."

Teresa let him lead her to the curb, then turned him to herself and hugged him. Then held him and cried the tears that had been teasing since Dallas. It was safe now, safe to let them go. "Davy, thank God you're here. I didn't realize how afraid I was until I felt your arms around me and was safe." She felt the rhythmic pulsing of his palsy beneath the sure strength of his arms and it made the terrors go away.

4

The speed of light is constant. Time is not. Time is relative.
At the speed of light, time stands still.

Albert Einstein

Within the millions of impulses from the brain there is a thread. It is the thread of time. It runs through each living hour of an individual's life. This thread of time does not know how old it is...

The hard edges of her crib hurt the baby when she rolled against them and her stomach was a hard knot of hunger. The last dried scum of old milk in her bottle was a sour reminder of what she needed. The cold and wet and fear held her tightly. Lost in an infant's timeless landscape, her suffering had no beginning or end. She cried out into the darkness; it did not answer back. She fell, but no loving arms opened to receive her. Fat, hot tears rolled endlessly down and her nose filled with snot. How to breathe and cry and stay warm was the suffering, but it was also what she did to fill the long, dark night.

Then the time must have moved on because sunshine began peeking in at her through the dusty blinds. Fragile cells deep in her brain recorded the terror of the long night. The fear and hopelessness locked themselves away, deeper and deeper in her infant brain, where she could grow up around them, and where, forever afterwards, being alone would set them free. Every now and then, fragile little cells of hope formed there too, only for the acrid fluids of despair and anger to rip them through until they hung like rotted shreds of ancient drapery.

The dry bottle of milk hadn't been any comfort since the last time the sunshine was there, but she held onto it anyway, sometimes biting the rubber nipple with her six good teeth – two on top and four on the bottom – and pulling it out to hear it snap. She had learned to roll away from the wet spot on the crib's mattress, or stand rocking against the wooden rail, but nothing relieved the cold from her wet legs and soggy diaper. Maybe that's why she liked to bite… it distracted her. The one blanket was a hopeless sodden wad in the corner.

The door in the other room opened and the baby sat bolt upright.

"Mama?" she called, throwing the empty bottle down hard on the ruined mattress, instantly forgetting the dark rage of the night.

Then again, "Mama?" She knew the door to her dark little room would open in a moment and happiness would return.

"Baby?" The voice was not Mama's, but was familiar all the same. "Are you all right, Baby? I'm coming for you." Miss Annie. Baby could tell now. Not Mama. But someone good who would hold her and fix the hunger and fix the cold. Someone. Baby gasped and then squealed in wordless delight as the door opened and Miss Annie stood there with her easy voice.

"My goodness, there's that baby!" Miss Annie exclaimed. "How is my sugar pie?" She walked quickly to the crib and gave Baby a hug and kiss over the railing. Her warm hands reached between the slats and found Baby's cold legs.

"My goodness, that baby's so wet, so soakin' wet." All the time talking and acting so happy to see Baby. She fiddled with the mechanism to let the side down. Mama didn't ever have to let the side down because she was taller. She could lay Baby down and change her before she even got her out of bed. She would lean across her, a tiny gold heart swinging from her neck, and Baby would reach for the blood-red stone that sparkled there in the middle.

Miss Annie was too tiny for that; she could barely even pick Baby up once the side was down. Baby could tell she was too heavy for Miss Annie; too big a burden. She would try to be still, try to be quiet, try to be whatever Miss Annie wanted her to be.

5

Life is like riding a bicycle. To keep balance you must keep moving.
Albert Einstein

MAKE ME AN ANGEL the jukebox boomed, too loud for the small afternoon crowd; yes, an angel... FLY AWAY FROM MONTGOMERY... Yeah, Rose thought, fly away... get the body she hated because it held too many secrets up and out of the ugliness... MAKE ME A POSTER OF AN OLD RODEO... Number HH12 on the old jukebox, Angel from Montgomery. Just what she would have said if she had the words. BELIEVIN' IN THIS LIVIN' IS THE HARD WAY TO GO, like the old song says. No shit.

The hot pink "Twin Palm Lounge" neon sign blinked its friendly backwards welcome through the window. Rose always liked the steady pulsing glow, but that *Palm* with no *s* was all wrong. Ought to be "Palms." How can there be *twin palm*? It was irritating.

It was dim and still quiet in the early afternoon heat before Jim turned on the air conditioner for Happy Hour. Only three or four regulars sat scattered around the small tables, the determined, unemployed drunks that had all day to take each other's' inventories. Jim, the owner, had gone to lunch and siesta. Rose knew the bar by heart, every quirk of every customer. But she was nervous being in charge alone all the same.

"Hey, Rosie," one of the dim shapes from the corner table called out. "Two more cool ones here 'fore we hit the road."

"Right."

"Join us, Rosie. A quick one for old times' sake."

Yeah, right. Get close enough for the alkies to see the sign on her back: "*Tell Me What You Think My Problem Is.*" Join 'em and get her inventory taken too, and slobber on each other about old times that she'd as soon forget. She liked a drink, Lord yes, but she wasn't an alkie like them, no. Just liked a drink to take the edge off. Lot of edge to take off these days.

"Can't do it boys. On duty." The words would hardly croak past the knot of dusty, hot desire for a drink. GOD GRANT ME THE SERENITY TO DREAD ONE DAY AT A TIME... Rose had a strict rule: she wouldn't entertain the thought of a drink before dark. Besides, she needed to run up to the apartment and check on the baby the moment Jim got back. And would have to be quick about it.

Let go and let God. Easy does it. One day at a time. Keep it simple, stupid... She chanted the mantras she hated; whispered them between clenched teeth.

Still, the knot grew and dried out until it was like a lump of sand that she had to swallow or die. It was hard living all alone out here, not knowing anybody who could help her out and the baby to take care of and all.

Hard, Lord yes, but better than home; there were too many hands at home, in that old house. Too many people and too many hands. And everybody brave but her; manning their battle stations every day, taking up words like guns and firing them at each other mercilessly day in day out. And somebody with hands on her all the time, like it was nothin'. Daddy and Hands – like father like son. Got to where she was afraid to go to sleep at night. That's what drinking was about; not what people thought.

No, better to stay out here in the desert. Jim was all right, didn't bother her as long as she did her job. And she knew enough to do her job. If something had to go wanting it was the baby. But Pop was coming out to stay a while, help out with things. That would help. *Pop's the only good thing was ever in my life and he hasn't got anybody either.*

The regulars were starting to get loud, picking a fight over some detail of political or athletic gospel. The booze talkin'. Innocent grains fermented and come to take over their tongues. Marijuana was getting bigger all the time and LSD and stuff invented in laboratories. But the drunks still had their standards.

Were they really different people on dry days, Rose wondered? Did the booze really talk for them? Or did it just give a voice to the anger and self-pity and sloppy sentimentality that was already in there? At the edge of the dry desert herself, Rose couldn't wait long enough for the answer to form up in her mind. Soon the chemical would come into her own brain and talk for *her* too.

"I'm no saint, but I love my baby. Gotta tell you, though, that sometimes I misplace her too. I forget there's no money and no love by keeping company with booze and the men who give it to me. I fall away into black velvet days and nights without problems, and without Baby. Then one day I just wake up, hear angels' wings beating the air near my head, like a trapped gnat or distant helicopter, and go out to find her. That baby is the only thing that will outlive my tacky life. She is something better than the sum of anybody's parts.

"You can tell an angel when you got no light of your own. They're company when it's lonely and they tell me when it's time to go get Baby. And their warm feathered presence gives me hope. When I am afraid, I hear the dull thudding of their wings. And I feel hopeful that something wonderful will – finally – happen. The grayness that is my life will run in brilliant colors. The angels will make it all happen, somehow.

"Even if they asked me what I wanted – mind you, they never do – I wouldn't know what to ask for. What is it I want? Something good from life. Like candy that you hold against the roof of your mouth until you salivate with the sweetness; tap it between your teeth. "*Al dente*," the Italians say. A little firm to the bite. I want a sweetness with a little bite. Stupid, I know.

"And I want the shadows to go away. There's somebody dangerous following me, sometimes I catch a glimpse of him in the doorway or just around a corner. If I stare too hard, he disappears. But I always know he's there. Dark figures haunt me, wait for me under the bed, scratch at the door. Was it something I did real bad? Having a baby with no father, maybe; but that ain't my fault.

"See that vase? There's just one little dot of glitter on a bouquet of bright roses. But I only see the tiny dot of glitter, the one spot of shining hope. Because of the angels. And because of the baby, my Teresa.

"Someone's always dyin' to tell me I'm a drunk. Look, I know what I am. But drinkin' ain't my problem. No. Just like the song says, living is the problem. BELIEVIN' IN THIS LIVIN' IS THE HARD WAY TO GO... drinking helps me solve it.

"But even people who wear dark glasses want to see the light."

6

Only a life lived for others is a life worthwhile.
Albert Einstein

avy cared for her like a child at first, seeing that she ate and slept and saw movies with old friends from the home, especially Jackie and Chaya. She sunned like an invalid under the warmth of his care and settled into her half of Davy's *Electronic Cottage* as if it were the most natural thing in the world. He put her name and signature on his bank card so she could get food and clothes, things they needed.

"Davy, I hate to use your money," she worried. "I'll pay you back when I get a job."

"Teresa…" Davy paused, looking for the right words, struggling to form them without too much distortion. "I didn't even realize I had so much; it didn't seem real to me, some bar-coded number in some bank only Jesse visits." He shifted and smiled his beautiful lopsided smile at her. "I'm pleased to be using it."

"I'm looking for a job," she persisted. "And I've applied for an art scholarship at the University."

"Yes, yes. But don't hurry. Take your time. Please just slow down." How to tell her he fervently hoped she'd never change a single thing?

Their friends folded themselves and their lives in around them as if nothing was changed since simpler, younger days at the home. Chaya was married to a trucker who was gone most of the time and had a two-year-old boy, Manuelito, whom they all called Manny. Jackie, a few years younger, was still single.

And all the while, Martha Ann's ivy prospered in their kitchen window.

The first Sunday of May, Chaya and Jackie took Teresa and Davy to church with them: First Baptist Church of Avila

"It's a comfort in a way, to be back in familiar surroundings," Teresa whispered to Jackie, "but I feel like I should wear sunglasses so God doesn't recognize me."

"Once a Baptist, always a Baptist," Jackie whispered back firmly.

"I thought that was Catholics...?"

God. Right after "go-cart" in the dictionary. A mystery. And Jesus, his *nom de plume.* The doctrines and scriptures of childhood were like teasing phantoms, there always at the tip of her tongue, the edge of her thoughts. But not solid, not strong enough to come and take her pain and guilt away. Still, it was peaceful to resume the clean habit of childhood nestled between her good friends.

The church service was like most church services – twenty minutes longer than anyone except the preacher had really hoped it would be, words raining down emphatically, little hammer blows of guilt meant to bow the unbowed.

The preacher's voice was beautiful and sonorous, but could not hold the rapt faces of the congregation, could not overcome the steady crescendo of their restlessness. Teresa studied his even features and powerful frame as he leaned into the heavy words. He was impressive in his physical person, stern and authoritarian, dressed in a severe but beautifully tailored black suit, holding a black Bible. His blond hair was light and shiny as corn silk, his brows dark and foreboding. His shoulders, broad and imposing as an athlete's, seemed to sag under some inner weight. His sensuous mouth was set in a faint conciliatory smile. He was as handsome and imposing as a movie star, but almost dismissive in his disregard for his audience.

She scanned the congregation to see how they felt about their nay-saying fair-haired preacher. Peeked at Jackie and Chaya to see if her raised eyebrow would make them see him in a less overwhelmingly spiritual light.

Teresa dropped her eyes to the paper bulletin the usher had given her when she came in. *Pastor: Ethan Stone*, it stated under a fittingly solemn picture of the man right there in the pulpit.

Prepare to meet thy God the bulletin admonished.

Evening dress optional Teresa penciled in beneath it with a little smiley face.

From where she sat in the back it seemed as if she was spying on a club meeting of some sort, a club of which she wasn't a member. Lapsed dues or something. She felt the faint blush of panic – the newness, the claustrophobic crowd – but calmed on feeling Davy's warmth right next to her. Davy made things simple. And safe. She could leave any time and he would go with her, stay with her. Davy was the one person she knew would never forsake her; she would sooner take her sins to Davy than this celebrity preacher.

"Every head bowed and every eye closed," the preacher began in the elevated pitch that meant a new order of business, the usual last item of business where the lost would be invited to come forward. "And no one looking about."

But of course, they were looking about. Peeping about like mad to see if any would be touched by the jaded old words.

"If you died tonight do you know if you'd go to heaven?" Even the preacher's mellifluous voice could not make the standard question new, and no one stirred as he went on with the usual closing plea. The same plea Teresa had heard hundreds of times at the church services in the home, until they were devoid of any meaning except a dim notion of some unadulterated soul that might be visiting and would hear them new, pristine, for the first time.

She wished she could hear them for the very first time. That she could cut the pain and sins out like paper dolls and lay them aside. Leave only the pretty pattern. She looked up and directly met the piercing gaze of the dangerously and suddenly handsome preacher. She was aware of a flutter of timidly raised hands around the big room, but she let her eyes rest boldly on the preacher a minute before bowing again.

The church was newly remodeled, the smell of paint and carpet glue still lingering faintly, carried by the huge rolling puffs from the central air conditioning, cold and dry and efficient. The committee had apparently solved the color choice problem by having no colors at all – bone white walls, tan cushions, sand carpet. Only the spray of spring flowers – *Given by the Carl and Elizabeth Brenner family in memory of Mrs. Martha Brenner* the bulletin said – gave any color to the monochrome pattern. It seemed that even the sedate congregation had taken on this subtle good taste; only a few daring a red dress or bright-flowered spring hat.

She liked the idea of brave islands of color afloat in the sea of monochrome conformity. A watercolor began to take shape in her mind, the first born there since the dark days in the hospital in Dallas: a central figure with a flowered hat even brighter and bolder than the one that had inspired her – a blaze of cerulean and cadmium – on a cityscape of bone white and beiges. She would bring to life the blazing field of poppies that the woman in her brave little church hat only dreamed of.

"And be sure," the preacher's strong voice boomed, waking her from the reverie, "to give each other the right hand of Christian fellowship."

Oh, God, Teresa panicked, too late. Was there still time? She looked behind her, spotting the two side doors. Yes, she could still escape without getting trapped in the long line that would undoubtedly be forming to shake the preacher's hand.

Once outside, she felt as if the dazzling noon sun woke her from a dream. The contrast of the hot South Texas sun already, this early in May, baking the sidewalks, and the cold dry expanse of the dim interior gave her an instant headache. A *Sunday Headache* just like the housemother at the home used to have.

The car interior was even worse. "Davy, how can you stand it? It's so hot out here! I'm not doing this to you again."

"I'm okay." He laboriously rearranged his braced legs and gathered the bulky crutches closer to his side to give Teresa more room on the driver's side.

"It was interesting."

"What?" Teresa felt dulled by the heat and the new headache.

"The sermon. It was on the radio. Last week's, I guess. Made me think."

"Me too. Made me think maybe life isn't for everyone."

"You didn't like Pastor Stone?"

"Oh, he is impressive. Intimidating, really."

"Do you think you could work for him?"

"From how far away?"

"His secretary?"

"Oh, jeez, Davy... why?"

"The job is opening soon. I do some financial planning for them and I heard they're looking for a secretary. I asked him to interview you for the position. He used to preach at the home, you know; he likes to help the home kids."

Home Kids. She hadn't heard that term since she left all those years ago. As opposed to Town Kids, who lived in houses with real families.

"You don't think I'm too irreverent?" Teresa grinned at him, masking the quick edge of fear. She couldn't work for a man who no doubt led the *Right to Life* movement in the community, who would shrink in horror from her secret.

37

And yet she could, so easily. She had all the office skills, the years of easy experience with church people. She could talk the talk and no one need know she hadn't walked the walk. It was time she pulled her share.

Davy answered her grin with a quick blush and dip of his head. "I think you're just what they need."

"Church secretary, hmmm... Yikes!"

"Just think it over. They know you'll need flexible hours so you can take classes at the university. That won't be a problem."

And it was arranged, just like that. It was the first time Teresa began to realize the influence Davy had in the community, especially in the church. When she walked into Pastor Stone's office a few days later, she knew she was there because of Davy's influence and not her own qualifications.

The pastor was standing at the window with his back to the door. The broad back in the inevitable dark suit seemed to dwarf the elegant room, didn't quite fit somehow. Like a large piece of misplaced or temporary furniture, left in a room until other arrangements could be made. His left hand, in his pocket, bunched the stiff coat fabric into his left elbow, his right hand rested delicately on the windowpane, just barely touching it with his fingertips. He looked like a sad mime, mirroring an invisible partner on the other side. Teresa paused in the open doorway, feeling she was intruding and shouldn't break the spell, though she knew he was expecting her.

That Ethan Stone was a preacher was nothing to Teresa, or no more than if he were a salesman or politician or accountant. She had been raised by preachers, taken her meals with preachers, sang and swam and watched TV all her life with the preachers that were steady traffic at the home. It was a business, a living – "nickels and noses" – complained the few who had been truly "called". So her trepidation at applying to him for a job was nothing.

He finally sensed her presence and turned. Because she was already still, wondering and staring, she caught the last glimpse of sadness in his eyes before he put on the mask of professional distance. An unmistakable aura of suffering, dumb before a silent God, clung to him as he turned to face her. Then was gone. In an instant, it was as if she had only imagined it. He came to her and guided her to the chair facing his own across a massive desk, quickly removing himself to his own side as if aware of the overpowering effect of his bulk in nearness.

"And so, Miss Teresa Chace," he said, smiling down at her name written neatly on the open daily calendar. "What can I do for you?"

Teresa's unease blushed itself into being. "Well, I came to see about the job; church secretary... I believe David Hurt spoke to you about me." She shifted, looked out the window at the hackberry trees and palms, arms dancing in the steady southwestern breeze.

"Have a seat, please." He indicated the chair. "Tell me about yourself."

"I just moved back from Dallas. Grew up at the children's home here; Davy probably told you..." She sat as primly as she could.

"Oh, how *was* that?" He eased into his own leather chair behind the massive desk.

"I was left there when I was five. Graduated from high school there."

"Yes." He turned his heavy gray gaze to her.

"Then went off to the big city to make my fortune." A search that culminated in the one thing that she must not tell him. She felt like a red neon sign lit up on her chest: "A" for ABORTION. Whatever troubles she might choose to share with him, that must never be one of them. Her stomach tightened with the secret.

"How long have you been away, Miss Chace?"

"I'm twenty-five now... went to Dallas when I was twenty... so five years nearly."

"And what brought you back to the Valley?" His face was pale, with just a thin blue vein traceable beneath the skin. His eyes, gray as lead, took on colors from the changing light of the window. Now blue, now green, now even a golden hue, but only for moments. Teresa fancied it had been the sadness he had faced when alone that had made them gray, and that they now wouldn't settle on that empty shade again, not while their owner had company.

"Let's just say the Prodigal Daughter came to herself." It was not safe to say more. She knew perfectly well that if he knew she'd had an abortion he would turn her down. And he was not the sort of man one confided such a secret to, anyway. So handsome, yes, handsome, she realized: and so coolly detached.

They both fell silent. The light from the window swept bright then dim then dappled through the room. The rich carpeting muffled the sound of footsteps outside the doorway; distant voices sounded like brass bells hanging in the slightest of breezes. Finally, Ethan spoke again.

"And you need a job? Now that you've come home?"

"Yes."

He turned his chair around and picked some brochures and leaflets up from the low shelves behind him. When he turned back and laid them neatly out before her, Teresa thought how he looked like a banker or an H & R Block tax preparer just doing his job. A calm, methodical answer to any maelstrom of despair and defeat. It should have been comforting, she supposed.

"Let's just start at the beginning, Miss Chace, since we don't know each other very well." His eyes seemed to have settled on a pale blue green. His mouth was set in a narrow line of determination. "Are you saved?"

Teresa's heart dropped as she looked at the booklet he held out to her, diminutive in his huge hand, *The Four Spiritual Laws*.

"I guess you've seen one like this before?"

"At the home we used them for bookmarks. We used to say there were eleven laws, but no one can remember the other seven. We were a pretty irreverent lot. But saved, all right. Yes."

Ethan laid his hand out, open, on the desk. His eyes had again settled on the flattest of grays, fixed on her face, yet somehow past it too. Lost in a moment like the one she had interrupted at the window. He laid the distracting tract aside.

"I'm sorry," she began, near tears, realizing the insult. "I don't know you well enough to tease you." She twisted around in her seat, started to rise, thought better of it and settled in again. "It's just that sometimes people make it sound so easy. Use this formula and your life will come together neat as you please. But it isn't like that..." Teresa's voice trailed off, wavering as if surprised to be pouring its heart out to a stranger.

"The devil isn't who we thought he was."

"No." That much she was sure of.

They both heard the distant rattle of Davy's metal crutches lurching down the hall, their eyebrows lifting as they turned to the open door.

"It's Davy," she beamed. Davy's pale hunched form staggered into view. Teresa sprang up and went out into the hallway to pull him into the small alcove office.

"Davy, what are you doing here?" she hissed in mock anger, herding him toward the office door.

"Spying," he managed to say clearly before his mirth sent waves of uncontrollable grimacing across his face and worked his jaw in silent echoes.

"Well, don't give up your day job," she poked him in the ribs with one hand even while she leaned against him, a steadying force as she steered him in.

"Pastor Stone, my roommate. You know him! Davy."

Pastor Stone rose huge and dark against Davy's frail form and took his trembling hand. "Yes. Mr. Hurt and I are acquainted. He does our financial planning; very highly regarded around here. Hello David." He motioned to another chair.

Teresa felt as if she were crushed between the great weights of presence of the massive Pastor and her frail Davy. As if they were defying some law of physics and could not be occupying the same space at the same time. She knew what it must have cost Davy to come here. Just for her. Yet she felt anew the impressive authority, the presence of this stranger from the pulpit.

"Davy grew up in the home, too. Like me, like most of us, he was never adoptable. He even had a mother. Has a mother." She reddened to realize how she was rambling. Why would it be so difficult to tell anyone about Davy?

"He's a CPA now, as you apparently know. Starting his own company..."

"Yes. I know about his new internet company. Actually, I'm one of his investors. Every businessman in this church sings David's praises. How is it going?" He turned his full attention to Davy.

"So far, very well. We'll be meeting with some underwriters soon about going public next year." Davy delivered the words carefully, then fell quiet.

Teresa immediately took up the slack of sudden silence. "Even back at the children's home, Davy never lacked for roommates. To the other kids it was like Space Camp at NASA with all that computer equipment."

The job was lost, she was sure of that. But, she comforted herself, it was just June; registration and classes wouldn't be until September and she had time to look for something else. Davy wanted her to slow down. She could tell now that she just wasn't ready. Was rambling on like a child.

And she could use the time to try to find out about her mother and the answers to the doctors' nagging questions. "Rose's Tamponade," the medical dictionary at the library named her condition. "Acute compression of the heart due to effusion of fluid into the pericardium." With the associated difficulties, of course. On and on. Another of life's little ironies. The stricture choking her heart named for the mother she couldn't remember.

"Teresa would make an exceptional secretary." Davy's words were so precise and controlled that she knew he had been rehearsing them. They brought her back from her reverie in a knot of embarrassment. Davy didn't know what a fool she had made of herself...

"It's settled, then." The rest was a blur that Pastor Ethan Stone commanded. Teresa found herself in the unlikely position of secretary to the pastor of the largest Baptist church in the Valley.

41

7

The secret to creativity is knowing how to hide your sources.
Albert Einstein

So then, you're our new scholarship student?"

"Yes. Teresa Chace." She extended her hand, but he had already spun around in his desk chair before he saw it and was now sat looking out the large third-story window. The campus was tinged with brown, the greenery sad and tired already in July. The few students walking within their view seemed to be moving through a heavy transparent syrup, the effect of the oppressive heat.

"I'm not sure how you arranged this opportunity, Ms. Chace," he said, accentuating the Ms. "But I hope you realize it is probationary. Not in the bag, so to speak." At last he turned back round to face her directly. "Never in the bag."

"I understand." She stood with her weight on both feet, tightly controlled, almost at military attention.

"In addition to your graduate classes, you will be responsible for keeping the exhibition room in order. I'll have the student who has been taking care of it show you around and get you a set of keys. Any questions?"

Actually, Teresa had a lot of questions, but they withered in the dry blast of Professor Stout's arrogance and apparent disinterest. She felt foolish holding the large portfolio of work she had taken such pains to get together for this meeting.

As if reading her thoughts, he waved toward the jumble of odd canvases against the opposite wall. "Shove those down a bit and let's have a look at some of your work. Get to know each other."

It took her several awkward minutes to make room on the display strip. Mostly there were large tablets opened to beginning students' careful, shaded drawings of draped fabrics and geometric shapes, their only individuality showing in the tiny hatches of shading, some strong, some feathery and delicate. An occasional one offered something different that caught her eye, but mostly they were unimaginative. There were two larger oils, bold, non-objective, nice enough. She preferred oils to acrylics herself, thought they smelled better and had a depth and warmth the acrylics just didn't manage. She only used the acrylics for something fast and bold, non-objective....

One watercolor caught her eye, made her forget for a moment about setting up her own work. It was of soft, delicate flowers set at an odd perspective to a small lake. But it glowed as if lit from behind with some unusual effect she herself had never seen nor tried; the sky dimmed out with white-hot brightness. A simple picking it up to set it aside turned into a much longer moment of time, holding it in front of her, wondering about the light. Even her tiniest sable brushes had never given her that delicate effect.

"Do you like it?" the professor's voice was almost sneering.

"Yes, I think it's lovely. Such an unusual effect with the light..." It's delicate beauty, leaning against the cracked, putty-colored wall, was a miracle. But she thought from his tone that perhaps he himself didn't care for it. There were so many things she couldn't do, so many things life was apparently never going to give up to her. But she could create small objects of beauty and find this in itself worth living for. And she could never resist the truth about it. That one watercolor was a jewel among the pretty pebbles before her.

"Ah, then we agree on something right off, Ms. Chace. It's mine. I put it there just today. To cheer myself up." He settled back with a self-satisfied sigh.

"Ah." There was an artist, then, behind the crusty 'department-head' exterior. Well, then. Fine. Things were looking up. She put up her own work. Two drawings she had done for the Einstein exhibit: one of Davy leaning against a doorway, using the arm crutch to counteract his perpetual lurching. Then two watercolors, landscapes from a very low angle, using the hot bright colors of a Valley summer, a lot of white heat. And then the large oil she had done for Davy, a non-objective piece of hard corners, cold whites and grays, institutional, entitled simply, *Hospital.*

He got up and came around the desk, in front of the little carved sign that said Doctor Richard Stout. "So it's 'doctor' then," Teresa thought. *Doctor Dickie*, she would find out later, most of the students called him behind his back.

"You need to get these matted," he said, tapping the drawings and watercolor as he walked past. Then he stood several paces back and spent a good deal of time on the oil.

"Well, you do work well in all media, Ms. Chace. No question of that. The oil is very interesting, as well as the perspective in the watercolors. And this young man," he paused and picked up the drawing of Davy. "Is he palsied?"

"Yes."

"Very nice. All the motion. And yet peace, too."

Teresa paused, surprised by the professor's sensitivity. And by her own pleasure in having it echoed in another person. "Yes. That is how he is," she said. And smiled to herself. "The real problem, here, Ms. Chace, is who are *you*? The artist must show their true self, their evaluation of the subject matter too, somehow. Peace? I don't think so. Just in your subject. And where is your signature, Ms. Chace? I don't see where you have signed any of your work."

"No, sir, I don't. That is, I haven't."

"All well and good, and entirely up to you, whether you sign your name, or make up one of those cryptic little monograms so popular these days. But your name, your face, your soul must be written across your work, Ms. Chace. Not so *we*'ll know who did it, but so that *you* will. Your vision is the only one you have, you know. Even a glimpse off in any other direction is a lie. Not a lack of talent, or a mood, or anything but a lie. Do you understand me?"

"I think so."

"When I create something beautiful, a slice of my own particular vision, I almost believe God loves me. When I love what I create, my creation very nearly loves me back. Do you follow me?"

"Yes sir." Teresa felt herself shrinking from the intensity of his passion.

"And you know the feeling?"

"Yes sir." Her voice was a dry croak now.

"So tell me... what happens then, Ms. Chace?"

"After the creation?"

"Yes, yes." He was impatient for her next word.

"Why then – wonder of wonders – you have this beauty, this magic shining orb, to keep. To shine for you. To show that you were there. That you lived and saw beauty. Or perhaps saw ugliness that you were able to transmute into beauty."

"Yes, yes, go on."

But she was afraid to say more, to break the spell of this truth. "That's it, sir, for me. To say that I was here."

He dropped back down into the creaky chair behind his desk. "A very handy thing to know about oneself, don't you agree, Ms. Chace?" The owlish eyes swam behind heavy glasses, staring, maniacal.

"Yes." The mania was unnecessary. She was weak with agreement.

"And you were afraid there was a wrong answer, weren't you? There isn't a wrong answer, of course, when you're talking about a vision only you can have. You will be amazed how many talented students you will see sweating over very impressive canvases who will never ask these questions. 'Everyone has his own specific vocation or mission in life,' Victor Frankl wrote, 'Thus he cannot be replaced nor can his life be repeated. We detect it rather than invent it.'" He stared at her hard.

"For now, Ms. Chace, I want to see your name on your work. Then behind it, shining out from all around it. I want you to do things that can fall out of your portfolio onto the grounds and when the janitor turns them in to me I will see the glow and hear it sing, '*Teresa, Teresa Chace*' in the way that a signature can never do. Only art."

She knew exactly what he meant, again. She put her hands, palms down, on her thighs and felt the bottom of her stomach lifting in breathless joy.

From her vantage point at the main desk, Teresa gradually became familiar with most of the people, all of the business, and many of the sorrows of the First Baptist Church of Avila. And developed an increasing respect for Pastor Ethan Stone as she watched him orchestrate his people. Most deacon meetings required only that he appear interested, object slightly to one or two points of slight excess (never the other way around), and act like he was signing reluctantly at the end so the deacons seated at the table would feel they had all been heard and accomplished their goals. Heading the education committee required mainly that he hand out the new quarterlies to the department heads, along with a word about the swell job they were doing. Most of the other committees concerned food or music and seemed to be efficiently and independently run, mostly by women.

He himself maintained his own strict privacy. What she learned about his personal life was from whisperings. Dim, anonymous voices echoing as if spoken into the huge, cavernous nave of a cathedral. They whispered that Ethan Stone had a beautiful wife away in Ohio with her family. No one said 'separation' or 'divorce,' but there were intimations and speculations. "Since they lost the baby," they said. There had been an accident, it seemed. The pastor's only child, a boy, had been killed. The source, she guessed, of the sad, gray gaze she sometimes interrupted in his alcove office.

There were always new frenzies for the church to be lathered into: conferences on evangelism, world missions, stewardship, banquets for fundraising, youth, seniors, and the endless covered dish suppers.

"Will I need a covered dish to get into heaven?" she teased him, without being quite sure he had gotten the joke. And wondering why she so wanted him to.

The purple swirl of evening gave out barely enough light for Davy to manage the front door key. The rehab center's van began to back away, then the driver paused a moment to turn the lights to bright in case he needed them. As the door finally gave in, Davy turned with what little salute of thanks he could muster. It had been a very long day and he was completely exhausted. Every movement now took a heroic act of will, the same will he used to ignore the pain from the raw blisters opening up around the newly-fitted leg braces.

The little apartment... he had never been so glad to see it as he was now.

The lamp they always left on – was it he for Teresa or she for him? – created a warmth as welcoming as its light was helpful. It looked more like a home every time he came in. How did she do it? The few things they owned seemed to be expanding: overflowing boxes and drawers that warmed and detracted from the dingy walls and bare floors. Teresa was a terrible packrat; having lost so much she couldn't bear the thought of giving up one other single thing. She gathered and stacked possessions in about her like a mad old woman who lived with 59 cats. Davy, the man who this mad woman did live with, smiled at her cozy chaos

Teresa's artwork lay, in its various stages, across the available tables, her garage sale "finds" made themselves happily comfortable in their new home. Davy had taken the larger bedroom so his computer paraphernalia would fit. The rest of the nest was slowly being feathered by Teresa. It made him happier than anything he could remember in his whole life.

He left the front door open and opened a window at the back; a determined little cross breeze began to filter away the accumulated heat from the day. The daily 'miracle of evening' was that so much heat could be dispelled so quickly. He noticed that it smelled of Teresa: her perfume, her potpourri candles, her paints and sprays and fixatives, even the lingering scorched aroma from her failed cookies of the night before. His life, which he had always worn with simplicity and good humor, must have been a desert. Only now, under the magic, invisible influence of this one woman's small hand, did it grow into this opulent forest of realities and possibilities. He had never known life could be this rich.

Of course, it was hard too. His routines with Jesse had been safe, comfortable; and it was all he had known for so long. Coming in from the rehab center at this hour would have meant a held-over hot meal, help with a hot bath, bed. Now he limited Jesse to the morning hours that Teresa worked at the church so he would not be interwoven into their lives.

Davy was so hungry that his stomach had given up and quit growling, numb as his mind. His bath would be another long struggle. He could cry from the exhaustion and the thought of trials yet to endure. Yet he was the happiest he had ever been.

"Go figure," he laughed into the darkness outside.

Yessss the never-failing southeast evening breeze sighed back to him. Davy felt a joy in the pain, even though he could barely manage to live it. His struggle, so daily and so unchanging, had a peaceful center now. This new life hovered somewhere just above reality; had a dreamy, unexpected quality, like a foreign film. He had simply never known it before.

He could barely remember his mother brushing his hair back, like Teresa did. Or just touching him, simply laying her open hand on his back or arm. The delicious feel of someone near enough that you could feel their breath. For years now there had been only the impersonal hands of people dedicated to forcing his body to surpass its limitations.

Even those few memories he could recall were tainted; tainted with the fear and futility his mother had breathed as the doctors fanned those first flames of horrid possibilities: Lesch-Nyhan syndrome, tuberous sclerosis; possibly neuro-fibromatosis or even ataxia telangiectasia. Many were names of the men who named the tortures: von Hippel-Lindau disease, Sturge-Weber syndrome. But finally there had been the reality, set forever in concrete, of "Spastic Diplegia" mixed with some degree of "Athetosis." Fancy varieties of cerebral palsy.

To think he had lain in that safe watery world nine whole months, perfect in every way. And, even crueler, to think he had seemed that perfect until he was over a year old and consistently failing to make those exciting milestones. His mother, already overwhelmed by the failures and rejection of her young husband, was then overwhelmed by sad facts about her son, facts which Davy was able to read for himself from a very early age, as his mind had been spared the complete indignities of his conditions: "Spastic Diplegia" promised "predominant involvement of the legs, which would be underdeveloped, show increased deep tendon reflexes and muscular hypertonicity, weakness, and a tendency to contractures." And, to make matters worse, an "associated corticobulbar impairment of oral, lingual, and palatal movement with consequent dysarthria."

Dysarthria; such an unlikely way to put the straining stammer that was his speech. Even the most able-bodied speech therapists sometimes stumbled over that one. "Athetosis" added interest: "the resultant slow, writhing, involuntary movements may affect the extremities...the movements increase with emotional tension and disappear during sleep." There were other varieties and combinations; some much worse. But these were the horrific words that described the neuromuscular difficulties of Davy's world. Even as they failed to describe Davy.

So, how was it that at his birth Fate had pinched off his prospects in only minutes? The cord squeezed a few moments too long? The doctor not too capable with the forceps? Nine months of easy perfection, then an hour of miscalculation and he was forever doomed to run at life like an overgrown puppy. By the time the damage was apparent the crime was so long removed that the answers were gone. Some little detail had kept the oxygen from the brain: a few critical moments and this... He saw it every day on his computer: every little detail must be just so, the marvelous complexity of the machine made no allowances. What you got out was only precisely what you put in.

But he didn't live with regret. It was all he had ever known. And until now, until Teresa, there had been very few things that the bumbling, open-mouthed charge of his puppy body had wanted to do that it couldn't. Now the hunger for more than his life had allotted to him was a frightening pleasure.

When he was a small boy, before he lived at the home, his mother had taken him to a big wedding with dancing at the reception. It was something like a primal experience for an invalid – the sudden exposure to something fierce, heady, magical, mysterious. Something he could never participate in. Of course, there had been many such experiences after that one: limits his body and others were always placing on him.

Stop! Life would cry out, and he would then only see himself as an enlightened but incapable lump of muscles that quivered and speech that didn't always form words. If only he had a voice, a voice that would pull people to him, not scare them away or make them back up in embarrassed self-consciousness. That was what the computer had given him: a bridge to bring his mind to the world, a way to participate in it. His voice.

Now everything was new and his and delicious. Never mind the blood drying on his pant leg, the body quivering with exhaustion and hunger and its own inability to correct them. It was all delicious. Teresa would never know what it cost him to share his life with her. Now he was open to anything, everything, open, once again, to the incredible pure blue blinding light of pain if he should lose it. What if Life cried out *stop!* once again?

Just as, years before, a carton of putty-colored plastic and metal and wires had entered his life and transformed it, had reached its glowing green face and dotted matrix of electronic words all around the country to bring him a world he had never known existed, so Teresa was like warm breath in a dark night.

There, on the coffee table, were strewn the bits and pieces of her art, traces of herself. He recognized the materials and beginning layout for a piece she was working on. What did she call it? A word collage. To be, as he understood it, a layered collage of translucent tissue pieces over the word "sorrow" in block letters beneath. The deep gold of the letters was on the board already, a thick coating of gesso and small ragged pieces of deep purple tissue already partially obscuring the word. The top would be deep, rich green, the green of old forest, yet new hope. "Experimental," she told him.

Waves of trembling added to his palsied gait and he became aware how lightheaded he was. In the kitchen that he felt he couldn't get to, he could see the red heart on the ivy Teresa had brought with her as if it were the distant moon, so near yet so inaccessible. Tears glided helplessly down his face, even though sadness was the furthest emotion from his complicated feelings. Just emotion, he decided, fullness of emotion and low blood sugar. One great gulp of uncalibrated air got sucked in as an unexpected sob and left in a slow moan, ugly even by his own jaded standards. He was glad Teresa wasn't here to see or hear. He decided to stretch out on the sofa and wait for her.

He was good at waiting, very good. Years of experience, waiting, dependent on others for his next move, had left him talented beyond most people. Not patience, really, but a practiced level of interior life that was ready any time his body failed him or his caretakers let him down.

Waiting for Teresa was his joy and his desperation. Waiting for her to hope, to heal. To love him? He would wait to hear her say she loved him or he would wait to see her walk away. He knew what he was. And he could wait.

Outside, the sun was a huge orange ball hanging heavy on the darkening horizon, scanty little puffs of dark clouds moving across it like horses and riders. Davy laid down on the sofa and watched the wispy dark riders pushing evenly, resolutely through the blazing horizon, listened to the distant insects as they changed shifts from evening to night, luxuriated in the heavy, humid robes of night falling around him. He monitored the periodic start and whine of the refrigerator and the neighbors' air conditioning compressor. He laid aside the arm crutches and folded in like a great mechanical bird alighting slowly, surely on the ground. He would wait. For Teresa. Waiting would be delicious.

When, an hour later, Teresa struggled up to the open front door with her portfolio, she looked through the screen and saw Davy sleeping on the couch. Still elated from her meeting with Professor Stout, she had been anxious to share it with Davy and was disappointed to realize he was asleep and then, mesmerized by his still form. Had she ever seen him completely at rest? Not a muscle was twitching or undulating in the familiar waves. Asleep, his face was lovely as an angel's; dark lashes sealed against his pale cheeks, his mouth relaxed, but curved and sensuous. And inert. Like a male sleeping beauty in his own glass case. Waiting. It was all Teresa could do to keep from reaching out and stroking that dear cheek, nearly a stranger to her now in its repose. To be so appealing and then wake again to the sure writhing and starting that was his daily fare. Surely it was only an evil spell?

Davy was more than someone to come home to. Davy was home. But she would not burden him with her needs, her life. Her love. She would stand alone if it killed her. He was on the brink of real success with his business and she wanted to help him, even if it was only by staying out of his way.

She finished wrestling her things in from the front step and quietly put them away. Seeing no evidence that Davy had eaten already, she prepared some hot soup and crackers, leaving them to stay warm, then settled into the big armchair next to the sofa to read the newspaper by the only lamp's dim light. Still Davy didn't stir. The breeze was cooler now and the heavy night sounds floating in through the open door settled in around them. Teresa's heart loped feebly, then recovered, leaving her short of breath. She massaged her chest over her heart, resting her hand there for the sense of comfort and steadiness. Her happiness with the day was a burden to it, just as sorrow or effort surely would be. Looking over at Davy, still sleeping, she realized her gesture matched his own. Both held their hands over their hearts in a silent pledge.

8

*Modern methods of instruction have not yet entirely strangled
the holy curiosity of inquiry.*
Albert Einstein

From what I can recall about the circumstances, Teresa, you're a lucky, lucky girl to have grown up here."

"Yes ma'am, I'm sure that's true," Teresa bit out the words, and thought to herself how that just wasn't the sort of thing you really wanted to hear from someone else. It was the sort of thing you'd rather say for yourself.

"Maybe you should just leave things like they are. Let sleeping dogs lie, so to speak." Mrs. Matrisciano rose up and squared her shoulders with authority. The air between them swelled with her certainty supported by all five meaty syllables of her improbable name on its little Formica sign. Strong and beefy and clean, like the proud doctors in Dallas who had never been sick a day in their lives.

"You were happy here, weren't you? Treated well?" She walked over to the filing cabinet as if to extract the slim file of Teresa Chace's past, but only tapped one nail against the side where a three-color sticker was asking, "Where will *you* spend eternity?"

Teresa's jaw worked a moment in silent anger. "I always have considered myself very fortunate. It's just that there's something wrong with my memory. I can't remember my own life. There isn't anyone to tell me about the things that were my life and now I've obviously forgotten them."

Her friend Chaya, along for moral support, touched Teresa lightly on the arm to force her to look at her, then gave her a widened stare that signaled the unspoken word "caution."

"Teresa," Chaya began brightly, "tell Mrs. Matrisciano what the doctors said."

For Chaya things were simple. She was Mexican and Catholic, both identities giving her a sense of the order of things that Teresa didn't have. They had been roommates at the home for a year when Chaya's mother had cancer, their twin beds separated by a lamp table with a clandestine candle burning to Saint Peregrine, the patron saint of cancer patients. A shiny little plastic prayer card nearby had a picture of Peregrine himself, a monk daintily lifting his cassock to show the wound on his leg that had been miraculously healed. Chaya went to Chapel with Teresa and everyone else, then faithfully lit her candle and offered up her prayers to Saint Peregrine. The two little orphan girls taught each other their prayers. Teresa could remember Chaya's life better than her own.

"In a minute, Chaya." Her teeth were still too close, the jaw hinting at what she really wanted to say. She waited for her heart to steady under the disarraying effect of the suppressed anger. It dipped and slowed and a tight band of darkness and pressure grew around her head. Her hand trembled slightly as she lifted it toward Mrs. M.

"I need to know, Mrs. M. I want to know. I've never bothered anyone about it before, but it is my life, and it was my mother who left me here, and I want to know the details. All I know is that her name is Rose. Rose Marie Chace. Someone told me once that she was killed saving me from a fire. Some said she drank herself to death. I even had my own private version where a crazy lady stole me and brought me here and my mother was still searching for me. You can understand, can't you, Mrs. M., how I would want to know the truth?"

Had her mother been a drowning woman who, with one last Herculean effort, saved her baby, pushed her up out of the morass that engulfed her? Or a fairy queen who forgot to put enough good into her infant daughter to be able to love her? Teresa despaired of finding a way to convey her need to people who didn't have it: there were just some things that big, strong people with plenty of everything were never going to understand. It was like a veil was over their eyes and they simply could not see – the way the Bible describes unbelievers.

She was tired of feeling backward in time with the light, spidery fingers of memory, working without proof, without evidence, feeling around for anyone who may have loved her. Her mother? There were different kinds of love, and some of them she had found since then. But it was never enough. And always the danger that it wouldn't last. They might die. Or leave.

Her anger worked her jaw in rhythmic waves and would not be swallowed. What would Pastor Stone – Ethan, he insisted she call him now – say about so much anger? Hundreds of sermons, his and others', she had heard in her lifetime, so many of them about anger. But nothing that said what to do with it. Only that it was wrong to have it. She must never be angry. It was too dangerous. Even if they got mad all the time, it was always safer to keep her own anger to herself.

"When I was younger I used to have nightmares where my real mama came to get me. But she was dressed in a black snake suit, the kind with a little point in the forehead and a tail. I knew snakes didn't have tails like that. Only the devil. She had white skin and bright ruby red lipstick, and when she opened her mouth to speak, her tongue was forked like a snake.

"Mother Garza said I was getting too old to be calling them in the night, but eleven didn't seem like such a magic number. I just liked to be sure someone would come.

"They always wanted me to call them "Mother," but now I understood about foster mothers. And that I am a "foster" child, different from a regular child. I've had Mother Steiner, Mother Hernandez, and Mother Garza. Mother Steiner wanted me to call her Mama, but I just couldn't do it. I wondered if real daughters could always call real mamas in the night." Teresa's face was hot and she was perfectly still, willing her eyes to stay dry.

Mrs. M. paused and turned her gaze to meet Teresa's steady one. One hand stole up to her throat and rested lightly there as she considered Teresa's words.

"I had a real mama once. I can remember waiting for her better than I can remember her. Nameless people would get my blanket and clothes and socks together to be ready at the time they said Mama would come. She must have come, sometimes, but I can't remember that. Only waiting and waiting while she never came. You know, she would have done that to any child, the counselor reassured me; it wasn't just me."

"No." Mrs. M. whispered, her own eyes damp with the tears that Teresa had willed away.

Chaya laid a hand on Teresa's arm and Teresa forced herself to be still, although she hated the touch.

"I cannot stand to be alone, though I don't want anyone to touch me. It is as if my skin is gone; if I am very careful the pain is not too bad. Everyone, sooner or later, tries to touch me, but it hurts too much. Sometimes, when I am bruised or cut, I look at the bloody place and wonder that it doesn't move me. Not like this secret pain inside. It hurts, but I know it will go away."

"Teresa. Honey...." Mrs. M. began, leaning across the desk.

But Teresa, unmoved, continued talking as if she had a speech that she must deliver. A speech designed to avert disaster.

"Maybe if I had been prettier, I thought. Or very talented. When I was very young I could sing and dance, make my eyes shine like I had swallowed the moon. But then the light started going out and they didn't know what to make of me. They had skin and didn't understand how it felt not to have any. So I learned that it is always better to smile. Not resist. Not care." Teresa took a deep breath and leaned back, her burden delivered. "But I DO care, Mrs. M. I want to know about my life."

"Well, of course, dear. You're a grown woman now; there's no reason you shouldn't have the facts that we have." She walked back to the filing cabinet and deftly ran her nail over the soft folder tabs and extracted *Chace, Teresa* as if it had been her idea all along, just a simple matter.

Anger does not achieve the righteousness of God. The scripture memorized since childhood taunted her. Davy was never angry. In their pasts, Teresa had watched him enduring things that made her angry on his behalf, but his own anger never seemed to form. Ethan seemed angry at everything in his sermons, although he never expressed anger in response to her or even to the endless inanities of church business. Why was she so angry?

"Of course, the details are pretty old now. We lost contact with your mother several years ago. There's really no telling..."

"Wasn't there anyone else. A father, grandparents?"

"I'm afraid your birth certificate lists the father as 'unknown'." Mrs. M. tapped the page lightly while she considered it. "There apparently was a grandfather... or great-grandfather... the relationship was unclear. And an elderly Hispanic man who seemed to take care of you quite a bit."

Teresa wanted to reach across the big desk and grab the file herself.

"He was quite elderly at the time; not in good health. I'm sure he must have passed away by now. As I recall, he didn't want to leave you here at all. He came to see you a month or so after you arrived, wanted to take you home, but the legalities... the worker noted his disagreement here on the record. He never came again, so I'm afraid we can assume the worst."

The old man in the mist of her dreams, holding her hand so she wouldn't become lost. His chest rattling with laughter at her every word and turn. "*Papi,*" her lips wanted to say.

And her soul could hear him answer: "Teresa. *Mi muneca. Ven con Papi.*" Real or imagined? No matter, she supposed, what he was really like. Or her mother, either. Just what they were like to her. No matter that she'd been safe all along; she'd never felt safe. Still, she was almost sure she could remember the old man – her great-grandfather, apparently. And water, something to do with water. But the image would not come clear.

Like children of the Holocaust, she wondered if her memories were really only dreams. No family album, no one to come to weddings and funerals, as if it had all never happened. "I am with you," says the Lord of hosts. But where were you *then*? "I will never leave you nor forsake you..." Again?

"The social worker that brought you here noted that your mother was in the habit of leaving you with people and not coming back for days. A drinking problem apparently." She digested the pages of the file slowly with her eyes and gave it to Teresa piecemeal.

Chaya touched Teresa's arm again lightly and smiled her Amway-hopeful smile. Why couldn't she just let Teresa read it for herself? But Teresa could not ask again, never mind that her anger was pushing her guts, right there, against her diaphragm and turning her breathing ragged.

"The last time, she left you with a Mrs. Cortez. The connection is not clear – she wasn't a relative or a neighbor either, apparently – but after two days the lady called the welfare office."

And that, Teresa thought, is how I came to be lost. "Is there an address for this Mrs. Cortez? Or a name for the social worker?"

"Now, honey, you know that same social worker won't be there anymore. Probably long since retired or moved on. But you can always contact the child welfare office. I'm afraid the baby-sitter's name is all we have here. Mrs. Cortez. Juanita Cortez."

"No address?"

"No, I'm afraid not. There are a few other names here. All Hispanic; no addresses." She smiled at an interior thought and then looked up at Teresa.

"That must be why you took such a shine to Mrs. Martinez. Carmen. You just wouldn't have anybody else. You spoke as much Spanish as you did English when you first came here, you know."

No, she hadn't known. How could she have known? "Did my mother...?'

"No, no, not as I recall. And she looked very... *mmmm... Anglo*." Mrs. M. searched for the right words. "Very fair skin, and auburn hair, nearly red. Real curly."

It was the first time Teresa was sure that Mrs. M. really remembered her at all. With so many children coming and going over so many years, she really didn't blame her. But it did feel good to be part of an actual memory. And one that made her smile.

"Carmen wasn't really an employee here; she was Mrs. Steiner's maid. But she really loved the children."

"I remember her. Tia."

"Yes, the children called her Tia. She was here for years. No papers, though. 'Wet', as they say. Nowadays that's a big crime, but back in those days it was very common." She laughed with short little spurts of her solar plexus, using only her diaphragm.

"*Mojada*?" Teresa thought it was funny; especially Mrs. M's embarrassment. "As in just swam the river?" She would have to tell Pastor... Ethan. Even he would have to laugh at Mrs. M's prim propriety revealing this unsavory fact. Just another little joke to melt the stony gray wall of his sadness, his own propriety.

"Well, like they do, she came over on her shopping card every Monday and went home every Friday. Her daughter still works here, but she's married to a citizen, so of course she's legal."

"And she's still here? Is her mother still alive?"

"Yes; in very bad health – cancer, I think – but she still visits sometimes, rides over with one of her daughters. Maybe we could arrange something there."

"Well, that would be a start." Teresa's anger started to release its hold a little.

"What about a medical history, Mrs. M.?" Chaya was anxious to stay on track; more concerned over Teresa's physical health.

"Very sketchy. There's the alcoholism, of course."

Of course.

"And no history for the paternal side." She tapped the desk absentmindedly.

Of course, again.

"I'm afraid the welfare people wouldn't have kept anything more detailed than that. You see, your placement here was always 'temporary'. There was never any legal release for you to be considered for adoption."

Temporary.

"Is there a reason why you suddenly need to know now?"

"She's had health problems," Chaya plunged in. "The doctors, up in Dallas, told her a medical history would help them in the diagnosis and treatment."

"Cardiac Tamponade." Teresa said it deadpan, and let it sit there, like it would explain everything.

"What?"

"Compression of the heart from fluid in the pericardium. The underlying cause could be genetic, in which case the medications and rest will handle it. Or it could be a mechanical problem with a valve."

"Well."

"Rose's Tamponade."

"What's that?'

"I looked it up in a medical book and they called the condition Rose's Tamponade. Isn't that something?"

"Yes, quite a coincidence."

Or not. Her inheritance, after all. Her mother's heart. A part of her mother that had, in spite of all her other failings, apparently gone right on beating.

She could feel it now, laboring under the struggle with her excitement and anger, limping erratically along, doing its best considering it had a hole in it. A hole in her heart, her birthright.

While Mrs. M. perused the folder, Teresa's eyes wandered to the wide window and to the bright day muted by the canopy of Mesquite trees, out across the flat fields and even flatter horizon. Papaya trees made cheery little green umbrellas across the yard; Teresa could remember how their hollow stems made great pea-shooters when they were kids, some hard seed pods of another plant, ideal peas. In her mind's eye she framed a picture: a girl with a wound in her heart, the blood flowing, turning on one heel, loose dress floating with her long hair in the breeze, like the lady on the old Mercury dimes, blood running out into the world like the scene in *Ben Hur* where Christ's blood runs down from the cross and is washed into trickles and streams by the pouring rain. She felt the colors red and black against blue, but knew that would never work. Would a cross be too much? It began to feel too garish, too much like a mural in Mexico. And where would the light be? The source of light was everything...

"Teresa..."

She jerked her hand back just as she raised it for that first bold stroke.

"Yes."

"You were a million miles away." Chaya's voice was a reprimand.

Yes.

"Mrs. M. was asking how you like working for Pastor Stone."

Yes.

She placed the errant hand over her wounded chest, to still it, to stanch the invisible flow.

"Very much. He's been very good to me. And Davy, too."

"And David?" Her narrow eyes opened and beamed. "How is our Davy?" Her delight and affection were evident and Teresa relaxed. Mrs. M. may have her own misguided reasons for hoarding her birth records, but she obviously loved Davy.

"He's amazing, like always," Teresa finally answered. "When did you see him last?"

"We talk on the phone from time to time, but I haven't actually seen Davy since, oh, last Christmas. Too long."

"You knew he'd had some surgery? On his legs."

"No! That rascal; he should have told us. How is he doing? I would have liked to help him out..."

"Oh, he's fine. That was way back in January. It's made a big difference for him. He uses arm crutches now but can walk better overall."

"He's gotten so independent. First that computer. Now he has that young .man to assist him. I understand he really has a gift for numbers... investments I believe he's working at... I don't know." The actual description of Davy's computer work mystified her, but her happiness at Davy's independence showed.

"Yes, he handles investments of his own and some accounts for others. He's even started an internet company for CPAs."

Their eyes met and Mrs. M. nodded. "He really is special."

"I don't know what I would have done without him." Teresa ducked her head to hide the quick tears.

"I'd love to see him."

"He'll be out here this evening. We're going to swim after hours. Dad Morgan said it would be okay. Davy loves to swim."

Mrs. M. laughed. "Yes, I remember that he did. Always. I can remember when we discovered what a lifejacket and swimming pool meant for little David Hurt."

"Freedom, he says."

"Yes. And to think that now he's a CPA; does work for the Home Foundation Board. They say he's a miracle on that computer; setting up different trusts and things. Dad Morgan was just telling us about all the different arrangements

David works out..." She leaned over and picked up a gray brochure from her desktop. "Charitable Remainder Annuity Trust, Lead Trust, Revocable Charitable Trust, Securities, Annuities, I don't know what-all." She cocked her head to angle her bifocals. "See? Here's Davy's name right here."

Yes, there he was, her Davy, "Financial Adviser." Teresa's eyes wandered to the window again, to the few mesquites and cottonwoods and distant palms bent in their chronic slant by the prevailing southeast breeze from the Gulf. Instead of rain, then, like in the film, there would be dark streaks in that peculiar southeast slant. And the terra cotta colors of the land. Her artist's heart put a Mexican village woman into the view, pulling a *cobija* about her as she stared into the setting sun. It would be strong and desolate; and the blood, the wound, hardly visible at all. The perspective was the problem. Even clouds aren't pretty when you're in them. Only slowly, as if from a distance, did she realize the conversation had moved on to the subject of Ethan Stone.

"Such a nice man," Mrs. M. went on. "Such a shame about his little boy. Tragic. Is he doing all right? I hear his wife went home to her folks for a visit and still isn't back. I do hope they're okay. I don't think anyone ever really gets over losing a child." None of the irony of words she had just spoken showed on her simple face. She laid the file down and smoothed it with her hands as if it had developed wrinkles. Or as if she had developed a sudden reverence for it.

"What exactly did happen?" Chaya wondered aloud, trying to draw Teresa back in.

"He's very private. You can tell he's sad, but he never talks about it. He's always in a black suit and looking very businesslike. A wonderful administrator, but impossible to read. I really don't know any more than what everyone seems to know. There was an accident and their little boy was killed."

They all sought the window then and honored the tragedy with their silence and sympathetic nods.

"Makes us stop and realize how very fortunate we all are. You actually seem to have a very nice life, Teresa, I must say. And David; I know he must be thrilled to have you back here. He was always very attached to you. You seemed to understand each other."

"Yes."

"If you need help with anything, please call me. I know you don't want to over-burden David; he's so willing but he does have his limitations, of course."

Of course.

And yes... my very nice life...

loved her so much. Then lost her. Then couldn't even conjure up her face, couldn't really remember the object my heart broke for. Like I had something wonderful, something miraculous, like a crown of feathers, maybe, or a jeweled sword. Then lost it. And without any evidence that it ever existed, I lost faith in it. Never sure again that the kind strangers cared for me, I had to learn to care for myself, think about my own comfort, my own safety. Anything could happen.

I've mourned all my life for someone I can't even remember. And now for a baby that is lost and a lover I mustn't take.

Lord, be tender with me. I wear the shame of the kind of suffering that people can't see. They think it's a problem of character somehow. I know you love me, God. But do you *like* me?

9

What does a fish know about the water in which he swims all his life?
Albert Einstein

The night sky was pure navy blue against the flat fields stretching away from the pool. Curdled banks of darker navy clouds obscured the tiny blazing stars until they twinkled and appeared one at a time, as if they were being set there by a passing presence. The air rolled in warm and humid from the southeast, settling the dried skirts of palm fronds in periodic sighs, moving the bank of clouds to reveal the hidden splendor of yet another star.

Davy and Teresa were children again, or carefree water creatures, mermaid and merman, in their own kingdom, swimming and playing in the warm water of the pool, the moonlight making diamonds of the water in their hair, iridescent bare skin. They held hands under water and made snakes of their hair and puffed-up fishes of their faces, then broke the water's surface laughing. Teresa wasn't afraid of the water exactly, but she didn't trust it like Davy did; he knew – had known since childhood – to make allowances: not to stay under too long, not to get too tired at the deep end, to stay with her. They met halfway in this watery kingdom where she gave up her human feet and he gained a fish's body that was surer than his own.

And then they were alone again. It amazed Teresa how different Davy was in the water. She had forgotten how surely the base of power and control swung in his direction with just that one alteration: gravity. Davy was already stronger than anyone knew. As he said himself, he had been in training most of his life. His motion, set into the buoyancy of the dark satin water, was transformed. No wonder he couldn't get enough of it. She wondered how he could ever bear to leave it.

She felt stronger herself than she had in months. She had somehow lost the ability or inclination to nurture herself, but Davy tempted her to eat and Davy gave her courage to work and Davy took her to his watery world and made her swim. Her own impulses to life and happiness, stunted for so long now, swelled under Davy's nurturing care. Or maybe the water had transformed her as well and she was the Little Mermaid whose feet would hurt like needles when once she walked on land again.

They floated like babies in the silent amniotic warmth, then thrashed like maniacs, skittering across the gleaming surface like water bugs. They baptized each other in hushed parodies of Dad Morgan's public ceremonies, their rising faces breaking up the slowed, honeyed light into tiny dancing dots. Underneath the water they were deaf and could not hear the world above, only the distant muffled hum of the pool's filter thrumming like some huge mechanical heart. Above, they scrunched their eyes to be sightless, and smelled the clean chlorine evanescence around them, imagined they heard the distant echoes of the tiny isolated village of the home putting itself to bed for the night.

Sliding through the water slowly, quietly, they came up to find even the moon obscured by the deepening bank of clouds. There was barely enough light to make their faces glow over the deep indigo mystery of water. They caught their breath at the same moment and, as if by unspoken agreement, floated in silent awe at the peace of the moment and sated languor of their bodies. In the whole world there was only blue and gold, and the sky hung heavy and low over them, its hidden stars holding their own breath as well. For the first time in years, Teresa relaxed and felt the water hold her.

"Davy," she whispered softly, not wanting to break the spell. "Do you remember me when I was little, when I first came to the home?"

Davy righted himself and bobbed silently beside her until his feet found the bottom. "I remember the first day I saw you." His smile lit the darkness.

"Did you think I was a Mexican? Or an Anglo?"

He laughed softly and placed his hand under the small of her back so she could float without thinking, without trying.

"I thought you were the prettiest little girl in the whole home. You had pigtails." His voice slowed and quivered. "And you never once made fun of me, like the others."

"But did I speak Spanish? I'm serious." She kept her voice stern and even.

"We all spoke some Spanish. But you spoke more than I did. You were always friends with the girls who had trouble with English. But you spoke English like all of us, not like it was your second language. I don't remember thinking you were Mexican. I just remember thinking you were cute." He poked her ribs and whooshed away, daring her to follow.

"Oh fine," Teresa yelped as the relaxed reverie ended. "Well I thought you were a total geek," she squealed and shot after him. She wanted to make him stay and hear her worries and her fears. And her secret. But they played. She did not want to be a burden to him. Weigh him down.

Davy threw a quarter to dive for, and Teresa watched it return the glinting light of the moon as it flipped over and over down into the darkness at the bottom of the pool. Languorous now from the floating buoyancy and peaceful night she only watched it and let herself float free until she felt Davy's hand close around her ankle and give a playful jerk down. Then he broke through the dark shimmering surface to chide her for her laziness and she turned to swim to the faint silver glimmer at the bottom.

But when she touched the spot it was not the coin, only a spot in the old concrete lining. She looked around, but did not see the coin and could feel the faint edge of panic in her chest; either she had not taken in enough air in the first place, or the distant darkness and hum around her frightened her. Davy had disappeared. She turned to the glowing surface of the other, safer world and broke gasping for air and thrashing for the side.

She felt Davy's hand around her ankle, his incredibly strong grip playfully tugging at her, pulling her under. She swam in earnest, the concrete edge of the pool a distant marker of safety. Something about the firm pull under water made her afraid; it was like a childhood nightmare where she was drowning and powerless. Irrational fear overtook her and made her thrash in panic until Davy, thrashing in his own slow pulsing motion, could feel the difference. Immediately his strong arms went around her bare legs to still them, held them to himself while he propelled her forward and up out of the water, toward the safe pattern of blue tiles at the edge. She gasped once to be so decisively free of the water and the panic at the same instant.

"You're okay," he whispered behind her.

"Yes," she panted, slapping one wet hand on the rough concrete curve.

"I've got you." His arms, skimming the naked edges of her legs, came up and encircled her waist as lightly as a dancer, then folded upon themselves until he held her whole body curved to match the shape of his own. She was surprised to be held in that way by Davy, but, then again, not surprised either. It was the iron tenderness of a man who loved her. Like the others who had held her before, but transformed by his love and the gleaming navy and gold lights of his water kingdom. For an instant it would have been the most natural thing in the world to turn to face him, put her mouth on his and take a lover there in their underwater kingdom. Why not? She was afraid for them both. Afraid she was not strong enough. Or that he was not. But afraid too of a life without him. The only love she'd ever known was lost love.

Then he too slapped one wet hand up beside hers on the edge. "Okay, now?"

"Yes." But her heart pounded all the same. She knew the world around her but could not feel herself in it. She felt like crying. Maybe she was crying in the easy anonymity of the water. Her greatest comfort had been that she could tell Davy anything. But she would not tell him this. He released her then and swung along beside her, steadying hands nearly touching on the pool edge, facing her. She reached for his free hand under the water with her own and held it there a moment.

He kissed her before either of them realized he would, a kiss at once as deep and hungry as that of any man who had ever kissed her and yet cut short by his innocent care for her and her own surprise.

"Davy," she whispered, touching his face with her hand.

He backed away from her slightly. "I'm sorry, Teresa. I know it's not that simple." He had broken his own vow of respecting the invisible boundary between them that kept them safe.

"No," she agreed, but kept his hand in hers close to her lips. "Not simple..."

His heart stilled to feel the tenderness in her, calming the rush of fear that crossing their boundary called up in him. He had been tempted for an instant to believe that the limits were not so necessary, that he could reach out to her and they could have more...

But no. There was no safety beyond those limits. For Teresa or for him. His unthinking passion was a danger to what they did share. He would never again endanger that. She would have to come to him.

When she was in Dallas and their relationship was by phone, it had been easy to preserve those limits. But with her close physical proximity every day now, it was nearly impossible. That they had been children together did not dull the longing of the grown man he had become. Now he knew the smell of her shampoo, the drape of her sweater, the damp nape of her neck under the ringlets of hair still dark from her shower. Now she was the most delicious, the most real thing in his life. The way her small hands felt against his back made him want to turn and worship her body with his own. But no.

He swam for the steps in the shallow end and pulled her behind him, making sure she was secure.

Teresa felt the determined shift in Davy's touch and dropped back from him. She had known only disappointment from physical passion. Then, at the worst and lowest point of her whole life, Davy had carried her into the safety of his protection. He knew her humiliation, her despair. Yet he said she was precious. Strong. And a survivor, like himself. She was rebuilding her life around that. Like a pearl. Neither had ever questioned his tacit assumption that their love would not be physical.

Now they were not so sure.

Their uncertainty was a weight between them in their watery kingdom.

"I could never ask you to share my life, Teresa," Davy finally spoke. "The life of a disabled person... well, it's no life for you."

"Or you," she said, crying in earnest now.

"It IS my life. And I am used to it."

"What..." she began. But he would not let her finish.

"You want a lot of things out of life, Teresa. And I want you to have them. Don't get me wrong," he smiled sideways at her. "You are the sweetest, sexiest thing alive... none of your womanly charms are lost on me, I assure you. But my life... well, it would mean sacrificing what you want from life."

"I don't know what I want out of life, Davy. But I know I would be lost without you."

"You know you have my love. I give it to you." He made a motion with both hands cupped as if bestowing a gift on her. "You are free to do whatever you want with it. Even free to love another. I want you to be happy."

"I am happy now," she said simply.

"But you deserve more, Teresa. More than I am. Or ever can be."

"I am happy now," she repeated against his doubts and her own fear, against their confusion.

She took his cupped hands into her own and brought them to her mouth and kissed them and leaned into him and they sat like children on the steps of the

66

pool, letting the water bob them lightly about in all the possibilities.

"For my part, Teresa, I promise that I will never kiss you again." He turned and smiled into her face. "Unless you ask me to."

"Davy, I want so many things and I am so afraid."

"I know."

They sat in silence until the gentle pulsing of the waves stilled and peace returned and enveloped them.

"Say my name, Davy."

"Teresa." His whisper was calm and sweet as a mother's.

"Say my name a hundred times."

10

A table, a chair, a bowl of fruit and a violin;
what else does a man need to be happy?
Albert Einstein

Teresa stood before a large blank canvas she had set up near the window. Her dark brows were nearly joined in the tuck of concentration between them. The graceful curve of her old wooden palette gleamed in her left hand, still empty, but colorful and shiny from years of oily layers of paints, the palette knife nicks permanently filled in with the dried residue of old paint. It was the first Saturday she'd had free to work on her own art and nothing would flow. First one idea and then another presented itself in a quick tease and faded before she could grab it with her mind. She could not get a picture of her own vision, with this stone against her heart. Yet only work would move the stone.

She saw the long, blue rehab van drop Davy off, watched him struggle up the sidewalk, his old canvas gym bag almost dragging along the ground as he staggered and swayed around its swinging weight. Saturday was his "Olympics Day" of physical therapy at the big rehab center a half-hour drive away. He always gave Jesse the day off and left his car in the drive for Teresa to use.

The Saturday buzz of the neighborhood made her own inertia seem more pronounced. And made it easy to resist her first impulse to go help Davy with his burden. He didn't like offers of assistance; one of his few touchy points.

Davy came in as quietly as all that hardware and his own limitations would allow and, seeing that she was working, came and stood wordlessly a moment, the gym bag heavy and rounded at the bottom like it had a bowling ball in it. Teresa held her concentration a moment longer, not turning to face him.

"The first stroke is the important one, you know Davy," she whispered, keeping her eyes focused on the blank canvas.

He bobbed his head and lifted his eyebrows in an unseen gesture that would have passed for a question.

"The very first stroke an artist makes, Professor Stout says, can be called 'Art.' From then on the brush strokes are just problem-solving." Still her hand did not reach out to make that brave first statement that would commit her to a new search for colorful solutions.

He stood and waited, the rustling and rattling of his involuntary movement finally coming to rest. Reaching out or speaking would start the unruly undulations again, and that he did not do. It was plain to him, in any case, that Teresa was troubled and he knew that she'd have to speak to him about it at any moment.

Finally he broke the silent spell. "You're working again."

"Yes." She turned to him, her eyes still foggy with concentration. "I'm getting braver, Davy. You make me feel safe, and it shows in my work. I pick what I like and what I want and trust my mind to make connections. That's what Professor Stout always says to do. You make me brave enough to actually do it."

Still they both stood motionless and waited for the words that would free them. Finally, Teresa let them out. "Davy, Carmen died. Mrs. M. called this morning. While we were talking about finding her she was dying. Cancer. We're too late."

He moved forward with the intent to comfort Teresa, but only wakened the waves to their cruel job of ruining any intentional motion. He eased up closer as best he could. He breathed in their closeness, as well as the smell of the old paint palette that was still waiting for Teresa's color choices. "Sorry."

"Yes. Well, that sneaky ole cancer is like that."

"She was a special lady." His own eyes were cloudy and guarded.

"I want to paint her." Something slow and solid, she thought, in all the browns and terra cottas of Carmen's race and northern Mexico desert home. "The way I remember her." At last, she laid a few strips of bold color on the wooden palette from the assortment of tubes on the table, mixed some of them with the tiny spatula-like knife, then selected a broad bristle brush and remixed an even more careful shade.

Finally, when the heavy bristle brush was full of the mixture, she reached out and put a stroke, nearly blood-red, in the center of her canvas. Then some quicker smaller strokes of darker reds and umber. "Dark to light, you know, Davy. Dark to light. The oils want to know the darks first." Her lips were pursed in a tight line, her brow furrowed in a set frown. She hesitated, stopped, agitated the brush a moment longer, then appeared to give up by tossing her brushes into the open jar of turpentine.

"Something will have to happen in my soul, Davy. Before I can paint this picture. Something that hasn't happened yet."

She turned to him suddenly. "We could go to the funeral. Come with me, Davy. I want to say good-bye to her, but I can't go alone."

"When?"

"Tomorrow."

"Across?" Local shorthand for the two hour ordeal of crossing the international bridge, sitting in line coming and going, then finding the tiny house in the crazy-quilt, of the rutted mud roads in a Mexican village.

"Yes. Reynosa. Tomorrow afternoon at three. Carmen's *velorio*. You know, like a wake."

He tried to keep the anxiety from his face; it was something he wasn't sure they could do. What good would he be? She could see the doubt settling in his eyes and added, "we can do it."

She gave her voice that teasing and pleading tone that she knew he would not say no to. His thin arms fluttered like the wings of a startled bird. Teresa knew not to look at him as he tried to regain physical control; spectators always sent his body into more and more spasm. She only sat and waited.

"So, when do we leave?" It was a done deal and they both knew it.

"As near as I could gather from the neighbors, the body is 'out' all afternoon and all night and family and friends come and go when they like. She said two or three o'clock would be good."

"Teresa, are you sure it's a good idea to take me? Won't that be too much commotion for a religious service? Maybe Chaya would go with you."

"Please." She pushed a sketch pad over to one side; the dappled morning sun shone down on the quick, rough lines of a woman sketched in against a dark, bold background. Davy had seen enough of Teresa's work to appreciate this was an early study and that the face would eventually shine with light against a brooding, troubled background. She was wonderful with light, and at capturing personality with just a few strokes, just a hint of expression around the eyes. And good at letting the colors talk for the person. Letting the person say, in fact, what they might never have had the courage or opportunity to say in real life.

Teresa rose and stretched, languorous as a cat, as seemingly unconcerned, and slipped around behind where Davy stood braced against his crutches. She must paint him like this; like a crane or other long-legged bird standing poised in shallow water. She stood right behind him and waited for the soft okay she knew would come, then slipped her arms quickly around his torso and gave him a hug. "Thanks, Davy." She could feel the muscles working in their ceaseless choreography.

Upon feeling her embrace, Davy started and blushed furiously, his head dipping and bobbing faster than ever. His soft hair fell forward and Teresa stepped back around to face him, reaching up to smooth it back from his face.

Slowly the crescendo of involuntary movement slowed and he brought his earnest blue gaze up to meet Teresa's. "I was set up, wasn't I?"

Before his slow grin could form they both heard the distinct whine coming from the gym bag at his feet. Color rose again to Davy's face. "Surprise," was all he could manage to mumble in his efforts to balance delight with physical control.

Teresa dropped to one knee and gingerly felt the bag from the outside. "What?" She could feel the unmistakable warmth and squirm of a live animal. Then another whine.

"Davy..." her voice went up at the end, as if in admonition.

"It followed me home," he managed to say. "What could I do?"

She opened the bag wide and pushed the canvas sides down over the warm, furry happiness that was now jumping about inside. A puppy, brown, black and white, and of unclear parentage. Teresa lifted it out and held it to her chest. "Oh, Davy..."

"It was a beagle in a past life, but there's other influences..."

"It's darling." She turned it over to examine its rounded puppy tummy. "She's darling." And held the puppy up to her own neck, running her free hand hungrily over the satiny coat of baby fine hair, pulling the floppy beagle ears back from the rounded head and squinting baby-eyes, still milky blue. It was a very young puppy, still smelling of its mother's milk, her licking-attentions, and musty littermates. "But where... how?

"One of the P.T.'s at Rehab had her, the last of a basketful. The runt."

"For me?"

He stepped around to face her, his face more serious. "A watchdog, Teresa. I have to leave for a few weeks. The underwriters are ready to meet with my lawyers and directors. We're going to take CPAS public early next year, right after Christmas."

Teresa stood silent, nuzzling the puppy under her chin. "Leaving? Next week? But..."

"You can stay right here; everything will be the same. The rent is all paid and there's money for the bills. Jesse is available if you need him for anything. Everything is taken care of."

Teresa sank down to the sofa, still hugging the puppy to herself. "Except that you won't be here."

"No," he answered, joining her on the couch. "It will take at least a month, maybe longer, just to meet with all the parties involved and start the process. Then I'll come home for a while. Then back to finalize everything."

"Will I be able to call you?" She had never thought about her life except as their life, in spite of her fear of a commitment beyond what they shared already.

"Of course."

She hugged him, the puppy sandwiched in between.

"Thank you for the puppy. She's so sweet. I can't believe it."

"Neither could the landlady."

"You called her?"

"Sure; I'd make a lousy street person. A brief lecture, a substantial deposit, and the adoption was final. She's got a layette, down in the bag."

Teresa dropped down again, still nuzzling the puppy in her neck, and fished around in the gym bag. "These smelly socks aren't hers, are they?" she teased. Then brought up a small sack of food, several small tins of moist food, chew toys, rawhide pieces, a red collar.

"Boy, this is a really well-equipped puppy, for such a new, tiny little orphan. How...?"

"Oh, there's always broke adolescents at the center, available for errands." Davy finally sank to the big armchair to get comfortable. "What do you want to name her?" The sadness was leaving Teresa's face as she settled the pup, who rewarded every movement and whispered endearment by licking her with quick darts of its bubble-gum pink tongue.

"Something impressive…"

"Spot? Tippy? Rover?" he teased.

Teresa stood and stared out the window, considering. "A people name, I think. Like a classy person of good heritage…"

"Queen Elizabeth? Jacqueline?"

She narrowed her eyes and scowled at him in mock anger. "Something good." She held the puppy up and away as if to protect it from Davy's irreverent attempts. "Maybe after someone wonderful?… I don't know. I have to think about it." She went to take the puppy out to introduce it to the grass in the backyard.

"Lincoln? Curie? Harper?" Davy was still calling out behind her retreating back.

After a discussion with the puppy itself during its lengthy search for the quintessentially perfect place to pee, she decided. When she came back in, Davy was still sitting, waiting to enjoy the show.

"I've got it."

"Garbo? Marilyn?"

"Morgan." She was emphatic, ending his teasing suggestions.

After someone wonderful.

After the only father either one of them had ever known.

The line of traffic at the bridge was backing right up to the shopping mall with its garish placards announcing the bargains in English and Spanish, as well as the current exchange of currencies. The sidewalks were choked with people, music blared from every cheap electronics store hawking off-brand boom boxes, and the windows were full of the bright polyester puffs that the Mexican women preferred: shiny miracles of synthetic fibers and outrageous taste, that appealed to the people starved of color by the flat, monochrome desert of northern Mexico. The green trucks of the border patrol agents cruised through, following tips or their sixth sense to detect aliens and drugs and contraband. Teresa wondered what the "profile" was, though she was confident that she and Davy didn't fit it. Teresa imagined that she could tell, simply by looking, which of the dogged pedestrians downtown and along the bus route were local and which were, like Carmen, *mojada*. The dressed-up girls with impossible spike heels and a studied nonchalance, one eye peeled for *la migra* and another for their patron, were obvious. As was the ubiquitous brown grocery sack, the real giveaway. Someone should counsel the shopping card girls to use fresh sacks with the logos of downtown merchants instead of old grocery sacks taken from their patrons' homes and worn soft as fabric with repeated use.

Teresa tried to imagine poor Carmen making the same journey every week, going to work for Mrs. Steiner at the home every Monday morning and going home the way she and Davy had just come every Friday evening.

"*Mojada.*" Nobody's what you think.

"Can you imagine that poor woman making this trip every single week, Davy?"

"Or even once a month."

A long sweaty hour later, they crossed the International Bridge and found the ramshackle colonia on the Mexican side of the Rio Grande. Teresa and Davy were dulled and blinded by the heat and brilliant sun and tedious crossing. They were both so limp with the heat and the anxious search down terrible streets for the tiny colonia that Davy was almost calm, as if his exhausted muscles had finally gotten the message that they should rest.

Teresa finally swung the old Ford into the tiny rutted dirt street the neighborhood children assured them was the right one, and the right tire sank into a hole just as the car pitched into the sharp incline. The lurch threw Davy against his door and Teresa held onto the steering wheel like it was a bucking bronco.

"Jeez, our alley's in better shape than their main road." They both looked mournfully down the incline into the neighborhood where Carmen's house stood, weighing their options.

"So, do we go for it and risk never being able to get this old crate out again, or do we walk?" But even as she said it Teresa knew she might just as well keep inching her way along, because Davy wouldn't be able to navigate the street, sharply inclined, no sidewalk, pocked with mud holes where housewives threw out buckets of water, the rest dusty with the hot, smelly, cloying dust of the city. A few desultory chickens pecked along the edge and flew up in alarm as the old Ford bounced by.

Davy, for his part, hung on to the handle and dashboard as best he could while Teresa picked her way slowly down, careful for the groups of children that were everywhere standing to stare. The street narrowed until they felt they could almost touch the houses on either side. They looked at each other with the raised eyebrows of silent alarm.

There was no mistaking the house, though, when they got to the bottom and the long Ford settled in at the "curb" like a big white bird coming to rest carefully, precariously on a post. People of all ages milled about outside, and Teresa spotted Carmen's daughter as she separated from the group and came to the car.

The short, dark-eyed woman approached them with her hand held out, already speaking.

"*Ay, Señorita, Señor. Maria, Maria Flores de Martinez, la hija de Carmen.* Remember? *La Directora*, she said you coming today." She dotted her native tongue with the English words and phrases she was sure of, touched Teresa's outstretched hand lightly, then reached naturally for Davy's with both of hers, trapping it a moment as if she knew how to compensate for his disability.

"*Si, como no.* Of course we remember you, don't we Davy?" Teresa took Davy's arm as they were swept out of the car into the somber swirl of mourners, then through many pairs of hands raised in greeting. Many offered the typical feathery handshake that, north of the border, would be called a "limp fish." They stepped into the dim interior of the tiny house.

Maria escorted them to two vacant seats barely three feet from the coffin itself. Cheap black fabric covered the coffin, intended to hide the shabbiness of the wood; the little plastic window on top allowed the family to view the beloved body that they could not afford to embalm. Even the coffin itself was short, like it had been custom-made with just enough wood to envelop the short Indian stature of La Senora Carmen Martinez. And yet the poverty did not turn to shabbiness because of the love and care that was evident everywhere in the tiny room that would barely hold the coffin and chairs for half a dozen mourners.

Carmen's face, through the little window, was not too different from the smiling face they remembered. It wore the satisfied expression – almost a smile – of someone at home among those they love. Yes, that was it: the satisfaction of being truly at home. Lying smiling in the midst of her attentive daughters, dark, silent sons, and dozen rambunctious grandchildren, Carmen still reigned over the family she had crossed that teeming bridge so many times to support, in her double life as an "illegal." *Mojada*? Not on this side. On this side she was a queen.

The unmistakable aroma of Mexican cooking wafted into the room from the tiny kitchen behind the curtained doorway. No matter the dish, the recipe always started with frying onions and tomatoes in some lard, with garlic and chilli sitting close by waiting for their turn to be thrown in. The pungent aroma tickled some deep memory. She was tiny, sitting at a table, comfortable Spanish eddying around her while her plate of food was served. A thick white crockery plate with a hot masa tortilla, then a big spoonful of steaming arroz, white rice turned orange with the tomatoes. And tiny pieces of chicken – wings, perhaps – nestled in sparsely among the rich rice dish. "*Come, mi'ija*. Eat, baby." Carmen? Or someone before that? The same someone who held her hand at the water's edge and showed her the ducks floating serenely by? "*Ay, Mamacita*," the voice cried out in her dreams, "*Te vas a caer*." You will fall.

The neighborhood forces of Catholics and Protestant Evangelicals and even *brujeria* – quasi-religious occult practices – combined into the unique service, the *velorio*. Loved ones came and went, offering prayers for the deceased and comfort for the family. Two large candles burned at the head and two at the foot of the coffin and smaller votives were scattered about, lit by the Catholic faithful, some of whom were still seated in the room saying the rosary as they pushed the beads steadily through their fingers and whispered the memorized words.

But because Carmen herself, along with many of her friends and family, had become Protestant evangelicals, there were no statues of the Virgin or saints, vestments for the clergy, or fancy drapings over the coffin. It contributed a basic austerity that was more at home with the poverty. Teresa stared at the humble little coffin, resting still on the aluminum 'X's of the folding legs under the ambulance gurney that had brought it over and would take it back on its final journey to the cemetery. There was a small cross on the floor underneath, fashioned of a loose white powder. Some magic *polvo* or powder for warding off spirits or something, no doubt. The contribution of the local *brujeria* superstitions against lurking evil.

Davy and Teresa kept their heads bowed, Teresa's arm resting on the chair behind him where she could feel the warmth from his back and its steadily undulating muscles. Teresa wished she was Catholic and had something to do; beads to push through her empty fingers, candles to light, saints to implore. She grasped for God through the empty symbols of her own faith and longed for the tangible symbols of the other.

And if she herself died tomorrow? No candles, no beads, no *polvos*. Only poor Davy and Chaya, maybe some merciful church folk along with Ethan, some people from the home.

Still, she would be ready. Death, her old lover, was not what she was afraid of. Fear was what she was afraid of. Aloneness. Not death.

She would be ready. Yes.

Or Davy? The thought made the sweat of the hot afternoon dry in a quick chill. She laid her open hand on Davy's pulsing back to comfort herself with his warmth. She felt keenly how frail and vulnerable he was, though strong in his own determined way. So brave and good. She felt him tremble beneath the thin cotton of his shirt and was newly aware of what it cost him to love her. How was she going to manage without him, even for just a month?

"Teresa," Davy whispered, turning to her. "I remember your grandfather. An elderly man, holding your hand... you hadn't been at the home very long."

Her heart quickened just a little and she held her breath to steady it.

"He spoke Spanish." Davy's face was dreamy, trying to gather and firm the memory for her. "I think I thought he worked there or something, but no... he was there for you. He wore a hat..."

"With the string in the back of his head, Mexican style." She couldn't be sure, but it was as if she was sharing the glimpse into Davy's memory.

"Yes. Mexican... but with light blue eyes. I remember him because I had never seen such light eyes in a dark man."

"I think I remember him too. Did we have a pond of ducks at the home? I remember him taking me to see the ducks. There were babies, little yellow babies."

"Yes." He smiled and touched her hand.

"I think I called him *Papi*..."

So it was true. The patchwork pieces were her childhood. The dreams were not made of fairy-dust, something that had never been. No. They were material remnants of love. She had a grandfather. *De este lado*, as the people here would say: From this side. This side of the river; this other world. These people she sat with, mourning *la dona Carmen*, were her people too.

Was this how it felt to the Jews who survived the Holocaust? Everyone dead and gone; disappeared. Only no stone to mark their passing; no Yad Vashem to memorialize them. Had they ever even existed, any of them? Something at her very center quivered with fear or loss. It was forbidden to mourn them. She, like the Jews she read about, felt guilty even though she could not remember having done anything wrong.

She thought of the dark Madonna, hooded, mysterious, malevolent, she was searching for. Rose, a show business name, a ghost, a fragment of a memory. And "Chace", a name she had looked up in every phone book of every town she'd ever been in. And maybe there were others.

Maybe Mrs. M. was right; better to leave well enough alone. Whose baby is anyone, anyway? Fisher Kings, every one of us, with our wound that will not heal. All we can do is keep it open, keep it clean. Let it bleed.

The room, full and dim as a rocky cave, blurred with the whine of the fan and the rosaries being whispered. The small clutch of people grew restless, Teresa and Davy both sensed it was time to go.

"Thank you," she whispered, a silent prayer. "Thank you for Carmen Martinez; thank you for the mercy of strangers."

Davy shuddered and Teresa let out a long sigh; the heat and humidity of the mid-afternoon claimed them and bore them away into exhaustion. She only had to lean forward a little to brush the side of the black cloth of the coffin lightly with her hand, say goodbye to another piece of her lost childhood.

"Goodbye, señora."

11

*She's certainly able to cry already,
but won't know how to laugh until much later.*

Albert Einstein

The only problem that still needs to be resolved," Einstein wrote his fiancée, "is how to keep our Lieserl with us; I wouldn't want to have to give her up." No, no, wouldn't dare to want exactly what he did want... to be free from his little girl. "And don't stuff her with cow's milk," the great genius joked. "Because it might make her stupid."

"I'd like to make a Lieserl myself sometime – it must be fascinating!" Yes, quite. And, though he had never seen his baby daughter, he already knew so much about the theory of her: "She's certainly able to cry already, but won't know how to laugh until much later. Therein lies a profound truth." Such affection for the idea of a daughter, when one doesn't want the actual daughter at all. Just the myriad truths she could, anecdotally, prove.

Why was Lieserl a secret for so long? The mother and the father cut away the child who trailed them, spoiling their elaborate plans. How could E ever equal mc^2 with a child there, wanting, needing?

But it is a child's nature to want and need.

And the secret daughter, could she be sitting in some foreign country, in her

79

frail nineties, trying to piece together the patchwork of her own life, denied the details, sharing someone else's memory?

Lieserl... *Tochti... Liebling...*

12

Out yonder there was this huge world...
Albert Einstein

The little girl stood facing the wall, a dark blue crayon poised in her two-year-old fist. She made a long, dark line then, quickly, an almost-circle. It is me, she thought – me in my color, the color of the plums in the bowl up high on the table.

"Baby?" the lady called from down the hall.

Hurry. She looked over her shoulder... no one in the doorway yet. No one big enough to take her crayons from her or her from her crayons. Two more marks, low down, smaller. These were her favorite things – her Humpty Dumpty doll with the long swinging legs, her cat Princess hiding in the grass. Those things were gone now; gone wherever it was that Mama was. She only saw her Humpty Dumpty doll and her cat Princess when she saw Mama. That much she knew; the rest was confusing.

She called out "Mama!" every time she heard a car door outside. "Mama!" every time a neighbor or the stiff southeast breeze touched the screen door. And finally, screaming, her chubby face contorted into springs of hot tears, "Mama, Mama, Mama," stamping her feet in rage.

But Mama didn't come.

Keys jangled and the lady's high heels made impatient hollow taps as she neared.

Just time now for some quick marks in her color that meant her name.

"Teresa!" The door crashed open and the lady was over her, talking too loud to hear.

"Oh, Teresa... Baby, look what you've done. What a mess." The loud rattle of her bracelets and stinging slaps for Baby's hands ran together in an unhappy blur. The smell of strong perfume and cigarette smoke on the lady's clothes made it hard to breathe. All the colors and all the smells and all the noise were the lady's now and soon she would take away her color on the wall, too.

She wanted to resist them but she was too small. Trapped by the high latch on the screen door and the towering fence of the back yard. Even the little yapping dog had more power than she did; scratching and whining, it could make them open the door to freedom.

No one ever picked her up or held her and rocked her except Mama. Now she didn't really like it when they tried. She couldn't have the one she wanted; she didn't want any of them now. But she could smell the ones who didn't like her, like a cat, and took extra pains to win them.

It helped to smile. They liked it when she smiled and sat still. Hated her rage of tears and stamping. Then they switched her bare legs with a little branch from the yard. Or left her to be alone in her room. Alone was the worst. Better never be angry.

Another time, another lady, not so busy, told her about the hot, wet plastic pants.

"*Ay, mi'ija. Three years old now y todavia con los diapers?*"

She patted the soggy, leaden rear. She had always hated the hot heavy wetness.

"If you go to the big potty, *hija*, I will get you some pretty *calzones*. Pretty little panties with ruffles. What color does the big girl want for her pretty new *calzones?*"

So easy? All she had to do was sit up on the big white toilet? No one had ever explained. So the nice lady got her the pretty pink panties with white ruffles. She never got them wet, ever.

And then it was her birthday and a whole box of beads and string was all hers because she was four years old now and old enough to play with them without putting them into her mouth. Maria said if she put them in her mouth even one time she would take them away. Maria is the lady that takes care of her now that Mama is gone.

"*Ah, aqui 'stas, mi'ija.*" Maria's voice always sounded happy, going up and down like gossiping. Baby held the beads she was stringing closer to her chest, hoping Maria hadn't come to make her dress or sleep or eat or something else she didn't want to do. She was making a pretty necklace of beads like Maria's, and she was almost finished. Teresa wished Maria wasn't so busy all the time, but she liked her happy voice.

"Look!" she held the beads up to show Maria, to please her, to buy more time.

"*Ay, que bonita*" she exclaimed.

To be just like Maria's necklace the beads needed a tiny Jesus, but Baby couldn't make Maria understand. She finally settled on the largest bead in the box, a smooth wooden one, highly polished. She drew Jesus on there with her dark crayon. Not what she wanted exactly, but it would have to do. And then she passed the beads slowly through her own fingers like Maria always did.

She had never known when or why they would come to get her and take her to another house. Twice the police car had come and taken Mama away and Baby had screamed and screamed. But only in her mind. Then she would be taken away to sleep in a strange bed; sometimes the black wall of sleep just fell on her tiny exhausted body before she could see where she was and resist. She wasn't in the habit of resisting anything. But oh how she did hate to wake up in a strange place and not know who to call.

Even when she'd been at home, she would wake up with her heart pounding, sweaty with fear, and run in to see if Mama was still there. She had never waked her up... she didn't want anything. She'd just stood and studied her sleeping form.

13

A question that sometimes drives me hazy:
am I or are the others crazy?
Albert Einstein

Call me Rose," she winked, stumbling slightly, and grinned in the direction of the dark sofa. "Lousy, two-bit honkytonk name I know, but that's me." She pulled a chair out from the old yellow Formica table and sat down heavily, as if completing a long and arduous chore.

"My mama must a thought I looked like a perfect little rose when I was born, huh?" Her husky laugh turned into a smoker's wheeze even while the grin stayed. "She herself was named Marie, after the girl the guy gets in some old movie, so she gave me the works – Rose Marie. They liked those movie star names back in the fifties. Now these hippies name their kids after dope dreams and worse – Blue Sky, Chastity, Peace. Maybe the next generation can name 'em after cars; those guys come up with good names."

She took a deep drag from her cigarette and made an elaborate show of cleaning the ashes from the tip into the heavy glass ashtray.

"Case of mistaken identity, that's me!"

"You are Rose," the larger figure on the sofa spoke.

"Yes. Yes, I suppose I am." Rose nodded as if this was news that saddened her.

"Where is the baby, Rose?" the younger one asked innocently.

"I thought you boys knew everything?" Rose squinted at them suspiciously and filled her glass with wine, picking idly at a chip in the table. "Now there's a name. Teresa. I thought it was pretty, classy, lots of syllables; a good, solid finishing-school name, don't you think?"

They did not move or speak in response and Rose smoked in silence, watching them through the curling blue strands of smoke.

"O.K., O.K.," she finally broke the silence. "I've sent her off."

She and the baby had been in and out of rooms and trouble. Now they were pushing her to decide whether to give the baby away. Or, "up," as they say in the biz. Give her baby up. Like you give "up" smoking or fats and give "away" your old clothes. She guessed you give away the things you don't want and give up the things you do.

"Remember when Baby was two? She stood in the middle of Mrs. Steiner's office grinning. The little twirling dance she did with two raised chubby little fists for balance. And me, hungover, wasted, but thinkin' all the time 'How can this be the last I see of those two raised fists, the last I hear those sweet white hightop shoes with their hard leather soles clicking across the hardwood floor like wooden shoes.' *Click, click, click.* Or *slll-i-i-i-i-i-d-e* and shuffle, then *click* again. I always tied them nice and snug so her ankles wouldn't wobble. When I'd take them off her socks would be stuck to her sweaty feet, pushed down between her big toe and the next one. I'd pick them out and hold them a minute to let them dry."

Rose began humming, then singing TAKE GOOD CARE OF MY BA-A-A-BY, DA DA TA DA...BE JUST AS KIND AS YOU CAN BE...her foot tapped and she hummed her own accompaniment between words and lines...AND PLEASE REMEMBER...TA DA DEE DA...TO BE SOFT AND TENDER...DUM DE DUM DE DUM...BECAUSE MY BA-A-BY BELONGS TO ME. She stopped and stared and held the smoke from her cigarette in her lungs a long time.

"And then you boys came and told me to go get her." Rose looked at them with the exaggerated affection of her increasing drunkenness.

"This time might really be the last. When I laid out her little clothes I was as sober as a judge. Mrs. Steiner was the one convinced me.

'Rose,' she says, 'you gotta think of the baby.'

Yeah; the baby's health, the baby's shoes, the baby's naps. Hell, even the baby's food sometimes.

'You can't just leave a baby alone, Rose,' she says. 'If they report you any more for leaving the baby alone, they'll take her away anyway.'"

Rose took a long, deep drag off her cigarette, studying the end as if there were vital information there she had to consider before going on. The shabby one-room apartment was lit only by the distant glow of neon. After studying the red glow of her cigarette, it took her eyes a moment to find the glimmer of the angels' heavy presence again.

"Mrs. Steiner said these early years are the most important. The formative years, she called em. Shit, you wanna see formative, live my life these last three years. She snorted a grim laugh at them through the smoke.

'But the baby, Rose,' Mrs. Steiner says. Nagging now. 'She needs security. And regular hours. And good food. Think of the baby.'

She says that like she thinks I don't think of the baby, and what can I say? I think about how sweet she smells when I snuggle my nose between her cheek and shoulder. How when she was a baby she had a little light inside that barely glowed until she saw my face. Then she giggled and grinned and I could see the six tiny pearls she had for teeth – "Toofless" I called her. She reached and the light grew all the time, til when I picked her up it shone like the sun. How the weight of her against my chest, the circle of her chubby little bare arms around my neck heals an ache that's there all the other minutes of my life. I've laid men across that chest, and jewelry, and fancy clothes, sometimes I just press it, rub it with my own hand like it's bruised and needs rubbing. But nothing was ever the right weight to heal it but that baby."

She saw the larger angel shift as if bored or unbelieving.

"It's true, all that thinkin' don't get her food on time or keep her pants changed. I haven't been too good gettin' all that stuff done Mrs. Steiner thinks is so important. But it isn't because I don't think about the baby.

"Same time, though, I know what I am. Mrs. Steiner says you gotta do something early, before six, 'cause they get set, you know. Like concrete.

"You boys believe me don't you?" She squinted her eyes against the new cloud of smoke and peered in their direction.

"Yes, Rose."

Satisfied, Rose continued.

"I bathed her first. Filled the sink with warm water and just enough soap to make bubbles. She always liked the bubbles; and she'd fit in that sink just like it was special-ordered to be her bath tub. I set her down in that water, started at the tip top of her fuzzy little head and scrubbed her down to her toes. Like it was important that she be real clean for her new family. Or like they do for dead people when they lay 'em out. I held her head tipped back with one hand and ran water from the wash rag over the top of her head, careful not to get any in her eyes. Like the preacher that Pop got to baptize her last year. Then put some soap and rubbed it until it made a fine little foamy cap; then I held the mirror so she could see her funny self.

"We made caps and hairstyles and beards. By the time we got finished her little fingers were all wrinkled up. I dressed her up real pretty in her little blue dress, the one with the tiny white buttons and undies to match. By the time Mrs. Steiner came, she was a picture. I fixed her up a little bag with her own jammies and that sorry old gummy teddy bear and her blanket."

Rose sat quietly and smoked. Then started to cry. "But I'm gonna get her back. Pop's mad as hell about it and he's going with me to get her back." She put the cigarette out, looking longingly at the filthy ashtray. "Gonna bring old 'Hands' with him, too; the man with the bucks. I made the mistake of calling and asking for a little loan. Poor old Pop doesn't have any money, 'course. Old Hands has cornered the market on all the cash. Now we're really at his mercy.

"I'm ashamed to say, boys..." Rose stopped and pushed her wiry hair back away from her face, then began the ritual of finding and lighting another cigarette. "Hell, I'm ashamed to even think..." But she could not say what was too shaming to think or say. Maybe it had only been dreams, she thought. Or her imagination. The hands at night, the dark, powerful shadows always waiting for her. And how much was her fault? Maybe it was all her fault. How could she end up there under those hands, all the time, in spite of her best intentions? Same way as with that ole booze, she guessed. Just too weak to fight.

Rose stopped and took a big raspy breath, then another drag of smoke, holding it for a long time before exhaling. She stared hard at the glimmer barely discernible on the sofa. "Get you boys anything?"

14

Without you, my life is no life.
Albert Einstein

With Davy gone, the old loneliness slithered into her life and told her lies. That she had not started over, but only run away. That she had killed her baby and God would punish her. That she was a reject and would never find love. She went through the same motions, saw the same people, did the same work. But without the prism of Davy's smiling presence, it did not add up to the same life. The same peace.

She made calls throughout the day, leads on names and addresses and long shots, but found no trace of Rose Marie Chace. In the evenings she went to classes and painted – eerie portraits of faces in the mist. She painted the upturned face of a dark gypsy beauty, the hair and eyes like her own, the bearing mysterious and sensual. And a chaste older matron, a discrete white bun at the nape of the neck, prim, eyes turned away. Tried to paint someone she wanted to be her mother.

"Be glad you can't find her," Jackie chided. "I'll gladly give you mine." And it was true. Jackie wasn't the only one of their friends with a mother that only gave her daily trials and disappointments. Teresa tried to be grateful that she didn't have a mother telling her what was wrong with her life or calling her from jail. But there was something insatiable at the center of her soul, begging for a name, an identity. An open link, begging to be connected to a longer chain.

"Righty-Tighty... Lefty-Loosey," she muttered to herself, trying to wrestle the lid off a new tube of acrylic paint. "But no Budge-y either way." She dropped the tube in disgust. Davy would be able to open it. He had very strong hands. Beautiful and very strong.

She took a large, dry brush and flicked it lightly around the fresh edges of her work. It was a baby. A tiny baby, swaddled in something that was turning out to be feathers. She just wanted to blur the faces of the baby and the huge angelic being that carried it. But carefully, lest she spoil the clear, unmistakable roses and loose petals that fell away into the dark night around them. The baby was being carried away, not cast out. The roses made it precious, beloved. "Well, then," she whispered to the glowing cherub. "Nighty, night for now. I've got to go to work."

She put her things away and left for the church. She liked to catch up on her work at night, when people weren't in and out, interrupting every thought. She was surprised to see the pastor's car still there, but thought maybe there would be an evening deacon's meeting or something that she had forgotten.

The cool dimness of the hall was such a relief from the humid heat outside that she didn't turn on the lights as she went toward the brightly lit office. So when she got into the office, her eyes swam in the sudden brightness.

"Teresa." Ethan's voice sounded relieved, distant.

"Yes. Pastor?" She couldn't see him.

"I'm glad it's you." He stepped out from the conference room. His voice was odd. He held his right hand in a turned-up fist, away from his body. He had wrapped it in a white handkerchief, now bloody.

"What happened?" Teresa stepped toward him, the rush of alarm quickening her steps.

"Searching, searching." He muttered as if to himself.

"For what? Can I help you find something? Here, let me see your hand." She took his hand and carefully unwrapped the cotton handkerchief. An angry gash of blackish clotting blood and white curls of laid-open flesh ran completely across the palm. There were no signs of fresh bleeding, so Teresa guided him over to the little sink in the work area and began to run clear water gently over the wound. "What were you searching for?"

"The best thing. Goodness. God maybe." He sounded so tired. Alone, searching for goodness, as if it were some distant thing waiting to be found, like a sword in a stone. It did make its own kind of sense, in a way.

She held his huge hand, palm up, and poured peroxide into the wound, opening his fingers to test the clotting edges and clean out the particles of old blood and tissue that would rinse out. It would be awkward to bandage, cut straight across like that, like a savage new lifeline, a fortune-teller's scar.

"Pastor," she began.

He swung her around to face him by pulling the wounded hand, knowing she would not release it. "Teresa, please call me Ethan. It is no longer a courtesy not to. Do it for me. Say my name!" His eyes were tired, the irises the flat gray of old silver.

"Ethan."

"Yes?" He smiled now, a rueful gleam shining out of the well of dark sorrow.

"Ethan, what is it?" She liked the way the sound of his name filled her mouth, began deep down in her throat, softly brushed her lower lip.

"Don't be afraid."

"No." It had never occurred to her to be afraid.

"I was taking out the file drawer. The metal rail has a sharp corner that ripped my hand when I stumbled. That's all." His voice was stronger now, more sure of itself. He didn't have his coat on, she noticed now. Had she ever seen him without the dark suit, right down to the Network News tie? She could feel the size and heat of his body so close to her, hear his labored breathing. She guided his hand back down to the sink, pulled a tube of ointment out of the drawer and laid a tiny strip down the middle of the wound. "I'll have to wrap it, Ethan. An adhesive bandage will never stay on across this fold."

He stared vacantly down at the wound. "All right."

He stood and silently watched her ministrations. "My hands were bloody like this the night of the accident. Both of them. Bloody. Just like this. See the scars?" He held his other hand out before her a moment then let it drop.

"Accident?" she asked. She knew and yet she didn't know. Not from him.

"We were in an automobile accident last year, Elizabeth and I. And our boy. Matthew." He looked at her with such force that she lifted her own eyes from her work and met his gaze. His eyes glittered as if feverish.

Teresa dropped her eyes and bent to finish bandaging the ravaged hand. "Yes, I know."

"Wouldn't you think, Teresa, wouldn't you," his voice stammered in staccato points, "that God would fly in somebody special to tell you that your son is dead? Your only son? But no, some guy who can't even pronounce your name comes in and looks as sorry as he can, considering he doesn't even know you, and..."

Teresa kept her head bent low over his open hand, although the last tails of gauze were already neatly tucked into the folds. Ethan took a deep breath and Teresa could feel a slight tremor in his hand. Then its weight grew as he seemed to relax.

"Well, I act as if it was his fault, when, of course, it wasn't. It wasn't anyone's fault, though I suspect Elizabeth and I blame ourselves. And each other."

"No," Teresa whispered, head still bent over the open hand. She passed one hand lightly over the bandage and the uncovered flesh of the curled fingers. Was that why his wife was away? Had their grieving been the thing they could not fix for each other?

"If I had looked in the rear-view mirror... if I hadn't let Matthew lie down to sleep in the back, without his seat belt... if we had pulled over when the traffic got so heavy. There are no ifs I haven't covered in some long night."

"No," Teresa whispered again. "You know it isn't your fault."

"There's a terrible price for being a preacher. Or a shrink, I imagine. When people come to you for counsel over the years, you begin to see patterns. You see the long trail of bad decisions, bad choices, stretching out behind them, leading them to their unhappy circumstances. They can't see them, mind you, and it would be cruel to point them out. But you see them all the same. Part of you starts to believe in a mantra that says 'you make bad choices, bad things happen.'" He took a deep, shuddering breath. Teresa backed away from him a step.

"And then the bad thing comes to you, like a skittish butterfly, fluttering about, randomly setting itself down on an arbitrary flower. You can't help but speculate what bad choices you've made. A horrible thought, I know, with absolutely no faith in it."

"Something bad happens and you figure you must have made some bad choices?" She wanted to be sure she understood him.

"Exactly."

"I guess Jesus just made some bad choices, so they crucified Him." Her voice was barely a whisper.

He took a deep breath, then let it out in a sigh. He leaned towards her, as if to whisper something, a secret perhaps. Without thinking, Teresa leaned over the few remaining inches and lightly touched her lips to his open palm, then laid her cheek against it a brief moment. He did not resist. They stood silent while the night held its breath around them.

"Food," Davy started. The June sun made white-hot mirrors of the chrome on the car. Jackie and Chaya fell into the car right behind Teresa.

"Now," Teresa added, whining.

"Picnic," Chaya added. Little Manny only squirmed on her lap, happily sucking on a messy teething cookie.

"Oh, I don't know," Jackie, always the prissy one, demurred. "Air conditioning sounds awfully good..."

"I know a great place we can have both. Someplace really pagan and naughty." Teresa stabbed at the accelerator, revving both the engine and the air conditioner.

Davy's question was only an expectant glance and lifted eyebrows.

"Pagan?" worried Chaya, not even sure what it meant.

"Naughty?" Jackie added, her alarm transparent.

"Let's go have a picnic up at the Don Pedrito shrine."

"Catholic." Davy's shorthand.

"Yes."

"Not pagan." He risked arguing.

"Don't tell the Baptists."

"Oh, yes." Chaya's face brightened. "I used to go there with my mother. She always took my grandmother and any sick neighbors who wanted to go. I haven't been there in a long time..." Her voice trailed off in nostalgic reverie, but her pleasure was plain.

"What is it?" Jackie was truly suspicious now.

"It's like a little chapel that's built where Don Pedrito Jaramillo lived back at the turn of the century. He was famous as a healer and now he's almost like a saint to the local people. Anyway, they have a little chapel where people light a candle and pray for his spirit to heal them. Or just pray."

"Are you sure it's a good idea to eat there?"

"So soon after church?" Teresa teased.

"It's a nice drive, a pretty, peaceful spot to eat outside. And the best barbacoa in the world."

An hour later they spotted the Barbacoa sign near the entrance to the Don Pedrito shrine.

The tiny store proved to be a combination drive-in grocery and yerberia. One whole wall was lined with gaudy religious candles, jars, tiny envelopes of polvos and various herbal remedies. A prominent poster leaned up against the counter with a small stack of cheaply printed pamphlets advertising Hermana Yolanda, who apparently could cure troubles with life, money, sex, and the *mal ojo* with equal ease and for the same reasonable fee, claiming the spirit of Don Pedrito himself helped her.

A hand-painted sign recommended a *barrida de blanquillo* to cure the *mal ojo* and a combination of yerbas for *susto*.

"*Mal ojo* is the evil eye, right?" Jackie asked. "But what's *susto*?"

"A nervous condition or shakes, supposedly caused by a bad scare." Chaya was matter-of-fact, almost bored.

"Maybe that's what happened to me," Davy offered. "*Super Susto*."

There were tall glass candles of every color, some in layers of different colored wax. "Check out the special Bingo candle, guys."

"Sort of a spiritual Seven-Eleven," Davy noted.

Teresa was laughing now. "Is the smoke for God? Who are these things invoking anyway Chaya?"

"Well, the original impulse was Christian, no doubt about that." Chaya indicated some of the many candles and signs and medallions that displayed a cross or the name of Jesus. "But, well, somewhere along the way it got to be sort of a general good-luck sort of thing." She set Manny down and gave him another cookie to keep his hands busy. "My people are pretty superstitious, I'm afraid. And a lot of them are too poor to afford doctors or real medicine. So they get help where they can." She gave them a dark, level look. "My mother used to bring sick neighbors here when I was a little girl. We'd drive up and nobody would be here, then we'd hear them calling to each other across the fields, from doorways, *'hay gente, hay gente'* and here they'd come to talk about Don Pedrito and the miracles they had seen here. It was always a surprise to see how many people came out from nowhere."

"They were probably all waiting to see Elvis' face on a tortilla or something." Jackie's distaste was palpable.

"Once a fundamentalist..." teased Teresa.

"I remember peering into a small dark room where they all swore they saw a light. 'What light?' I kept asking my mother...'what light?' I couldn't see it. Mother was real mad at me all the way home for asking what light."

A tiny elderly lady with crooked teeth stepped into the open doorway and smiled at them; proud as if company had stopped by to visit her personally and see her lovely things. She spoke little English, but Chaya ascertained that she was one of the descendants of the original owners who'd been there when Don

Pedrito lived there – and 'acting cashier.'

After the bilingual tour and discussion of everyone's maladies, they left with two paper sacks filled with oozing, delicious-smelling barbecue tacos, a tiny paper sack of herbs for Chaya's headaches and a small tin of genuine coyote fat because Davy couldn't resist. "It's that or the snake oil remedy."

The old lady came around the counter and took Davy by the arm. "*Tienes angel,*" she said, smiling up at him. Then reached out, held both of his restless arms until they stilled under her gentle pressure.

"What?"

"It means 'you have an angel,'" Chaya explained. "Sort of a folk way of saying you have a lot of presence. 'Charisma' maybe. Something like that."

The woman closed her eyes and prayed a short prayer, sort of a benediction.

"*Ay, mi'ijo,*" she cried at last, opening her eyes. "*Que Dios le bendiga.* God bless you."

He smiled at her, his white teeth a surprise in his contorted face.

"So, where's this air conditioning?" Jackie complained. The tiny store was cooler than outside and dim. But not cooled by any artificial means, just a canny use of shade, cross-breeze and thick concrete walls.

"In the shrine, the chapel itself. Come on."

At first the tiny chapel looked like any other, charming in its gaudy poverty, candles lining the altar reminding the visitors and no doubt God Himself of the many requests laid before Heaven there. It was true, the air was cooled by an ancient window unit. Fresh flowers were everywhere, in homemade bouquets and fancy florist's sprays. Don Pedrito himself, the most famous healer in Tex-Mex folklore, lay sleeping under a concrete vault painted to resemble him in life.

When they convinced Jackie it was the actual body of Don Pedrito sleeping there, she allowed that a picnic outside might be pleasant, after all. They found a shady spot on the grassy lawn and spread their things out around them, little Manny on his mother's lap to keep him from wreaking havoc on the precariously-balanced food and drinks.

"When we were kids we'd eat out here," Chaya said. "Before my mother got sick. Mostly now when I think of my childhood I think of the home."

"Me too." Jackie was tighter about home memories, less sentimental.

Davy nodded yes in a way that only Teresa would have recognized as affirmation. The challenge of eating the greasy taquitos of barbecue wrapped in flour tortillas had left him tired and thirsty and his legs were cramping badly, unaccustomed to their double duty now that Davy was determined to spend the whole afternoon without the braces.

"My childhood," he finally spoke, "was an uninterrupted line of training. Physical training, bowel training, 'activities of daily living' training. All the "therapies": physical, occupational, speech. If I had started from the same gate as you guys, I'd be in the Olympics by now."

"They did all that when you were so little?" They all turned to Davy. None of them could remember him ever talking about his illness.

"Yes; my earliest memory of anyone besides my mother is the first of many occupational therapists sticking my plate to a table with wet clay, strapping a spoon to my hand, and weighting my arms so they wouldn't fly around."

"That's probably why you're so patient now." Jackie offered, always looking for a neat label or explanation.

"Yeah, we handicapped kids were a captive audience. Couldn't cut and run. Cut and walk, maybe, on a good day."

"Mrs. M. was bragging on your talent with financial planning the other day..."

"I rest my case...."

"I was telling Ethan about the home the other day," Teresa began.

"Ethan?" Jackie's voice rose in an unspoken admonishment.

Teresa blushed and turned to her, missing Davy's quick look as he dropped his gaze to the food before him.

"Since when is Pastor Stone Ethan?"

"Yeah," Chaya added.

"Jeez, guys, I work with the man every day. When he takes his coat off it's Ethan. Puts it back on, Pastor again. Magic."

"So are you getting to be like friends, or what?" Jackie's voice was still too high.

"He makes me nervous," Chaya added. "You don't call him Ethan to his face do you, Teresa?"

Teresa shifted uncomfortably. "It's hard to explain. He's finally started to tell me a little bit about what happened..."

"To his little boy?"

"Yes... all that." She turned to look at Davy, but he did not raise his eyes to meet hers.

"This is nice, even if it is pagan," Jackie interrupted. "But I still feel kind of guilty."

"Gah, Jackie," Teresa mocked her in a teasing whine. "Klaus Barbee didn't have guilt like you have guilt."

"Moral propaganda is lost on happy sinners." Davy murmured. Then lifted his sweet blue gaze to them and smiled. The smile of innocence. The smile of home.

The chairs where people waited to be counseled by their pastor were not ten feet from Teresa's desk outside Ethan's office. She sometimes visited with them while they waited and while they made appointments, and grew accustomed to hearing the beginning and summarizing conversations as they came and went from Ethan's private office. Without ever meaning to eavesdrop or pry, somehow the general shape of their individual problems gradually came clear. And so did a working knowledge of Ethan's stock responses. For the most part he gave them the rules that applied to their behavior and told them he would be praying for them. And the people liked it; they came again and again. Teresa liked it too; liked that there were fences around all the wild pastures of disappointment and despair. Liked that there were answers, and men like Ethan – strong and solid and sure of himself – to point them out. It was comforting. Even though the prescription seemed hard, sometimes impossible, at least there was a prescription. And someone confident enough to hand it out.

But it worried her, too, that the same people were back over and over again with the same problems.

She and Ethan talked in between flurries of appointments and church. She felt the old power pulling her to this man, found she wanted something from him that it wasn't right to want. Discovered a sense of safety, security in his size and domineering control over the people and the Word. His distance, almost coldness, was not born entirely of his loss. She was sure of that. But it had surely stunted something in him, something that was dying now for lack of nurturing.

"It was the kids," Ethan explained his odd behavior that evening. "That whole week of vacation bible school, with so many children Matthew's age. I couldn't look at them without thinking 'that's the size Matthew was,' or 'Matthew would have been five now, like this group.' Those thoughts are never far away, of course, but so many children..."

"Maybe it's not the same, but that's the way I always thought about my mother. I could vaguely remember her, you see. How much was memory and how much fantasy would be hard to say. It was like she died when she disappeared

96

for good. But I saw her everywhere."

Ethan paused and turned to her. "No one ever adopted you?"

"Apparently my mother never released me for adoption. Couldn't raise me, but wouldn't sign release papers for me to be put up for adoption either. Maybe she thought she'd come for me, who knows."

"You never saw her while you lived at the home?"

"No. A woman who worked there said she saw my mother there once, at a Christmas party. But I never knew she had been there. They have strict rules for visitation. Maybe she didn't qualify; I don't know."

"I suppose not."

"How old did you say Matthew was when he died?" This new intimacy made her greedy... hungry for more.

"The accident was in January. He was going to be five in April. He was already angling for a bicycle." Ethan's lips bunched up over to one side of his mouth in a thwarted little smile. A smile that caught itself and turned into a grimace.

"And you and Elizabeth didn't have any other children?" Teresa tested the name and sent it out like a dove, to see what sign it would bring back to her. And nailed the teal gaze to her own.

"We talked about it, were sort of planning to, soon. After the accident, people would say things like 'you can have more children.' It felt like being slapped. Even talking about it seemed to cheapen Matthew's memory. And then we grew so far apart. Well, we just quit talking about it at all." He sighed and sank to the chair next to her.

"They say that happens, when a couple loses a child." She mustn't go on with this, mustn't say more. How she herself knew only too well how you never got over losing a child. How unfair it would seem that his cherished one had been taken, when she callously gave over her own. How could he ever forgive her when she couldn't even forgive herself?

"The balm I had offered to others – so many tragedies over the years – just would not heal us after Matthew was gone. We blamed each other, I suppose. For not having the power each thought the other had. Power to keep things held aright. We thought our power kept us all suspended safely in a net. Then we found out that anything can happen."

"Yes, you're a very powerful man; you do give people the impression that you could heal them if you wanted to." Every sense she had was full of him: his peculiar scent of soap and aftershave, the rich color of his eyes and hair caught in the sunlight from the window, and framed by his resonant voice. The preacher's voice. Forbidden, taboo, too strong.

He looked at her a moment, as if he could not understand what she had said, and then went on. "Then the waves closed over our heads as if nothing had happened. Life went on, just like they always say." He threw up one hand, palm up, as if tossing a ball into the air.

Teresa hugged the stack of files they were organizing to herself and watched him when he spoke, thought of her own secret burden and its daily toll. There were small stacks of papers he was sorting and handing to her, and even the weight of what he was saying didn't keep him from his efficient method. His eyes scanned the stacks, then the pages, then extracted the proper ones. He talked almost as if he were reading into a recorder, never expressing the powerful emotions that must be buried in the words he spoke. The dark suits, the colorless office, the ritual, the jargon, the whole gray web of his daily life seemed to hold him suspended in a slow, cold pantomime. Ethan the Preacher. But where was the man?

"You can't sustain that state of alert forever, but it seems cheap to just go on as if nothing had happened. In the midst of the crisis, of course, it is as if God suspends and protects and carries you forward. You assume it is for some great purpose. Then – plop – there you are again, in the dailiness."

Teresa focused on his face; his dull gray eyes glimmered faintly now with the teal of the nearby drapes. She was mesmerized, both by his still-raw pain and the sudden insight that the man Ethan Stone and his "office" as pastor were not one and the same. She didn't think he knew it himself.

"We absorb so many varieties of pain and disappointment into our lives," he continued. "Splinters, tumors, pain, death… until we hardly notice them there anymore. You build a callous and cannot feel the pain. Cannot feel anything, really."

"Was there no one to pastor you?"

"No, no one. I even 'broke off relations,' as the diplomats say, with God Himself. I couldn't pray, or read the Bible, or any of the comforting things I had counseled others to do. It seemed like if I just stayed very still, tried not to call attention to myself, maybe the whole thing would cease to exist, maybe I would cease to exist."

Yes. She knew.

"Then I was afraid God would find out. Though what I thought He could do to me after that, I'm sure I can't imagine."

"You were afraid God would find out what?"

"What I was thinking, how I felt."

"God's always happier with the truth, don't you think?" Though she could not bring herself to tell Ethan, or even Davy, about the abortion, she had told God over and over until she was sure he was tired of hearing about her repentance, her contrition. It wasn't God's love she was afraid of losing.

Ethan looked at her, his mouth twisted to one side again. "I'll tell YOU the truth, Teresa. I wasn't concerned with God's happiness one bit. Mine had ended and I hadn't yet figured out how to go on living without it and I could not forgive God. Not just for my own suffering, but the world's. At the same time, I was embarrassed to have finally tripped over that same old stumbling block I'd been leading others around all those years. Suffering."

"But here you are now..."

"Well, habit saved me, as is so often the case. And someone reminded me that God had done all He could do for suffering by coming in the flesh Himself. I didn't know what it meant for me exactly, or for anyone. But it was enough to hope that I could come back here and work. Work that I'd always considered His work. And that maybe He would reveal it to me in the work somehow. That I would know the answer as I spoke it to someone else." He set the papers aside and smiled at her.

Teresa moved closer to him, let his body come between her and the sunlight streaming in the window behind his desk, sat down facing him across the desk. "I want to tell you ..." She wanted to tell him about the abortion. Wanted to see if he could absolve her. Wanted to let him touch her, touch her own pain and remorse, the way she reached out every day now to try to touch his grief.

"What? What is it Teresa?" He stood in God's place and gave God's Word, surely he could take away the pain. Was that what women wanted when they wanted the priest?

But she could not bring herself to tell him. It wasn't safe. Something in her knew that; even as her body and mind hungered for this other thing, this dangerous intimacy.

He tried to drop back into cordial conversation. But it didn't work; not for him, not for her. He reached toward her with his bandaged hand and then let it drop. "You are so..." he whispered, staring at her as if in pain.

But Teresa did not let him say it. She looked aside and let the moment subside, like the silent swell of a wave out past the sandbars that would break it.

"That wasn't exactly true, what I said about no one being there for me." He worked as he spoke again, safe behind the pile of work and habit. "There was someone. The pharmacist at the all-night drugstore where I used to go for Matthew's prescriptions and friendly advice about earaches and tummy-aches. Crusty old guy; used to be a medic in the Navy. Practices medicine without a license, really, luckily for me. At odd hours during the long nights when I couldn't sleep, sometimes I'd drive through, like in 'real life' before the accident, and talk to him." Ethan's voice was dreamy, far-off, his eyes covered over. "He laughed real wheezy, like he had emphysema. But hearty. I think I just wanted to go hear him laugh. I'd just sit in my car with the engine idling, buy some small thing I didn't really need, and we'd talk. I could say any little thing, and he'd laugh that wonderful raspy, hearty laugh." Ethan chuckled at the memory. "He never knew what he did for me. I couldn't tell him; that would break the spell. Such grace from strangers when those I loved could not touch the pain."

15

I have no special talent.
Albert Einstein

A job opened at the university the same week that Teresa admitted she should leave the church job. It required a recommendation from Professor Stout and his assessment of her work so far. Exactly the kind of lopsided situation she tried not to enter into with the egotistical professor. An open invitation to him to speak his mind. He wouldn't make it easy, she knew. But somehow, she always felt that in the last analysis he was on her side. He took his students seriously – sometimes too seriously – and there was no doubt her own work had matured already under his tutelage. Nevertheless, she prepared to keep her head down.

"Miss Chace," he proclaimed loudly, announcing her arrival to himself. He threw down the pen he held and screeched backward in the ancient desk chair; let there be no mistake that you have interrupted the great man, his manner said.

"Yes sir." She had learned never to apologize to him, for interruptions or anything else. It only made it worse.

"May I help you?"

"You said this would be a good time to pick up the recommendation form and do the last interview?"

"Yes, yes, of course. Have a seat." He slid the form in question out from under

101

the paper chaos before him on the desk and twirled it around with a flourish to review it quickly. Scanning the pages with his eyes, he muttered *blah, blah, blah* under his breath. "We do seem to have the nuts and bolts here, Miss Chace," – he still refused to call her Teresa – "and only lack a few inspired words from the great man. That's me!" He looked up at her, grinning at his own sarcasm. "You've more than met the requirements in all media though, of course, you have an obvious preference for watercolor." He scribbled a few lines.

"Anything you'd like to say in your own defense... or add for your own aggrandizement?"

"I'll leave it to you, sir."

"Wrong answer," he nearly yelled, squawking like a game show buzzer. "Too cautious, too self-effacing. Confidentially, Miss Chace, they don't want another cautious, self-effacing person in this position." He leaned toward her and spoke in a conspiratorial stage whisper. "They want someone brave. That's all an artist is, you know. Someone brave enough to say he is an artist. Even small children draw and paint, many with an admirable level of expertise and originality. But to be an artist you must have enough ego... confidence... *huevos*, as the local folk crudely put it... to say that your vision, nay, your choice of ways to execute your vision, are valuable. Are yours valuable, Miss Chace?"

"They are to me, sir."

The force of his belly-laugh threw his head backwards. "Exactly. And you are an artist because you SAY so."

They worked out a few stilted lines of description for the hiring committee and wandered into the area of subject-matter. "That is one of your personal gifts, you know, Miss Chace."

"Sir?"

"The subject matter. You are very talented in your treatment of light, of course. But your subject matter is your strongest suite. You have a gift for enclosing your subject in your mind, making it truly yours, owning it, before you share it on canvas. Your work is never just a picture of something; that they can do easily with this artsy-fartsy photography."

"To tell you the truth, I've never thought about it before."

"No, of course you haven't. You're young, you own everything. And it's a spiritual quality, it seems to me."

He turned to the strip of drying paintings behind him and indicated Teresa's: iridescent blues and greens, a watercolor done wet-on-wet, of the watery world of the mermaids' king and queen, weightless in their secret watery kingdom, their bodies gleaming with shedding water and light, the king fixing golden combs into his queen's floating hair. Dots of light shone like diamonds in their hair, the rest was darker, lost in deeper realms of possibility. "Lovely, a quality of fantasy, yet strong sensuality."

She looked, feeling heat rise in her face and neck. She could plainly see for herself now, with the perspective of time, the strong intimacy, perhaps even sexuality, of the picture.

"A very strong image for such light treatment in the colors, yet look at their faces." His voice rose in delight. "They are children! The childlike innocence of their faces set in such a strong context is brilliant..."

His eyes became foggy with introspection. "As I was saying, that comes from a spiritual quality; one that an artist has... or doesn't have. And not one that can be taught. Still..." he resumed scribbling on the form, "it would be a good selling point to the committee." He paused reflectively. "But don't take them too seriously. Critics are just pigs at the pastry cart, as someone once said."

The hot wind of late August sucked at the heavy double doors of the large studio in a fresh gust, as if someone was trying to get into that cool, dim haven. Teresa could see the tall easels of the life drawing class standing like a spindly forest between Professor Stout's desk and the opposite wall of huge windows. The palms and hackberries outside were a frenzy of green motion against a sky too hot to be blue. This was not the month for landscapes, she thought. The greens were too dried out and tired, the blues too faded with the blazing humid heat, the muddy waters of the canals too low and scarce, the fields too bare and crusted and empty in the merciless heat. Still... if the heat could be conveyed somehow in the soft wash of a watercolor, the pale motion was beautiful in its way...

"You could loosen up your work still," he mused as he wrote. "Let the lines go freer. Quit trying so hard for the image and go with the looseness, effortlessness." He stopped writing and peered up at her through his thick glasses. "No one wants to go to the ballet and see them grunt."

Finally, he signed the form with a flourish. Grinning up at her he added: "They'll hire you."

"You think?"

"I have my ways." He put his finger to the side of his considerable nose and plainly winked.

"Thank you, sir. And thank you for your time and all the trouble. I'm learning so much from you, Professor Stout..."

Before she could finish, he asked "What, exactly? What is it you have learned from me? I would really like to know." It was a challenge, a dance between his ego and his aversion to flattery. But she was ready for him.

"To sign my name, of course, sir. In more ways than one. And to choose my line and color based on what my eye likes. To trust that impulse. I wasn't so confident of that before."

"I know." He gathered the papers, stapled them and handed them to her. "Miss Chace, just one more thing."

"Yes sir?"

"You've heard it said that art imitates life?"

"Yes."

"Don't forget Stout's Corollary." He held his finger up as if in warning.

"Yes?"

"Life swallows art."

I'm not the smartest person in the world. But then, the smartest person in the world (documented IQ:171) is writing a newspaper column. I aspire to more than the smartest person in the world. I aspire to combine my pain, my soul, and my IQ... until the sum of my parts swells past anything intelligence has to offer. Something the waves won't quite close over when I'm gone. Maybe that is art. Maybe that is love.

And my heart rocks in my chest and terrifies me until I cannot work. I'm not really afraid of death; maybe just a little afraid of dying while doing something stupid, an ignominious end. That ole shame come home to roost. But not afraid of death itself. Maybe I could find the things I've lost there.

Davy was so tired that he had tremors on top of his usual tremors; numb with the things that can go wrong with the fragile vessel of the human body. Especially his. What was supposed to have been a simple checkup at 1:30 had turned into a marathon of hurrying and waiting and demeaning little interviews.

Dependent on these medical "experts" for his survival and any hope for the future, he also loathed the inhumane system they worked within. Forced to wait long hours, herded like cattle into rooms full of other patients waiting to benefit from the same august personages. Cautiously reviled by the lower echelons of students and residents, then forced to endure the embarrassment of their own revilement in turn, by the "specialist" he had gone there to see in the first place. The whole entourage then swooping in moments before closing time to brush aside any personalizing details David had offered the lower echelons and dole out only a crumb of information or possibilities.

Possibly more surgery, certainly more tests, new braces. Come back in two months. Small return on the investment. During the long hours in the stuffy waiting area he made mental note of the unlikely people who were called into the inner sanctum every few moments by the bellowing nurse: Joan Crawford, George Washington, as well as the more usual. Teresa would be pleased by the company he kept.

He would have to try harder not to be bitter. Certainly no one can truly see another's burden. Certainly those young doctors who sail and play racquetball and drive German cars don't truly see his own bent form. His panting, pulling, pushing, precarious form lurching through life. Over the years of his training he had become friends with physical therapists and nurses, but never a doctor; the doctors persisted in treating him as though he were not quite bright. But Davy was used to people not seeing him, looking away discretely.

As he let himself in to the apartment, the evening light was failing fast. The interior was dim, but he preferred it that way. He usually turned on very few lights when Teresa wasn't there. Not that he minded the blaze she preferred burning in every room. His house was dim, Teresa's was blazing, and the house they shared was a good-natured compromise as they each did what they pleased on the trail of the other.

He pulled out the makings of a sandwich. He never ate in public, so by now he was ravenous. Curiously out of sorts, nearly in tears, and ravenous. The individual components of the sandwich escaped him, the thin slices of ham too delicate for his trembling fingers to separate and the fresh slices of bread too fragile to survive the frantic wide misses of his quivering attempts to bring them together. He ate the fragments that survived his assault, like a toddler victorious over his first finger food. The milk was going to be beyond him for now, he could tell.

Maybe he would have to go back to his old schedule with Jesse helping him on clinic days, seeing him home and fed and bathed. He had rearranged all that so that Jesse would not be woven into his life with Teresa in any way, but he didn't think he would be able to keep it up. He tried one last time to pour the milk into a wide mug, until the mess exceeded his thirst and he gave up. He stood at the sink and trembled violently and ducked his head over and over in his own curious frantic submission. He was beaten by a cup of milk.

"Let it go," he said to no one. Or only to the dim shape and faint hum of the darkening kitchen. All apologies to Emil Coue, it was quite possible that every day in every way he really wasn't getting better and better.

"And when a poor, palsied SOB trembles," he said, pulling his new prescription from his pocket, "you've got trouble." He smoothed the small paper bag out on the countertop, considered the alternatives, then just swallowed it dry. Then passed the empty mug under the running faucet a few times and washed the pill down with tap water.

In a neat little artistic frame on the back of the sack, the pharmacy had printed the Hippocratic Oath and the serpent on the staff.

"Was Hippocrates a hypocrite?" he challenged the darkness as he waited for the pill to go down or choke him, waited to see if another marathon with the mug was necessary. He thought he had got enough ham and bread down him to satisfy the printed warning against taking his pills on an empty stomach.

The oath was longer than he thought, parts of it shocking in light of modern times:

THE OATH OF HIPPOCRATES:
I SWEAR BY APOLLO, THE PHYSICIAN, AND ASCLEPIUS AND HEALTH AND ALL-HEAL AND ALL THE GODS AND GODDESSES THAT, ACCORDING TO MY ABILITY AND JUDGMENT, I WILL KEEP THIS OATH AND STIPULATION:

But then, Apollo doesn't carry much weight in modern medical circles, as I understand it.

TO SHARE MY SUBSTANCE WITH HIM AND RELIEVE HIS NECESSITIES IF REQUIRED.

Are you kidding? These guys don't even want HMOs.

I WILL FOLLOW THAT METHOD OF TREATMENT WHICH, ACCORDING TO MY ABILITY AND JUDGMENT, I CONSIDER

Notice the standard changing here... where is Apollo when you really need him?

FOR THE BENEFIT OF MY PATIENTS, AND ABSTAIN FROM WHATEVER IS DELETERIOUS AND MISCHIEVOUS

But racquetball and German cars are O.K., right?

FURTHERMORE, I WILL NOT GIVE TO A WOMAN AN INSTRUMENT TO PRODUCE ABORTION.

No, I'll go her one better. So much for Hippocrates.

WHILE I CONTINUE TO KEEP THIS OATH UNVIOLATED MAY IT BE GRANTED TO ME TO ENJOY LIFE AND THE PRACTICE OF THE ART, RESPECTED BY ALL MEN AT ALL TIMES.

Legal precedent for sailboats and beamers.

BUT SHOULD I TRESPASS AND VIOLATE THIS OATH, MAY THE REVERSE BE MY LOT.

Amen. And the horse you rode in on.

He sat at the table and tried to settle on a particular stack of papers to study. His preliminary proposals and paperwork were starting to come in for taking his internet company public. CPAS would be the ticker symbol. CPA Services. Certified Public Accountant or Cerebral Palsied Accountant, either way it was nearly overwhelming. Almost too much to think about. Like Teresa.

The advantages and disadvantages of going public had to be carefully weighed. They needed access to the permanent, noninterest-bearing capital in order to expand and increase public awareness. But it was a lengthy and exhausting process and would lay before public scrutiny every detail of the game he had played privately, heroically, for so long. There were thousands of decisions that could only come from him. And he had his investors to think about. If all went well, he would make several people a lot of money. Many of them were good friends; all of them had become involved on Davy's word almost exclusively. He wanted to be sure they were rewarded for their trust and their patience. Even Pastor Ethan Stone.

Ethan Stone, the man who had won for himself everything that he, Davy, had ever wanted. Davy had set Teresa free to love someone else. Even though he had loved her since he could remember. And now it seemed that she was falling in love with his very preacher, his pastor, his friend. Teresa, who was so hungry for love, so needy in that way, wanted the preacher. Wanted what she shouldn't want; wanted Ethan Stone to love her more than God, more than his calling. It was impossible. And he didn't doubt that Ethan wanted her, he could see it growing there in his careful face. Davy wanted her too; wanted her in his body, in his soul. But he wanted her free, even free to break his heart. But now, he could not let himself think of all that. Not now. He would have to store it away where he kept the other parts of Life that eluded him.

For now, he had a lot of homework to do. He was in the process of soliciting bids from several investment banks for the position of the lead underwriter of CPAS' public offering. The board would evaluate the proposals and choose a lead underwriter at the next meeting. Next week. There wasn't time for self-pity. Then he would assemble accountants, lawyers, financial experts... all the pieces of the pie. He would not allow himself to think of the things that were not meant to be. He would go forward with the things that he could make happen.

16

No one can read the gospels without feeling the actual presence of Jesus.
His personality pulsates in every word.
No myth is filled with such life.
Albert Einstein

Esmeralda was Teresa's first "town friend," as the home kids called non-resident acquaintances. They had adjoining stalls when they showed their lambs at the annual livestock show during high school. Teresa always admired Esmeralda's dark Hispanic beauty and her no-nonsense approach to things.

Esmeralda, unlike her exotic name, every syllable of which she wanted pronounced, was steady and peaceful, domestic to the extreme. She had married and settled only a few blocks from her childhood home in Port Isabel, just over the causeway from Padre Island. It seemed odd to Teresa, driving to visit, that so much staid tradition lived such a few blocks from the wild resort atmosphere of South Padre Island with its flawless beaches and "Party Naked" spring break tee shirt shops.

The invitation to lunch on the weekend had been a surprise and Teresa was glad to have a chance to see her old friend. Talking to Esmeralda was satisfying. More than just a social volley like with Chaya or Jackie. Contemporary as she was in every discernible way – "Super Chicana" they teased her – it was still as if Esmeralda's mother and grandmother and great-grandmother all stood just behind her with their long dark skirts and no-frills wisdom born of experience, necessity, and the Catholic church.

Teresa sat on a stool at the counter while Esmeralda finished putting together some chicken envueltos, finally offering Teresa her choice of a dollop of sour cream or yogurt on top of the shredded mound of lettuce.

They talked as they ate, catching up on the last five years as if it were a couple of weeks, Teresa putting a gloss on her "trouble" in Dallas, Esmeralda a gloss on the fact that she was childless after three years of marriage, practically a tragedy in her family. Teresa opened the flour tortillas and discretely nibbled at the individual contents. She was having trouble swallowing; the chunks of chicken were out of the question.

"You're not a vegetarian, are you?" Esmeralda finally asked.

"After four years of the livestock show, I thought we all were, Teresa answered, twirling the clinking cubes of ice in the sweaty glass.

"Oh?" Esmeralda missed the joke. "Lacto-Ovo or what?" Always up on the latest.

"Yeah. Lacto-Ovo-Beefo-Porko." And she forced down a creamy chunk of chicken to put Esmeralda off. It was too complicated; she just wanted to enjoy herself today. No problems.

"So, how's Davy?" Esmeralda's voice rose in arch innocence.

So, finally she could not skirt any more corners.

"Davy," Teresa murmured. "Davy's good."

"How is it working out... living with him?"

"Good. Fine."

"Come on, Teresa. It's not like you to hold back. How is it, really, with you and Davy? I can tell you love him, the way you light up when you talk about him. You've always loved him. But something's wrong. I can tell."

"I do love Davy. So much that I'm afraid I'm going to hurt him."

"How's that? He adores you."

"Yes, I know. I think sometimes that he is the best friend I've ever had. He's been there always, like a safety net..."

"But more than that." Esmeralda only spoke what they all knew.

"Yes. More than that. Or, more than that if he were... if I could..." Teresa's eyes filled with tears.

"Oh, honey, I know. You don't have to say it. I know."

110

"It would be asking a lot. And everyone always seems to be warning me not to burden him."

"But Davy loves you. He will wait forever, if that's what it takes for you to know, to be sure."

"Does he? I think maybe even he knows it would be too much."

"I don't know. It's been a while since I've seen you two together."

"And now he is pulling back; I feel it. I've hurt him already; I don't want to hurt him more." Teresa dropped her eyes, refused to meet Esmeralda's steady dark gaze.

"How could you?" And then it came to her at once. "There is someone else? You're seeing someone?" Her dark eyes widened with this possibility she hadn't considered before.

Teresa wondered if that was the way it felt to have a mother to talk to about things. Not a "house mother" who met all her needs but never left space for what was really on her mind. Or Mrs. M., who always had her own agenda. Wouldn't a real mother listen to the spaces? Ask what she had on her heart? There had to be room to say the real things, it helped if someone begged to hear them, unformed though they were. Would that make you feel like a real person, with a right to live in the world?

"So tell me about him."

"He's tall. And blond, but the sort who tans anyway. Heavyset in a way that says 'here's a man to be reckoned with.'"

"Just bigger than life," Esmeralda teased.

"Well, yes, he really is." Teresa considered the estimation as if it were a question. Ethan *was* bigger than life, in a way.

"He thinks a lot of himself; and yet he has an air of sadness about him all the time. A new sadness from real things in his life. And an older one, too. Yet he can still do his job; ministers to the believers." She slipped the last in slyly.

"Believers?"

"Yes. Oh, did I fail to mention that he was a preacher?"

"Oh, Teresa." Esmeralda's voice turned down at the corners like her voluptuous mouth.

"And what do you find so shocking about that?" Defensive.

"There's more; I can feel it coming." Esmeralda's dismay was real enough, but her acceptance genuine enough that Teresa wasn't afraid to go on.

"What? You think I'm going to tell you that he's married? That he has a little wife who doesn't understand him and two small innocent children? That I'm the home-wrecker?"

Esmeralda didn't answer.

"All right. One child, recently deceased. And I'm not the home-wrecker yet."

"Are you, ah... *involved*, yet?" Esmeralda asked, leaning into the "involved" a little heavier than the other words. Discreet, as always. Careful.

"Oh, no. Nothing like that."

Teresa could see Esmeralda preparing a lecture, then thinking better of it, realizing Teresa hadn't asked for her approval or blessing or anything like that. And she had never been any match for Teresa's strong will.

"So, what's he like?" she finally relented.

With a little victorious throw of her head, Teresa sat down. "He's a stuffed shirt; you'd love him. A fundamentalist of the worst kind."

"And what kind is that?"

"He believes it. Believes what he's read, believes what he's heard, believes what he believes about it. He's interested in God like some people are interested in politics. But not really friendly with Him, either. Know what I mean?"

"I guess so..."

"God, man. Everything. The whole Judeo-Christian worldview capped off with not smokin-drinkin-dancin-and mixin with people who do."

"So why did he let you in the door?"

"Don't be so narrow, Esmeralda." Teresa grinned past her mock offense. "I don't smoke, drink, or dance. And I'm willing to quit mixing with those who do.

"And he's big, as I said. Just taller than everyone else in a room. And the most gorgeous voice you ever heard. That's what did it, that voice. He whispers and you feel as if it's only for you, but I'm sure they can hear it three doors down. He booms and the rafters answer. Public and intimate at the same time."

"And do you know all this from personal conversations or what?"

"Several sermons, two speeches, and some board meetings. And working together every day. People melt and virtually ask him to lead them. Come right up to feed out of his hand. He tells them the hardest things they'll ever have to hear, and they come back and beg for more. Coming from him in that golden voice, no one resists. No one. I think it's the black suit."

"Uh-oh."

"No, no." Teresa looked more alarmed than she felt; to reassure Esmeralda, to reassure herself. "Perfectly safe. He's so intent on being good, looking good... It's not personal. You could wind him up and he would be that kind, that considerate, that appealing, to anyone. It isn't just me."

112

"But it is you..."

"He's everything I ever thought I wanted in a man, including just out of reach. Just out of reach." Teresa made a grasping gesture with her hand and dropped her eyes at the memory of Ethan's sad ones. "And the most interesting, sad, blue-green eyes you ever saw."

"So what are you going to do about it?" Esmeralda's eyes pushed her like an open hand. Be smart; be careful. Like a mother.

"I start my new job in two weeks."

Esmeralda considered this a moment and then nodded her smiling approval, reached over and touched Teresa's hand lightly.

Teresa raised one finger in stiff oratorical style. "Tis a far, far better thing I do than I have ever done..."

17

The great moral teachers of humanity were, in a way,
artistic geniuses in the art of living.
Albert Einstein

Jesus Saves," rang out the old hymn. And the congregation fluttered down to their pews; a light crowd, due to summer vacations, Teresa guessed.

"Jesus saves," echoed Pastor Ethan Stone in the tense seconds just beyond the quieting of the people. A few stray coughs scattered themselves around the sanctuary. Because it was not quite full, the coughs echoed and lingered longer than usual. Longer, even, than the beautifully articulated opening address of the Pastor.

"Jesus saves," he agreed with himself quietly, head bowed deeply into the open Bible, arms grasping either side of the winged pulpit. The bicycle position, she had heard young seminary students in Dallas call it. Did Pastor Ethan Stone learn this opening posture in seminary, she wondered, or was it a natural consequence of true heartfelt awe before the Word and the power of Jesus to truly save? Or had the distinctions blurred after years of blending them?

"We will take our text from the gospel of John," he began briskly, breaking the torpidity of the crowd. Pages rustled and heads bobbed over the familiar thin pages. "The third chapter, sixteenth verse."

The heads settled quickly back in satisfaction. They knew this one. This was an old familiar friend. Teresa laid her hand lightly on the passage in her old Bible. It was marked with a variety of different colors of ink and pencil. At the home they had even had T-shirts with this entire verse printed on the back: *For God so loved the world, that he gave his only begotten Son, that whosoever believeth in him should not perish, but have everlasting life.*

As the Pastor wound up into the first of the four points of his message, Teresa's mind fell back from the forward thrust of the message, back into the sonorous key laid so perfectly at the first: Jesus saves. From what, precisely? Eternal damnation, to be sure. From fire, flood and pestilence too? Not always. From guilt, then? Guilt, falling as it does, between the slats, the firm, solid boards of certain sin and free will. How does guilt relate to its cousin, conviction? When He saves you from damnation – eternal damnation, mind you – it must be an eternal remedy He applies. No beginning. No end. I am standing, then, Teresa thought, in the "eternal" right now. Damnation, then – of any kind – cannot touch me here. Because He saves. Saves me from it. A straight line that would have been a circle could she have seen its huge entirety.

Nothing Pastor Ethan Stone said on the subject that sunny Sunday morning exceeded, in power, the message Teresa preached to herself in that one point. And the pastor still had three to go. But she listened to them because of that voice, that voice of determined, liquid gold pouring out from behind the sternest brow and saddest eyes she could remember. Her mind would not wrap itself around the logical order and meaning of his points, but it devoured the insistent energy that drove them forward. It was as if he sang for them; the meaning was more than the words.

Teresa sat on the very last pew in the corner; she could barely see Jackie and Chaya sitting across the sanctuary. Ethan in his pulpit was a distant drama. He wasn't just Ethan from back there, but Pastor Ethan Stone. No, more than that. He was Pastor Ethan Stone plus all those nodding, swaying heads in between that pulpit and her pew at the back. A composite. Which explained, perhaps, why he seemed to be bigger than life. It wasn't just his physical size.

She let her attention wander to the neutral expanse of the sanctuary, its careful blend of affluence and tackiness. Really, she noticed for the first time, there was nothing of beauty there, only a combination of deep pile carpeting and muted fresh paint and vaulted airy spaces that gave an impression of opulence.

Even the stained-glass scene behind the baptistry was as stiff and Puritan in line and content as the pastor's three-piece dark suit. Three huge arrangements of silk flowers were carefully arranged in brass urns with wads of moss hiding the wires and styrofoam of the florist's craft. Huge banners, flags of the countries where the church supported missionaries, were draped across the back, above the doors. Sewn, Teresa imagined, by the older ladies in the "Busy Hands" group.

She thought of her and Davy's shabby little apartment, half of an old house. Their two tiny bedrooms, two minuscule baths made for them a duplex within a duplex. (How far down could they divide their lives and still have anything left?) At least here, in church, each person's space expanded outward into the unnecessary vaulted spaces. Their souls could rest or stretch or fly, unencumbered. God's house was not anybody's house, after all; it was everybody's. She was at peace here, with Him, the sole bearer of her secret sin.

Ethan's perfect polished sermon sparkled on, waxing louder and surer when the massive air conditioner cut off and waning again when the oppressive heat wormed its way back in and kicked the compressor back on. The first Sunday in September and still as hot as August. The summer lethargy and the hypnotic rise and fall of the sermon made her sleepy. She began to read the odd bits of paper that she had stuck into the pages of her Bible. Quotes and pictures torn from magazines or jotted down in her own hand.

Deviation, proclaimed one, *from the truths of the blood begets neurotic restlessness*. Then, lighter, smaller, *Jung*. Yes, that Carl, he sure had a way with words, didn't he? And the next, smaller, the flourishes more pronounced: *We all know that Art is not truth. Art is a lie that makes us realize truth – Picasso*. Why wouldn't church words stick to the ribs like that?

Not that Ethan's sermons weren't interesting. But the careful, correct, polished sentences divided up among four or five clear points were too neat. So slick, they simply would not cling to her mind. Not like Jung, for example, or Shakespeare: *What a piece of work is man!* Harsher words with rough edges of truth or dare that had the spiny jabs of sandburrs.

"The Bible uses the image of the shepherd to tell us of God's love and care." Ethan's voice rose and fell with an elaborate rhythm timed to prevent boredom and accent the main points. He drew the lovely pastoral scene of biblical days and peaceful hillsides. Teresa was lulled into the re-created setting.

"When one lamb would refuse to stay with the flock, the shepherd was duty-bound to search for him until he found him. That one lost lamb was of paramount importance to his shepherd."

Yes. The lost lamb. A picture worth a thousand words. And the tender shepherd searching, without rest, until it was found. God was so good with pictures, loved a story.

"There were too many dangers to let one lamb be off playing in the rocky hills alone. There were wolves, mountain lions, ravenous from their meager living in the barren hills. There were unexpected crevices and canyons the lamb's young eyes could not discern. The true shepherd, the proven, trustworthy shepherd, could not let even one of his charges stray from the security of the flock."

No, suppose not. She herself, wounded, sinful, always came back to Him, trusted Him. More than she trusted anyone. More than she trusted Ethan or even her beloved Davy.

"Still, there was always one. Always a little lamb that would not stay with the flock, that wanted to go his own way."

Mm, h-mm. There was probably a Greek word for it, but Teresa recognized it all the same.

"What could the shepherd do?"

With more than a little interest now, Teresa capped her smooth, hard black pen, sliding her fingers along the cold barrel slowly, deliberately, waiting. What would a good shepherd do?

"He broke one of the little lamb's legs."

Teresa gasped and dropped her free hand to the cushion beside her. A flash of alarm and embarrassment flushed her cheeks and she looked about to measure the damage from this shock. None; the people seemed to have missed the horror of the point.

"He broke one of the lamb's legs, so he couldn't walk. Then carried him around his own shoulders until the leg healed. That little lamb's feet never touched the ground for the weeks it took for his leg to heal. He was totally dependent on the shepherd for his food, his water, his movement. For his very life."

Well, yes, she guessed he would be, poor thing.

"And then, finally, when the leg was healed and the little lamb could stand and walk on his own again, the shepherd would put him down. And that little lamb would never again stray from the flock, would never even leave the shepherd's side." His voice strained with emotion, trying to emphasize the trust. But Teresa's thoughts snagged on the broken leg, the helpless lamb's broken leg. Snagged like fishhooks on a hidden log, they would not move past or back up or loosen themselves from it.

Was that, then, what held her to Him after all? Fear? She knew, oh yes, without a doubt, what that broken leg felt like, the pain when you had to walk, even the relief to be carried. To beg, do not break my leg again. Oh, don't touch my heart, don't. My heart is broken, do not touch it again. Then snapped herself back. It was only Ethan, after all. Only another sermon.

A Nazi-shepherd. How sweet.

Well, no denying that fear's a great motivator. Teresa felt motivated to leave. But she realized too that her own suffering had saved her from a worse life. Brought her home to the goodness of her beloved Davy and the remorse of her earlier loss to heal.

"A sheep not following the shepherd's voice is in danger," Ethan explained. "Wandering around, not following the shepherd, will lead to death from predators, or falling off cliffs or being lost to food and water. Many things." Ethan stepped back a bit and took a deep breath, then sighed.

"And that is why our Shepherd, our Lord, allows such hard things to happen to us, isn't it? To save us, He has to carry us and hand feed us." He quiets and looks around the room. "And as that sheep learned to depend on his shepherd, so do we."

The crowd stirred a bit and Teresa could feel the insights and sighs and learning in their midst. She felt her own tears welling and thought of the worse things her own sufferings prevented. How wrong the path she was on, how beautiful the one she followed now. She herself nodded "yes" in her own spirit as the congregation sighed in theirs.

God – You wouldn't break my leg again would You? I choose to love you; believe You love me. Or choose to believe it anyway. But I'm so afraid of You. If a shepherd broke a wayward lamb's leg to keep him close... I'm afraid You'll break my leg again. Oh, God, please don't break my leg again. I'll do it Your way. I will. I choose to. Because I am afraid.

Did You wish I would do it for love?

Have I run the race?

More like I've survived... being dragged by a wild horse, my foot caught helplessly in the stirrup.

Fought the good fight?

Well, I can take a pummeling.

Will fear take me to the finish line, God?

"Love wears you down a lot faster..."

Why aren't things ever as they seem? People what they appear? Probably even Norman Rockwell knew the bitter truth.

Teresa squinted up at Ethan's large frame swaying behind the elevated pulpit, thinking how she would paint him now. Watercolors, her favorite, would be too soft, too forgiving. Now she would paint him in hard angry lines of acrylic, bold and dark and narrow at the brow, a dab of light where there was no denying his fair hair. One fist raised to make a point, break a leg. The other hand an open palm, lowered, empty. Beneath the darkened brow, just above the horizontal slash of mouth, the soft sad gray gaze she so often surprised in his office. Looking out, waiting for the grace he could not apprehend.

Would the pastor close his hand if she were to fill it with a stroke of light? The picture in her mind would not say. And what if she were to tell him he shouldn't say such awful things about God? What if she were to tell him her own horrific secret, that she had destroyed a tiny, innocent life on purpose, while that of his own small son had been taken in spite of all his goodness.

The air conditioner kicked on just as Ethan's stern visage dissolved into the standard closing plea: "with every eye closed, every head bowed" that often ran to eight or nine pleas and many eyes peeking and bored. Oh, well. Church wasn't supposed to be fun, anyway. If it was enjoyable, people would just think it was too good to be true. Maybe it's just a concentration of spiritual misery and infirmities like a hospital is filled with physical misery. And just about as much fun. But credible, nevertheless. And what else could you do when you were sick?

Look at Professor Stout at school. He always told the truth and look how obnoxious he was. How can any human being be a "pastor" anyway, not to mention a "preacher"? A professional Vehicle of Truth. But Teresa couldn't help but notice that her heart ached with trying to match Ethan's painful words to her life, and lifted in a puff of joy at Professor Stout's pronouncements about Art.

The people rose as one, singing again to drive home the message, "Faith is the Victory." Time to slip out, through the heavy back door, before the right hand of Christian fellowship threatened. Teresa stood paralyzed for a moment, the obedient child nervous to do the right thing, to take this hand the people offered. But her fear incited a small rebellion; time to get away.

There was no longer any way for Teresa to tell act from feeling from fear and so she slid once again past the people, mouths rounded in the *ooooo* of "overcomes the world." They laid their hymnals against their own breasts and swayed backward a bit to let Teresa pass, mouthing, from memory, the refrain: "Faith is the victory that overcomes the world."

The blazing sun – merciless now, in the peak of summer – made dizzy waves of the sidewalks, and Teresa had to make downcast slits of her eyes so she could make her way to the car without being blinded by the glare. She didn't know how Davy could stand the heat, waiting in the car. They came early to claim one of the rare spots of shade, but still, it must be over 100 degrees.

Each time she tried to look up she could see only shapes of blinding light – the chrome and windshields and mirrors of the parked cars. She thought of Professor Richard Stout's acrylics, spaces of incredible light burning shape into the canvas in such an odd way. White-hot like this summer day at noon. Bold. He had the bravery to tell what he saw; tell it without asking what it meant. Show it.

If one wanted to show the character of God, Chekov, how would he show and not tell?

"Jesus revealed the character of God."

Oh yes.

Her heels tapped, lonely and clear, on the deserted sidewalk. Squinting forward now she could make out her car, Davy sitting straight, hunched over his paperwork. Tears formed from the glare and clung to her bottom eyelashes.

"Davy," Teresa sighed, sliding into the car beside him.

"Good message?"

Teresa watched Ethan greet the deacons as they arrived for the regular Monday night meeting. He managed to make his beautiful voice warm and familiar in each individual greeting, yet aloof as he managed the business of the meeting. He was careful to touch each shoulder in a gesture of friendliness, but he didn't seem to have any real friends among them. But he always gave them bread from his own hand, even though he sometimes gave them stones from the pulpit. He waited until each was seated at the gleaming conference table with its basket of fruit as a centerpiece.

His eyes tonight were distant and gray, only gleaming with the rare teal when his gaze settled on Teresa. He knew she understood the dull intricacies of church business now, and drew her into a kind of intimate disdain, like they were sharing an inside joke.

She was impressed with the incredible retention and patience of his mind as he brought to fruition seeds planted weeks earlier with each individual "leader" of the church. His success, she could see now, was that he was so strong and slow and sure, so even. He made them feel safe; it was all just as expected, all perfectly right and good, everything was going according to plan, always a slow nod of agreement even when engaged in a major disagreement. They filed out exactly one hour later, satisfied.

Sitting so near Ethan day after day, passing to him the facts and files and messages and tips she knew would make him successful, she realized that she felt safer with him too, protected, somehow, from the vagaries of the world. It was partly his size, of course, and partly the rigidity. A strict fundamentalist, his fixed certainty gave him a solidity that was both intimidating and irresistible.

"I know now why people don't like fundamentalists," she told him matter-of-factly after the last deacon had left and they were clearing off the long conference table. She pulled the huge basket of fruit toward her to carry back to his office.

"And why is that, Teresa?" He knew by now not to be too serious with her.

"God-satisfied looks very much to an observer like self-satisfied. Know what I mean? Smug." She continued gathering pens and tablets, clearing coffee mugs, not looking at him.

"Do we look smug?"

She made a face at him that said it went without saying. Then joked with him to bring the light back to his teal eyes. "Say, Pastor, what does 666 stand for?"

He smiled cautiously and answered: "The number of the Beast."

"Do you know what 668 is?"

"No..."

"The Neighbor of the Beast."

His laugh boomed into her ear as she leaned in front of him to gather the papers on the table. She touched his arm lightly as she went around him. Her own small hand against the dark sleeve of his coat looked naked, defenseless.

"How you've spoiled me, Teresa. I hadn't laughed in so long, or even smiled. Maybe I never did..."

"Doctor Faustus, call your service please," she pantomimed a paging operator. "Doctor Faustus, call your service..."

He turned and looked at her, uncomprehending, then let his face open into red-faced mirth. "Teresa," he whispered, in fake chastisement.

"Watch out for the forbidden fruit," she told him, reaching for the teetering basket.

Ethan's own sure hand steadied it. "You're wrong about my deacons, Teresa."

"Oh, Ethan." She wished he would hold her. Defend her with his fierce simplicity. But she was afraid of him, too. How could he preach about broken lambs' legs? How could he? Maybe he wasn't the same man.

"They're good men. Some of them used to be close friends." He took the stack of tablets from her, but did not stop walking the perimeter of the long table.

"Was that before or after you figured out you could love them in the Lord without having to spend time with them?" She did not look up to see his face.

"Teresa," he began, then dropped it. It was true; what could he say to her brash truthfulness?

"Strong people so often forget how they got that way."

"Yes." That he accepted. And reached out toward her as if to take her hand. Then thought better of it.

"Pastor?" she asked softly, not meeting his eyes.

"Yes?"

"God didn't break my legs, did He?"

18

There exists a passion for comprehension...

That passion is rather common in children, but gets lost...

Albert Einstein

If Mama doesn't come," she asked, "whose little girl will I be?"

"*Ay, Mi'jita*, such questions. Of course your mama will come. For such a beautiful little girl as you. *Mi pequeña muñeca, mi guerita bonita.*" Mrs. Cortez held Teresa to the reassuring pillow of her bust and rocked her, hard, while she stroked her hair. Teresa was five years old, but still tiny and shy as four. She molded herself to the older woman's breast and stared, dry-eyed, out the screen door. She had trusted so many times, been betrayed so many times. She did not know if she would trust again.

"Will you give me a cookie, Tia? *Por favor, una galleta?*" Teresa's accent, when she lapsed into Spanish, was as clipped and authentic as Mrs. Cortez' own.

"*Ay, si*, Baby," she cried out, happy there was something she really could guarantee. "*Otra galleta para la muñeca!*" She sat Teresa aside and struggled to her feet, her own groaning indistinguishable from the ancient rocker's.

"I will stay here with you, Tia." Teresa spoke as if she had weighed all the options and decided. It wasn't a question.

"*Que preciosa* Baby," the woman cried with a delight that was perhaps tinged with pity. "You love your *Tia Juanita*?" And she patted her on the behind and fussed with the little ruffled dress again.

Teresa nodded solemnly as she continued to eat the huge, hard butter cookie. Its sweetness made her fury taste better in her mouth, honeyed it until she could swallow it, too. Then she stood, silent and pensive, while Mrs. Cortez talked to Child Welfare on the telephone. She understood as they discussed the problem but she didn't care.

No, she didn't care.

Still, the last of the doughy cookie wouldn't go down and Teresa began to tremble. Then stamped her foot in a tiny, powerless stab of anger. Tia came and told her 'no' too sharply.

"*No, no, mi'jita.* Don't do that. Sit down here and be a good little girl."

She was a good little girl. She trembled but she did not cry. She was a good learner – she knew when to speak and when to be silent, so they would not leave her alone. When she was alone, she fell away into darkness and there were never any loving arms to catch her, hold her. In her dreams she was standing in an open field with everyone she loved and something – a bomb, maybe – came down and murdered all the others. Murdered them and swept them away.

"It's been more than a week, *casi* two," Tia told the social worker over the phone. "And still that *borracha*, that drunk, she don't come for the baby."

19

Long live impudence. It was my guardian angel in this world.
Albert Einstein

I wasn't gonna drink today. I had a plan. Where did I put that plan? Let's see here now."

Rose swayed, hit the bureau corner and dropped to the floor too easily, as if it wasn't even a surprise.

"Whoa... pride cometh before a fall." She took a minute to appreciate the humor, then sat as if collecting herself to rise. Then a morose look came over her face and her shoulders slouched into futility; she sank back down to stretch out on the floor. She spent her last ounce of ebbing energy reaching for the bright crocheted throw on the couch and pulling it down to act as a sloppy, itchy pillow.

"Oh, well. The day's shot now anyway. Might as well have a little nappy. Just rest a minute." And she began to cry. She still missed the baby. But it wasn't safe to bring her home, not 'til ole Hands took his dollars and got the hell out of town and out of their lives. He liked that baby too much, ole Hands did.

"Messing with me is one thing," Rose said aloud to the empty room, jabbing her cigarette for emphasis. "But he better never touch that baby. Maybe I was partly to blame for what he did to me; but I don't even want him to breathe the same air as my Baby."

"Never," she hissed again. Then she drew her feet up, laid her cigarette in the overflowing ashtray, rolled over on her side and curled up like a dog. Like an acquiescent dog, kicked one too many times; kicked past caring.

"God, I know what I am. Forgive me. Don't keep the angels from coming, God. They're my only friends except Smitty, God, and we both know what he wants. I'm payin' more than that cheap ole wine's worth; but I got nuthin' else." Her face contorted into silent sobs as she talked to the faded floral swirl on the old couch inches before her face.

"Pop will be mad as hell when he finds out, but it's better this way. Hands can't find her there." Her eyes glazed over and stared cold and unblinking. Wanted someone to run to, yes, someone to hold me and make me safe, but not Daddy... Gradually the begging became a sodden whining and Rose finally dropped off to sleep.

The evening shadows slowly stretched into wedges of darkness, dividing the shabby apartment into isolated spots of spray-painted white enamel, scuffed wood veneer, frayed sofa. And a woman – younger than she seemed – curled into the warm humid comfort of the night. The night song was Spanish cursing, broken glass, tires crunching on loose gravel. No insects, no children, no breeze through lacy trees, no sound of any living thing giving comfort to any living thing except a sweaty, drunken, temporary kind. Occasional headlights froze scenes in the tiny apartment: plastic flowers on the Formica table with rusted chrome legs, pink waitress uniforms hanging from a peg on the back of the door, congealed Spanish rice and pinto beans on the stove, empty wine bottles neatly stacked in the grocery sack that served as a trash can.

Rose dreamed soggy, dark dreams. Suffocating; someone's huge mouth on hers, his boozy tongue snaking in, then down there doing dirty, secret wet things. She is agitated and angry, but powerless to defend herself and powerless to rise up and have another drink to make the taste and feel of shame go away. Someone's hand is over her mouth, like she keeps her own hand over her mouth when she cries. But what can she do? There is nothing to be done... so much pain, so much guilt, nothing to be done. Finally, in her dream, she disperses into the air, like a Fourth of July sparkler, with a fine hot flame letting darkness overtake her.

And still the night wore on. The lights, the curses, grew fewer and fewer. The velvet darkness deepened and completely overtook the small room, the heaped form sleeping there. And finally, in the leaden hours when even evil things sleep, they came. The angels. Huge, filling the room with their presence. Yet barely visible. Or visible only when a stray beam of light caught them just so, like the mercury in a glass thermometer. The kind of glimmering light that any other light would eclipse. "I can see them," Rose often told her friends and rapt drunks at the bar, "because I got no light of my own. You gotta be really low, really down and out. If you got any light of your own, you can't see 'em." She insisted, they nodded. But still she knew they didn't believe her.

As the massive forms settled into the dense air around Rose, she stirred, moaning just a little. Their motion beat the airwaves into a pulsing sensation, like distant helicopters.

"You're here," Rose mumbled without opening her eyes.

"Yes."

"I knew you'd come." Rose rolled onto her back, keeping her knees up to take the pressure off her lower back. That back had really been giving her fits lately; she thought maybe those pills the doctor gave her for the pain got her drinking again. She knew not to try to lay out straight. The hand that had been pinned under her was numb, but she ran her other hand over her face, rolling dried matter out of the swollen corners of her eyelids. Then slowly, she ran the back of that hand down the opposite cheek where she had been drooling, slack mouthed, all night. Still she kept her eyes shut, as if her squalor didn't exist as long as she couldn't see it.

"I'm afraid I'm a mess," she said to the heavy presence.

"You are Rose," one of them said back. Then silence.

After a moment Rose began to laugh, the deep rattling, husky laugh of too many cigarettes. Did he mean 'you are ROSE' or 'you ARE, Rose'? Finally, she felt her face sufficiently wiped and her dress sufficiently rearranged to where she dared open her eyes and sit up.

"Ah, you're still here." She hoisted her body slowly up the arm of the sofa, until she was sitting.

"Yes." It was the darker one talking, she could tell. The older one. The younger one was just the faintest glimmer and hardly ever talked. He smelled of peppermint.

"Well, don't go 'way; gotta run to the head." She turned and looked back, held up one finger and squinted back at them. "Stay right there, now."

"Yes."

In the bathroom surprised roaches scuttled away when Rose switched on the light. She shrank from the sudden glare, felt her way to the lavatory and rinsed her face with cool water, holding it in cupped handfuls over her eyes swollen with booze and crying. She avoided her own gaze in the dingy streaked mirror until after she had used the toilet and smoothed her wrinkled dress and adjusted the tights she wore instead of hose. Even after all the little modifications, she was disgusted by her reflection when she finally looked. Her hair was an angry auburn halo that made her skin look green, somehow. Then she remembered her guests and hurried out, plucking out bobby pins and smoothing the frizzy curls.

After the bright light of the bathroom, it took Rose's eyes a few minutes to adjust and find the angels, though she could sense right away that they were there. She was dying for a cup of hot coffee, but was afraid they would leave if she turned on the lights and stirred about. She had things she'd been wanting to talk to them about.

"So where were you boys when I needed you?" She thought of them as masculine, although neither had characteristics that said anything of gender. Just a presence heavier than she was.

"You know, when I decided the baby would be better off with someone else for a while. You knew about that, didn't you?" They always seemed to know everything else. Stuff she didn't really want them to know.

"Yes."

"Well, why didn't you stop me?"

"That is not our Way, Rose. You know. We are only messengers."

"Well, that's just spiffy. A good message might've been 'keep the baby!'"

"Why did you leave the baby with someone else, Rose?"the younger one asked. Innocent as a child.

"I... well, I guess I was afraid. I know, I know, I shouldn't be afraid. 'Fear not' you guys always say. But I was afraid something might happen to her. With me like I am. And Smitty always hanging around. And Hands. Nobody decent around to see to her except Miss Janey and she's old and getting tired of me, I can tell. Now that Pop's sick, things are tough." *And if Pop dies*, her pulse coursed in her ears, *whatever will become of us?*

"Your fear has served you well, Rose."

"It's a great motivator, all right, I'll give you that. So why do you guys always say 'Fear not'?"

She rose, brightening. "Say listen, you boys mind if I smoke?" Even as she asked she rummaged around in her purse, then on the end-table piled with papers and knickknacks. She found a single cigarette, limp, missing some of its tobacco, and lit it hungrily. "One more nail in the ole coffin, right?" In the brief flare from the match she could no longer see them, but her eyes recovered quickly this time and she caught the huge faint glimmer.

She watched the small plume of smoke curl around herself, as ephemeral as her angels. She filled her lungs with it and held her breath a moment. "Whew," she finally hissed, releasing her breath. "For a minute there, I was afraid I might breathe to death." She laughed out loud and the thousands of cigarettes she had smoked in her life laughed a distant rattle of their own.

"Just look at me, a lousy drunk who can't even raise her own kid, talking about happiness. Don't let me run you boys off. It's just that when I start feeling too bad sometimes, I start telling the truth. And then, who knows what might happen, right?" And she laughed raucously, ending in a spasm of coughing.

Still the heavy presence did not speak.

"Just don't be mad at me, boys," she was crying now. "Ask God not to be mad at me, okay?" Frank tears rolled down her eyes now, staring into the darkness.

"If God was like that, Rose, as severe as people think, all the good people would be prosperous and all the bad people would be dead." The dark one spoke, and his substance was solidified for an instant. Rose could nearly make out the imposing height, flowing hair. Then there was only the glimmer again.

"And the world would stop rotating on its asses. Oops – axis." And she convulsed in laughter.

"It's not enough to trust God, Rose. You've got to trust that He is good." The younger one again. Pollyanna.

"Trust? I have a kind of resignation, doesn't really feel good. Is that trust?" A floating, face up, that she knew to use to go through the waves. But it felt scary. That couldn't be trust.

"So, your life is full of pain, Rose. Don't wait to draw a bucket of life without pain in it, Rose. The pain is what makes it the water of life." Then there was that heavy thudding noise like distant thunder.

With a start, Rose realized that the angels were gone and someone – probably Smitty – was banging on the cheap hollow door. She was exhausted; Smitty was the last person on earth she wanted to see now. But he'd be peeking in the window, looking for her. He'd see her there on the couch talking to herself. He'd stand out there and yell and make a scene until the neighbors complained, maybe even called the cops. Better go ahead and let him in. Always better not to make a fuss.

The other Rose opened the door for Smitty, invited him in. The slovenly, dead-eyed Rose Marie who cooked up short orders and tended bar at the *Neon*

Flamingo or the *Twin Palm*.

"Hey, doll," Smitty pushed past her, muttering past the cigarette dangling from his lips. Both hands were full, one with a paper sack of groceries, the other with a six-pack.

"New hours, Smitty?" Half bored, half angry.

"Nah, I told you doll... we're pulling out at 7 a.m., be on the road a week, taking a refrigerated load straight cross country." He always talked trucking to her as if she'd be impressed or something.

"Thought we'd have time for one last little fling." He flipped on the little table radio on the counter and grabbed her up and twirled her around in a tight two-step. She was repelled by his greasy T-shirt and the smell of diesel clinging to him. His nails and fingertips were permanently blackened by his first love, the huge chrome tractor trailer that, this month, sported a red cursive *Rose Marie* across the driver's door. But she danced. What choice did she have? He'd be gone tomorrow. A week, did he say? And he'd leave her some groceries and a little extra money to buy some things she needed. Yes, she could go for Teresa first thing in the morning.

And Rose watched for dawn as Rose Marie danced with Smitty, and drank with Smitty, and made the shabby sofa out into a bed to give Smitty everything he expected. Until finally dawn did come, or just the faintest tinge of dawn. And the last of Smitty's cigarette rolled away from his blackened fingers onto the threadbare old carpeting and pile of papers. The faint glow grew stronger – or was it just the coming dawn? Rose couldn't tell for sure. Then beautiful swirling clouds, like mountains she had passed through once on her way east with her grandfather when she was just a girl. She could put her hand out in the clouds as she did then, and feel nothing, just lose herself in it. And lose her grandfather if she only stepped away a little. And poor Smitty grew fainter, too, as the swirls picked him up and rolled him away, groaning. But she didn't care; didn't give a big cheesy rat's ass about Smitty. No.

Coughing. The haze she had seen with her grandfather had not made her cough like this. What could be wrong? And something snapping, cracking, like wheels crunching over dry sticks, and a light brighter than the creeping dawn at the window. Or could it be cellophane, crumpled closed then left to open on its own? Rose opened her eyes, expecting maybe to see the angels. Or something else extraordinary.

Even when she finally realized there was a fire, she did not know what to do about it. The part of her brain that would cry danger had long since been worn down and snuffed out. And she could still see the beautiful foggy dream of her clean childhood before her and was loathe to look away at the real danger enveloping them as they lay there. She did not even remember that Smitty was with her, once he had rolled away.

If she could just go back to sleep, she could be that young fresh girl again, hiding in the mists. The invisible cool droplets would spray her cheeks while she ran in her dream, and cool her cheeks now growing warmer and warmer. She would just breathe it all in with one big deep sucking breath and....

The searing pain woke her. Even lungs toughened by thousands of cigarettes couldn't stand the shock of that blast of dense smoke. They felt like they were turning themselves inside out with the coughing and retching. Rose was frantic now, and immobilized by her fear, and leaden with alcohol.

"Hey, anybody in there?" A strange voice boomed at the door, something came crashing in at the window. Rose was dimly aware of a siren, lights, crashing sounds. But it wasn't enough. Just when she thought she'd seen the dawn, the sleepy dark dream overtook her again.

20

People are unable to view this situation in its true light,
for their eyes are blinded by passion.
Albert Einstein

You guys smell like a giant macaroon," Teresa groaned. "You're making me hungry." The air in the bus full of teenagers was thick with the aroma of coconut tanning lotions. With Teresa's feigned objection, they slathered on fresh layers and waved open bottles of it under her nose.

"Quick, Pastor, the window!" Joe Cantu, the youth leader, cried, leaning across Ethan to open the window.

"Youth Group to Beach" the bulletin had said. Hah. Teresa rolled her eyes at the gross understatement. How could four little words be so deceptive; what the bulletin called an "activity" turned into this roiling, teeming, swarming crowd of towels and chips and radios and fried chicken and sweaty teenagers with noses coated white, chunks of their clothing cut away to expose fresh white skin for the burning.

"*Like a virgin... touched for the very first time,*" the tinny words floated from the radio of the nearest pulsing body, swaying to the tunes church kids weren't supposed to sway to. Madonna; hardly church-approved. Teasing, Teresa leaned over and sang along with the melody: "Like a pagan, doomed to hell forever more."

Getting out into the stiff, clean Gulf breeze was like magic, driving away odors, hairdos, and shirttails with one push.

"Pastor," Joe shouted back toward the bus, "bring the little ice chest from under the front seat, will you?"

Ethan nodded slowly and reached his long arm to grab the chest. It dangled as easily as a purse would on her own arm, Teresa thought.

Joe had asked Teresa to come along days before. Only today did it become necessary for him to draft the Pastor also when some other chaperones couldn't make it. Ethan looked so stiff and out of place in his old clothes that Teresa almost giggled out loud. She knew for certain it was the first time she had ever seen him in anything except a black suit. She balanced her easel and paintbox while she tried to gather the remaining towels and lotion.

"Here, let me help you," Ethan offered. He took her easel and paintbox firmly with the same hand that dangled the ice chest and strode toward the table the kids were commandeering at the edge of the dunes. Already, Joe and the young couple who had come to help had tablecloths and food spread out and a little wagon train of drinks set around their site.

Teresa stood and squinted into the sun, breaking suddenly from behind heavy clouds. It felt so good to breathe the clean air, stand braced into the wind while it wrapped her straight hair back into curling tendrils. Her heart sped just to see the perfect lighting out over the horizon as a dark cloud bank moved in and enclosed the glaring white heat and azure. Maybe it would rain later, but she would have her picture shaped by then. It was perfect.

After the scramble of lunch and sandcastles, Teresa took her things away to begin work, pacing back and forth from the shoreline to find just the perspective she wanted for the picture. Color and light always, for her, sprang from some hidden well, offering few choices. But the subject matter, or the precise slice of it that she would paint, the angle that would be the eye, the shape – that was the thing. It had to have the right shape.

Once she had chosen the best spot – almost behind a dune, down low to give a lot of sky – she worked quickly. Over the hour or so that it took to sketch out the shapes and begin to lay in the broad strokes of color, the dark clouds stalled in the shadows that broke into surprising slants of gold and white rays, then closed again in darkness. A fine wet spray filled the air.

"Won't that need to stay dry?" Ethan's voice broke her concentration just as the beach umbrella he carried blocked the light across her canvas. Yes. The mist, wonderful on her face and arms, would soon be too much for the canvas.

"Thank you. Yes. Put it right here." She buried the handle then angled it back to give the full view of her chosen angle.

"Here." Ethan brought a piece of wood from nearby and folded his towel around it to secure the handle, propping it to make it hold its angle and be firm in the wind.

"Perfect. Thank you." Ethan's nearness stopped her brush; she waited, still, leaning back away from the canvas.

He knelt just outside the shielded dark circle of the umbrella, not six inches from Teresa's right hand poised in midair with its brush.

"Oils this time?" His voice was reverential.

"Acrylics. A watercolor would have been more fun, especially in this light. Simpler, more spontaneous. But my professor wants some work in acrylics.

"Ah."

Teresa pushed her sun hat back with her free left hand, careful to leave enough peripheral vision to watch Ethan as she squinted into the horizon between brush strokes. She turned once to look into his face. His eyes, trained out across the horizon, were washes of steel gray pushing back the last glimmer of teal – exactly like the darkening surf. What did he see there?

As if he read her thoughts, he said, "I'm trying to see it the way you do."

Ah. Still her hand would not lay down another stroke.

"I've stopped your work. I'm sorry; go on. I'll just be getting back to the kids. It's that they all went off to play volleyball and my hand is still... Well, you know about my hand." He held it out a brief moment and it was as if the kiss of the night of his fresh pain hung there between them. He dropped it and rose.

"No. Don't go."

"But you can't work."

"I'm fixin' to have a vision. I can tell." She smiled up at him.

He chuckled as he dropped back down to the sand.

"You never have visions?"

Ethan's deep laugh pulled free from his quiet decorum. "That's the most charming thing about you Teresa."

Her eyebrows made a question.

"That what you say is never what anyone else would say. Always a surprise. I deal with so many people in my profession. But so few of them surprise me. Never with what they say. Sometimes with what they do, but never with what they say. They're too careful for that, most people; especially with the preacher."

The leaden clouds parted and she laid out the broad wash of foamy teal and white for the shoreline. She worked silently for several moments, not turning this time to see if he was watching.

"You know," she finally spoke, her eyes never leaving the canvas. "The problem is that you have to use words too much in your profession. They get to be tiresome, I imagine. Yet, when it gets right down to it, why else would people go to the preacher, if not for words? What else could you do from your side of the pulpit?" She leaned back and studied the shape, then mixed a pink tone and touched the slanting light, made it bounce visually off the canvas. Sometimes it was just that touch of unexpected color – a shade that wasn't even there to see in the original – that made a painting come alive.

"The 'foolishness of preaching' the Bible calls it." His voice was low, intimate.

"I worked in an ice cream parlor once. Ate ice cream until... well, you can imagine. I still haven't recovered my taste for it. But what's a preacher to do who's sick of words?"

Ethan stood to survey the group of shrieking bodies he was responsible for. Their music from the radio and rhythmic thuds of the volleyball, punctuated by shrieks and loud guffaws, told him it was business as usual. He stretched and worked the muscles of his calves with his good left hand.

"I didn't realize. You're probably getting cramped kneeling there. Come on, let's go for a walk and stretch. I need to get a fresh eye anyway. It's at that point." She set aside her paints and brush and closed the lid on the paint box, kneeling over it like a little girl.

She turned quickly then to step out of the protective canopy of the umbrella and ran into Ethan's outstretched hand, reaching to help her up. It surprised her, embarrassed her even, that she didn't even think to look, never expecting help. She took his hand, too nonchalant, too no-big-deal and rose quickly to her feet, clearing the dark circle.

When she reached her feet all went dark and she thought she might faint. "Wait," she whispered and held Ethan's strong hand with both of hers. "Got up too quick."

He must have felt her sway slightly and steadied her with his bandaged hand against her back. "Teresa?" His voice was tinged with alarm.

"I'll be fine. No problem." Why didn't the little dark muddle leave like it always did? She opened her eyes wider, staring, trying to light the darkness that had overtaken her. Her heart rolled erratically in her chest, righted itself and then, with one deep breath, the feeling passed.

"What is it?"

"Oh, nothing, really. I just get these spells sometimes if I get up too quickly or something. You know." And she was already walking toward the water's sleek edge.

"I'm going to go check in with Joe and the group, see how things are going. Start walking that way. Stay on the water's edge and I'll catch up to you in a bit."

Yes; he would catch up to her. After carefully tending to decorum, appearances. She would be glad when her notice was up in another week and she went to work at the art department. She was beginning to feel guilty for what she hadn't even done.

Teresa found the thin foamy tongues left by the waves where they warmed and bubbled on the hot sand, kicked her thongs back a few yards and began to slowly push through the water. She loved to face out into the surf, eyes closed, the breeze merciless and steady, clean and heavy with dampness. She felt she could turn into it and be swept clean forever.

When she opened her eyes again, she looked out, far away into the waves that no longer broke and fanned out into the foamy slapping shallows around her toes. Out past the last brave sandbar where they rolled and pitched and sucked and hollowed out and reached and fell to do it all over again. Out into forever. And it made her so afraid and sad that tears rolled down to mingle with their salty cousins in the spray. Even the ocean could not be the good, clean, sturdy life she wanted. Every wave a threat, every picture she painted of it a promise nothing could keep.

"A penny for your thoughts."

Teresa jumped slightly at Ethan's voice behind her, then reached to wipe away the dampness that still clung to her lashes.

"Are you all right?" He reached for her instinctively.

"The ocean makes me sad," she said, turning back to face the horizon. "It always has, even though I love it. So big, so endless, so dangerous. And still so incredibly beautiful and inspiring. It frightens me." They stood and stared out at the horizon; the roar was a comfort to their silence. The dark clouds were heavier now with rain, the light mist picking up strength to become stinging needles in their faces as they walked.

"Joe says we might as well leave in a bit. The kids have had plenty of sun and they can't do much if it rains. They've voted for pizza and home."

"I'd better get my things protected and get back to help pack up."

"Joe says you're staying here?"

"Yes, that was the deal. I want to try a watercolor. My friend Esmeralda lives just across the causeway. When I'm finished I'll just walk to the pavilion and call her."

"Ah. Well, come on. I'll help."

When they got back to the big umbrella it was beginning to drip with the moisture. "It's a good thing you brought this over for me. My things would be soaked." Teresa pushed the paintbox and easel over so she could sit under it and look at the painting with fresh eyes. Ethan still stood off to the side.

"Come on under if you're getting too wet."

"I'm okay here," he said, kneeling to look in at the painting too. The sky ran in muddied teal and blues, broken into patches of hopeful slanting rays of light. The clump of yellow flowers at the top of the nearest dune was foreshortened in the front, brilliant with the last warming rays before the dark bank of clouds moved in.

"It's lovely," Ethan said. "So very like this day... as it has changed moment by moment! So very like the beauty and danger you spoke of."

"I'm learning to leave the danger there. My tendency was to rearrange everything, leave it all goodness and light. My art professor is always on me to leave the dark as well. I think I thought the pretty pictures would protect me somehow." She ran her finger softly around the edge of the canvas.

"I gave my life to something that I thought would protect me, too." Ethan's voice was grim.

They both laughed softly. Rueful, knowing.

"Look." Ethan reached his long arm in under the canopy to indicate the sky in the painting. "See how the sky is so gray and heavy and broken – there over the yellow flowers – where the sun can barely get through?"

"Yes?"

"That's how I saw everything after the accident: I could remember the sun, how it was that people were warmed and gained strength for that next step. But it was hidden from me."

"Yes."

"And yet you show yellow flowers." He dropped his hand.

A fresh strong wind pushed into them and they closed their eyes against the blowing sand. Then it passed.

"You are so brave, Teresa."

"I am afraid all the time."

When the last cooler and boom box and towel and whirling adolescent was loaded onto the bus, Teresa stood on the sandy road and waved until it was out of sight. The sudden vacuum made her feel so alone and distracted that she didn't want to get back to work just yet. Why had she wanted to do this in the first place? Probably just to prove to herself that she could. But watching Ethan and Joe and the kids recede into a small dot in the distance made her feel the ocean at her back as if it were a tiger. She would turn and face it and its persistent roar, but it was harder now that she was alone.

Already the steady brisk breeze was carpeting the spot with a fresh layer of fine sand, erasing the footsteps of the boisterous group only minutes departed. Way off in the distance she could barely make out the causeway connecting the narrow island with the mainland. Teresa imagined that she could see the church bus making its way across it like a tiny plodding beetle.

Then she turned back to the blowing sheets of fine sand, Padre Island mutating and erasing its own history as she watched. La Isla Blanca the early explorers called it because of its white sands, foamy white waves and white heat of the sun by day and the silvery incandescence of its moonlit nights. Now it was a hazy wash of gray streaked with blue and the early tinge of sunset as the clouds broke and cleared. Teresa was happy to see the sky again, she had been looking forward to the brave blaze of sunset that the ocean itself always magnified.

It was warmer, too, as the clouds broke up and the air dried. Teresa dropped her terry cover-up and took off her shoes. She wanted to try to capture the last of the vision before her in the dying light. She slipped out of her sandals and, dressed only in her thin cotton sunsuit, spun and opened her arms to the wind and the roaring waves. Not a tiger, after all, but only the infinite, ceaseless waves. She sprinted to the top of the largest dune and studied the landscape, then sank to her stomach on her beach towel and studied it again.

The perspective changed everything, the heights making her aware of the sliver of sand as an island, connected to the rest of the world by just the tiniest of bridges, the lower view making her feel small and safe. She wished she could swim out into the breaking waves, feel the power of them crashing over her, sucking at her feet. She must have felt it once, she knew it somehow. But she was afraid.

Professor Stout would expect her to bring her work to display; he seemed especially intent on fixing her interest in perspective as well as light. The lighting was a gift, she sensed it and executed it in all her work almost without thinking. But the perspective she still did by rote, by conscious effort. That was what she wanted to feel, to get into her soul now. She rolled over on the towel and studied her painting with a fresh eye. Good light, good color, and a nice capturing of the mood, as Ethan had said. But still the perspective was too safe, too common. Only the tourist or craftsperson's head-on view, no personal vision. Still... she savored and protected it from her own critical scrutiny, like a baby. She knew its faults, but she loved it.

The look on Ethan's face when she had given notice had matched her own feelings: sad, but relieved. They both knew it was the only thing to do. Their brief, common path had led them to a point of tacit longing that neither would speak or deny. Somewhere along the way of hope and help the right hand of Christian fellowship had turned into something else. A maze where every turn ended in pain for someone. Then the dark misery of the age-old laughing stock: a preacher and his secretary in love.

It was impossible. Their necessary daily proximity, where each felt the warm breath of the other, the shared sorrows, they were too much. They both knew they could not play out the drama they were hinting at in front of the hundreds of ever-watchful faithful, either. No, no, they would have to separate, try to save themselves. Not satisfy the brooding presence that waited to see them fall, the dark and hungry specter that especially loved to take a preacher down. Professor Stout had offered her an assistantship and, with it, a way out.

The clatter of Teresa's boxes and paints was swallowed up in the thick air and dull roar. Amid the flapping of the loose scallops of canvas around the umbrella and the periodic crying gulls she began again. Wait to judge, only paint, only see, she told herself. She allowed the forming picture to swallow her; more than an hour passed before she looked up from her work, and then she only did so because there was a shift in the weather.

The wind picked up intensity and the light faded. Heavy dark mist replaced the sunset, then sheets of slanting rain. She was certain now that there was a shift in the wind; something was blowing in over the turbulent Gulf. A sudden wave of cold and apprehension made her shiver. Had anyone checked the weather forecast? Was it a storm, or only a passing squall? She froze, not knowing whether to wait it out or start walking for the jetties to the safety of the restaurant there and call Esmeralda to come for her. Finally, a crack of lightning made her decision for her and she leapt to her feet.

"Teresa."

Her heart thudded as she spun around. She was at once relieved and terrified. It was Ethan.

"I'm sorry," he stepped back quickly. "I frightened you."

"No. The storm frightened me. I didn't know what to do..." She gathered her things quickly while Ethan folded the umbrella and took the heavier case of paints.

"I was going home when I heard the weather report on the radio. It sounded serious."

They stood still a moment, as if to gauge the wind, their intentions. Ethan reached out and touched her hair. "There's tiny flowers all through your hair. You look like a wood sprite."

"Or a mermaid," Teresa answered laughing, trying to ignore the warm caress of his hand on her hair.

"I thought maybe you'd be gone already..."

"No." They were both paralyzed; breathless.

"I had no hope of not coming back to look for you but prayed all the way that you wouldn't be here." Still neither moved.

"I was just finishing up." She looked down the road and saw his car. To be sure he wasn't just a vision, or that he hadn't just materialized there, Star-Trek style. It was Ethan's car, all right, and it was Ethan. And they were alone there as the blowing sands prepared to erase whatever they decided to do about it.

The wind and rain let up for a moment and Ethan dropped his gaze and stepped out of his frozen silhouette. "May I see it?" He held his arm toward the painting.

"Oh. Yes." She picked it up and held it out at the right distance to catch the fading light. "I'm not totally happy with it, but I think I learned something."

His eyes formed a question.

"About perspective."

He looked back to the picture and then out to the roiling sea and then back again. "Teresa..."

"The colors and light are good, I think, but the perspective is insipid, don't you think?"

"Insipid?" And finally he smiled. "Insipid," he said again, as if rolling it around his tongue, tasting its veracity.

"I've been trying out different things, trying to work on that. I couldn't work up the courage to swim out into the breakers, though. And that is what I really wanted to do." She knew she was chattering because she was nervous, but she could not make herself stop. "Do you think I could put my things in your car?"

"Yes, you'd better."

They put her things away and walked out to the wet sand. Walked until Teresa was tired; talked. And stood facing the roaring tiger, now silvery in the deepening night.

"Isn't it beautiful?" Ethan murmured, as if seeing the ocean for the first time.

"Yes. And scary."

"You're not afraid of it now?" He looked down at her, surprised.

"It's just so infinite." The waves thundered at their feet, then clutched at the sand in a foamy retreat, whispering *Sh-h-h*.

Ethan walked away from her a few paces, kicked off his shoes and rolled up his pants legs. Then carved out a big circle with his toes. He went over and took her hand and led her into the circle with him. "Just look at our part."

Oh, if you only knew how it is with fear. My fear. But she laughed and stepped with him into his circle.

"Yes, I think I can handle this part."

He drew another one within it. Smaller. And pulled her in again.

"And now?"

"Yes." It was barely large enough for four or five others had they been there.

The last ember of evening gave way to nightfall and darkness, the moon giving everything a suffused and eerie glow. Easy to see how moonlight might be responsible for madness.

Still they did not touch, only talked and held their faces into the heavy mist. And then he drew a circle large enough only for them.

And she stepped into it.

"Are you still afraid?" He ran his huge hand lightly down her bare arm.

"Not in here." But she shivered.

"Cold?"

"A little."

He bent at the knees and scooped her up into his arms as if she were a child, and she clung to him, and he spun her slowly, carefully, resolutely around and around, and the circles spun in upon themselves and they were both lost in it, floating. There was no perspective, no expanse of sky or sand, only the constant roar of the sea pounding like a pulse in their ears. Like pilots with vertigo, they pressed against each other trying to get their bearings without landmarks.

Teresa held Ethan's head, pressed her cheek to his and held it there, smelling the scent of his skin before the wind whipped it away. And then he set her down again, gently, easily and they stood swaying, not daring to breathe. She forced herself to think of Ethan; he had everything to lose. The old thought was barely born before she jerked her head back.

Davy.

But no. Their love was something different; not this crushing hunger. Still, it was as if his pulsing presence were beside her a moment. It moved in the wind as if to speak, but did not. His knowing eyes stared a moment, then turned. He would deny her nothing.

"We barely know each other," she whispered. "Or who we really are."

"True. Both of us wounded by our lives, though. And need each other."

"There are many kinds of love," Teresa said, her voice almost hushed in sadness for a moment.

"We do have one of them, don't we?" Ethan whispered, holding her closer.

Finally she moved against Ethan, her head pressed to his chest, her hands pulling his in to their sides. And the sigh could have been his or hers or only the whisper of the waves. His power was her power now. In return she would give him everything.

"This is the safest I have ever felt," she whispered. And it was almost true. She was safe from everything except him, his passion, his judgment.

He loosed his hands from hers and enveloped her, pulling her closer. Her own hands, trembling, found their way to his wide back, then rolled up into fists she tucked into the hollow between her neck and his midriff. Then they relaxed and she leaned away from him to look up into his face. It was not too late; they could still turn back, go home.

"It's not right," she said

No, he nodded, but held her even tighter

"*Te adoro*," she said, knowing he didn't speak Spanish, feeling safer not to share it yet. "*Nos necesitamos el uno al otro.*" Her voice sounded childlike as she reverted to the language of her childhood.

He rested his hands lightly on her shoulders and she picked one up and held it to her mouth. He held her other one to his. The sighing ocean pulled at their feet.

They moved slowly, barely daring to breathe, savoring every second, seeing each other in the silver magic of the moon, tasting the salt on each other's skin. Giving each other a thousand tiny chances to say "enough."

The rigid and gloomy preacher was gone and, in his place, the gentlest of lovers, powerful but shy and careful to touch and taste and ask for every breath and kiss with his own before he took one from her.

"I was so afraid you wouldn't be here," he murmured into her hair. "And so afraid you would. I had no idea what I was doing, what you would say." She could feel his breath warm on her scalp.

"I never thought you would come; you were so sure..."

"You aren't afraid?"

"Only of the ocean." They laughed and fell back to look full at each other again.

"Ethan..."

"Yes?"

"Take me into the water."

"Now?"

"Yes. Just a way. Just so I can be where the waves break." It was their last chance and she knew it. Their love could turn to play and safety or be forever taken out and covered by the sea.

They waded out into the water, then he picked her up and carried her on his shoulder like a baby, out until the thin foam of retreating waves hid his own feet, then until the dark swirl and eddy pulled at their hips. Teresa clung to him; impossible now to tell the difference between fear and thrill. He carried her far above it. She laughed, then cried with the emotion and Ethan's nearness, his solemn security.

By the time he stood where the waves broke there was no protecting her from the water. She turned and put her legs around his body and clung like a small child, inching her way up his torso so her head could be higher and higher and further from the waves. She laughed and cried until he was afraid he was frightening her and carried her back in closer to shore, where he could hold her and set her down to feel the firm sand beneath the water with her feet. Then picked her up close to him again. By the time their mouths finally found each other they couldn't have said whether the salty kisses were tears or ocean spray. Ethan was the strength she had lacked and, because of her, he saw the crashing beauty for the first time in his life. The bottomless waves were content to have them in their sure grasp. Down, they whispered, down, down.

"I'm not afraid now."

"No."

"You never were, Ethan, I'm sure of it."

"Not of the ocean, only of you... of us."

"Yes."

"I know what this makes me, Teresa..."

She shrank back from him.

"But you... Oh, Teresa. Just to be alive again. You don't know what you've given me."

"I want and need you too. Take me home with you."

He pressed his body into her and she felt hers answer *yes* as in that moment they were lost. Past the point where their minds had anything to say to their hungry bodies. He dipped down into the dark swell of water and she could feel the dangerous undertow then the slow lift of the wave. The merciless ocean was all around them, washing over them, pushing them up, then pulling them down, changing everything.

21

A man should look for what is, and not for what he thinks should be.

Albert Einstein

"We are, all of us, alone."

The opening words of Ethan's sermon were barely more than a whisper, the congregation hushed.

"Not just physically, but mentally, spiritually alone," he continued. "And so we are afraid." The congregation murmured in agreement. Teresa sat stock-still between Jackie and Chaya, rapt, sketching the outline of his body in her mind, imagining that she felt him around her, on her, as he spoke. Imagining that she smelled his clean, masculine scent so far across the crowded, air-conditioned expanse of sanctuary. Knowing she could not hold him forever.

"What is so terribly frightening about being alone?" He paused, but didn't look up. "No one there to confirm, affirm. Our thoughts… drops of water sliding incessantly to the sea. With no one to say anything, we are left with our booming doubts echoing forever, grazing us as they pass, wounding us again."

Was the message for her? Or something born of his own healing pain? She could not tell where he was going, but let her mind be carried, floating, floating as on a gentle wave.

"God sent John the Baptist to the desert with only locusts and wild honey. But he sent Peter into the crowded streets to find a stranger named Cornelius who would serve him the very food he loathed and feared. And Paul went both to the desert and the crowded cities. All of them, as we are in our souls, alone. Yet, like us, determined to follow our Lord. Because we know Him." Ethan's huge hands balanced outward, palms up, like gigantic scales weighing both sides of each point. Still Teresa could not make her mind stay with his message, only with his body and its strength and hungry tenderness.

And then the closing prayer, a prayer that Ethan once had deacons give, delivered now himself: "Thank you God for your grace and its odd portals of entry into our lives. And forgive us the sins our lonely, wounded souls sometimes commit."

Yes, that last was for her, she knew it. And was frightened for them both. She could hear Ethan reaching for grace.

Yes, God. How does your love come to us in our great need, through our great sin? Tell us, because our lives are your life. We have had you in a box that will shatter with this fullness. We've come full circle to the chronic guilt your death was meant to cure, so we know we must have lost the way somewhere along the line. Where are you now, God? In the orderly and pristine traditions, even the perfumed, dark Mother where you frown through colored glass? With the dark-suited terrorists who shout your name in the streets? Or, miracle of miracles, here, right here in our lives, permeating and filling our lives where you have finally tracked us and thrown us down, spent hares. Will we live in spite of our fallen, wounded selves? IS your forgiveness wrapped in your love?

When Teresa got home, Ethan stood in her apartment filling the small space with his dark, brooding presence, still in the same black suit. Hands in his pockets, he paced around the room reading the titles of the books on the shelves, studying the few small art prints on the walls while she paused, looking confused... "It was Davy let me in," he smiled.

Then he opened his arms to her.

But Teresa did not go to him. Looked nervously around the apartment.

"And went discreetly off to his room to work on his computer, right?"

"Actually, he left. With a young man. Jesse, I believe his name was." Ethan turned her face to him then nodded and sighed sadly. He knew she heard his heart behind the sermon. There was no mistaking his passion for her. Or his guilt for feeling it.

And then, at last, he held her close, breathing in the faint perfume of her dark hair.

"Ethan," Teresa began, faltering. "Ethan, there's something I have to tell you." Why? Why did she have to tell him? For absolution as if he were her priest? So she need not fear the secret lurking there any longer? Or only to see how deep his new-found grace would run...

"You're so beautiful," he murmured, as if he hadn't heard. When he felt her stiffen and nod her disagreement – as she always did – he leaned away from her and studied her face. But Teresa would not meet his gaze.

"You don't think so, do you?" He brushed her hair back from her face. Her look said "no" all too plainly.

"Why?"

She left his arms and busied herself about the tiny room. "When you've never looked like anyone that you can remember, you can never tell. Your family around you must be half the mirror. You know, your nose is a little big, but it's like Mom's whose is even bigger. The freckles are Daddy's and we're crazy about Daddy..."

"You can't believe me when I tell you?" His voice was sad, wondering.

"I don't think so."

"Teresa, you are so adorable, so beautiful."

Teary, she turned away again.

"I wish you could just believe me. Beautiful inside and out..." He pulled her to him again and rocked her gently, held her head to his chest with his huge hand.

"Have you ever discovered you have broccoli on your teeth twenty minutes after you've met some really important people?" Her voice was a whisper, as if only musing aloud. "No way to call them back and meet them over again with white teeth. Their eternal image of you will be with an asinine green grin."

His chuckle bobbed her head again his chest. "Yes."

"I feel that way all the time." She leaned away from him so she could look him – steady, intent – in the eye. "That's as simple as I know how to describe it."

"When you find your mother, maybe you'll find out how you came to be so adorable." He smoothed her hair back and kissed her on the cheek and neck. "Then you'll believe me. Then you'll know."

"I wonder. It's hard to say, about mothers. About love. About anything. I mean, I see mothers on TV that look like someone who would look at me and

147

love me and we could talk. Confide. Be easy because we knew everything, could say anything. Like Davy's mom, even. You can tell by the way she looks at Davy that she loves him. She nearly swallows him with her eyes. People don't know what they have when they have a mother who loves them."

She sat him down at the tiny corner table and lit a candle made with seashells and scented with sandalwood. The soft light threw dancing shadows, made the plain things beautiful, glinted off the gilt edges of the Bible lying there among Teresa's other books and pamphlets. Ethan reached out and stroked it softly with one finger. His gesture seemed to act as a cue. She sat on his lap and kissed him fully, slowly on the mouth even as he spoke, then backed away to look him in the eyes again, his sad, gray eyes. "So, tell me about your pale problems."

"Teresa," he began, slowly, carefully. "What do you want from God?"

She answered softly. "We could both hear your heart in your sermon today. We both knew how much we needed that loving comfort, even those passions. And you know the Lord will forgive us, although for me that's one blessing I will have to study and learn to trust. My genuine heart love is Davy. Always has been. But I was always afraid it would be too much for him. Yet the loneliness overcame us both. I have not met your wife yet, but I can tell you love her. And I know in my heart she loves you."

"Teresa…" he lowered his head, then looked up, the sadness surrounded with guilt yet a genuine love for her. A gratitude, a desire. Yet the truth they both knew. "I knew you would understand." He nodded, reached out and stroked her cheek

"Yes," she whispered. And touched his hand as it touched her so gently. "I know we both know."

Ethan nodded, shrugging his shoulders gently. Then dropped his hand.

She could not prevent the tears. "What I want is a pin. Or a badge, maybe. Something that says I'm all right. A good person. That God likes me anyway, he really likes me. 1-800-JUSTIFY. Something I can wear. Take it out and look at it to remind myself." She stood and paced a few steps then stood beside him. She closed his eyes with her hands and kissed them with a tempered passion. I want my baby back. The love of a preacher, maybe, she whispered in her soul. My life with you in it, and a life with Davy that might not even be possible for him… But God would not nod and say yes to that. And so she held all of it back from His pastor.

"You're afraid of God, then?" He softened under her touch, relented and warmed to her once more.

"Afraid? Sometimes." She thought about it in earnest for a moment. "Maybe just afraid of the terrible things people say about Him. But I love Him, too, like He really is my father. He for sure is the only one who isn't always telling me I need to be different."

"Yes, I believed that once."

"And now?" She stood near him, breathed in the scent of his strength and his masculine heaviness.

"Now I'm afraid to ask any questions. Something's missing. Gone. My first innocent faith is gone." He laid his open hand on the small table, palm up, empty.

"I know where it went, Ethan." She sat up straight to face him. "If it's gone, I mean. It has to be here somewhere. The First Law of Thermodynamics, according to Davy: Energy hangs around." She shivered a second to say Davy's name in Ethan's powerful and intimate presence.

"So if it's left me, it's still around somewhere in the universe," he smiled slowly, his eyes lightening.

"Nothing as abstract as that..."

"Then where?"

"I have it."

She was firm, tipped her head at him in emphasis.

"You have it?"

"Yes."

"My faith?"

"Exactly." She thought he would look happier. She kissed him gently on the top of his head.

He kissed her, lightly, tenderly, as if he were kissing a child goodnight. "Teresa," he whispered softly. "Teresa, I see it so clearly for you. Then I start again, telling myself the prodigal's story, seeing my own sin. I can see that it is the story of the Father's heart, Teresa, when I see it for you. But when I see it for myself...."

"I know, Ethan. Don't feel bad. Even the Pharisees thought God was as self-righteous as they were. You told us that yourself, last Sunday." She would not let him fade from her again, didn't want to live this night without him. Whether he loved her or not, his hunger for her felt like love. Rising, she pulled him up to standing too, taking his hands as if they would dance, kissed the open palms, clung to him then backed away and looked up at him, at the pale gray haunted eyes.

"Don't be ashamed, Ethan. You loved your little boy and you lost him. Never be ashamed you loved him so much. That it hurts you so bad." Maybe she even whispered it to herself. Her mouth opened slightly, tried to form the words to tell him of her own secret sin, but she could not.

He held her for a very long time. Held her until she felt her own heart thudding against his chest. Until finally she broke his grasp and leaned back to look up into his face.

"Tell me the good news now, Pastor." This is important, she told him with the steady stare, mark this. "I've heard enough bad news about Jesus Christ to last me a lifetime. All the shoulds, musts, oughts." Her hands trembled in his and her breath came in shallow spurts. "I want to shake all that off me now, just like an ol' happy spaniel comin' up out of the water. And you shake it off too, Ethan. Let's shake off all the stuff we've heard, all the bad news, every molecule of the water except for the very drops we were baptized in." Do you hear me, do you know, her eyes begged. And she could see the pain leave his cold eyes, feel his hands gently hold hers tighter and tighter. "Jesus has a good personality. It's not Him people hate..."

And then Ethan, so gentle for so long, so careful, so circumspect, slammed his weight against her in the full force of his passion. Teresa was afraid for a moment. Afraid she might break, or disappear altogether under the sheer intensity. His huge frame, so tender always until now, was overwhelming, flung, as it was, against her smaller, more fragile one. Her heart beat erratically, then rearranged itself and began anew, stronger, more hopeful. She floated out of the fear. The fear of being alone. Ethan wanting her, desiring her, was like God wanting her, pulling her to Himself. He was passionate and hungry for her. It was almost like love. And she let herself float out of any thought or feelings at all, away from any thought of herself. Or even Davy.

"Come home with me, Teresa."

Home. Yes. Even though we both know now. Two lonely hearts do cry to each other.

Waking up next to Ethan in the pretty flowered bedroom was a jolt. The night of passion was like a dim dream except for Ethan's huge frame curled around her own. The morning sun turned the tangled sheets pink and still he did not move. Teresa pulled the sheet up a little further over his chest and tucked it firmly in around him, hugging him tightly for a moment. She felt an animal desire for him, for his closeness, that was not sexual. Just wanted to cover his mouth with her own, press her own body over his, draw him to herself. But she held herself back. Only paused a second to comb his hair back from his face with her fingers and breathe deeply, taking in his scent, so familiar now.

"I should leave." The dawn was still young enough; it would be safe.

He only shook his head and turned on his side, taking Teresa's hand and holding it with his under the pillow. "I had terrible dreams – nightmares – only you can erase them."

She curled up and fitted herself against his broad back. "I know how complicated this is for you."

He took her hand and lifted it to his mouth. "I feel as if everything I ever did until now was a fraud." He turned to her and took her small head in his hands, kissed her deeply.

"This," she said, kissing him back, "is real."

"Yes," he breathed. Teresa could feel his strong fingers pressing into the shape of her skull beneath the skin.

"I can't claim I don't know what I'm doing," he went on. He shifted away from her, the mattress protesting. Then turned to face her. "But I don't ever want to be alone with the rules again." He held her alongside him, all gentleness again. Careful; the Ethan she knew the best.

"No." The rules were somehow swallowed up in the relationship.

"I've been so careful, so compartmentalized, all my life. Kept things in strict confines, so as not to let them get out of control. Just kept the rules, without caring about them, because fear wouldn't let me do otherwise." His voice was sleep-drugged and slow, as if he were talking out a new dream before he truly woke.

"Yes, it's really hard for trust to get in the boat when fear's already there." She hugged him to her. "But not impossible."

He enveloped her and pulled her tighter to him until every place she felt her flesh his was there to meet it. "Imagine... just try for a minute to really imagine Jesus holding you, loving you, Teresa. As surely as I am holding you now. Would you still be afraid?" He pressed against her and pulled her tighter to him.

She tried to imagine it, for Ethan. But the answer was the same as always. "Yes."

"Why?" He loosed his caress and looked her in the face again.

"I have love crossed with fear and anger. Can't count on love, can't trust it.

My life hasn't worked the way yours has, you know. Back when I decided I couldn't trust 'love,' it was probably true. I know the decision to never express anger was a wise one. I've seen what happens when I do. A child needs so many things... Well, let's just say an angry child can't get them."

"I suppose that's right."

"Believe me. I spent years performing: thought, word, deed. Always performing. To hide the anger. To disprove the guilt – somehow these things were all my fault. Never imagining for a moment that I was innocent. All that work on the disguise, all those years in hiding. Only to find I am innocent. That's what God Himself was hunting me down all these years to tell me."

"He used you to teach me the same thing."

"The 'vicarious nature of this faith,' as you tell us from your own pulpit."

They became shy again, both of them aware of the terrible irony, the incongruity of deep spiritual truth discovered in the warm bed of adultery.

"What was it you wanted to tell me last night?" Ethan suddenly remembered.

"Confess. Confess. I wanted to confess to my priest." She looked hard into his eyes, checking for enough grace to bear what she would tell him.

"Yes?" He really was interested now.

"Come on, I'll find some breakfast while you shower."

"And then you'll tell me?"

"I hope so." She smiled a smile with absolutely no mirth in it.

She put on the shirt Ethan had worn yesterday, the crisp white shirttails falling to her knees.

"OK. The kitchen's over there," he pointed to the right out the doorway into the hall. Then he himself disappeared to the left.

The hallway was lined with family portraits: wedding pictures and old folks and the golden-haired elfin boy they had lost. Teresa tried not to look, but they were irresistible the way they wove a picture of the family life of the Stones. The family life that she, Teresa, had never had.

She wandered out into the living room and hall once again, absorbing the grace and orderliness of someone else's life. And not Ethan's either. No, there was very little of Ethan in this well-appointed home. Elizabeth Stone seemed to have feathered the nest largely alone. Tracing the sounds of Ethan showering Teresa found that the pretty flowered room he had taken his lover to was not the master bedroom of the house. No, his marriage bed was a huge king-sized brass bed layered with gauzy frills and assorted pillows. And untouched.

Ethan had taken his lover to bed. But not his marriage bed.

It made her catch her breath, but she could not say what she thought. Even to herself. So she went slowly back to guard the simple breakfast of toast and coffee until Ethan came to the table in a tee shirt and old khakis.

"Ready." He sat heavily into the chair.

Teresa watched Ethan chew his toast; his teeth met so perfectly that he ground his food with a resonant fury and determination. Anyone who chewed food that thoroughly, she thought, was someone you wanted on your side. "Tell me."

"Ethan, I don't know why I have to tell you. But I do. "

A cloud of detachment fell over his steel gray eyes, and he focused on his food as she talked.

"While your son was being taken from you..." she began, halting.

Ethan's head snapped up and he focused now on her.

"I was doing something... unforgiveable." Tears welled in her eyes but did not spill. "Murdering my own... no... they took... I asked them to take..." There was no way to tell it right.

"What...?" Ethan's gray eyes were flat, closed off to her. "What are you trying to say, Teresa? What did you do?"

Her mouth moved silently again, tried to form the truth out of the horrific words; tried to say loss and grief and regret instead of murder. Finally she just whispered the one, dead word: "Abortion."

Ethan finished his breakfast with his eyes fixed on the plate, not saying a word. He looked up once, pursing his lips as if he were about to speak, then dropped his gaze again.

Teresa thought *If he doesn't say something to me now, I will not be able to breathe. I will die.* She felt her cheeks grow hot as if with a fever, her mouth grew dry. Still Ethan did not respond.

It's over, then. She was not the kind of woman a man like Ethan Stone could ever love. She knew it all along, but now the wanton hope lay around them stillborn.

When Ethan finally spoke, it was as if he were only wondering aloud, not speaking to her. "I wonder what people do want from religion, from 'church'?" His brows were knit into businesslike concentration. His face was a stone he could not throw at her sin because of his own.

"Only to huddle together around the flame, I guess," Teresa whispered. "Like winter calves." She turned away from him and gazed out the window.

Ethan's face softened. "Like winter calves," he echoed softly.

153

"Exactly. Even knowing that it might turn into rules. Or condemnation. We sometimes end up very disappointed calves."

"Teresa," he finally said softly, "thank you for sharing your heart about that. I honestly do not have words for what you have done for my broken heart, my soul. To see and love someone so wounded by life… well… I will never be the same kind of preacher again. However our lives turn out, know that you changed mine forever. In a good way. A holy way, really. Sin and all.

"I always knew there were many sinners in the Bible that God loved and honored anyway. Kind David killing a beautiful woman's husband so HE could have her?! Jesus' most beloved woman follower a prostitute? So many things like that. But I was stunted with pride thinking I just didn't do things like that. Now I see it in my people, feel their sorrowed souls open and heal when I share that kind of regret, sorrow, pain." He shook his head, sighed and held his hands up like he did in the service earlier. "Now I know what they suffer and what they need. When I bring all this of ours to the Lord and recover from my wounds and pray for yours… no words. This is what I am here for. Yes. Now I know." He looked up at her tenderly. "And I know you do too. Do we understand it all entirely yet? No. But I can tell we both know and accept it in a deeper way now." Tears streamed down his face.

"And you know I've always loved Davy?" she whispered.

He smiled.

"And you know you love your wife?"

He ducked his head and sighed. Then looked at her again. "Yes. We both nearly died of the grief when our boy died, we could not help each other. We still don't know what to do or how to process it. But I have a genuine desire in my heart now to heal things."

Teresa felt so surprised and weak, she sat down and stared at Ethan and then out of the window. "Yes," she sighed. "But what you and I had? What we shared?"

"Makes us like other people. We can accept, forgive, love, lose in a stronger holier way than we ever were able to before. That is what I think in my heart. My soul."

They sat quietly a few moments, then seemed to nod 'yes' to each other, wiping their own tears from their eyes."

"Time for me to go home then, Ethan," she said softly.

"Will Davy be there?" he asked.

She flinched to hear Davy's name from Ethan's mouth. "I left him a note."

She gathered toast crumbs with her middle finger, considering.

"What he must think?" Ethan said sadly. "We have known and respected each other so long."

"Ah, Ethan. Whatever Davy thinks, it will go to his grave with him." She knew Davy would never judge her. But could he still love her? She realized again how important it was that Davy love her. She wanted, in fact, to be home with him now at this instant. Safe.

"I can imagine how this looks to him."

"What about Elizabeth?"

"My wife?" The color left his face, temporarily. He sighed. He shrugged his shoulders. But then the hope and color quickly returned to his face.

22

Black holes are where God divided by zero.

Albert Einstein

A nd when I got free"... some things you can't share... "I got all the way free!
Looked back, a surprised astronaut, on the tiny world behind me. I laughed;
I howled. My sins, fierce and filthy up close, were hidden away under a cloud of
something pure and white. Like drops of blood fallen into a cup of steaming milk. It
was disconcerting to see my whole warm world, my womb, so tiny. When the box fell
away, would the God I'd kept there fall too?"

She has made her choice, then, Davy said to himself. Their love was not enough,
not the right kind. Could not be. He had been foolish to dare to hope. He knew
himself so well, had purchased peace so long. And yet allowed this other desire
to grow in him. No. No. Back to the narrow slice of Life that was left to him.
Back to peace.

He crushed Teresa's note from last night in his hand and dropped it into the wastebasket. "Gone with Ethan. Don't worry." And then a hastily scrawled heart and a flowing T, her new signature on her artwork.

So. That was how it was. He hadn't meant to be so greedy, to want so much from life. He would share whatever part of her life she left for him and let the rest go. It had only been a dream, a wordless desire. An ache. He had known all along it was too much to ask. He had loved her as long as he could remember. And then wanted her with all the fierce lust of a lifetime of denial. And then set her free to choose something better, safer, stronger. Ethan could give her the steady, steady unpalsied embrace that Davy would never have. He had other gifts, his own passions, his own desires, but he would not ask Teresa to accept them for his sake. But he had so wanted her to want them for her own.

"I've been knocked down before though." And what made him weaker in the knees made him stronger, more resolute, in his will, his own brand of fierce determination.

"Morgan," he whistled softly. Then picked the puppy up and nuzzled her a moment. "I've got to go now, sweetie. Watch over our girl for me, now, will you?" Tears pressed against his eyes but he said no to them. No with his ever-stronger will. No to the kiss stolen from a mermaid in that watery kingdom, so near and so far away. No to the physical hunger for Teresa's touch, the desire that was almost stronger than his will.

Was Ethan actually free...? To properly give her what she sought, what she needed?

But he would not let himself think about Ethan.

He arranged the bank book, today's mail, and five crisp, new hundred-dollar bills on the tiny table by the phone where Teresa could not miss them when she came home.

Then he shouldered his hanging bag and left this cozy nest and false dreams, shut the door on the last wisps of the delusion he had entertained too long. Locked the door and waited at the curb for Jesse to come and take him to the airport.

Only hours later, when Teresa let herself in with her own key, she could still feel Davy's presence, but she knew she would not find him. Only Morgan, alerted by her key, was already there wriggling and snuffing in excitement and reprieve. She cuddled her a moment then turned her into the tiny yard at the back.

"Davy, are you home?" she called out in a phony cheery greeting. Her voice was dead in the empty apartment, no reassuring answer of any kind. The note she had left for him on the entry table was gone. She pushed open the door to his room, knowing he would not be there.

Davy's room was brave and strong and gentle as Davy himself. It was strewn with her own artwork and books and notes sprinkled haphazardly on top of his own strict orderliness – computer peripherals, printouts, ledgers and exercise equipment. Financial statements and printouts were everywhere. She was amazed anew at his fierce determination and accomplishments.

She ached with the emptiness, wishing Davy were here. Home. Wishing she could hold him, that he would hold her and tell her he loved her and everything would be all right.

Wishing he was not suffering. Not for her own sake any longer, but for his own. So he could believe in what he had to offer her. What he was to her.

She sat down on his bed, felt the sensible brown comforter as if she could feel his warmth there. And finally curled up in a ball on the side where the sun from the shuttered window made a lattice of light. She would wait for him. Like he always waited for her.

She lay in the spot of striped light and let Morgan, returned from the yard, nuzzle her and lick her neck and finally settle in at her feet in a sleeping ball.

And she slept and dreamed dreams streaked with gray.

Davy:	Do you love me, Teresa?
Teresa:	You know I'm so fond of you, Davy.
Davy:	Do you love me?
Teresa:	I care for you.
Davy:	*[his head hangs down in shame and disappointment, but he is willing to take what she has to offer]* So, Teresa, you care for me!

Her own words in his mouth sounded weak to her.
He was her life.

23

Few people are capable of expressing with equanimity
opinions which differ from the prejudices of their social environment.
Most people are even incapable of forming such opinions.

Albert Einstein

"You're a little early, aren't you brother?" Ethan opened his front door to Bill Carpenter, his most trusted deacon and almost-friend.

"Yes, Pastor, I am." He stood there a minute as if undecided whether he should enter or not. "Truth is... well, Ethan, I'd like to speak to you a moment in private before we go over to the meeting."

Ethan was as surprised by the "Ethan" as he was by the tall man's obvious discomfort. Bill Carpenter was a man unusually at ease with the world and at peace with himself, and had, until this moment, been content to use the usual Baptist "pastor" or "brother" when addressing Ethan.

At that instant, even as he let him in the door, Ethan knew that Bill knew. He led him into the study, felt his own heart pounding at his ribs. He had never allowed himself to pull anyone beyond the circle of acquaintances and trusted co-workers into the circle of friendship. If he had allowed himself that luxury, Bill Carpenter would surely have been the man. If he was to lose his pastorate, everything, then he was glad Bill would be the one to take down the first brick.

In fact, as he looked back on the incident later, Ethan would be unable to decide if the deacon had ever really even accused him of anything. The dam had simply broken at the first words and Ethan was very soon pouring out his soul before the stooped and saddened man before him that night.

"And so," Ethan concluded, wiping away the persistent dampness around his eyes, "as they always say, I really don't know how it happened. Or why. Or what to do now. I know what God thinks. And I know I don't deserve to serve Him anymore."

"Ah, Ethan." Bill Carpenter's voice was full as a tenor's, as gentle as a sigh. "You've just discovered what every minister of the gospel discovers – his own inadequacy and imperfection."

"I see those guys on television, read about them in books... whiskey priests, daring to continue to put Christ in the mouths of their people..." Ethan said, shaking his head almost violently as if to deny what he himself spoke. "Well... now it seems I am one of them. I have no excuse. There truly is something hovering, something beady-eyed and hungry, swooping down at any scent of weak flesh."

He was near hysteria. Take the preacher down, take the preacher down. Something lived in the outer darkness that wanted only to take the preacher down; jealous, perhaps, chewing from the center of what it lacked, like neighbors will tear down their neighbors with bigger houses, newer cars.

"On the other hand, Ethan, as your friend..."

Friend? Was he really a friend, not someone sent to find him out and reveal his sin to the world?

"... I really must say that you are different now. You must feel that it has seemed to people like you've been... I don't know... frozen, or something, for a long time?" He struggled for the words. "Ever since the accident."

"Yes."

"Before that you were very rigid, but you were young and full of hope. When your hope died – in that accident..." He grew more confident. "When your hope and peace died with Matthew, the rigidity was not enough."

Ethan flinched visibly, with the actual speaking of Matthew's name, and with this kind man's characterization of his state for the last year. Yes, all true.

"We hurt with you, Ethan, but you would not let us near you." He shook his head slowly as if in fresh grief at the memory. "But you're different now. Alive again. Willing to risk being alive, anyway. We both know you will have to make some decisions, that you can't go on this way. But something important is happening and God will use it for the best. You'll see."

"Rigid... yes." Ethan rose and paced slowly around the small study, training his breath to come naturally again. "I don't think I put God in a box, exactly, Bill." Breathe in, slow, slow, he told himself. Now breathe out. Don't think, just talk; you have nothing to lose. "More like I found Him that way. Or He was presented to me that way. But I thought the box was part of Him, that's for sure."

Outside, the light of the November day was beginning to fail, leaving the tropical foliage flat and unrealistic. Ethan could almost see it the way Teresa would, had the habit now of trying. The stillness there, and rare crisp chill, matched his own.

"Teresa taught me to see Him without the box somehow. I timidly, fearfully, began to take the box apart, plank by plank, never sure which part was really God and which was box, never knowing if He would still be there when all the planks were gone." He turned quickly to face Bill. "We're not talking sin here, now, Bill. We were perfectly innocent. Or at least Teresa was. I think I loved her from the first day – something about her freedom, something about her need. And it wasn't that love that was wrong. No; that much I'm sure of."

The somber deacon only nodded. It was so still and quiet they could hear the distant humming life of the house itself. Vague electrical buzzes and hums, water sighing in the pipes, the breeze nudging the windows.

"I didn't know what I would find with the box gone. Teresa, so lost and yet so free, she knew what parts were only box, that's for sure." He laughed and it was a melodious treasure in the somber room. "She knew He didn't speak to His people with tracts and formulas, she knew He would let me name my pain and suffer with me, knew that being a 'fundamentalist' was no guarantee of anything. Anything at all." He shook his head angrily, opened his huge hands to his deacon as if in supplication. "Most importantly, she knew He would never break a lamb's leg..."

Bill Carpenter rose and stretched, stood at the window to watch the last light as though it were the dying embers of a fire. His tall, thin frame was stooped, his eyes alive with questions he would never ask, his fingers lightly tapping the left breast pocket that hadn't carried cigarettes for years now. He nodded as if agreeing, but did not speak.

"You know, Bill," Ethan finally spoke. "I don't think even God liked that box. When it was gone and I dared look at His face, it was smiling, tender, accepting. If I ever looked at Him before, when I imagined Him, He was very stern. When I lost my son, I blamed God for it and could not be reconciled. What I thought, before I knew Teresa, was that if I obeyed all the rules and tried to be a 'good' person God would keep us safe. All of us. I guess I thought it was a 'deal': I do my part, He does His part. None of it had anything to do with what He had done on the cross or my faith.

"I don't know now how I could have called myself a minister. Minister of what? Certainly not God's grace. Now it's different; now I can see my people. I look out at the congregation on Sunday morning and can barely speak for awe of them. Even the ones who I always suspected came to church for distinctly non-spiritual reasons... there they are, week after week, with their empty cups raised up to receive something from God. It is a miracle. An aging couple sits there at ease, either side of their daughter who has Down Syndrome. Single people, many of them fresh from seeking love and acceptance in all the wrong places, come to the altar and start all over again. Men who have slapped their wives, women who have taken it out on their children. I don't think I ever saw them before. I speak to them now and feel them lean toward me, eager for any crumb of God I can give them. Before, all they got from me was a stone." In his earnestness he didn't even notice the pun.

Now it was dark outside, the scattered lights of the neighborhood faintly twinkling over the fence line. The neighborhood dogs called out the status of their yards, announced the distant sirens before they became audible.

"Don't be too hard on yourself, Ethan." Bill Carpenter's voice was nearly a whisper. "You've been a very good pastor. It was only yourself you were not kind to."

"Thank you, Bill," Ethan said, reaching to touch the deacon's arm as he had done so often. "I only wish I had come to you earlier, even back when Matthew died. I didn't want anyone to see me like I was. No faith, no hope, none of the things I had exhorted others to have. It wasn't even pride, I don't think. Just a vast desolation."

"I should have been bolder, Ethan. I knew – we all knew – that you weren't doing well. We prayed for you, but we should have come and sat with you in your sorrow."

"Yes, like Job," Ethan laughed softly. "Maybe that was how it started with Teresa. She was the first person that was IN the sorrow with me. I had been alone for so long. Elizabeth and I just could not be good for each other." He looked over at his new, self-avowed friend. As if checking to see if more would be too much, for tacit approval to continue. It was the first time he realized the room was almost dark now. He stepped back to flip on the ceiling light, flooding the room with its yellow glow.

Bill sat down, his head bent over so far that Ethan wondered if he might be praying. Then he looked up and lifted his brows as if expecting to hear more.

"I was empty. And lonely. The usual excuses. But then Teresa is something more than usual..."

"Yes, she is. I've thought so myself. Smart and vivacious, yet so needy. You can feel it, just to be near her. Broken."

Ethan smiled. "Yes, there's plenty of material there to reach a pastor's heart. And that's the way it all started, of course. I wanted to help her. She was the bravest, sauciest little thing I'd ever met. I didn't have to know her a week to see how badly she had been hurt by life and how she continued to hurt herself, by feeling she'd deserved it."

Only days later, before the Sunday night service, Teresa too knew her cozy little world had ended. Knew it right away. She recognized the voice, having never even heard it. It was the only voice that fit.

Teresa sat on the back-corner pew, waiting. The usual rustle of activity in the foyer at the rear of the sanctuary crescendoed itself into a bevy of delighted voices. Teresa did not turn around; she was not ready to see for herself the person that belonged to the distinctive voice. The pleased cries of "Elizabeth!" were enough. Enough to confirm the identity, then clues that would tell her... she didn't know what. She turned to face the side wall, allowing herself just a peripheral slice of the scene.

"Elizabeth, oh, honey, where have you been?" One elderly lady cried plaintively. It sounded to Teresa as if she might weep with pleasure and relief.

"Mae, sweet, I'm so happy to see you," Elizabeth cried as she hugged the woman to her. "And to see you looking so well... your knee is nearly healed, I can tell! Let me look at you." She held the older woman out at arm's length as if admiring her face, her form, her dress, taking her all in with a warmth Teresa knew she herself could never have mustered. No, not even if it had been her own long-lost grandmother. Something much more than the usual right hand of Christian fellowship.

"And here's Mrs. Wingert, too," she called to another lady, only slightly younger, standing shyly behind old Mae. "I understand congratulations are in order... another perfect little granddaughter. You lucky thing, how do you do it? Order boys, get boys, order girls, girls it is."

Teresa could not tear her sideways stare away from Elizabeth's graceful form and melodious voice. Or the growing little crowd of people drawn to her. She was warm and magnetic. And lovely in a prim, well-scrubbed sort of way. An Ivory Girl ten years later.

"Lovely, isn't she?"

Teresa jumped, felt herself blushing to be caught gaping. "Yes, she is. Pastor's wife?"

The intruder was one of the deacons, though Teresa barely knew him. He wrote something on a small card he held on his Bible for support, then put it away and stored the pen with a decisive little click. "Yes. Elizabeth Stone. Been away at her folks' all summer. Sure glad to see her back. She's a wonder."

He tidied up the row of hymnals and visitors' cards on the pew in front of Teresa and began work on the next one while they both watched the crowd swell around Elizabeth. Teresa sat frozen and nodded, not speaking.

"Be best for Pastor, too," he continued. "Don't know if they've had a little trouble or what, but he's been off his feed ever since she's been gone. Be good to get things back to normal."

"Yes, I'm sure that's right." Teresa tried to be polite to the older man while still dwelling on every word the prodigal wife was saying to the parishioners as they welcomed her back to the fold. A steady stream of children, too, came to her and were sent away with a story and a stick of gum or a *Tic Tac*. Then Teresa could no longer make out the words for her own blood rushing in her ears and the garrulous deacon filling the slots with cards and the pauses with words.

Did he know? But, how could he? Ethan had seemed confident that there was no hint of suspicion anywhere, that he would know. She was beginning to get paranoid, then, because she sensed that this man's voice betrayed more than casual interest.

It became harder and harder to breathe. The cool, holy solace of the sanctuary evaporated. She was a girl again, standing in the church at the home where, despite its emptiness, she did not feel all alone. A child again. *Una niña.*

As the space fills with people, it gets harder to breathe. A boy across the aisle belches and I can see the dark gasses and germs floating over, mixing with the air. Then I can no longer breathe any air without those dirty microbes and I have to get up and leave.

When we all come here together we sing. JESUS LOVES ME, THIS I KNOW... The words always stick in my throat and I cannot say them. I make my face and

164

mouth go on as if singing, but no words come out. Jesus loves good children, not bad girls who nobody wanted. I have been unable to charm anyone into wanting me, loving me. What chance of charming God Himself?

They tell me more and more that I am funny and they say it in a way that I see they don't mean weird. They laugh at my jokes. "Funny" is the only thing they don't make fun of.

You can laugh or you can cry. Hanging upside down, the world is a very funny place; you can hang there and laugh and no one can tell you're crying. Even when I cry and cry, flushing out accumulated sadness, I can tell that the world is funny. God, for example, says He knew me in my mother's womb.

Smile. Be smart. Be funny. She learned what she had to do. Her performance didn't win love, exactly, but a kind of affection that was better than nothing.

"God is love," she had told them, laughing. "But get it in writing."

It was easier when she was a child.

Elizabeth Stone rounded the corner where her people sat admiring her, took Teresa's hand and held it in her own warm and gentle one while she asked the deacon to introduce them.

24

The tragedy of life is what dies inside a man while he lives.
Albert Einstein

It was club day and Esmeralda met Teresa at the door in high heels and a shirtwaist dress.

Teresa grinned as she went in. "Got time to talk a minute before you have to go be sworn in?"

"Actually, I left myself enough time for a sandwich. Let me fix you one too. I'm leaving in... thirty-five minutes. Don't let me forget the time with your great rap, now, Teresa."

Teresa followed her into the kitchen with its big bay windows, etched glass sparklers hanging on nylon fishing line. She sat at the long breakfast bar, near the telephone and Esmeralda's neat stack of mail and newspapers.

"I figured I'd be hearing from you soon. Enough time has gone by now for you to really be in hot water."

"Oh, yes. You won't be disappointed." She slid the top glossy magazine off and read the colorful cover of the second: "Twenty-one Styles for Summer" and "Mensa: The High IQ Society."

"So, which do you recommend, Esmeralda? Style or Mensa?" Teresa asked as Esmeralda bent into the refrigerator.

"The IQ club, right?"

"Yeah." She flipped the pages lazily, waiting for Esmeralda to quit fussing and sit down with her.

Esmeralda laughed. "Did you know that in Spanish *mensa* is the rough equivalent of 'blockhead'? *Estupido, tonto*," she added, tapping her own skull and making an expression of dullness to indicate their meaning.

"Really? Oh, well. Call yourself 'wonderful,' and in some language in the world it'll mean dumbass."

"For sure."

It was always a wonder to Teresa that she didn't shock Esmeralda. How had they ever become friends? Beneath that elegant, capable, Super-Chicana exterior was a person willing to be both good and honest. But what did Esmeralda like about her? Worse, how could she even tolerate her? Always late, always embarrassing, always with her life in a mess and old paint under her nails. Esmeralda, with her long nails so beautifully lacquered and shaped. A mystery.

"How are your art classes going?"

"Maybe I should have been a writer instead."

Esmeralda laughed. "Oh, no, Teresa. I've seen your work; you are very talented. Although I do seem to remember that you were very good at writing when we were in school. Didn't you used to write a lot of poetry?" She pulled out creamy lined napkins and laid them on the counter between them.

"Yes, I did," Teresa laughed. "And always about death. 'What does an eleven-year-old know about death?' the teacher always asked me. 'Write about what you know.'"

But she had known. Known that in her dreams she was running in huge empty rooms, full of strangers. Someone was always chasing her, she was always in danger. She always wanted to scream and save herself, but her voice stuck in her throat. Sometimes she was buried alive, helpless to call out, or she was hacked to pieces. She would wake up with her heart pounding so hard and fast she was afraid it would burst out of her chest. When she stared to write about what she knew, there was nothing else she could think of.

"Mustard or mayo," Esmeralda asked as she arranged the wheat bread on matching plates. All of Esmeralda's dishes matched and Teresa knew there must be more than eight of each piece.

"Yes."

Esmeralda looked at her sideways. They always had this little ritual. Esmeralda asked in either/or, Teresa vacillated and tried everything.

"So, tell me..." Esmeralda turned the neatly stacked sandwiches into tiny triangles and built a pear salad on a lettuce leaf with *Philadelphia* cream cheese in the middle.

"Well, there's no future in it, as you warned me already..."

"Oh, Teresa, I didn't mean it to sound like that, never meant to judge you." She stacked the sandwiches neatly. "To tell you the truth, I was glad you had someone to take care of you. No one else ever has..."

"Except Davy."

"Oh, Teresa, I love Davy too. But you know what I mean..."

"Oh, I do. Yes, indeed I do. And I wanted that from him too."

"From the preacher?"

"Yes. He seemed like a man who could take care of anything. I wanted him to take care of me."

"Not love?"

"Love? Gosh, Esmeralda, I don't know. Love? How would I know? Love is all I ever wanted. Sex for love up close, friends and work for love medium distance, my art for the anonymous love of the world and all the strangers in it..."

"Is he in love with you?"

"Ethan? He loves part of me, but not all of me." She paused and thought a moment.

"Not all of you?"

"You know, like Davy does."

Teresa reached for a sandwich. They fell silent while Esmeralda made lemonade and filled the glasses with ice.

"I met the wife."

Esmeralda stopped a moment, to consider. "Did she know?"

"Oh, I don't think so. I think she just chose that moment to ease herself back into Baptist society and, fate being what it is, there I sat, right in the middle of it."

"Teresa, how horrible for you." Esmeralda stared out the window as if trying to re-create this unhappy scene in her mind.

"Ah Love: 'Stronger than Death and harder than Hell.' No. That's the bad part. It was not horrible. The only horrible thing was that she's... well, she's wonderful. You'd like her. I liked her. Everyone in the whole church adores her. She's even more popular than Ethan."

"You're kidding."

"Yeah... weird, huh? I thought that she would be, well, stiff. I knew she wouldn't be like me. So I guess I thought that meant I wouldn't like her. I'll tell you what it felt like. Remember the movie 'Yentl'?"

"Yes. Streisand."

"Remember when Yentl/Streisand was still disguised as a boy and became inadvertently married to a beautiful young girl."

"Yes. Amy *What's-Her-Name...*"

"And the really gorgeous hunk had been in love with this Amy, but she dutifully married the boy Yentl that her parents had chosen for her, making every effort to see to 'his' comfort and happiness. Tried to please 'him', with her years of training in the feminine arts... Remember what Yentl said?"

"Can't say I do."

"Well, here was this utterly feminine girl, the kind she'd made fun of, mocked, all her life: so much so that she'd bobbed her own hair and was traveling about as a boy. After hours of this Amy, her heart just melted. She said to herself, thinking of the guy who had hoped to win her: 'I can see why he loves her.'"

"The hunk?"

"Yes. Yentl could see the beauty and allure of the very thing she had been shrinking from, avoiding, rejecting, in her own self."

"And Ethan's wife was like that?"

"Well, she had that effect on me." Teresa took a breath and added, "I can see why he loves her."

25

When the solution is simple, God is answering.
Albert Einstein

The Free-Fall again.
Falling, falling away.
Spinning and falling.

Alone.

Spinning and falling away.
Out into nothing.
Where no one will help you.

Alone; forever. No loving arms to catch you, hold you.
No loving arms will ever open to receive you as you fall.

At first, Teresa thought she was just coming down with something, a chest cold, or flu. Her chest felt tight and odd, like some virus was sniffing around deep in the little bronchioles, looking for a foothold. But nothing ever developed, no cough came to satisfy that heaviness deep in her chest.

Then she speculated that it was only the old fear and loneliness creeping back into her life, as she had known they must from the moment she'd heard Elizabeth Stone's warm voice, back into the spaces that had been filled with Ethan's solid presence. Their time together had been so rare, his solemn presence so filled with guilt, yet it had spread out between them and stitched her life into something hopeful.

Loss, mourning; always some loss or fear of loss. Afraid, even, that she would lie, unloved even at the last, in her grave. But what can you do about feelings? She must not think about it. Her head and heart could not hold it. It was too precarious, trying to love someone. Always the dizzying possibility they could reject you.

Davy was gone on business, calling only briefly to check on her. Her job at the university took up most of the days. Her art was maturing under Professor Stout's maniacal tutelage, but now the resonance of it all was wrong.

Just like in her chest.

Ethan could not come to her, of course. His wife was home, with him. Oh, he called once, too brief, too circumspect. They made eye contact when she slipped into her pew in the back Sunday mornings. But that was all. And now, anything could happen.

That was it, then, she decided. Anything could happen. Little girls can wake up without a mother. Big girls can wake up without a lover. Anything. And wouldn't that give anyone a heaviness in their chest?

Then there were "attacks." Every symptom of fear and death fell on her like pieces of plaster from an invisible ceiling. Davy called Jackie and Chaya and made them promise to make sure Teresa saw a doctor. They tried on the old labels, were enamored of the symptoms – "hyperventilation" or "palpitations," sometimes even "arrhythmias." The old dilemma – was she crazy or sick or bad?

One of the kindlier doctors explained the difference between crazy and neurotic, neurotic coming with a little friendly chuckle that meant it was more socially acceptable. Crazy apparently equaled psychotic, which equaled ignorance of your own state of being, out of touch with reality. Neurotics know there's something wrong with them. "They know they're crazy!" They had both laughed good-naturedly together. *Junto. Muy divertido.* So funny. Neurosis.

She was waiting for the previous doctors in Dallas to send her records. Just in case, Davy begged her. It became simpler to just stay at home. Not so many risks.

Today, however, there was no question: she'd have to go to the doctor. She

171

made it there, too, with only the specter of the falling pieces behind her. Never gone completely under with it. Gone in, tight, only slightly shaky, endured the hour and a half of waiting in the grim gray waiting room, and seen the doctor, also grim and gray, and made it back to her car. Then it got more difficult. Home was so far away; no one there knew about her "condition." What if she fainted, fell right here? Would strangers look into the car window and know she needed help? Or would they think she was only sleeping? It would depend on the way she slumped down and over, she supposed. Or on the alacrity of the passers-by. In any case, it depended on something she couldn't control.

That's how the panic started. Then grew and grew until it trapped her with it there in the car. It spread and squeezed and sucked up all the air and left her desperate and breathless, pressed against the cool glass of the driver's side window, gasping. Still it grew, swelling against her throat until she couldn't swallow or breathe. It was just a matter of time now. Should she try to get off the road and into a parking lot, try to spare any she might take with her when she lost control of the car? Or stay on the road, hoping to beat the clock and make it home. And then what?

But by the time she let herself back into their apartment, she felt foolish. Why, it hadn't been that bad! Certainly not the worst she'd ever had. Couldn't she have stayed in town just a few extra minutes to pick up some groceries? Oh well, not worth going back now. She was weak and hungry and sleepy in that magnified way that she always was after the dying drills. Even more. This time she had real news. "The good news and the bad news." But which was which. Her mind reeled, but it was such a relief to have it back that it was a peaceful sort of reeling. Turning over and over and over the facts and possibilities. It was a good thing Davy had insisted she go to one more doctor.

"Teresa?" Davy's voice was soft. His desk chair creaked and slid, then there was a moment of clashing metal as he organized his arm-brace crutch and got free of the chair and desk.

"Oh, my God! Davy, you're home!" She ran to him and hugged him, nearly toppling them both. Tears leapt to her eyes.

"Oh, Davy. Thank God you're home."

"Rough trip?"

"Yeah."

"Do you need anything?"

She cast her eyes back and forth as if considering. "Prozac, or the Lord's soon return," she finally pronounced.

His milky blue eyes smiled with the humor his mouth could not smoothly manage. She smiled and touched his arm just so. Any more would cause a spastic overreaction.

"Yeah, a rough trip. But I'm okay now that you're here.

Teresa glanced at the table, already covered with Davy's books and papers. "What did I interrupt, Herr Professor?

"Just my stock reports." He moved to shove them to one side.

"So how IS the Dow Jones this week?"

"Up a little. I'm trying a new theory of tracking new gain trends."

She stopped to look over some of the printouts. "Goodness; so many numbers, so little time. Do you risk your actual money in the market, Davy?"

"Well, just the principal that I set aside for that."

"And you've still got it?"

"Oh, that's doubled or tripled since I started. But I just leave it in there to write covered calls."

"Covered calls?"

"Options. I make a little along the way, as if I were a broker. There's very little risk, and it grows steadily."

"So what's the new experiment?"

"Just locating stocks with emerging gain trends; I developed my own data base. Someday maybe it will develop into something... But enough about that. How are you? What does the doctor say?"

"Oh, we've got time for that yet. Let's just sit and stare a minute. How long will you be here?"

"Two weeks."

She tried to keep the disappointment from her face. Would he never be back to stay? She gathered some larger books he had marked and set them behind her on the floor. "I'll put the heavy artillery back here. What's the topic this week?" She slid gratefully into the old wooden chair that she had redeemed with a calico seat cushion. Home. Peace. With Davy it wouldn't matter if she did have broccoli on her teeth.

Davy smiled and moved the stack slowly aside. "The second law of thermodynamics."

"Ah!" She yelled and threw her hands up in mock despair. "Just when I'd begun to accept the first."

He ducked his head in hard silent laughter. "You'll like this one even better."

"*Mm-hmm.*" She leaned back and closed her eyes.

"'The entropy of the universe tends to a maximum.'"

"Entropy. Good word." She stopped chewing and looked attentive. Thought about what it could mean. She liked the way it pushed deep into her throat before the tongue threw it forward and lips caught it back again. She remembered the first law: saving its own energy. EN – gathering, swelling; TRO – tossing forward into time and the world; PY – stopping it, before it went too far.

"Great concept, this, Teresa. You'll love it." He laid his taco down and collected his focused attention.

"I know that look... too well," she teased. "I just remembered; I have an appointment." She looked pointedly at her watch and made as if to rise.

"Come on Teresa. It's simple, really."

"A root canal," she insisted, still rising.

"Five minutes," he insisted, mirth exploding behind his eyes.

She sat back down. "Five minutes, Davy. If I haven't grasped it in five minutes you're out and I'm going to read twenty minutes of *Medieval Mystics* to you."

"Deal." He touched the piles of books and magazines slowly, reverently, as if to collect his thoughts by infusing them freshly through his fingertips. "Entropy is the measure of disorder or chaos in a system of energy. No matter what work has been done the energy is still all there somewhere, if you remember from the first Law of Thermodynamics?"

"Yes; was just whipping it on the good preacher the other day."

"Well, entropy is the random resting order afterwards."

She chewed a moment and let the silence expand. "Your time's almost up Davy and I'm still mystified... 'Mystics for the mystified'..."

"Like the ice melting in your tea, there, Teresa..."

"You're grasping now. Who'll it be this time, Davy? Dame Julian of Norwich or my namesake, good ol' Teresa? Or, we haven't heard from old Bernard in a while..."

"You'll never understand the Big Bang Theory, Teresa, if you don't grasp this."

"Oh, no! Bring in the Biofeedback and under-the-pillow subliminal tapes..."

He panted in suppressed laughter. "Time flows in one direction only, see, and yet scientists see the increased complexity of high-entropy states. So that's when they realized the universe must have had a beginning. Hence the Big Bang Theory." He dropped his hands as if his point was made to such perfect satisfaction that it must be plain, his face flushed with the effort and excitement.

And because it was plain to him that he was succeeding in making Teresa relax and forget for a moment, in her light-hearted teasing, whatever the trouble was that he'd seen haunting her eyes when she first came home.

"Davy, Davy, Davy," Teresa shook her head slowly, as if sadly remonstrating an errant child. "Do you really get so excited over the scientists deciding the universe had a beginning? Julian, Teresa, Bernard... they all knew it over 1500 years ago!"

"Their faith told them. You don't even have to have faith to see it now, Teresa."

"Yeah. Now you only have to have a Ph.D."

"Like Einstein said..."

"No!" Teresa stopped him with a sudden shriek. "I do NOT want to hear from the great icon today, thank you very much." She touched a finger lightly to Davy's lips as if to seal them. "Nobody's who you think they are..."

The famous man who cared so much for mankind and so little for his own child.

The huge black and white panels hanging in the museum haunted her still. Lieserl...

But Davy had brought her back again. Her color was better, the smile her own. Almost he dared to laugh out loud.

They cleared the dishes and picked up the ordinary business of the day.

"Mrs. Matrisciano called, Teresa. She really wishes you would call her back." Sad and apologetic, knowing she wouldn't.

"First, the news."

David scraped his slow way back to the table. "Yes?"

"Well, there's good news and bad news..."

"Bad news, first."

"My heart condition is getting worse; nothing to worry about unless I stress myself or get pregnant."

"Good news?"

"I'm pregnant."

The nights came earlier now, the trees along the flat horizon like black lace against the bruised mauve sky of earlier evenings.

Abortion?

175

No. Not after the pain of the lost baby she had named Regret. Not when she could already hear the tiny floating stranger singing from its dark, watery world low in her pelvis. Tiny, innocent notes like the crystalline tinkle of silver against a stem of crystal. Already it kicked and swam and floated in front of the ultrasound screen, turning to face them when they spoke to it through her abdomen. The shiny snapshot of the ultrasound picture captured it from the side as if it slept in a tiny hammock. Already the picture was dog-eared from her enchantment.

"A baby, on top of everything else, Davy. It is too much. You should throw me out into the street."

He covered her trembling hand with his own.

"Your hands, Davy. They are so strong, yet so gentle." She looked him in the eyes. "It is worth everything I've been through to have your unconditional acceptance. Your safety."

They sat in silence for a long moment, then Teresa spoke, her tears nearly betraying her. "Don't you wish you had never met me, Davy? Never taken me in? It is all too much."

"Oh, Teresa, no," he answered, shaking his head. "I have no regrets. No regrets. Except that I cannot be... other than how I am. You deserve so much more."

"Hush." She leaned over and held him and cried in earnest.

"Will you tell Ethan?"

"Only if he comes to me. If he never comes to me I will never tell him."

"Never?"

"Never."

26

Before God we are all equally wise——and equally foolish.
Albert Einstein

Davy sat in the dim foyer and waited for the deacon's meeting to end. Yellow light from the small square windows high on the oak doors made shadows around the room and a pyramid of deceit in the middle of the floor. Then the vague rumble of voices surged as the doors were flung back and braced by the departing men.

Davy struggled to his feet and stood at the doorway, nodding to the men as they passed.

"Can I help you?" one asked.

"No, no. Thank you. I'm just waiting for a word with the pastor."

Ethan finished the paper he was reviewing with one of the men and stood to leave. His eyes dropped a moment as he noticed Davy there in the doorway, then he raised them and nodded.

"Good night, then, Ethan," the other man, older and quite bent, shook Ethan's hand and turned to leave.

"Let me walk you out, Sam," Ethan offered, taking the older man's arm.

"No need. See you Sunday."

And then there was nowhere to look but into Davy's unwavering gaze. "Good evening, David. What brings you out at this hour?" He circled the large conference table scooping up the few remaining tablets and papers while Davy stood in the doorway.

"I'd like a word, please, Ethan."

"Of course." He kept his head down.

"Here is the 'red herring' I promised." He tossed a folder down on the conference table in front of Ethan.

"Red herring?" Ethan finally met his gaze, a question on his face.

"The preliminary prospectus for CPAS... they call it that because of the red lettering on the cover that identify it as preliminary."

"Ah." Ethan picked up the folder and considered it. "So it's going to happen for you, then, eh Davy?" He was impressed and relieved and hopeful all at once.

"It looks like it. And as one of my original investors, you stand to make some serious money when it does."

"This is really great, David. I mean it. For you. For everybody." He breathed deeply and motioned as if to leave and began walking toward the door.

"There's one more thing, Pastor. Before we go."

"Yes?" But Ethan kept walking as if to follow along at a conversational distance behind his departed deacons, turning out the light in the room as he drew near the doorway.

And the darkness and the pretense came together in the same instant with the deliberate and unmistakable clanking of Davy's crutch thrust across the doorway, the rubber tip catching the frame and locking it into position. "About Teresa."

Ethan stopped and stared down at the metal crutch horizontal in the doorway in the dim light of the security lights. It was rigid and still as an iron bar, no longer subject to its owner's palsy.

Their silence was finally broken by the distant rattle as the exterior door closed behind the group of departing deacons, then the mechanical hum of an empty building. Each man could hear the breath of the other, smell the other's scent, sense the other man's tense will.

Then Ethan turned the lights back on and backed into the room. Davy let the crutch drop to the ground again and moved noisily through the door, pulling its release and letting it hiss closed behind him as he approached Ethan at the long table.

"I understand your wife is back." Davy's voice was just above a whisper.

Ethan instinctively leaned toward him. "Yes," he breathed, as if only exhaling heavily.

"And Teresa? What about Teresa now…"

"Oh, David. What you must think of us…? Of me? I've grieved over our sin, what you must think of it. Teresa assured me…"

"It's not your sin that worries me. It's your love." He leaned heavily into the arm crutches to face Ethan squarely. "Do you love Teresa? Will your love sustain her?"

Ethan's face was devoid of color, his eyes dead. He drew his brows down into deep consideration, then looked down at Davy full in the eyes. "Do YOU love her David?"

"I would die for her."

Ethan sighed and sank down heavily into the leather chair nearest him.

"You know I am not free to love her… like that." Ethan sighed.

"Then you have to stop now."

"You say that as if you mean it for my own good, David."

"I do."

"And can your love sustain her?"

Davy swung through the crutches and stood looking down into Ethan's pale face. "Preacher, I am crippled, but I am not the little crippled boy people think I am." He lowered himself down into the chair nearest Ethan's. "I am a man like any man, with the same hopes and fears and lusts and soul that other men have. I see out, but other people can't see in – can't see me – because of my body. People are afraid of my handicap… YOU are afraid of my handicap… because… because… you are afraid of your own. We are all challenged, preacher. You should know that by now."

"Yes." Ethan's voice was a trembling whisper.

"Teresa and I have loved each other since we were children, but she is afraid of my handicap too. She is afraid I am not strong enough." He pushed himself back in the chair and made himself as straight and tall as his disease would allow. "But I am. Stronger than either of you knows. Crippled is what I am, not WHO I am."

Ethan stared down at his desk.

Teresa knew what it meant when she opened the door against the rainy morning. The clouds were so heavy and close in that they looked like giant pillows waiting to catch Ethan's faint and trembling form heaped up there on the front steps, looking smaller than she would have imagined his large frame could ever look.

"Teresa," he started, then dropped his gaze. He needed a shave and seemed to have slept in his clothes.

"Yes," was all she said. Yes to him, to the soggy, leaden day. To the sure gnawing thought that she would say yes now even to the moment when they would say goodbye forever.

"I've come to say goodbye."

"Yes." Teresa stepped back, swayed, and held the door to let him pass. His overcoat brushed her as he passed into the dim room and she smelled the faint aroma of Ethan's rearranged life.

His eyes, weighted and dull, flickered around the room. "Is David here?"

"No. He's gone back to New York. His company is going public soon." Glad to have him stand there and fill the room with his presence, his voice, his aroma, his light from the scanty reflections on his golden hair.

He only nodded and stood examining her things. He ran his fingertips lightly across the titles of her books on the shelves. He stopped at the new stack of medical books at the end. "Why so many medical books?"

"I'm a hypochondriac."

He smiled and kept his eyes running over the new books of mystics Davy had brought her. "And these?"

"I have a broken heart."

His smile deepened until the bleakness left the beautiful teal eyes. Finally, his huge hand rested on the small embroidered homily on top: "All things shall be well; all manner of things shall be well."

"Who?" He was mesmerized.

"Julian of Norwich. A female mystic. I don't believe you have those in your church," she laughed softly. "Davy found it for me in a little store downtown. He knows I love her writings. From the 14th century. 'Showings' she called them... things God showed her about Himself."

"It's beautiful."

She was pleased that he found beauty in the small shabby room. She didn't like grandeur; preferred comfort, security. But it was nice when people were interested in her things, found beauty there. Like her artwork.

But she was grasping, beginning to try to keep him there a moment longer, to find the thing that really would 'make all things well'. She knew she mustn't, couldn't. Her words against his word; no, too puny. They wouldn't keep him. He could not love a woman who murdered her own child. She could not love a

180

man who could not love her.

The part of her that ached for him, that stood closer to feel the weight and solid masculine leather smell of him was shrinking away from him even as he spoke. His size, his sorrow filled the little room; she stepped back, stood away from him, and tried to breathe the air that was not yet permeated with him.

"Teresa," he began, taking her hand as she stepped backward. "There are so many things I need to tell you."

"I know." She could hardly breathe. She wanted to turn her back on him then, walk away and leave him before he could leave her. Spare herself that, at least.

"You'll have to help me. You, more than anyone, you know who and how I am. I've wasted so many words, used so many, but the ones I need fail me. I can't find them easily. You know that about me. I've loved that about you. That you could take me into your world, see past my words."

She felt his grip tighten and realized that he now held both wrists, up in the air, as if she had been about to strike him. She continued to pull back anyway, needed more space between them to say what needed to be said.

"Ethan, don't say it. I know. I already know."

He looked down at her, his eyes tight with the hidden sorrow. Like a wounded animal looking at her with trusting despair. "You know?" Wondering, as if he couldn't grasp what she had said.

He pulled her harder and it seemed as if her feet would leave the ground. She whispered now, "I know she's back. Your wife's back. Elizabeth." She said the name so it would be there, a solid presence between them in the small, dim room. "And you will do the only thing you can do. You'll do the right thing. I always knew you would." She twisted now, turned away as if in shame.

A low groan was his answer, and he pulled her back and into his arms like a small child, pressing her head against his shoulder. He began to weep, huge unabashed sobs and shuddering gasps of air. Now her feet really did leave the ground as he held her, then gripped her under her arms and held her up above him and turned, slowly, one complete revolution, leaning backward to balance her weight against his middle while he looked up at her, his face contorted with convulsive sobs. It was as if they were at the ocean again, in the waves, only now he was more afraid than she was. And now she would not cover his quaking mouth with her own.

Then in one impossible motion he eased her down until her feet were once again on the ground, and on until his own knees were on the floor and she seated in the big overstuffed armchair nearest to him. They ended the dangerous moment like that, Teresa weak with exhaustion, Ethan kneeling at her feet, his head on her lap, weeping as if he would never stop.

"Can you forgive me?"

Forgive him? She had not expected that. Would he be able to forgive her if he knew that the life they had created lay there between them, barely as big as her own tiny fist, swimming in its peaceful, watery world. It was Ethan who should forgive her.

"I am sorry that I let you come with me to a place I knew we couldn't stay. Sorry for the price you'll have to pay." She felt strangely powerful and peaceful.

"I wanted to give up everything for you. I very nearly did. I wanted to be the one who would love you enough to give up what was most important to them." His voice broke and shook, almost like Davy's.

Yes. The bleakness of her life swept over her like a wave. She willed herself to allow the memories and feelings – attached like ticks – to come to her, not numb out. Go through them, feel them; maybe they wouldn't kill her or hurt as bad as she had always feared. Maybe the pain wouldn't last forever. All she had done – all anyone could do – was fit the pieces of her life together as best she could. Tried each piece – like a jigsaw puzzle – various ways until it fitted in with the rest.

Only Davy had loved her like that. He had given up his privacy, his autonomy, he had done the things it was hardest for him to do – all for Teresa. And, then, finally, he had given her up, too. Teresa knew, even in the face of disaster and one more loss that she was borne up, protected, loved.

Slowly, slowly, over what seemed like hours, they sobered and came to themselves. She no longer had to tell herself to take each breath. Ethan still grasped her knees, but gradually ceased sobbing and relaxed. She felt his heavy body go limp against her, until finally neither moved nor spoke. She ceased stroking his hair and let her hands fall to her sides, began to breathe with quiet regularity. His head on her lap warmed her abdomen and she knew their baby could feel its warmth. She was tempted to tell him, to pull his ear up to her barely swelling abdomen and ask him how he could not know, ask him if he couldn't hear its tiny crystalline song. But she was too weak, exhausted. And slowly the memory of her decision came back to her to stop her. It was better, for everyone, if he never knew.

No passion ruled them now; that they had ever fallen seemed a dream. This, now, was simply the way they were. But for their fall, they could possibly have had this, too. Warmth, comfort of presence at chance meetings, bedside vigils, emotional moments of church business. But now it was gone and they both knew it and were shaken more by what they had lost than what they had done.

"You know, we could be like this now and be virtuous. Sacred even," Teresa finally broke the silence.

"Yes." His voice was so small she could barely hear it. "We forfeited the right to the best thing. But I know one thing." He raised his head to look at her. "God is good. And merciful. He knows our frame, Teresa."

"Yes."

"I didn't know before."

Yes, she knew. They had both confused religion with their spiritual hunger, thought the rules would redeem them, keep them safe. Had pinned the hard truth on each other. Religion kills. Only the Spirit gives life. Love does, indeed, cover a multitude of sins. Only Davy's kind of love enabled them to apprehend God's own love.

"I was keeping the rules to keep from having a real relationship with God." He pulled himself all the way up now, to stand and then drop into the chair facing her, nodding his agreement, rubbing the last dampness from his eyes and face.

"I'll get us a cold drink; maybe sandwiches or something." She lingered one moment longer, pressing her hands to the last, rapidly fading warmth where his head had been. Then lightly, ever so softly, over her abdomen. And finally to the chair arms to push her leaden body up.

When she returned with a tray of sandwiches and iced tea he was exactly as she had left him, but calmer, dry-eyed, staring. She set the tray down on the shabby coffee table and was glad for the unexpected brightness, nearly opulence of her dishes against it. A delicate bone china with the tiniest blue flowers and gold trim for one plate, a heavier, more ornate pattern of cobalt and gold for the other, the crystal glasses also different but similar. She liked the effect of them all, mis-matched but pulled together with the saffron linen of the napkins. Garage-sale discoveries wheedled out of frantic housewives with grudging change. At that moment, she was prouder of them than if they'd been handed down from her grandmother.

They ate in silence. It seemed as if Ethan's spirit and substance slowly returned. Gradually his gaze, averted since his breakdown, came to rest on her face for seconds, then to meet her eyes. He was different, he looked out of them differently. He certainly saw her differently.

"Teresa," he began, a sigh taking the last syllable. "The long night facing God with this was easier than facing you. It was as if forgiveness was something He had been standing there trying to hand me for a long time. I understood that God has a will for me, not I for Him, and that He could erase my sin at a glance. But what of His will for you, Teresa?"

He looked away sharply and shook his head. Then he looked back at her with the powerful certainty that she loved. And a self-deprecation that was new.

"I'm all right, Ethan. That's the only way I know how to say it. Even though I've known for some time the right thing, the only thing, to do, I did nothing."

"No." His voice was small, subdued.

"And I found you and pasted a colored picture of my bright and shining prince over your real face. Saw in you a love I thought had passed me by. But I didn't see you. If I had seen you the way God does, Ethan, I would have..."

"Don't say it, Teresa. We are who we are."

"Yes." She took a long drink of the tea, then held it away from her and traced rivulets of the condensation forming on the sides down into collections that fell in heavy drops, like tears, onto the linen napkin on her lap.

"You just can't think how you have changed me, Teresa. 'Adultery,' people call it, with a sneering whisper that separates it out of 'normal' sin into a small dark category worse than the others. But I can plainly see that my lack of charity, my failure to entertain strangers, my harbored resentment, my doubt... all was one dark stream.

"I will not commit this sin again, Teresa, God helping me. Not against Him. Not against anyone. But I see it now in the dark stream that runs through all our lives. I am in it with my people. I touch them, feel their violence and lusts, smell their fear, their broken lives, and it is the same dark stream that I am in, buoyant, but only by grace. I had myself so 'set apart,' sanitized and deodorized by my fundamentalism, that I couldn't see my people, feel them, smell them, taste them, hear them."

Yes, Teresa nodded her assent. Had even set himself to cast a stone at her sin, her secret. And who was she to withhold her forgiveness from him? She who misunderstood love and trust and had never loved him as much as she loved Davy, had nearly ruined him.

He looked up at her, the sadness and the hope fusing into a green light that lit his eyes from behind. "Now I am afraid all the time."

Teresa's voice shook with emotion. "We all are."

27

Imagination is everything.
It is the preview of life's coming attractions.
Albert Einstein

Christmas came, unbidden, and fell on Teresa like a stone. Mrs. Matrisciano called and invited her to join the holiday activities at the home, but Teresa declined. She did the semester art show at school and a buffet at Professor Stout's. Davy stayed in New York to spend the holiday with his mother.

And then winter slid into its only serious month – January. Once or twice the temperature dipped into the thirties and threatened the farmers and citrus groves with a slight freeze. And it drizzled until the sidewalks were dull with pounded mud, the palms an ironic reminder of the tropics they had heralded weeks before. The north wind worked at the old windows in their apartment until it built up drafts and eddies that refused to be warmed by the little space heaters. Even Martha Ann's tiny ivy in the kitchen window seemed stunted and cold.

Teresa huddled with Morgan on the sofa under an old blanket, trying listlessly to sketch, watching MTV videos to spark ideas for her work. But the damp cold made her fingers leaden, slowed her mind. It was 68 degrees in the house, and the little heater was bravely nudging it on up towards 70, but the cold had seeped into her bones and would not be so easily dislodged. Her very soul seemed to be frozen, unyielding to the prodding of sight or sound or the monotonous scratch, scratch of her lead pencil.

Davy rarely called anymore and she in her turn had lost the will to call him. The rent and bills were paid by some arrangement Davy had with the bank and Jesse, and as less and less seemed demanded of her, gradually the less she did.

On the TV there was an odd video about an old man trapped in a boarded-up room. The old man grew older and weaker; still he struggled. It was her old theme. Even with the volume turned down to a whisper, she recognized the theme. Like a ballerina able to dance in the dark.

She reached for the remote control and raised the volume to try to catch some of the words as the aging man struggled and struggled to free himself.

WHAT I'VE FELT
WHAT I'VE KNOWN
NEVER SHINED THROUGH IN WHAT I'VE SHOWN

So many mistakes. And now even Davy was lost to her.

NEVER BE
NEVER SEE
WON'T SEE WHAT MIGHT HAVE BEEN

She would never know now. Could not even muster the strength to try and imagine what her life would be. If she lived.

NEVER FREE
NEVER ME

The song went on as the old man pounded on the walls of his cell-like room.

SO I DUB THEE UNFORGIVEN

Teresa sat up right to try to catch the words over the screaming guitars.

THE OLD MAN THEN PREPARES
TO DIE REGRETFULLY

Yes, she had known it was coming. Her old theme song, the adolescent's lament. Not easy to pull into a painting, though...

One January afternoon, Davy called. Teresa clung to the receiver like it was a life raft, hope welling up inside. Trying to keep him talking.

"Do you know any dead people, Davy?"

"Pardon?"

"Dead people. *Los Muertos*."

Davy, knowing Teresa, knew to take the question in earnest. "Senora Carmen... my grandparents, but I barely remember them."

She leaned over and let the steam from the hot soup she had just prepared warm her nose. Then settled back to start on the thick chowder that she wouldn't enjoy eating. It had never bothered her one iota to thumb her nose at nutrients, but she wouldn't steal them from the tiny baby floating within the closed dark world at the center of her being. She pictured it hanging inside her uterus like a round pink bat, connected only with the sanguine rope of umbilical cord and her own will to sustain it. Him. Her. She wouldn't let the OB doctor tell her.

"Maybe when people die, they leave something of their soul with those they leave behind. Maybe my mother's dead and I will become like her in ways I can't imagine."

"I remember my dad perfectly well, but nothing about him has insinuated itself into my soul, for sure. I'm saved, though, by being 'a little crippled boy.' Got to start my identity over all clean."

"Yes. I was always trying to imagine who my mother had been, who she was, so that I could weave a tighter identity for myself. Was she a Madonna or a Whore? Never mind, was all I ever decided. And went on as before, putting one foot in front of the other."

"As of today?" Davy laughed.

"Yes, today." And she smiled too. For the first time in weeks.

"Davy," she dared, finally. "When are you coming back?"

"I don't know if I am, Teresa. Things are going really well here and they want me to stay on the board of directors the first year..."

The rest of his explanation was lost. Her ears closed from the inside, squeezed shut by tears.

The TV chattered on in the background, a program special called *Delancey Street* where ex-cons learned how to dress, look, act, talk, and work like normal working people. "Wasn't it hard?" the insipid host asked the young ex-con.

"Well, it wasn't easy," he drawled thoughtfully. "But it was easier than bein' in prison. It was easier than bein' an asshole."

Yes.

Outside the evening sky struggled into night, dark wisps of black clouds spoiling the molten flourish. The old battle of good and evil worked out in the stratosphere as the silvery lining of mauve and vermilion succumbed to darkness. Unusual splendor, Teresa thought, even for God; the first hot, mad strokes like Van Gogh, then the softer blaze as if heaven herself had left her doors open.

The lacy mesquites and rosewoods bobbed gracefully and delicately in the wind. They were bent and gnarled and susceptible to all sorts of disasters. But she preferred them to the stolid oaks, perfect and straight and strong and always the same. Then, even before she realized her soup had cooled, only blackness and her staring reflection in the window's glass.

And with no more preparation than that, the phone rang and changed everything, again.

Teresa picked up the phone now as if it were the heaviest object she had ever been forced to handle. What could it be after all? She knew it wasn't Davy. It was only poor, officious Mrs. M. who sooner or later would be able to see for herself what Teresa, her poor little orphan charge, had gone and done. Teresa had only thought to spare her by avoiding her until she lost interest.

"Yes. Hello, Mrs. Matrisciano. How are you?" Teresa's voice was careful, proper, sing-song.

"Teresa, honey, I've missed you. How are you?"

The pleasantries she had expected soon gave way to what she never expected; Teresa, who thought she was past surprise, wavered and bent under the easy trickle of words.

"You found my mother? Where?" What did it matter? But the years of unanswered questions flooded in upon her.

All her stories spiraled up from the years of wondering and speculating and remembering. She laid the phone down gently, carefully, lest it spill the last glowing embers of its heady news, lest she shake the words and see them run and quiver and turn into other words, lest she wake and find it was only her longing, after all.

A nursing home in Corpus Christi. Mrs. M. would take her there. Inside her mind, longer versions spun wildly.

The real mother had died to save the child.

No.

She was a prisoner.

No.

She was a princess.

No.

The real mother gave up the baby to save her.

Yes, maybe.

The real mother gave up the baby to save herself.

Yes, also possible.

The child could have saved the mother.

Who knew?

The mother could have saved the child.

Her head began to hurt with the spinning possibilities. The mother could have been a drunk, just as they said, and gave her up for men and booze. Or she could only be sick, incapacitated. She would have come for her if she were well.

But if she were the bad one, the not-princess mother, then she had saved the baby anyway, saved her by abandoning her.

Truth is ambiguous. That much she knew for sure. Stories were only stories. How she, Teresa, came to be everybody's baby. Everybody's, that is, except her mother's. But the truth would not come so clear or clean. So easily.

Years of waiting had left their mark and Teresa was not to wake so easily from the dream. It felt like something quick and new, too precious yet to touch or even consider in any practical way. Just a new chapter to the long dream: an error, cast out. But part of God's design, as Blake so kindly put it. Sister twin to poor Oedipus, turning, in spite of every blessing, to ask "Who am I?" The connection – broken for so long – snapped and sparked and threatened as its raw edges were brought nearer.

"Teresa," she spelled now at the bottom right corner of her paintings. Just Teresa. In chaste self-effacement, demure, understated. Teresa. Just barely legible, tiny.

No, the dam did not break yet, not like it would in the days of reality that were to come. But Teresa began to move slowly and laboriously out of the mist. When it broke she would see everything clearly. Gone now were the tyrants of

189

her unredeemed fantasies. Her mother real and her mother imagined.

The weight of the unhappy years, the uncertainties, pulled at her feeble heart and warned her; then was gone. Never again would she feel she had no background, or only a dim dream that may or may not have really happened. Her deepest instinct was, somehow, satisfied. She wasn't even in a hurry now, to urge Mrs. M. to come for her so they could go. No, it was enough just to know. She couldn't even tell if she needed to do anything about it. She would of course, and then the stones she was still laboriously setting down into cement would prove too fragile against the flood. Then she would know everything. For now, she knew enough.

Mrs. M. arrived right on time. Teresa had intended to watch for her and run out to the car, but got busy and failed to notice the big station wagon until Mrs. M. was already standing at the door. She was wearing a black and white stripped polyester dress smoothed at the wide hips into the unnatural telltale arc of a girdle. Teresa could hear her pantyhose swish as she entered and then her heavy heeled pumps too loud on the bare wooden floor between area rugs.

"Oh, what a cute place you and Davy have here," she gushed, looking around eagerly at the small apartment. Teresa was surprised to realize she had never even seen it before. As many times as she and Davy had talked about having her over, she felt guilty now to realize it had never been translated into an actual invitation.

The day, nearing the end of January now, was warmer than it had been for a week or so, and Teresa considered for a moment that she was probably overdressed in the bulky sweater; she would get too warm before the day was out. But she was anxious to get started and said nothing, slid onto the wide vinyl seat and buckled the seat belt low on her lap. At four months the pregnancy did not show in her abdomen really, but Teresa was always acutely aware of the tiny swimming passenger. She touched her abdomen lightly, and then her breasts, where the difference was more noticeable. But not in the bulky sweater, not where Mrs. M. might notice. No.

Mrs. M. chattered happily about the nice weather for the drive, the fortuitous meetings and comments that had resulted in her locating her mother, the daily business at the home. But she didn't seem to require many responses and left Teresa mostly free to think and consider the scrubby terrain of the coast, already perfectly flat and nearly sea level in its last resigned approach to the Gulf. Only two signs ever spoke of Corpus Christi at all, the tiny town of Vista Bonita never. Yes, Rose had somehow avoided the sprawling seaside jewel of Corpus Christi – "Body of Christ" – for a little Texan winter-haven called Vista Bonita – "Pretty View." Well, who could know?

The ride was only two and a half hours, but by the time Mrs. M. steered the old station wagon off the highway to follow the "*Corpus Christi 12 Miles*" sign it seemed to Teresa that she had been on the road all day. Not that she was tired physically; just exhausted in her mind already by the irrepressible flood of speculations and reservations and anxieties about Rose Marie Chace, her mother. If she squinted and focused her mind just so she could almost remember her, maybe a curly halo of auburn hair, high heels. Or maybe not. Maybe those things belong to the parade of other women who cared for her, some of whom asked that she call them her mother. It was all too confusing.

Now, the prospect of seeing her was numbing. She wouldn't be sunning herself beside her villa, after all, but in some undetermined condition in a nursing home in a tiny beach town. She had an idea Rose always liked the beach; sandy, roaring shores figured prominently in the dreamy snatches of memory. And left her tiny daughter, somehow, with a lifelong fear of the ocean. And now she was in a nursing home near the ocean, and not in there from old age. Rose would be now only 45 or 46. Why, then?

"...and you children were the only children I would ever have," Mrs. M. finished an anecdote that Teresa could not remember the beginning of.

"You never had any children yourself?" Teresa wasn't really so surprised.

"I knew I never would when we married – health problems." Even now, after all the years and the things she'd no doubt seen, the older woman blushed at the memory of gynecological tragedy. All these years later her voice still rang just a decibel higher with the pain.

The last miles were eaten up in rustling maps and traffic and straining to make out signs worn and torn by the merciless salt air and then they were, suddenly, miraculously there. *Vista Bonita Care Center*. Just like that. Only a long, one-story building of yellow brick with four groups of palms and lawn of St. Augustine – "carpet grass." Nondescript, bleak, obviously not where the wealthy retirees chose to wait it out. But where Mrs. M. assured her resided the person of Rose Marie Chace. For a second her heart rolled ominously in her chest, then righted itself. Teresa drew a deep breath.

Mrs. M. cut the motor and, in the sudden silence, whispered, "Teresa." And turned to face her, her hand covering Teresa's own. "Are you ready for this? It could be anything, you know. It could be bad. You're prepared for that?"

Yes. The princess had long since withered and died. She entertained now only the delusion of a regal older woman with silver hair, confined to a wheelchair, but joyous to be reunited with her long-lost daughter. An artist, perhaps, who still had her best oils with her in her room. But the possibility of a bag lady did peek around the corners of the better dream.

"Now or never," she smiled at Mrs. M., and opened the car door to the stiff, fresh gulf breeze. The wind snapped her hair back and then, when she turned, tickled her face with it. She was glad for the bulky sweater.

Inside, the care home was dreary and thick with the unmistakable smell of baths and bodily functions and food masked with disinfectant aerosols. No one was at the front desk, so they wandered on into the hall of rooms, lined with wheelchair patients with the hungry eyes and extended hands of beggars. Metal trays were everywhere, filled with linens or medications or food. The air was filled with conflicting voices, some cheery and some long mournful moans as if in torment. And an occasional bit of radio music, mostly the *Tejano* that the Hispanics preferred. A place, Teresa thought, out of Dante. For people who had good intentions.

A pleasant young nurse rescued them and extracted most of Teresa's life story while searching Rose's chart, tending to several whining interruptions. The diagnosis was grim: cirrhosis of the liver, organic brain syndrome. But the nurse's manner of relating it was so cheery that hope still bloomed. Then she led them down the long hallway to a semi-private room with two faded tags: "Martinez" and "Chace." Just like that.

"I'll wait outside, dear," Mrs. M. offered. "Maybe I'll even go back to the lobby to wait for you, so I can sit down."

So Teresa was left to cross the literal threshold of her dreams into the reality of Rose accompanied by a cheery stranger. The young nurse turned to her in warning: "Rosie is home sometimes," she smiled, touching her finger to her own temple. "And sometimes not at home. You understand?"

Yes.

"We call her Rosie. I hope you don't mind."

No.

As Teresa felt the dreams of her mother melting like the bad witch sprinkled with the water of reality, she found that she had loved them even if they were not true. She would mourn them now too. *Goodbye lovely smiling lady in the trees,* hair streaming through the clouds. *Goodbye stern and proper Victorian matriarch,* silver-haired and proud. *Goodbye* to all the hopeful dreams.

Hello Rose.

28

If you want to live a happy life, tie it to a goal, not to people or objects.
Albert Einstein

Teresa pulled her eyelids wide, unblinking as a lizard, to take in everything at once. But still it was her nose that reached out to know her mother first; the smell of alcoholic desolation was so strong that Teresa didn't know if she could stand to go closer. Was it the little old lady curled in the first bed, Rose's roommate? Or Rose herself? They made their way around the foot of the roommate's bed, past her beggar's hand reached out to them in greeting, and went to Rose's bed by the window.

Rose too had beggar's hands; but hers were tied to the bedrail with canvas restraints, cupped palms up like a beneficent saint in a Bible picture. Her pillow was no longer under her head and so her head was thrown back into gaping, snoring submission. The sour, fetid odor seemed to emanate from that open orifice, was almost visible in its heavy acridity and stench; Rose's rotting liver, no doubt, sending out its last dying gases.

The young nurse didn't hesitate a second, proceeded to fix Rose's pillow back under her head so her mouth would stay shut, straighten the scrambled covers, all the while calling loudly to her: "Rose, Rosie, come on honey. *Roooooosie.* Wake up. You have a visitor. It's your daughter, Rosie, come to see you." The light Hispanic inflection on the words blunted them somehow, made them seem less stark to Teresa, standing paralyzed at Rose's bedside. Your daughter here to see you. Just like that. Succinct end to a very long story.

Rosie, however, while perfectly willing to be seen, was not going to see anybody that day. She cleared her cloying mouth around its few dark teeth with loud *M-mmmm-hmmmm*'s and coughed a deep, rattling unproductive cough, pulled at the restraints a second and dropped back into unconsciousness as deep and roaring and infinite as the ocean's. Her left foot was tangled in the covers and so left bare, its waxen yellow nails grown long, the skin splitting with edema and curly clotted spider veins. When her eyes opened for a few seconds, they were so swollen and had such dark circles under them, that it looked like she had been hit right in the center of her face.

"It looks like Rosie isn't going to wake up and join us today," the nurse lamented cheerfully as she fixed the shades on the window and straightened the bedside table.

"This is Rose Marie Chace? You're sure?" It was ridiculous, she knew, but all that came to mind to say. What to say to the ruin and desolation of that face, the death of the fairytale Queen.

"Oh, yes, honey. This is Rose all right. Sometimes she talks a little, tells a little joke... Don't you Rosie?" she raised her voice turning back to Rose once again.

Nothing.

"She came with very few things. And she's been here a long time." The nurse, looking apologetic, looked quickly through the contents of the little bedside stand, then closed the door and walked over to the tiny closet. "They're in here, I think." She extracted an old worn suitcase and popped it open before Teresa could protest.

Inside were only some clothes, a few cheap cosmetics and lotions and a stack of papers, most of which proved to be insurance and Medicare forms, bills, postcards, a few worn photos of nameless people. Only one photo was in a frame and it seemed to be of Rose herself, younger, smiling. The locket Teresa now wore hung at her throat. Teresa's hand rose unbidden to her own throat and touched it there even as she saw it plainly in the photo. Another dogeared shot was of an old stooped man in a hat, his face bare discernible. *Papi*; Teresa knew it. But she could not bring herself to actually lean down to take them. The nurse stirred the things quickly and, judging them to be of no importance, clicked the suitcase shut efficiently and swung it back to its hiding place in the minuscule closet.

To Teresa it was as if it hadn't happened at all; she would wonder later if it had. It was kind of the little nurse to help her at all; she had no right to ask for more. For anything. She had no right. It can't be. No.

Teresa turned away to go, then turned back. Was she a child? Had she been dismissed? The nurse was covering Rose's naked foot, tucking the wild halo of graying auburn hair back behind Rose's ears. Seeing Teresa standing there, frozen, she only smiled. And waved. Then covered the disgusting, ravaged foot with the clean white sheet. Not like the plump, pristine feet she had imagined the disciples offering to Jesus to be washed. Not like them at all.

No.

"Come again another day, Miss Teresa," the nurse sang out. "Sometimes she is awake."

Yes. So casual, so simple. Come another day.

Teresa backed toward the door and made as many grateful remarks as would come to her. Thank you for your time. Thank you for your kindness. Thank you, thank you, thank you. Rendered obsequious by a common act of kindness. As she backed toward the door and freedom and good, safe Mrs. M. waiting in the lobby. She couldn't recall ever having hugged Mrs. M. before; she would hug her now. She even thought she could hear the swishing of her heavy thighs in their girdle and hose, rustling briskly, officiously to her down the hall.

"*Que Dios la bendiga*, Miss Teresa," the nurse called after her. "God bless you."

And yes, it was the ample form of Mrs. M. swishing its way toward her, gathering her in its spongy arms.

"It can't be," she whispered. And allowed herself to be gathered up and removed and put in the car and taken away from the cold reality of Rose.

And so she was not alone when the dam broke.

I choose to forgive her. Forgive her. Let it go. Let it go. Let it go. There will never be enough love in the world for you, Baby. You missed it somehow and now there will never be enough. So let it go. Go on. Fight. Live. How can you forgive someone you do not know? It would take a lifetime to learn to forgive. And I don't have a lifetime. I have five months. Five months until my own baby will be born, and I will not keep this poison in my veins until then.

Rage, Baby. Rage. Blow the top off the careful pot of rage that has simmered for twenty-five years. What could it hurt now? Who could it harm? Who would you even tell? Send the crashing china flying, break through the walls, rail, rail.

What to do with so much anger? It seemed to live a life of its own, wanted someone to own it, receive it. Who then? Who to blame; who to receive so much rage? The rotting relic in bed 304B? What could her rage do that Rose hadn't already done to herself? The kind strangers who saved her and raised her against all odds and for no discernible reason other than their good intentions and yet could not wrap their hearts around her own in the nurturing affection you could call "motherly"? Those who had rewarded her for being smart, laughed with her for being funny, smiled at her for helping out so much? The world that mistook performance for meaning, rewards for love? Herself? Yes, that was a safe target. But what, exactly, had been her crime? Where, precisely, had she gone wrong?

And still the anger grew, swelled and rolled and pushed at her guts and heart like molten lava, too hot for the cold mountain that held it, about to blow and run and ruin in all directions. She knew it now, recognized it from the haunting sorrows of her life, the whispered accusations, knew it from the filthy floor of the convenience store and the barren halls of Grace Community Hospital. Remembered it from the nightmares of her childhood, the snake lady and the evil figures who chased her. Recognized it as the tormentor who made her lips quiver when she told it to smile.

What to do with it? "Hostility," brittle-footed Dr. Clay had called it, him and his legion of beefy cohorts. Like "hostile" was just another feeling – sad, happy, hostile. Anger? No, no. Anger is when the neighbor's dog chews up your paper three mornings in a row; anger is when your best friend dates your lover behind your back; anger is when you get fired for something your co-worker did. No, it needed its own word, this dark, roiling, steaming, sulfurous mass of toxic feeling that crushed her heart until it stumbled, squeezed her lungs, set the nerves and muscles of her arms and legs to twitching and jumping instead of smoothly pumping up and down. It turned her blood to poison and her saliva to salty, acrid solvent that melted gum in her mouth. Until her brain was forced to put up emergency barriers to keep itself from being destroyed by the poisonous, venomous toxins, until she could not feel herself in her own life, until she thought she would die only because she could sense she could not survive under these crisis conditions forever, until she knew she would faint.

Be a good little girl. Forgive others as you would have them forgive you. Let a smile be your umbrella. You're a lucky, lucky, lucky girl. God grant me the serenity... The hopelessly distant proverbs that melted at the enormity of her distress, then skittered off like cowed dogs at the hot blast of her rage. It blasted every distant thing that dared approach it, scorched even the pathetic comforts of her own affirmations, blackened the cool, innocent memory of Ethan's passion, of Davy's steadfast love. Everything good and decent from twenty-five years of living wilted under the long hot sulfurous plume of dragon's breath.

She wanted to break something, hurt someone, scream an ugly choking scream, not like movie stars scream, but like wolves howl when trapped in bone-crushing steel traps. Wanted to break every dish in Heaven. Throw a pie in the face of God.

And she wanted Davy. But he had neatly removed himself from her life.

Teresa looked down at the pale skin of her wrist, thin and translucent, stretched just as it had always been over the delicate blue vein snaking across the wrist and up the thumb. Amazing, the things that happened and the body just ticked resolutely on. Blood raged and pounded in her head, yet the same quiet blue thread pulsed across her wrists, just like always. And if she were to cut that delicate blue thread, the air would turn it red every time.

She looked out the window, but her eyes fell short in their focus and were mirrored in the window, the image she had avoided all her life. Framed by the dark hair fading to the red glint of the dissipated floozie Rose, the same glassy-eyed stare, the mouth hanging slack, numb from too much of something life had dealt them.

"Did you know her then?" Teresa finally lifted her head and asked Mrs. M.

"Yes." She left her hands firmly on the steering wheel and kept on driving as if their lives depended on it. Her eyes swam behind the thick glasses.

Teresa thought of dozens of things she could ask her. What had she been like? Had she loved her? But nothing formed itself in her mouth and she only sat with her hands upturned in her lap while Mrs. Matrisciano picked her way steadily through the traffic and then, mercifully, back onto the highway. Visions of the hundreds of other children from the home blurred her focus. Not enough love for any of them. Anger still gnawed at the pit of her stomach like hunger. It would not even soften into fear or sadness; just bitter rage that so many were sent with so little into the world that would require so much. Her heart hammered with a dangerous strength and rhythm that it hadn't had for months now, made steady by her anger, fed by the same adrenaline that made her head spin and threaten to come apart.

"Will you tell me everything?" Her question to Mrs. M. rang with her bitterness.

Yes. Her nod was barely perceptible.

"Teresa, dear." Mrs. M. reached for Teresa's limp hand, pressed it lightly.

Teresa turned to her, her eyes bright with the adrenaline, shining with the challenge to Mrs. M. What could she say, after all?

"Teresa," her voice was a thin, aching croak. "I always wished you were my little girl."

29

To dwell on the things that depress or anger us does not help in overcoming them. One must knock them down alone.
Albert Einstein

I am eleven years old, nearly twelve, and I cannot say that I am angry. It is too dangerous. They get mad all the time, but there is no room for my anger. It is safer to keep it to myself.

I've been having nightmares lately. Mother Garza says I'm getting too old to be calling them in the night, but eleven doesn't seem like such a magic number to me. I just like to be sure someone will come. What is a nightmare, anyway? Fear is the only thing I am afraid of. I will be twelve next week and maybe then I will be braver.

They always want me to call them "mother," but now I understand about foster mothers. And that I am a "foster" child, different from a regular child, or a "daughter." I've had Mother Steiner, Mother Hernandez, and now Mother Garza. Mother Steiner wanted me to call her mama, but I couldn't. I wonder if real daughters can always call real mamas in the night?

I had a real mama too once. I can remember waiting for her better than I can remember her. Nameless people would get my blanket and clothes and socks together to be ready at the time they said Mama would come. She must have come, sometimes, but I can't remember that. Only waiting and waiting and she never came. She would have done that to any child, the counselor told me; it's not just me. Since then I've had 'Mothers'. Mother Garza takes care of us foster kids here at the home. Twelve of us. Other houses are full of foster kids too, and they have their own "parents."

In the nightmares, my real mama comes to get me. When I open the door, she's standing there dressed in a black snake suit, the kind with a little point in the forehead and a tail, even though I guess snakes don't have tails. Only the devil. She has white skin and bright ruby red lipstick, but that's all of her that I can see. The rest is covered with the black suit. When she opens her mouth to speak to me, her tongue is forked like a snake's.

That's the really horrible thing about the dream, that forked tongue. When that happens, I call for Mother and Dad Garza. But I still don't wake up and open my eyes. I stare and stare at the horrid snake lady until she is pushed back, back far away into the night sky, back until she is just a dot of light on the horizon. And I tell myself to remember, always remember, that a dot of light on the horizon is evil. It may look like a light, but it is evil and I will always have to be careful. I try to scream, but it feels like I have cotton stuffed into my mouth, muffling any sounds I make.

Going back to sleep is like drowning. I go out into the water and feel it sucking at my bare heels, trying to get a good hold on my ankle, trying to pull me down. Exactly like a hand, an actual hand around my ankle, pulling me down. And I am aware that it is my fault, I have gone too far out, or I am too weak a swimmer. I don't have the power. I deserve to drown. The ocean is roaring at me and I look out and see that it never ends. If I let the hand take me down, I will suffer forever because there is no end to the ocean.

When I scream, Mother Garza comes. And sometimes Dad Garza too. He doesn't mind so much; I am his pet because the kids all say I look sort of like him with my straight dark hair and upside-down pouty red mouth and eyes that can't decide if they are brown or green. Maybe I am a Mexican they tell me, laughing. "*Media Mexicana.*" But I remember my mama and her white skin and fuzzy red hair.

I cannot stand to be alone, though I don't want anyone to touch me. It is as if my skin is gone; if I am very careful the pain is not too bad. Everyone, sooner or later, tries to touch me, but it hurts too much. Sometimes, when I am bruised and scraped while working with the animals or playing soccer, I look at the bloody place and wonder that it doesn't move me. Not like this secret pain inside.

The soccer bruise hurts, but I know it will go away. This deeper, secret pain might go on forever. I understand why they don't know what to do about it; it's not their fault. I'm sure it's my fault that I have no skin and am in awful pain. They tell me it's not my fault. And they try to stay away.

Maybe if I had been prettier. Or very talented. When I was younger I could sing and dance, make my eyes shine like I had swallowed the moon. But now the light is going out and they don't know what to make of me. "You want to cry?" they say sometimes. "I'll give you something to cry about." But they don't, not really. They're not really mean. They just have skin and do not understand how it feels not to have any. I am wax and their hands are so hot. They mean well, but I soften and melt in pain when they touch me. So I've learned that its always better to smile. Not resisting. Not caring.

Sometimes, sitting in class at school, I bite off little pieces of paper and chew them. Then spit the wads out and lay them side by side along the edge of my desk. Some need an extra little twist and shaping to make them round and uniform enough to stand beside the rest. I think I must need some shaping, too, to stand beside the rest.

In science we are studying the brain. How all the little neurons are like a computer with a chemical factory. What we learn makes a groove in it; if we repeat something many times it will make the groove deeper. Our brains are full sized by the time we are six. I try to imagine all the things that are already buried in there, in that jellied ball of gray matter; try to remember my mama, my life before. It says in the book that memories are made by some chemicals named glycoproteins. And they never go away. I thought memories were something else, something more lovely or magical than a thing called glycoproteins.

I've been writing poetry lately, and it always comes out about death. What does an eleven-year-old know about death my teacher asks me. Write about what you know. But I'm nearly twelve and I know. Know that in my dreams I am running in huge empty rooms, full of strangers. Someone is always chasing me, I am always in danger. I want to scream and save myself, but my voice sticks in my throat. Sometimes, I am buried alive, helpless to call out, or hacked to pieces. I wake up with my heart pounding so hard and fast I am afraid it will burst out of my chest. When I start to write about what I know I can only think of those things.

So I don't think I'll be a poet when I grow up. I feel naked when they see my words. It's easier to draw and paint, where I can tell the truth, but only I can read it. Or draw sturdy buildings and make them just like I want them, with huge stone arches and big windows. Miss Berrigan's art book says that ancient architects claimed that "the arch never sleeps." I like that: you build it and it doesn't depend on anything but itself. That's its power. Arches never sleep. Glycoproteins never go away. Oceans never end.

Here at the home, the church is open all day and usually empty. I can sit in there and no one tries to touch me but I do not feel alone. I don't think God exactly lives there, though they call it His house. But the part of Him that He is willing to let us see is there. Colored light slanting in dusty spotlights to the altar. Plain, simple, quiet goodness and gentle power; sort of like Dad Morgan. Safe. Until the people come in.

30

How was I able to live alone before, my little everything?
Albert Einstein

avy's letter wasn't much comfort anymore, but it was the only comfort she had without Davy. Teresa curled up on the old sofa with Morgan to read it through one more time. She hadn't imagined how much she would miss Davy. More than she missed Ethan, whose life had never been so intertwined with her own. She buried her fingers in Morgan's soft fur and inhaled her sweet puppy scent. Maybe she could make a memory that was good. Morgan's warm pink tongue rewarded her with diligent affection. Yes, she could start with this small good memory, like rummaging in the bottom of her purse for a cherry Lifesaver. She thought back to school science and hoped her glycoproteins were working.

Teresa smoothed her trembling hands over her tee shirt. The warm mound of abdomen, just starting to swell into a visible bulge in the fifth month, was comforting. No one could really tell for sure that she was pregnant yet – at least no one, including Jackie, had said anything – but Teresa could sometimes feel the tiny flutter of life.

She waited for it now; but was disappointed. Only the faint flutter of the paper she held and the harder, more precarious flutter of her heart. All somehow a result of the sad reality of finding her mother. The river of grief and rage had poured itself into all the cells of her body, translated itself into rivulets of trembling discontent. The sense of impending doom and quaking inertia that the Mexicans called *nervios* or *susto* and the Anglos called anxiety. Inadequate words, in any language.

The facts were plain enough and she was stuck with them. She had turned a corner and before she could turn away from it had seen once more the snake woman of her dreams. She could neither piece her reactions together, nor look again at the mirror. Even though she told herself that it wasn't so much, it wasn't so bad, she could not stop the venom in her veins.

Maybe, read Davy's letter one more time…

> *Teresa,*
>
> *The "road show" is going well, although it is exhausting. The presentations to investors and underwriters about the public offering are getting pretty slick. Oddly enough, the people involved do not seem troubled by my physical handicap; maybe it even lends me a kind of intellectual status in these Hawking days. Since we are going to market CPAS nationally we have to meet the "Blue Sky" laws in every state. It's a monster endeavor that eats lawyers like candy. Everything's a go with the SEC and the registration statement will become effective in a few more days. Sooooo, guess it might really happen.*
>
> *It was so great to talk to you by phone last night. You asked why I never get angry. To be so angry, Teresa, there must be ruined expectations. Mine were never high. I suspected the truth about my body at three or four. I was always aware that I looked like a drooling drunk to passersby. Now I spend most of my hours in consideration of which muscles to release and which to contract. My smile laughs at itself even as it is born – ridiculous. My sobs could be a chuckle. Could be. My voice went deeper at adolescence but still cannot hit a note reliably. I cannot even hug myself when I am afraid. You are right; very little can surpass all that and cause the anger that is ruined expectations. I have my regrets, of course – I wish I could have held you, or at least smiled at you with my own soul's smile rather than this exaggerated grimace – but my expectations were never high.*
>
> *Or maybe you are only now wondering about your own anger and what it could mean and what to do about it. You may be surprised to know what I have to say about that, Teresa. I say it's good. Pain always gives advice. And it will not go away until you take the advice.*
>
> *You were a baby playing on the beach. When the waves came and took your castles you had no words, no defense. You found yourself alone and wondered what*

you had done, how you had become lost. When strangers kicked sand into your face, you had no self to defend. You became careful, so careful. I was there; I saw you. You were too smart to risk your anger then.

And for a time, in Dallas, I know you wanted to die. Part of you still does. But little girls mustn't die or kill themselves just because they are angry; there wouldn't be any left. Shake your fist! At the sky, at the world, at the strangers (and lovers) who kick sand in your face. At ME. You were never afraid of me, Teresa, and my spastic imprecision, and I always loved you for that. Your anger does not make me think you are bad, but strong and brave and honest. Because I care for you and want you to be free.

Fight, Teresa. Fight.

Yes. Being seen by Davy was like being seen by God.

Her soul was bathed in the cool water of Davy's acceptance. He knew her like no one did and didn't condemn her. And she knew he was right. She would go on; with Davy or without him. With Ethan or without him. She would fight; to live and to sustain the fragile life within her. She would do whatever she had to do, even if it cost her her life.

The anger would not kill her? She trusted Davy; she knew he must be right. And all that fear?

"Come on, Morgan," she called the puppy from her warm burrow on the sofa. "One more trip outside then I'm outta here."

Half an hour later, she drove the old Ford out of the narrow gravel drive and into the afternoon sun. Late February now, it was a springtime day, early, as spring always was in the Valley. Everywhere the landscape showed new spring green budding out to overtake the winter browns. Already the palms were sprouting new tops for the burnt brown fringe on their skirts. New rows of broccoli and cabbage waved in lines of teal and purple, rescuing the flat brown landscape from monotony. Some of the citrus groves were being pruned to remove old, dead branches, giving the rest a chance to live. It was a pretty time of year, full of promise.

Like a sleepwalker, she found herself on the street of Avila Baptist Church, only dimly aware of what she was doing. When she saw the parking lot full of cars she realized it was Sunday. She sat in her car, staring across the street, imagining the growing crowd inside. She didn't really want to go and hear all the old rules; she had wanted Ethan but never loved his sermons. And she despised the generic right hand of Christian fellowship. But her need was so great now, born of fear and loneliness, that it knew it would be met. Had to be met. A kind of raw faith, after all. She swung into the parking lot and was out of her car before she could think. Before she could lose her nerve.

The prospect of seeing Ethan – even from her seat at the back, even as a tiny preacher-puppet moving up on the distant stage behind his armored pulpit – was unnerving. But she wanted to see him; to see things all of a piece. Only please, God, she prayed under her breath, no broken lamb's legs today. She wouldn't be able to take it.

The sanctuary was more crowded than she could remember seeing it; the older 'Winter Texans' were still here enjoying the sunny February and the locals were between holidays. Teresa sat in the back corner near the door and waited for the crowd to arrange itself, studying the shapes and colors of the adults, the faces of the small children, avoiding any stray glances from people she knew.

Finally, she released her eyes to seek out the familiar dark figure settling in on the stage as the song-leader stepped to the pulpit. At first she did not recognize him. It simply didn't look like the Ethan Stone she had known so well. A tan suit had replaced the dark ones, which had never been right with his coloring. This made his hair gleam lighter in the overhead spotlights, softened the lines of his face. And was he thinner? His face, from so far back, seemed more wide-eyed, opened out.

She remembered the first acrylic she had painted of him: hard, dark lines of bold colors, narrow and creased at the brow in anger or admonition, a dab of light for his fair hair, one fist raised in anger or admonition, the other hand lower, open and empty. Even then, she had captured the soft sad gray of his eyes, looking out his study window for a grace he could not apprehend, and painted them in carefully above the bitter slash of mouth.

She had drawn him after she knew his passion, quick dancing sketches more reflective of her own passion for him than any qualities of his own. And tried to paint him, but could not decide on an aspect long enough. No perspective. She needed to see him from this distance of the back pew of the church, his many parishioners in between, the gloomy Word, as he managed to make the Good News sound, on his lips. Once they were together she was too close and could not see him clearly enough to paint him.

Today, she could plainly see, he was different. She could use her beloved watercolors to paint him today. A soft beige wash, not so different from that of his church and congregation, to begin. Gone the angry slash of mouth; now his lips were vulnerable as her own. She would exaggerate the space between the eyes now, dashes of teal at the outer corners. Only a shadow – a touch of Natural Sepia, perhaps, or hint of Burnt Umber – would still be in the brow, where the lines of disappointment had lived so long.

The congregation slogged through the opening hymns with the song-leader, the offering, and various prayers with the lay people. They were halting, stilted, trying to keep from being "vain and repetitious," as they viewed Catholic ones. Then the familiar slow flutter as the congregation settled to their seats and turned their faces expectantly to their leader, their fair-haired pastor. Teresa's heart slammed into her chest and rolled into an erratic pattern that made her feel faint until it corrected itself. Then her head cleared and her mind reached for the words she had come to hear.

"You don't know how much danger you've been in," Ethan was saying. Or was it Ethan? Could it be a blonder twin, a younger, simpler cousin? Only the voice was the same. He didn't even ground himself to the ornate pulpit while he spoke but stepped down the wide landing to meet his people halfway, like a celebrity. "... how many times He's saved you." He shook his head for emphasis. "While you've been thinking how well you were doing."

She lost the next words in a blur of surprise and then heard him say "I woke up this morning" like he was starting all over again, a new message. Then stopped.

"Just think," he exclaimed, his hand flying up in delight. "He didn't have to wake me up another morning!"

The crowd murmured and Teresa sighed with them. Yes. This was what they all felt God would say to them.

"You are where you are because He has been so careful, so tender with you. His Word promises not to give us more than we can bear; and He knows all we can bear is His tender mercy. In spite of all our sins." He dropped his head and paused. His next few words were lost in the rustle of the congregation straining to hear them.

"He will care for you forever." His voice dropped even lower. "Even if he has to part the water." Then rose to an open-handed exclamation. "Even if he has to get water from a rock." The murmur increased as the congregation caught on. Ethan dropped both hands. "Even if He has to die for you..."

Teresa felt her body relax, felt a smile tease the corners of her mouth, turned tight for so long now. And then she felt the slow sure tumble of the tiny life within her. Ethan, this new Ethan, full of grace, would never know what he had done for his own baby swimming, innocent and content, in Teresa's womb, no bigger than its mother's closed fist. She did not fear the coming words. The cruelty seemed gone. The smiling blind fetus within its watery world tumbled again in relief and freedom.

"When the Lord told Abraham to give up Isaac, there was no promise attached. He just told him 'Give him up.'" Ethan held his hand out in admonition, then turned it over in supplication. He stepped down once again. He was nearly on their own level now; when he reached his hand out to make the point, it looked as if he might touch the rapt faces on the front pew. The floodlights made splashes of golden light of his hair as he paced back and forth, handing them this truth, this drink of cool water.

"We have been abused by the enemy of our souls. But, people," he nearly shouted. "He is not who we thought he was. The enemy of my soul," his hands touched his own chest, "and the enemy of your souls," his huge hands opened out to the still congregation. "Is Fear. We are so afraid of what He will say about our sin, that we will not face Him so that He can set us free."

They all shifted, almost in unison. And Teresa shifted with them. She and the tiny stowaway, innocent product of sin.

"You are traveling under sealed orders. You have to go without knowing where you are going or what you will do. It is a relationship He wants from you. Not religion. You have to walk and move in the mystery. Take the risk of faith."

Teresa lost the rest of the benediction; the people rose as one. She looked to the lights and Ethan was already gone.

And so she came to him later, in the early evening, when she knew she would find him in the church office alone. The lights were dimmed, as if everything was prepared to be locked for the night. But the one light she had trained her eye to, the one she had to see, was still on. Ethan's office.

There was no one else in the church. The new secretary's typewriter was covered and the desktop cleared of papers. And past the small alcove was the broad, dark back she had known so well. Ethan stood at his desk with his back to her, preparing, no doubt, to leave for the day.

"Pastor," she finally spoke, though it was barely a whisper.

Her name was on his lips before he could turn around to her completely – "Teresa!" His hand went out towards her, then dropped; the color left his face and the sparkling teal of his eyes deadened, confused. "Teresa," he said again, and the slow flame of color returned to his cheeks.

She could see the stronger emotions struggling to send a message of caution to his face; for a moment she felt the old thrill. Then hardened herself, remembered the deep reservoir of bitterness and fed on it.

"Pastor, do you have a minute? I need to talk to someone." She let her breath and eyes give weight to the "Pastor" and the "someone." Let there be no mistake.

And Ethan saw it there and knew. Even as he settled her in a chair across the huge desk from his own, he sent the flushing passions of his face and fluid eyes away and finally faced her with the warm, objective distance of a pastor. As he had faced so many, as he had faced her that first day, months – a lifetime – ago. A man prepared to be something more or less than exactly a man. A priest prepared to speak for God. He betrayed his steely intentions only once, for an instant, as he glanced at the open door to the alcove and seemed to consider whether or not it should be closed.

Finally he was still and his eyes, gray now, settled on Teresa's. He laid both hands precisely, calmly, on the desk, raised his eyebrows in question as a gesture to begin.

"Everything is a mess. I'm so bitter or anxious or whatever it is that I can't study or paint." She flailed her arms around her a minute in agitated exasperation.

He was quiet, afraid perhaps of where it was leading.

"I found my mother," she finally gasped, the disgust apparent in her inflection.

"Didn't you want to find her?" His voice was careful, neutral.

"I thought I did, yes. But not her." Her face turned aside with the strength of the twisted grimace of her mouth. "I wanted to find the lady I had dreamed about all my life. Not a dissipated old alkie in a nursing home."

"You saw her? Talked to her?"

"Mrs. M. found her, drove me up. It was a mistake. She couldn't even talk. Dying now, apparently, after years of lying there with a pickled brain."

"You found your mother." He spoke the words in slow surprise, deliberation, looking away as if considering the ramifications of what she told him.

"It was Rose all right. But not the mother I was looking for. I wanted to find someone who would look into my face and tell me how it all connects. Explain my life."

"And she can't do that." His voice was a careful monotone.

"Can barely open her eyes." She waved her arms again in a vain effort to convey the disappointment at finding this human detritus, this embarrassing old rag doll whose brain was long lost in the alcoholic poisoning of her body.

Ethan took in a long, deep breath and blew it out softly through pursed lips, looking toward the darkening window then back again to Teresa, his eyes the rich and dangerous blue of the ocean.

"And there's nothing I can do," Teresa stammered on. "Can't change the facts. The facts that feel like they might finally murder my soul. There will never be anyone who will love me, make it be all right, accept me like I am no matter what." Even as she spoke the words she felt them twist in her mouth like a lie. Davy loved her, Davy accepted her. He just couldn't make it be all right. Just like she couldn't make Davy be all right, no matter how much she loved him.

"No, you can't change the facts, Teresa." He spoke slowly, softly, but with a new confidence as if he had asked someone and knew the answer. "But it occurs to me that there are two things you can do about it."

She was surprised to hear him answer her, surprised, indeed, that there might be an answer. It eroded her anger for a moment, made her docile.

"You can see God that way." His voice was firm. "And you can be that way yourself."

Her eyes filled suddenly with tears, hot salty reaction to his answer that she didn't even understand. Something broke deep within her. Her heart fluttered under the weight of hidden sorrows and broke the wall that had hidden things so long, leaving her breathless. All she had ever known about love was how you can lose it, kill it, and not expect it. Then hate herself for that. Then hate the lost lovers. Now the confusion between her true love for Davy and her infatuation with Ethan's godly new ways was an insurmountable wall she could not climb. Ethan rose and moved around the desk to her, but only stood, huge, quiet, beside her while she sobbed. She did not dare to look up at him, but could not help enjoying the weight of him pressing into her side, though he did not touch her. She cried until she was not even ashamed to go on crying.

"What we had, Teresa..." Ethan's voice broke and he could not finish.

"What was it we had?" Her voice was a quaking whisper. "Only a beginning and an end..."

Ethan reached for her, then dropped his hand. "We had 37 days."

Yes.

"You know that I love you, Teresa." Ethan rested his hand lightly on her hair, tenderly. "I would give anything." He paused and hammered the word out again: "Anything. If we had never sinned..." Now it was clear that he too was crying.

"If I could know you forever and love you in the very best sense of the word."

"I don't know why you love me," she spoke in ragged spurts between deep, wracking sobs. "Why anyone would..."

His eyes, dark now with misery, cast about the room as if the balm he needed would appear to him. Finally, he only whispered, firm, sure, stroking her hair lightly: "You don't need to know."

Teresa was still a long moment and then dragged a huge ragged breath past the knot of grief, her head still bowed into her hands and face still wet with tears. And then she laughed. Tiny and rueful at first, a tentative little chuckle. Then another long intake of air and she was perfectly still. And then raised her face to Ethan and laughed the laugh of joy and mirth that had always delighted him.

"Good answer, Pastor." And smiled with the simple satisfaction of a small child. A wounded child, tenderly consoled. Her shoulders still caught in the rounded shudder of grief, tears still made wet spikes of her dark lashes. But the laugh was full of her hope and his comfort.

While Teresa helped herself to the box of tissues on his desk, Ethan went and stood at the big window. He wiped his own eyes once with his white handkerchief and stood staring out into the falling night. Only a faint blush of evening remained on the horizon.

"You are right, of course, Teresa." Ethan still did not turn to face her. "You are not anybody's baby. No one in this world is going to step forward and give you what you have been looking for. But do not take the cross lightly, Teresa. Only God says that you are His child and He loves you and accepts you. Only God says that. You are not an orphan. I am not an adulterer. We are His children; lost in the forest somehow, for a while. But His children forever." He turned to face her. "The meaning of our lives is buried in that fact."

She tried to pull her mind back from its racing flight from despair, tried to focus on what he said. But could only take the words into a safe, numb corner of her brain and store them. She did not deny them, but could not wrap her mind around them, make them live and change her steps, her heart. Not yet. She could tell that Ethan could see something that she could not see yet. Like there was a veil or filter she was looking through. She could only see the way she had always seen. Through the veil.

He sat heavily in his chair and fastened his teal eyes on her dark ones. "You taught me that, Teresa."

She had known him as lover and as pastor; still the sure intensity of what he told her was a surprise. Or was it new?

"Knowing you so well, wanting you so much..." He did not finish but turned away. "I became more like you – warm, full of life, searching. My rules were not enough anymore. Controlling people with fear seemed cruel for the first time and I became obsessed with filling them with grace. All because of you. I had not lost my faith, exactly, but I had twisted it around into something His love never intended."

"Ethan," she whispered, her tongue caressing her lip, her eyes closing against the impossibility. But it wasn't Ethan; it was her pastor.

"Don't say who you are Teresa, don't look in the devil's mirror and say 'this is how I am.' Only God knows how you are." Pastor Ethan Stone spoke to her with firmness, sureness, like he used to do. But with a love and grace that was new. "People say 'God allowed it to happen' whenever there is sorrow. It makes Him sound mean. The truth is, God is love. If you want to see Him in it, look where the love is."

"And this anger? This bitterness? It's poison, I don't want it..." But she would not finish. She would never tell him. Never. The purity of this new Pastor Ethan Stone only strengthened her resolve.

"A love relationship accepts anger as well as sweetness. God wants a love relationship. We learn, like Job, to accept adversity as well as good from Him. He accepts our anger. When we understand that He loves us, then and only then can we set it aside."

"That's what Davy tried to tell me. But Davy never gets angry."

Ethan smiled. "You're wrong about that. He was certainly very angry when he came to see me."

"He came to see you?"

"To see what my intentions were. To save us from ourselves."

"Oh," she whispered. And then softer, "Davy."

"He loves you very much."

"Yes." Another precious love lost to her.

Silence enveloped them, new tears coursed down Teresa's cheeks.

"You're disappointed about your mother. You wanted so badly to have someone recognize your worth, declare your right to breathe the air. You even had a plan, someone in mind to do for you what a person simply cannot do. No one can justify your existence, Teresa, declare you beloved once and for all. But God already has. Keep that close to your heart. Your mind doesn't grasp it now. But you know it's true and it will seep into your soul and make you free. It will." His face was earnest as a child's and he laid his open hand on the desk as if playing the last best card of a good hand.

Closing the door on the false hope she had pinned on Ethan somehow opened the door for her art once again. Primitive, innocent... like man before tools, before weapons, compelled to draw his life on the walls of his cave. Bigger, bolder pieces, not so perfect and sweet. She left the jagged edges, the unfinished faces where life would not answer the question art posed. And learned to let it be. There were two weeks before Davy was scheduled to be home again, and she filled every day with plans as she painted.

Only days before he was to come, Esmeralda came for the afternoon.

"*Ay*, Teresa," she chided, stepping over the clutter of canvases and easels and supplies. "How can you LIVE in all this..." But her voice died out when she turned and saw the pictures themselves.

"*Ay, mira...* Davy. *Que guapo!*" She drew her breath in loudly and shook her head in silent admiration. Studies of Davy were everywhere, in every stage: pencil drawings, charcoal studies of shadow and light, chaste watercolors, garish acrylics. "They are beautiful," she whispered, leaning over to hug Teresa.

"Thank you, Esmeralda." She dropped her brush into a jar and stepped back to survey the group with Esmeralda. "I didn't start out to draw Davy at all, but once I opened up to begin that's what was in there. All Davy."

"Out of the abundance of the heart, the mouth speaks," she quoted scripture.

"And paints," Teresa added.

"Here's Davy holding a lamb, just like the picture you always see of Christ," Esmeralda exclaimed, running her beautifully manicured nail reverentially down the side of a small painting.

"Look closer," Teresa said, grinning.

"Oh my God, it's a puppy," she squealed in delight. "How sweet!"

"Not just any puppy," she said, pointing to the furry ball asleep on the couch.

"Oh, how adorable. She's yours?"

"Yes, she is. Davy got her for me before he left. For company."

"What's her name?"

"You'll love this," Teresa said. "We named her Morgan."

"For Dad Morgan," Esmeralda exclaimed. "I love it. Morgan. Yes, it's perfect."

"I don't know what I would have done without her."

Teresa's eyes filled with tears. "You won't believe what I've done now."

Esmeralda turned and took Teresa into her arms. "I know, *mi hija*, I know. That's why I am here." She swayed gently and patted her like a mother on the back.

"I love it when you speak Spanish to me, Esmeralda. Did I ever tell you that I dream in Spanish sometimes?"

"*De veras?* Was your mother..."

"No. I found her."

"Yes, I heard."

"*Pura gringa.*"

They both laughed and parted, Teresa wiping her eyes with one hand and leading Esmeralda to a chair with the other.

"Sit. Sit. I'll tell you all about it. How did you know..."

"I have my sources," she grinned.

"Did your sources know about the rest?"

"No, but I can guess. The preacher?"

Teresa nodded solemnly, pulling her own chair closer to Esmeralda's. "But it's over."

"Tell me."

"It was some insane thing I just had to do. Try not to judge me, Esmeralda..."

"*Ay, no, mamacita...*"

And so she told her everything. "I know you tried to warn me. But I fell in love."

"Yes."

"Not with Ethan Stone at first. But with his office. With his position, his strength. It was as if he were a priest and I was some poor peasant girl doomed to follow him out of reverence for his holy office. I wanted absolution from him, justification. Things he did not really have to give to me. I know that now. But he was beautiful."

"Yes, I can understand that. The abortion murdered part of your soul, I know."

"I so desperately wanted forgiveness. Wanted to erase the whole thing." She looked coolly into Esmeralda's dark eyes. "Wanted that baby back."

"The aborted baby?"

"From the instant they scraped it out of me, I wanted it back."

"Yes, yes. I imagine you would."

"You cannot imagine what remorse, what incurable, agonizing regret that was. I had just murdered the very thing I loved and that could love me naturally..."

"Teresa, what are you saying?"

"The holiness, the absolution... the baby. Everything I wanted intersected in the person of Ethan Stone."

"And him?"

"Oh, he wanted something from me too. But not something he would leave his wife for."

"But how?"

"Esmeralda, it's done. It's over. He is a changed man. He really is."

"And you?"

"I am carrying his child."

Esmeralda sighed and they floated silently in the afternoon light, each awash in the enormity of what she was saying. Finally, Esmeralda turned to the sketches and paintings on the easels around them. "And Davy?"

"He knows."

"Is that why he left?"

Teresa nodded. "It is too much. I know it is. But he is due home in a few days. We will have time. Maybe in time he can forgive me. I cannot imagine my life without him."

"No." Esmeralda studied the drawing of Davy's face turning away.

"I will never tell Pastor Stone, Esmeralda. Never. Davy understands that. And I want you to promise me that you understand it too."

"Yes. Whatever you say, Teresa."

"He is back with his wife and everything is as it should be."

"Yes. Only you are alone."

"Just for a few days more."

Days later, when she came back to the little apartment from the grocery, Davy was home, settled into the sofa reading a book. She saw in his posture, as if for the first time, the struggle it took for him to do such a simple thing. She walked over and planted a loud kiss on the top of his head then folded herself down at the other end of the old couch, stretched out and put her toes next to his thigh to warm them.

"Good book?"

He closed it, as she had known he would, nodding in the affirmative.

The lurid colors and bold fonts of the cover gave it away. "A thriller?"

Davy's slow grin answered her testiness. Their disagreement over reading material was not new. "A legal thriller. Murder, mayhem. You know." His grin overtook the muscles of his jaw and turned into a grimace, but his eyes still shone. "Very clever!" He was baiting her now and she knew it.

"I don't think it takes a very elaborate or clever plot to kill someone. Our hold on life is already so tenuous... just let nature take its course." She sighed and stretched and snuggled her toes deeper under his thigh. "Rob anybody of his defenses and he'll be dead soon enough; won't take a rocket scientist to off him."

"It's my chance to be brave, Teresa. I identify like mad with the hero and feel what it would be like to fight off the dark monsters of my own life and be brave."

"That part maybe..." she sounded dubious.

"And the lawyers..." he continued, grinning.

"Don't even get me started," Teresa interrupted, poking him hard in the ribs with her toes. She was suddenly so relaxed and exhausted that already her voice betrayed her with its sleepiness. Had she even slept since Davy left? She could not remember for sure.

He reached over her to the afghan throw on the back of the couch and pulled it down over her legs. She pulled it in around herself, murmuring her thanks, and curled deeper into the worn cushions. "I've missed you, Davy," she sighed.

"Yes."

"It's home again, now that you're here."

"Teresa," he whispered. "I have to tell you something."

Her body stiffened. She could feel the sadness in his voice, his reluctance to tell her what he must. No, please Lord, no. Not Davy too.

"What?"

"I'm moving. They want me to be on the board of directors for CPAS."

She felt the weight of her strained heart and a brief wave of nausea. Not Davy. No.

"Where? When?" She stayed as still as stone, would not look up at him. Would not ruin the glorious moment he had been working towards all these years.

"New York. Right away. They've hired me to run the company during the time they take it public and for a year. Stock options. Contract renewal possibilities. It's too good to turn down. I've come to settle things here and pack

217

up. And say goodbye." He lowered her hand to the sofa beside her.

"Oh." Her voice was a tense squeak and she force herself to draw a deep breath. "Oh, Davy. I am so happy for you." It was too much; the baby was more than even Davy could bear. And now she had lost him.

"I have an obscene amount of money from the IPO already, Teresa. And a salary you wouldn't believe. I want to buy a place for you. For you and the baby. And leave our arrangement with the bank and Jesse for taking care of things..."

"Davy, thank you. You don't have to worry about me. Go and enjoy your success." She finally dared look up at him. "You will come and visit, won't you? After the baby comes?" She told herself to smile, told her eyes to open and close, her mouth to speak, her rigid body to act normal. He had done so much for her; she would not ruin one second of his time, his achievement with her despair. But... How would she live without him?

He took her hand as an answer and they stayed silent for a long moment. Then Teresa snuggled down into the sofa and closed her eyes. "We have so little time, then?"

"A couple of days."

She considered several responses, but let them die in her mind. "Tell me a story, Davy. About Einstein. Something relative." She closed her eyes and snuggled deeper into the covers. "We'll have a nap, then think about all that."

"How about the Special Theory of Relativity?"

"That should do it," Teresa laughed, feigning a light snore.

He relaxed and settled back into the sofa as well as he could. "Everything came from two pretty straightforward assumptions about how the universe works. One, that the laws of physics would obey the central law of Galilean relativity; they would have the same forms in all uniformly moving, inertial, reference frames..."

"It's working; I'm SO relaxed," Teresa breathed deeply and snored louder.

"Second, that the speed of light will be observed to be the same for any inertial frame, needing no other frame."

"Yes." Teresa's drowsy voice chuckled softly.

"Slower velocities such as sound remain relative and the speed of light became a new absolute quality of the universe."

"The speed of light... odd to imagine light even having speed, isn't it? You'd think it was just there... or just not there..."

"Mmmhmmm," Davy willed himself to be at peace, to lull Teresa into his peace with him.

"Can you ever forgive me, Davy?"

"It's not like that, Teresa. You know that."

"Everything in me is ready to love this baby, Davy."

"Yes."

It was as if the tears leapt from her eyes to his now. And the hope and grief and love knotted up in his throat and he was silent.

Teresa gave up hope and burrowed back into the cushions.

"I love this baby already. But I grieve for one... that died." Even now she could not think of how to tell him. Abortion was at once too clinical and too violent – spoke only of the body that was lost, not the precious soul. "When I was so sick..." she faltered.

"Shhhhh," he put his arms around her, rocked her with the sway of palsy and his love. "I know; I already know."

"About my abortion?"

"Yes. I nearly drove the doctors and nurses crazy in Dallas getting what information I could from them. No one would tell me much, but the bits and pieces finally made their own picture." He kissed her lightly on the top of her head and smelled the delicate perfume of her hair.

"I tried to talk to Ethan about it, as a pastor, you know; but I just couldn't. You're the only one that secret baby is safe with Davy. The only one."

He lifted her hand to his face. "Thank you."

"But it haunts me. Part of me is so afraid God will punish this baby for what I did to the other. I know He is not like that, but still... I need to let it go."

Yes. "Did you name that baby, Teresa?"

"They would not tell me if it was a boy or a girl. They knew but they would not tell me. So I call the baby Regret." Tears slid from the corner of her eye and across the bridge of her nose.

"It's all right, Teresa."

"I was afraid that I only wanted this baby to make up for that one, Davy. And I want to love her for herself. She deserves to be loved for herself, not as a replacement or something."

"No."

"But it is only that I mourn the lost baby."

"Yes. I will mourn too, Teresa. We will remember the lost baby. We will remember it, name it, offer it up to God. Share this baby with it and divide our love and it will grow to be larger than both of them."

"That's what I want, Davy. But how?"

"In your heart, Teresa, was the baby a girl or a boy? Just ask your heart..."

"A girl." Teresa sat up, crying harder now.

"And if you could have named her?"

"Lieserl, I think." In memory of the little girl the great man did not want... the man that brought light as the standard of the universe.

Not Regret. Only love that had become lost to them somehow. Only a twist of the impulse that made it, that made the universe.

And Davy found candles and Teresa helped to light them and they named the lost baby Lieserl and amid the flickering shadows as night fell around them Davy read from the Bible and they gave her infant spirit to God. Teresa wrote her name in beautiful flowing script on a piece of art parchment and folded it around a small clip of her own dark hair and Davy enclosed it in the old Bible he had carried since the home. They wrote the date of the abortion on the gilt and maroon plates at the beginning reserved for family trees, then "Lieserl" beside it, and closed the Bible forever.

"It is done forever, Teresa," Davy said, closing the heavy book around the lock of hair. "We will keep it for a treasure, but put it away."

"It is not a secret,"

"No, not a secret. A treasure that only we can know."

A treasure.

And finally, Teresa laid down again, put her head back on Davy's lap and let the exhaustion and peace take her to a new sleep.

"Sing me a song, Davy." Her eyes were closed, her voice dreamy. Her fist lay turned up and open, like an exhausted child's.

And so he summoned the peace from his very soul to relax the appropriate muscles and tendons and vocal cords, and told himself it was only a game, like the computer charts, and found that if he dropped his voice to its natural depth and nearly whispered, it sounded like a song. It was a song; Teresa nodded and smiled. In the deep whisper that came from a different place than anyone else's song, and with the wide vibrato of his palsy, it was new, almost like a hymn or lullaby, but recognizable.

Teresa at last nestled against the warmth of Davy's body and his song.

31

Life isn't worth living unless it's lived for someone else.
Albert Einstein

Teresa's heart fell with each soft thud of her shoes as she walked down the hall to 304B. Bed B was her mother's. Not the brooding angel whose streaming hair waved from the trees, or the snake lady, forked tongue naysaying every turn. No. Just a middle-aged dying woman, skin waxen and yellow with the liver's slow demise.

She stood quietly in the doorway a moment. Rose was asleep. Or in the wide and rheumy-eyed staring stupor that was her life now. Her wrists were still tied mercilessly to the bedrails, acquiescent now, her hands arched, as still and graceful as any of Rodin's. But her pillow had long since sought its own way and Rose's head was thrown back in open-mouthed surprise. Her swollen abdomen, under the taut sheet, looked like Teresa's own, the ascites caused by the failure of everything vital matching the tender arc of the success of the force of life.

Life, Teresa thought, rubbing her own abdomen lightly, where one never sought it nor expected it, nor understood it. But life, pressing itself on you, nevertheless.

There was a force in the room, closed in with the heavy stale air that had been rendered so by the smell of bodily excretions and the chemicals employed to dispel them. At first, pressing her body into the room, gasping for more scarce molecules of oxygen, Teresa did not think she could immerse herself any deeper to approach Rose's bed. She swayed and caught the doorjamb and realized she was afraid to go in. Afraid, in fact, to even put one foot in front of the other. Her heart taunted her with its erratic loping.

"Rose," she spoke finally from the safety of the doorway.

Then, "Mother?" Barely a whisper.

When Rose did not stir she advanced two sliding steps and began again. "I am afraid. Davy tells me I am brave, but I am afraid nearly all the time. It is only my fear that makes me act so brave." She slowly raised the volume of her voice as she neared Rose's bedside until it sounded like the usual bland chatter the nurses used with the patients.

"My fear makes me act cocky sometimes, you know?" She busied herself about the tiny space, tidying up the bedside table, straightening the blinds in the window. Invisible ropes pulled up tighter around her throat. She forced her hand to reach out and smooth back Rose's fuzzy halo of graying auburn hair. It looked as if it had been burned in a cheap perm but Rose had surely been too sick too long to have had her hair done. She barely stirred as Teresa talked.

"I don't know what to do. To do anything, anything at all, might spell the end of me. Do you know what I mean, Rose? Do you?" Her voice and outstretched hand trembled slightly, with anger or with the fear that fed the anger.

Rose closed her mouth with a loud sigh and shifted to find the re-routed air, settling once again into rest. Teresa stood rigid and silent, feeling her own baby roll gently in its watery world until Rose settled into her stupor once again. Joy and pain both pulled at her wounded heart where before there had been only a free fall.

"Ethan was so surprised to find the Devil was not who he thought he was, Rose. Imagine my surprise to discover the same about God. Not, after all, *que sorpresa*, a grouchy policeman I slip stealthily past, eyes averted lest he ask to see my license. Not the Giant in Jack and the Beanstalk – big, dumb, but so strong you'd better not mess with him. Who did I think He was that I would not even meet his gaze, much less grasp the hem of His garment?"

If she had known all this to begin with, she thought, she would not be in this position now. But then this sublime joy, conceived in Egypt, would not be born in the promised land. Grace, once again, worked its eternal mystery. Grace torn from the larger loaf and handed, morsel by morsel, to the hungry. Ethan. Davy.

Teresa.

"But enough about me. As they say in the movies, Rose, where have you been all my life?" The slight tremble moved to Teresa's lips now and the lifelong knot of grief threatened to break its way out. Like a mighty river, wider and deeper than the banks meant to hold it.

Socks are lost; one from every pair. People stub their toes. Flu lays out millions. Cancer sneaks into the hidden cells of one of every four people. Car wrecks claim the only child of doting parents. Strangers put bullets into the brains of babies. And, somewhere within that long litany, mothers leave their babies. Mothers leave their little girls.

What would it have been like, to be loved? Like Mrs. M. said when they found the litter of baby possums dead in the rain gutter: the mother just had 'em in the wrong place at the wrong time... too much rain.

In truth, there had been love. Dad Morgan, who they all clung to like a father, Mrs. Garza, the first teacher who told her that she was smart, the black lady who shared her lunch with her when she sat terrified on the bus. Miss Berrigan, her first art teacher, who gave her hope. Martha Ann... The grace and mercy of strangers had been everywhere.

But the particular love of a mother had eluded her. Teresa stood staring silently at the dying woman lying in submission before her. Tears rolled down her cheeks unheeded as she grieved for the beautiful woman with the streaming hair smiling beatifically down from the trees, pushing aside the clouds with her sighing. Broken-hearted not only for her own lifetime alone but for the days rolling out before her now wallpapered with this yellowed dying memory.

We are who we are.

The words came to her as if whispered on the slant of sunlight stabbing through the window. She reached out and lightly touched the tied maternal hand, covered with dark red bruises and filthy nails, slid her own hand to the swollen belly. She closed her eyes again. Some things are so bad that there's nothing you can say about them. Nothing you can do. Things so bad... all you can do is forgive them. Like the infant Lieserl.

And there was another truth: It wasn't really Rose that was going away. It was the idea that there was safety or security in the world she was losing. Rose was leaving, but Rose's presence would never have fixed her, wouldn't have changed anything. She was doomed from the start to wander the world with a bleeding wound no one could see, and even the beautiful Rose of her dreams could never have fixed that. No.

She could see herself walking along the sandy shoreline of Corpus Christi with that Rose, saying the things that had never been said between them. But still she could not picture the deep layered kernel of shame and fear healing. Could not picture the river of rage leaping its banks and leaving anything but debris.

This poor swollen statue with the tarnished halo of hair, cuffed to the bedrail for crimes committed in a haze of alcohol and circumstance. Her liver paid the price. Her trapped hands paid the price. The poisoned center of her being, floating up in putrid breath, paid the price. Her own baby, standing angry and grieving, paid the price.

Not fair; no.

It would be so simple to lift the errant pillow accidentally, carefully, over the fragile face and downturned mouth...

"I'm thirsty." The startling blue of Rose's eyes, ringed in rheumy red, opened suddenly and Teresa was so surprised that for a moment she didn't realize that Rose was speaking.

"Thirsty," she repeated. And the upturned helpless hands drew their fingers in and opened them out again.

The little ritual of giving Rose a sip of water and a spoonful of ice seemed like it took an hour. Teresa wished Davy were here. Or at least waiting in the hallway. She was working without a net now.

"Maybe I will paint you, Rose." Yellow and red now with darker umber dying all around. Teresa waved an imaginary brush against the canvas of the coarse sheet stretched across Rose's flaccid breasts. Tried to imagine Rose as she was before. Could she, in fact, dimly remember her? Was the fiery cloud of hair the same as this dingy version before her now? Were those gnarled hands the ones she could vaguely remember making little caps of shampoo bubbles with her hair?

Teresa touched the tiny gold heart around her own neck, felt the indentation where the red stone had once been. She stepped back as if from an easel and waved a faint, imaginary line of delicate gold across the vulnerable throat of the painted Rose. She had to keep the lines loose, as Professor Stout admonished her: effortless, flowing, don't want to see the ballerinas grunt, he said. Then a tiny golden heart of forgiveness, the blood-red stone making a red cross of reflected light in front of it all.

Once settled again, Rose turned the unnerving blue gaze on Teresa for a long moment, then away towards the wall, mumbling and waving her hand. Teresa reached across to free the restraint on that side and Rose gesticulated and muttered and then looked back at Teresa in fear.

"What is it, Rose?"

"Angels." She motioned back toward the wall, a surprised smile gradually replacing the fear. She wiggled her fingers awkwardly and giggled an odd throaty giggle. Almost girlish. Rose, nearly absent from this world, participated somehow in the next.

Teresa had seen patients weave invisible works and swat invisible flies in Grace County, but not with this vestige, however dim, of delight in the process. Under the hopeless, helpless, putrid, edematous flesh of this cirrhotic woman was a soul, a soul that still sensed humor and delight. Teresa stood transfixed. She could almost sense a presence in the room too. Rose's delight was contagious, even though her lips turned dusky blue and the distant death rattle in her chest brightened in a wet crescendo.

A young Hispanic nurse came in laden with towels and sheets. "Good morning, Miss Rosie," she called out, too loudly, too gaily, and playfully tweaked Rose's toe as she walked by with her burden.

"Time for her bath, now, Miss," she said again, this time to Teresa. "If you could wait outside a minute."

Teresa started out, obediently, then the nurse called her back. "Or you can stay. I don't think Rosie here minds a bit, do you Rosie?" And she touched her fingers to her own temple and gave Teresa a sly wink across Rose's splayed form.

Rose started and collected her phlegm and what was left of her wits, clicking her dry, cracked lips. "What?"

"Rose," Teresa said. "Rose, it's time for your bath." She freed Rose's other hand from the rail while the nurse prepared the basin and towels to bathe her there in her bed. A bed bath, just a simple morning bed bath like they gave to many patients many mornings.

Rosie's brain was damaged by too much alcohol to ease her pain, you know. But she is still with us." She turned and leaned closer to Rose and raised her voice a bit. "Aren't you, Rosie." Then laughed and patted her shoulder.

Rosie laughed in return, but never looked in their eyes at all. Just mumbled a bit, holding her hand up as if in a friendly conversation. Then said clearly, "Is it Christmas already?" The nurse chuckled a bit.

"Ay, no, Rosie. Christmas is long gone. It's April already. Pretty spring day. April showers bring May flowers."

The tepid water and rough scrubbing woke Rose even more and she talked about people that weren't there, then, clearly, a joke. "What," paroxysms of coughing, "do May flowers bring?"

Teresa and the nurse looked at each other in stunned surprise.

"Pilgrims!" And laughed until she choked again, laughed at her own laborious joke brought up from the dim pit of memories.

"That's a good one Rosie." The young nurse smiled.

Yes. A good one, indeed. How, from the melted synapses in her pickled brain, had it surfaced, intact?

They heard the loudspeaker paging "Ana, Ana, come to the front desk. Ana."

"That's me," she said, apologetically.

"Go ahead," Teresa urged her, leaning over to take the washcloth from her. "I'll finish up for you here."

Ana was only too relieved and dashed out to the busy hallway, leaving Teresa alone with Rose.

She allowed her mind to float away from any notion of Rose and settle only on the physical needs and realities of the moment. A bath for Rose. To wash her, yes. As if warm soapy water could affect the deep poisoned core. And to say goodbye.

"But what would a bath have to do with goodbye, Rose? Huh?" She cooed and talked to her in lilting singsong like to a baby, innocent and ignorant.

For long tedious moments the coma claimed Rose and Teresa had to bathe her inert form like a limp, unwieldy doll, wrestling her as if she wanted to win something from her. Sometimes Rose would laugh, starting the squeezing wet rattle in her chest anew. Or cry softly, moaning and whining barely decipherable words.

Someone's radio down the hall played raucous *Tejano* music and the metal trays and pans and carts accented every beat from the hallway. Rose's roommate, 304A, shuffled around her own bed talking to herself and wrestling with the mountains her age had made of the molehills the nurses referred to as "activities of daily living." Periodically her whining protestations wondered why her invisible visitor hadn't kissed her. "You've been here an hour and you haven't even kissed me." Children or husband or lover long vanished?

"Just kiss her honey," Rose said distinctly in an instant of perfect lucidity. "She don't know where she is." And then dropped back down into the heavy sleep of her permanently anesthetized brain.

Teresa froze and then slowly began to laugh out loud. "Why Rose, you're really in there aren't you?" And the laughter grew until tears streamed down her face and she could barely catch her breath. And Rose chuckled along in good-natured agreement for a few seconds, nodding agreement and waving sign-language to her angels across the room. And they laughed too.

Then there were only Rose's two wretched feet to wash. Teresa bent Rose's left leg up and placed the plastic basin of soapy water close to it, then lifted the left foot carefully in. She held Rose's calf along her own arm, grasping her swollen ankle firmly with her own right hand, washing Rose's foot with the other. Her toenails were thick splitting yellow like hardened old wax; the skin tight and shiny, cracking in places with the edema. Teresa concentrated on that foot, scrubbing at the hardened layers of dead skin thick as a shoe sole.

"Rose."

Only silence and sighing breath.

"Rose, do you remember having a baby?"

"Baby," she sighed clearly.

"I'm going to have a baby soon." She lifted Rose's foot gently out onto the towel and enfolded it there while she carried the basin around to the other side. "And I want to know if you can remember your own baby. Can you Rose?" When she finally dared look up Rose was smiling at the wall.

"What do you see there, Rose?"

Rose reached one hand toward the wall as if clutching something, then, once extended, turned her hand slowly over and opened her palm. As if letting go of a trapped moth.

Teresa lifted Rose's other foot gently over the side of the basin. It was covered with spidery veins and there were places where the skin had finally done what it had threatened to do – burst under the tension of the body fluids trapped in the tissues there. Teresa eased it into the fresh warm water and squeezed washrags full of water over the lower calf. Gently, slowly she rubbed the thick callused soles and toenails, then brought that foot too out to dry in the fresh towel. Slipping a fresh cotton hospital gown over Rose's thin arms, she was sorry that there was no nice clean gown of Rose's own to put on her. Only the cotton one, un-ironed, stamped "*Vista Bonita*."

Teresa rested and surveyed the room and Rose. The stimulation of the bath must have kept her alert, because now she had faded off into her coma again. Teresa folded a crisp new sheet down over Rose's chest and laid her arms on top of it. Then reluctantly retied the wrist restraints. Rose did not resist, but only closed her fingers as if she had recaptured what she had so happily given over to her angels.

Teresa waited and watched Rose as she slept, her putrid aroma already

227

beginning to overtake the pleasant scent of her bath. Then gathered the bundle of soiled linens and pulled back the privacy curtain to leave.

"Hi, honey," the confused octogenarian in the next bed called to her. "You haven't even kissed me yet."

Teresa opened her mouth to correct her, or explain, or... then instead she just walked over to the elderly woman and kissed her firmly on the cheek.

She would have to learn to hold things lightly. As lightly as Rose. Even her own baby. Lightly as Abraham held Isaac. Holding too tight, trying too hard to be safe. That was the danger. Only the cross, as Ethan said, should not be taken lightly.

We are all orphans; somewhere in our souls we know it. Abandoned by love we thought would save us.

"What do you mean, quit?!?" Professor Stout yelled and swung around to face her.

"I'm sorry, I know I've let you down. You don't know how much I appreciate the scholarship and job..."

"Quit," he thundered again, incredulous. "What could possibly..."

"I managed to really mess up my life... Life does swallow art, just as you warned."

"So, what.... are you going to give up art and work on being a well-adjusted good person now, or what?"

"I won't give up my art, Professor Stout..."

"Well, that's something, at least. If you could just give it up, like that, then you were never an artist." He whipped his chair back round so his back was to her again. "Art is what you do because you have to; it drives you and leaves you no choice."

"I just can't work... health problems..."

He turned and stared at her with his maniacal, owlish stare, demanding a better explanation.

"One of which is pregnancy." Finally, the truth was the only thing that would do. He knew no one in her personal circle of friends, no way his knowing could reach out and damage Ethan.

"So?"

"Another of which is a bad heart."

He looked at her even harder, as if his eyes would bore a hole into her. "In what sense?"

32

Be a loner. That gives you time to wonder, to search for the truth.
Have holy curiosity. Make your life worth living.
Albert Einstein

Teresa didn't have the energy to sketch, had lost even the impetus to turn the pages of a book or magazine. She lay stretched out on the old sofa, propped up with enough pillows to give her lungs a boost, Morgan curled in deep doggie dreams at her feet. She would have been short of breath at this stage anyway, petite as she was, but the strain was also beginning to show on her heart. Its weakness left her quivery and tinged with blue around her mouth. The doctors' admonition to maintain bedrest had hardly been necessary; her distended belly left her little choice.

The coffee table was strewn with pamphlets and vitamin samples from her recent visit to the obstetrician and, among them, her Bible. She found that it was easy to be spiritual when you were sick; the most natural thing in the world. Teresa picked up the little cardboard "Gestation Calculator" wheel – no bigger than three inches square – and spun the dial around for the thousandth time. She didn't know why she found the scientific calculator of conception dates and birth weights such a pleasure. The red arrow for *Conception* she had always been able to turn precisely to that day in September when her life and Ethan's had slammed unexpectedly into each other's; their precautions after that made her laugh, looking back. How determined they had been – hell-bent, you might say – and how poised the universe, to create this new life in just that way at just that time. The preposterous unlikelihood made her laugh.

"You know, baby, you were a pushy little thing from the start!" The hard mound shifted and rolled in answer and Teresa laid her hand flat against it to savor every movement. "What were the chances, huh? But there you were, ready to leap into being with no more sense of decorum than that! Well, you showed 'em, didn't you, baby, you showed us all."

What were the odds, after all? The cardboard wheel, the lines and dates and arrows so precise, so scientific, showed the day so plainly, showed that now, in May, the growing fetus was nearly *Term*, weighing around 4 lbs 12 ozs. and was 42 ½ centimeters long. Teresa had no idea how long a centimeter was, but could picture a small bundle that weighed nearly five pounds. The wheel said it would weigh slightly over five pounds in a few more days. Then, somewhere around seven pounds, sometime in early June, the darkest red arrow proclaimed, would come the magic day, the ideal center of the shaded red section called *Term*. Actually, she could spin it to the exact day in June, since she was uncommonly certain about the exact day in September, but the doctors had warned her they might have to do a Cesarean section before that if her heart wasn't holding out too well.

She had begun to lose interest in the wranglings of the cardiologists and obstetricians and internists and surgeons and more cardiologists; her body and mind shut down and concentrated on the one thing they knew now that they must do.

She would, she understood now, have this baby, even if it was the last thing she ever did. And the thought no longer frightened her. It was, in fact, the great certainty of her life. She had spun the little cardboard wheel daily, obsessively, since December, and she would spin it resolutely on until the end. Term, rather. Until the red arrow said *Term*. Whether it would be the end as well no longer concerned her. Let the doctors confer back and forth about that. She knew, for once, exactly what she had to do.

She slid the knit panel of her pants down and the cotton blouse up to expose the whole rounded curve of her belly. The navel was totally extruded, even lying down, and she pressed one finger to it just to watch it spring back like a tiny water balloon. Jagged slashes of wine-colored stretch marks radiated out toward the bones of the pelvis, all pointing angry red fingers back at the guilty navel standing there exposed and ridiculous. She reached for a squeeze of lanolin from the debris of the coffee table, smearing a dot of it slowly, gently around the hard mound. Odd to feel the skin so fragile and taut over the rock-hard burden within.

It was an incredible joy to watch her body do the very thing for which it had been fashioned. The bones of the "pelvic girdle" – pelvis and hip joints – loosened, then sank into a new configuration under their weight. She sometimes had to stop a movement and re-create it with the new angles in mind, or they would creak and pop in protest. Her breasts, nearly twice their former size, were sprouting tiny silver striae of their own on the sides from their weight. A thin dark line had appeared near the navel and disappeared into her dark pubic hair, a line straight and fine as if the doctor had drawn it on for some specific medical purpose. Would it go away after the delivery, she wondered?

The skin of the tight mound glistened with the lotion and it was easier to see the contours, almost possible to make out the baby's position. She imagined it often, sometimes accommodated by the baby's swift kick or slow roll, little clues it sent as it swam in its secret world. Well, its swimming days were over now, as it was getting a little pressed for space. Now it was just a little stretch and slow roll to the other side. Or kicks, right into the solar plexus, sometimes down into the bladder.

"Wake up, baby," she whispered, pushing gently on the larger side with the palm of her hand. Running her flattened hand down firmly, pressed into the lotion-slick flesh, she thought she could make out an elbow or knee, some tiny hard ball of flesh that rolled slowly by.

The phone rang. Esmeralda.

"Teresa? Were you sleeping?"

"No, just lying here building dungeons in the air."

"You OK? I haven't heard from you lately..."

Suddenly, Teresa felt the baby's familiar thudding roll, punctuated with determined kicks. Now on her right flank, then all over.

"Swell," she whispered, stock still so as not to break the determined little gymnastics. She moved her hands to new spots, as if picking out messages from beyond on a ouija board, one painful letter at a time.

There was nothing for her to do now but wait.

Hours later Teresa woke only enough to realize she had been asleep; the radio was still softly playing. She let the darkness claim her again, the words of the disc jockey a blur but for the name Madonna. "Like a virgin," Erotic lyrics undulated within the sly, slutty whispers of her voice, "touched for the very first time." *Mm, hmmm,* Teresa laughed. Just like a virgin. Who would want to touch what had been touched everywhere by everyone?

And then she fell away again into sleep and dreamed of virgins and whores. Never like the rock icons said it would be. Always filthy afterward. She knew.

But no. It wasn't like that. She gripped the hard crystal of her own innocence, and Ethan appeared in her dream. Even Jesus wasn't mad at the harlot, he told her; He was mad at the sanctimonious men who judged her.

Then there was Rose, floating supine, fixed, now, in her hospital bed for all eternity. Rose leered at her with twisted red lips in her dream.

Deeper, deeper, Teresa's sleeping soul elegantly guided the dreamer. "No good," the voices whispered. "A failure; no right to live, anyway." Her body pulled back, aware of the anger and lust and sorrow it had carried for so long.

In the dream Ethan put a jeweled robe around her shoulders.

And then left her. Alone.

Mrs. M.'s voice intruded, uncommitted, stilted, like a public radio announcer: "I always wished you were my little girl..."

But her loneliness was the loneliness of the very planet she clung to, floating in the blue fluid of space, sorrow for gravity, spinning forever in silent loneliness and shame.

She was a little lost sheep. No. A slut. Touched for the very first time...

She woke up because her heart had stopped.

But it hadn't stopped, had only kicked her hard, once, in the chest, and then refused to beat again for so long that the alarm sounded to the cells of her body. Once, twice, it kicked again, then rolled and begged for the oxygen it lacked. Teresa could only lie there, past fear, and contemplate her dreams.

Morning was announced by the birds twittering around the hibiscus and oleanders outside the window. The first light, still rosy and ethereal, forced Teresa's reluctant eyes open. Morning. May. As she rolled to her side and forced herself to sit up, the slow rolling of her abdomen reminded her: *Live.* Put one foot in front of the other. *Live.*

Before she could make her way back from the bathroom, the phone's shrill ring broke the rosy peace of morning.

"Teresa." It was Mrs. M. Hushed, contrite. "I'm so sorry to disturb you, honey... But I knew you would want to know. Your mother passed away last night." They were both silent a long while, then she added, as if to be sure Teresa understood: "Rose is dead."

Teresa leaned over to turn the little radio up louder to listen to Ethan's sermon. She pretended that she was there in person, rustling with the congregation, coughing with them, and bowing during the prayer segments. There... and yet enclosed in her apartment... with her artwork and her ruined esteem.

Then Ethan's resonant voice began with a prayer asking all to realize their presence in the Lord.

Teresa shifted heavily, tried to picture Rose in the presence of the Lord, laying aside that putrid flesh. Laughing as she did, in spite of her awful life. Teresa remembered her crusty laugh more than her ruined flesh really. Then Teresa leaned over to arrange her paints on the little table next to her. Ethan's voice seemed different. Like a new Ethan; almost as if he wasn't the same man.

She smeared wide brushstrokes of deep blues on the pad of art papers, then smeared the heel of her own hand through them where a sky could be, blotting them repeatedly making faint shapes of paler blue, like clouds. Then held the finished print away from her and angled it in the light. A good beginning. Did it need a dark figure somewhere on it, experiencing the blueness?

"Some of you have an orphan heart," Ethan's voice rose, the little radio buzzing a moment with the increased volume. "Some of us are wounded by the sorrows of life."

It was as if he were there with her, leaning across into her face to make his point. Teresa's heart sped in earnest now. Was it really Ethan?

"God has already adopted your spirit, it is safe in the holy of holies. He is adopting your soul too, where it sits alone in the innermost rooms of your heart and mind. Someday, he will even adopt your body..."

Teresa could hear him pause and then hear rustling sounds.

"Last year, when my son died," he began softly. The rustling stopped as if the congregation held its collective breath. "I looked for comfort everywhere." Still no one stirred; they too had looked everywhere for comfort.

"People," he said into the microphone.

Then: "Friends."

Then, softer: "Brothers and sisters." A bare whisper. "We all have wounds and losses and sorrows in this fallen world, don't we?"

Teresa could hear several of them cry out "Amen."

"I know and love you all and have for many years. But I was never open enough, not buried in the Lord's ways enough. And now I know what brings us to Him closer than anything else and keeps us clinging to His garment more than ever. Our sorrows. Our needs." She could hear him step away from the pulpit and move down closer to them.

"You all know how much it hurt my wife Elizabeth and me to lose our boy." His voice quavered and Teresa stilled completely, knowing there were tears. She could picture him staring out at the sea of faces that reflected his own sorrow. "And I know many of you have lost treasures like we did."

A few soft sobs filled the hushed silence.

"But we are all still here, aren't we? Loving the Lord who has taught us the true riches of our lives." He paused again and the silence of the congregations was as hushed as her own. "And now we are learning to share our losses and sorrows while we live as unto Him the best we can anyway."

A few more sincere *amens* went up again.

"Lord we know those beloveds we lost in this life are with You now. And we choose to live out our days best we can, trusting You to keep them until we are with them again." The silence was only broken by a few sniffles.

"And Lord," Ethan whispered, "we all have our own crown of thorns just as You did… whether it's loss or shame or sorrow or pain. We carry our own crosses as You did Yours. It makes us appreciate the eternal love and enormity of what You did for us." He stopped a moment, and Teresa could picture his tears falling.

"Lord, we know this world is fallen. Full of sorrows we cannot change. Blues we can only sing, not remove. But we trust You to turn them all to Your good somehow. Whether it is what we did wrong or what was done to us, You turn everything of us believers to Your good, as it says in Your Word."

He was silent a moment. Then a faint murmur went up and steps could be heard. She could picture him walking back up to the podium, then pausing and turning back to the congregation, reaching his large hands out, palms up, smiling around the damp tears still glistening on his face. Then starting his sermon.

"I learned recently that even Einstein lost his first baby. No one knows for certain what happened to her. Seeing quotes from a recent museum exhibit about him that included that sorrow, I felt a desire in my heart to know what helped his blues. Still crumbled in my grief, one of his famous quotes caught my attention: 'There are only two ways to live your life. One is as if nothing is a miracle. The other is as if everything is a miracle.'

"I remember leaning back, thinking of our broken hearts and my own shame and sorrows in response to it, then something of that lake of sorrow began to shine in my soul instead. I could feel our little boy's smile envelope my tragic unraveling because I was driving the car when the wreck happened. And leaning over him as he died. Too great a wound back then. Too much. But now the Lord's Word saying: "ALL to His good" and that smile of my son shining in my soul... well... no words. Different.

Then the truth of that verse was able to shine light into that dark place in my wounded heart. The Lord doesn't cause the bad things. But He does turn them to His good. Our way? To hear His will and do it. We may not see the eternal value of that in this fallen world. But someday? Forever? We will.

"So, I am learning, beloved brothers and sisters here today. I am learning. And praying you can too. There is a beauty underneath the sorrow. A way we have not traveled yet. I am beginning to learn my way. And I am praying you all begin to learn yours as well.

"So our Lord's Word for today says the very thing we need to know and live in: Open your Bible to Romans 8:28. *We know that God causes all things to work together for good to those who love God, to those who are called according to His purpose.*"

He was silent a moment, then closed his Bible. "Let us know that and live in it best we can. It is the meaning and the way to survive and live as unto Him."

"God has given me the greatest gift he can give to a pastor – the ability to feel the pain of my people. My heart was broken." He waited and Teresa held her breath along with the congregation. "Is your heart broken, too?"

It was almost as if she could see him, his fair hair a dot of light against the darkness of the stage behind him, his words spilling out like blood. She looked at the marks underneath her hand, at the darker silhouette she'd added against the darkness of the sea behind. Her stage. Her blood.

"I didn't need anyone to tell me what I had done." His voice grew fainter for a bit. "And you don't either." The faint rustling of the crowd was like dim applause. "We know how our hearts got broken, don't we? And we know where we have looked for comfort."

A few dared a faint "Amen." Teresa nearly whispered it herself.

"A friend told me once: 'I'm not afraid of God so much; just the awful things people say about Him.'"

Teresa shivered at his reference to their exchange.

"People," he nearly shouted again. Teresa froze along with the invisible congregation. "God did not break our hearts."

No, she barely nodded. And the congregation waited in mute submission to hear their shepherd's voice.

"But he cracked open Heaven," and there was a loud slap that could only be Ethan's open hand on the pulpit, "and poured out mercy for everyone. Comfort is UP, people. Not to the right or to the left. Comfort is in the love of God. The God of all comfort."

Yes.

"Even Einstein had a certain wisdom about that in his remark, didn't he? There are only two ways we can survive our sorrows. Knowing everything is lost. Or believing God turns all of it to His good. There are only two things Goodness can do about evil, after all. Stop it. Or redeem it. If God had stopped it He would have doomed us to be robots instead of beloved children with free will. And people..." His voice was nearly a whisper now. "Think how we love our children." The rustling swelled, showing that they were doing just that. "We want them to have everything. Everything. Even freedom. But how can we keep them safe? Where could we keep them, what could we do, to keep evil away? Put them to sleep and set them in a glass coffin like Snow White? Build them a tall castle tower like Rapunzel's? We don't want that for our children..."

Teresa's lip quivered to think what it cost Ethan to put words to the pain of his own loss. Words that his people could put like salve on their own wounds.

She could see her own mother, Rose, free to drink and abandon her child and then just fly away on the undiscriminating wings of an angel. And herself, free to condemn her or to wash her feet. She could see Ethan and herself free to look for comfort where they could, regardless of the consequences. Free to look up, after all. Free to mourn. Free, even, to run into the sea that could devour them.

"You don't have to say His name out loud," Ethan was saying. "Or a certain way." No one moved or coughed, no organ music faded mechanically in and out. "Just say it."

Yes.

The rest was a blur.

"Keep looking up," the shepherd admonished his sheep. "Up, up, up." And the piano and organ swelled into a crest that carried the myriad voices as they sang:

ONE GLAD MORNING, WHEN THIS LIFE IS O'ER
I'LL FLY AWAY...

The taped message was cut off there, to conform to the radio time slot. The obligatory music faded and gradually turned into the normal business agenda of radio, while Teresa sat and wept. Wept for the shiny brass so easy to mistake for gold. Wept at the humility of being loved. By Ethan. By Davy. By God himself. So easy to mistake sex for love, so easy to mix alcohol with it until you couldn't tell life from love from disaster. So easy to come back... so heartbreaking that anyone would love you enough to still be standing there when you did.

Ethan, in revealing himself, had revealed the truth. The pristine simplicity of it was like clean mountain air. A child's simplicity. Her own simplicity, before the world cracked and ran out like a great fetid egg. The world that she had been trying to scoop up and put back in its delicate shell ever since.

She wept, even without knowing about the rest of the service that the trimmed recording left out. Without knowing that Ethan told his people goodbye, that he and Elizabeth were going back east near her family. His intention, he told his rapt sheep, was to be chaplain at a large teaching hospital where God had called him to be what his degree said he was – a spiritual doctor. Where he would comfort others in their sorrows the rest of his life.

In the huge concentrated complex of human suffering he could stand with people in their sorrow, hold the hands of those leaving this world and shy of the next, hold those they left behind. Say yes to the boiling cauldron of pain he had before only denied or judged. She could not see that his eyes and the eyes of his people filled with tears, that he came slowly down the steps of the stage from his pulpit and joined his people at the altar. That when he knelt, his people herded in around him like winter calves in the cold.

All she knew for sure was the Lord's best gift of love in her whole life... Davy. She wept, afraid she had lost him. Davy... Davy. The only desire of her heart was for Davy to be the way the Lord turned all their sorrows to His good.

Then she was felled by the pain in her abdomen and lack of oxygen as her heart began beating erratically. She grabbed her cell phone and called 911.

33

The years of anxious searching in the dark, with their intense longing, their alternations of confidence and exhaustion, and final emergence into light—only those who have experienced it can understand that.

Albert Einstein

The delivery room, already filled with more people and machines than seemed possible, filled now with the cold, salty smell of blood and cloying animal realities. The exact same smell, if she could force her senses around the grim medical intrusions, of any animal giving birth in any cardboard box. Teresa swam in a blur between the huge pressing waves of the hydraulic panting impossibility of pain and the dizzying, dropping troughs of drugged relief between them. A dark curtain waited, threatening always to fall over her mind, but she willed it back, strained to push out the compact living reality into the cold, buzzing room, teeming with the effort to keep her alive.

By the time the baby finally appeared, the array of people flocked around the delivery table were more interested in Teresa herself. A grim doctor, swathed in green cap, mask, and gown, caught the baby in green sheets, swung it, floating, in space a moment, then deftly passed it to the nearby nurse, also in green. A forest of baby-catchers. They barely remembered to shout *"It's a girl!"* to the semiconscious mother panting in exhausted ecstasy.

Teresa strained to see over the green sheets draped around her raised knees. She watched the baby's tiny face, at first shut tight against the rude passage, explode into a screaming protest that shook its bluish tinged body into red health and filled its lungs with this new, waterless life. A girl. Still trailing clouds of glory, or only the ropes of umbilical cord, not fragile, like in the maternity book drawings, but knotted and strong and still pulsing, strands of red and blue and flesh like a garish party braid. Then she was free.

They wiped the baby roughly and wrapped her tightly in her own white blankets. The nurse wafted her briefly by Teresa's head so she could see for herself that she was perfect. Then took her off to the side to put drops in her eyes, a plastic hospital bracelet on her tiny ankle. Teresa could hear her shrill screams punctuated by gurgling sobs as the nurse sucked out the mucous from her minuscule nose. Then away. Somewhere far away where even Teresa's determined ear could not follow.

They kept her awake a moment longer as they kneaded her abdomen until it produced the placenta, the bloody, gelatinous mass with which she had sustained her infant daughter for nine months, now trash for the steel bucket. Then she slept or fell away into darkness.

"Cardiac Tamponade," the young doctor pronounced to the sheaf of papers and charts before him and the tight group of medical personnel surrounding Teresa's bed.

"Yes, Rose's Tamponade," concurred the older doctor, looking up over the top of his reading glasses.

The cardiac monitor buzzed loudly, and the nurses scurried to reset it, looking to the doctors for orders.

"Ventricular arrhythmias stepping up now..."

"Let's set the lidocaine up a bit."

"Yes. Reset the pump for..."

"We're up to the max now; we'd better get ready to make a move before we get an arrest and lose her right here." Their voices picked up volume and pitch in alarm.

"Prep for pericardiocentesis?"

They all nodded reluctantly, weighing the risk of letting Teresa's exhausted heart go on like this any longer, versus subjecting it to the added stress of the surgery to remove the fluid building up in the sac around her heart. Watching the downhill slide of the EKG readout, they gradually relinquished the hope that it would improve or even out. Clearly, something had to be done. But in her weakened condition, and with the blood loss from the delivery, no one was anxious to try.

"It's a no-win situation," they moaned, even as they set the flurry of activity into motion that illustrated their choice. They had to try. With hope or without it.

"Another 5 mg of morphine?"

"No, can't risk any more, respirations are pretty shallow already."

"Okay, let's get her prepped. Make sure the kit has a 16-gauge needle and a stopcock."

"Will it be subxiphoid approach?"

"Yes; prep here," the older doctor said, making a loose circular motion over Teresa's chest.

Teresa, weak and drugged, listened as if from a great distance to the flurry of efforts to save her own life. But what little force of will was left in her mind she spent on the memorized perfection of her baby girl. It was like a dream, but the tiny screaming body, covered in blood and something white like smeared cottage cheese, was too graphic to be anything but real. Nearly bald, pink right away with screaming rage at the abrupt entry into the bright, cold world. Trailing the pulsing rope of cord. Her baby. Her own body had done what she willed it to do; she had produced a perfect baby girl in spite of the odds. The perfect pink goodness that survived the dross was pushed out into the incredulous world.

She could barely remember the struggle now, the endless parade of doctors and nurses arguing her case before some unseen magistrate: would the continued labor be harder on her heart than a Cesarean section; what messages did the stubborn little fetus send through the wires glued to its prison walls to receive its vote? The rest was a narcotic blur. She didn't even think of what it had cost her, only took her mind around the miracle over and over and over again until the weight of joy pressed on her heart and became too much.

The oxygen hissed and sighed softly as it misted around the mask lying loosely under Teresa's chin. The heart monitor made its ceaseless beeps and blips and clicks, and an occasional alarm when Teresa's vital signs didn't please it. The various noises blended together into a comforting, melodious song, a song the nurse bathing and attending Teresa did not seem to enjoy. She frowned at the streaks of the monitor, charted its disappointments, cursed softly at the IV pump. Then she bathed Teresa's face and torso and painted a rusty colored liquid over her chest.

Teresa became more alert with the bath, oddly euphoric. The nurse – *"Emma Garza, LVN"* the gold tag gleamed – expertly laid aside the wires and catheters and tubes to scrub one arm at a time, then the torso. It helped Teresa shake off the effect of the drugs and the incredible fatigue. She pushed aside the stiff coil of green plastic oxygen tubing and mask.

"You better keep that on, honey," Emma said, replacing the hissing tubing. The rough white washcloth hung up on the gold chain around Teresa's neck, snagging badly enough to stop her for a moment.

"We need to take this necklace off," she said, as she picked the single offending white thread out of the loop that held the tiny gold heart to the chain.

When she finally freed the tiny heart, she leaned down to inspect it more closely. "Must be pretty special to you."

"Yes. It was my mother's." Teresa's voice was barely a whisper, but it felt good to have a conversation with another human being, after being talked over like she wasn't there most of the night and morning.

"You feeling a little better now?" Emma asked. "Long night." Then laughed a big, hearty laugh, raspy like maybe she was a smoker or had an old cold. Her graying hair was in a big, loose bun and her large bust made a smooth line with her stomach and abdomen, giving her the look of a very competent Victorian lady.

"*MMM-hmmm*," Teresa answered sleepily.

"Can you remember having the baby? You had a pretty rough time of it..."

"Yes." Teresa said, her voice a weak whisper. "A girl."

Emma laughed her comforting laugh and snapped out a fresh hospital gown.

"Is my baby alone? When do you think I could see her?"

"Soon enough. You need to rest now. And I can personally guarantee you, that baby won't be lonely. There's fourteen brand new people squirmin' around down in that nursery, practicing their crying for when they get home. Don't you worry."

No. Her baby was not alone. She was sure she could remember the tiny heart of the necklace swinging from her mother's neck as she leaned over her. She could certainly remember waking up in her crib, crying and crying as no one ever came. Crying until she didn't care anymore. But not her baby.

"I don't like to be alone," Teresa whispered. To Emma, to herself, to God.

"Well, you're not alone now. That baby came out yellin' and that's good; she'll stick. Not one person who ever lost a child got over it – not even God – so be glad yours is yellin'." She laughed heartily and snapped the clean sheet in the air over Teresa's trembling body.

"Do you speak Spanish?" Teresa asked Emma weakly.

"*Pues, si, mi'ija,*" Emma smiled down at her.

Teresa smiled and closed her eyes.

She could remember endless echoing empty rooms, rooms where she looked and looked for Mama, rooms where she waited but Mama never came. Endless nights at strangers' homes, fear filling her throat so she could not sleep, could not eat.

"No. Now I have my baby. Babies change everything, don't they?"

Another nurse came in holding a sheaf of papers and another clear plastic bag of IV fluids. "Emma, are you about done here? The doctor wants us to run her blood gases one more time and get her up to surgery as soon as they call." She hung the plastic bag – *Dextrose 5% in Water* with an assortment of added things scribbled on a label with black felt-tipped pen – and wrote something on a piece of paper taped to the wall.

Teresa kept her eyes closed, listening, and waited for the other nurse to leave before she asked Emma what it all meant.

"It means," she answered brusquely, pulling up the stiff new top sheet and blanket, "that you're all cleaned up and prepped for surgery." She laughed and patted the taut sheets and then Teresa's leg. Maternal; competent.

Teresa liked Emma's comforting presence, her hearty laugh. Something about her made her feel that she could tell her anything. Everything. And she would stand, both feet held square and solid with the ground by the heavy, white-stockinged calves. She could tell Emma that she had known the danger a pregnancy would be to her heart condition. Her broken heart. She was sure she needn't tell her there was no Mr. Chace, her chart was no doubt clear on that. She could tell Emma all that though; nothing would ruffle that solid, resolute energy.

Maybe she could even tell her how she had looked for her mother everywhere. Lovers, strangers, the wind. How her mother grew and grew until she had loomed over everything, larger than life. How she sometimes glimpsed her in the trees, hair streaming out behind her in the breeze, mouth opening with the largest branches to say... To say what? Now she sometimes sees her there, hovering on the horizon, head draped in veils. Now she never looks at Teresa, knowing that her opportunity to please her is gone.

Could God be her mother instead? And she, Teresa, someone's baby at last?

And then she dozed again, her blue lips relaxing into a slack smile, dark hair left in damp ringlets by the mist from the oxygen mask.

There was a soft tap on the door and an old Hispanic man peeked in. When his body followed they could see that he was a priest. "*Hay, perdon,*" he apologized, realizing it was the wrong room. Then, thinking again, he approached the bedside. "You are Catholic?" His smile conveyed a sincere wish that by some miracle she was.

Teresa smiled and raised her open hand to him. "No, but I can use the help."

"You have problems, *mi hijita?*"

"My heart. I am going to surgery now, for my heart." Teresa's words were thick with the narcotics and she was dreamy, eyelids weighted and gently closing between sentences.

"*Ay, que lastima.* You have a church? Or you want that I pray with you?" He chose his words slowly, halting and careful to find the ones he was sure of in English.

"Yes. And yes," Teresa smiled.

"My prayers, they are in Spanish. That is okay?"

"The best," Teresa nodded. He was as old as her grandfather in her dreams, her *Papi*, the one who loved her and held her hand.

They bowed their heads and she was swept into the lilting cadence of Spanish supplications. When at last he finished, he smiled again and patted her hand. "*Seguro que no eres Catolica?*" His smile now was mischievous.

"We were raised Baptist," Teresa began dreamily. "They always made a big deal about the cross being empty because we serve a risen Lord. They made it clear that he wasn't really in the bread and wine..." She touched the beads of the oversized rosary hanging at the old priest's side, ran her fingers lightly over the raised body of Jesus there on the cross at the end. "But to tell you the truth, I always missed the weight of his body on that cross; his presence..." Her words spaced themselves out slower and slower, her eyebrows fighting off the heavy lids. But by the end she was asleep.

Teresa slept and dreamed of Davy. And he reached his strong arms around her and held her...

"I don't mind dying, Davy," she whispered. "Really I don't." They held their breath and froze.

Her lips, in their grayish blue circle, pursed once, then didn't try to talk again. She slept. Life, once it makes up its mind, really is insistent, irrevocable. How could it have been only one year? It was as if her whole life had prepared her only for this. And now it was all leaving her. Or she was leaving it. Ebbing slowly away. The nurses were kind, careful to avert their gaze as they sifted through the array of hardware around her. But she could feel her own heavy, erratically loping heart. Her broken heart; overwhelmed and broken, finally, with rage at the inevitability of loss. Her heart, exhausted by the best thing it had ever done, ebbing slowly away. Well, then. Let it be. She would rest. And continue with the dream.

In her dream she now floated down a river, slow, deep, treacherous. She was alone in a small boat. Her mother, her hair a reddish gold halo around her head, called her from the shore. Her face was blotted out by the bright light. Teresa got closer and her mother helped her step over onto the bank, firm and lush. She knew for the first time what it was to belong, what it was to be safe. Then she woke again. And remembered what it was to be alone, enveloped by fear.

"Say my name, Davy," she murmured in her sleep. "Say my name a hundred times."

It was even colder in the operating room. The snap of rubber gloves and beeping equipment and frenetic hustle and bustle evened out into a blur that she was barely aware of in her drugged sleep. She could feel them pushing, pushing on her chest, the sting of a needle. And the tense commands of the doctors.

"Steady, steady. Keep the suction constant now!"

Freezing; the deepest cold she had ever known.

"I feel the pulse from the sac now," one doctor begins, tenuous. Worried voices concur.

"Pull back...."

"It's clotting."

"Oh, God, no."

"We're getting some serious PVC's here guys."

"Stand ready to defibrillate if necessary."

"Lot of fluid here; suspected there would be."

"Blood pressure *casi nada men*; give her some *Levo* and up the IV. Can you work faster? She can't take much more."

Finally there was only blackness. And the terrible cold.

I hadn't realized how many sounds were in the world until I began to rise. Then there came a moment when there simply were no sounds. Now I look out over rolling foothills and a distant mountain range, all bathed in the purple haze of evening, and realize there is no engine noise, no effort noise. Just a floating heaviness, like the instant a ball reaches its nadir and turns to fall, that split second, stretched out into long velvet minutes. I am weary, yes. But not tired. Bone-weary like you get from life and its cares. Weary of the search for love and the empty blackness of the freefall without it. Weary of the fear and weary of the anger that leaps from fear. Weary of the very weight and smell and feel of my own flesh; happy to just lay it aside. Go home. Home to mercy, to tenderness.

But memory jerks me awake in strobe-light milliseconds and I do not want to leave new love. Don't let it happen again, God, please. Never again. The small comfort of the holocaust survivor: Never again. No number tattooed on my forearm to remind me of the pain. Just remembered pain, stored away, not in words, but in electrical impulses, enzymes, little chemical tracings like the glistening trail of a snail, nearly invisible but for a certain glint of the light.

I don't want to love anyone too much. And then lose them. I am so tired. It is too much. All I ever wanted was love. Intimacy. With God; with Davy. To open my palms and lay them flat against his, press my mouth to his mouth, my body against his. To know and be known. Will God's own blaze make this flame of my desire grow pale? Does He wait, patiently, lovingly, to envelop my tiny flickering flame in His blaze? SOFTLY AND TENDERLY the old hymn says He is calling us... COME HOME, COME HOME, YE WHO ARE WEARY COME HO-O-OME, he invites us. The weary and the meek. Davy. Who, like Einstein, assures me that mass is interchangeable with energy and cannot be lost, only changed.

Now that I do not make an effort, I can do anything. My own light has dimmed and the darkness is evident; I can see angels glimmering, feel the light smiling touch of true affection. No voices mock me here, no evil waits, polite, discrete, to destroy me. The beauty, the stillness, the effortless satisfaction, they are gifts. Because of love. The angels say so. I could not see them before, while my own light still burned.

I feel my heart failing and wonder why it doesn't hurt. It's like being pinned under a great crushing stone, but it is not pain. There is nothing to do but lie back and let God name me and meet my need.

In this silent world there is a pool, like dark glass, filled with my own tears, reflecting back to me the image of someone I never knew. I was right about one thing: mirrors are a lie. There is only one mirror that is not the devil's.

I am what I am, and in the closing moments of my life I nod and say Yes. Yes to joy, Yes to pain. Yes to the God who sees my suffering and brings me home to Himself with only this eternal Yes carved into my heart.

One star, blazing, falls away from the others. I am taken away again, yes, by angels fierce and proud.

Not because I am lost, but because I am loved.

34

When you feel a little better, you must make a drawing of her.
Albert Einstein
(after the birth of Lieserl)

Ethan Stone's large frame, even without the usual dark suit, seemed out of place in the small group gathered outside the hospital nursery window. He was taller and blonder than the young Hispanic fathers, and solemn compared to the beaming young mothers walking gingerly up and down the hallway in new bathrobes. His new calmer spirit was evident in his casual shirt and slacks and brown leather loafers. The stiff formal preacher air of his usual black suit was gone and he was another tender-hearted man just looking at the babies.

He paced up and down in front of the glass, hands in his pockets, then finally settled into a spot not taken by new parents or hospital workers stopping by to cheer themselves at the sight of those glowing bundles of new life and promise.

Once or twice he nodded to doctors or nurses who thought they recognized him, though without the dark suit they weren't sure. Then a slow hum built around the nursery as the nurses put babies near the window to be admired up closer. The people congregating on Ethan's side of the glass scanned for their own babies and exclaimed passionately to each other, mostly in Spanish. Ethan studied the rows of identical little clear plastic bassinets. Then remembered when his own Matthew had been born and there had only been a few...

But no, he would not think about that.

He shifted awkwardly from one foot to the other, jingling the loose change in his pocket, scanning the beehive of activity inside the nursery. Then settled his gaze on the neat row of tightly wrapped forms. Past three shocks of wild, black hair and one round face red with the frenzy of crying, he spotted her. Slightly smaller, less hair than the rest. The black lettering on the bassinet card read: "Baby Girl Chace, June 21, 5 lbs. 3 oz., 18 inches." His heart thudded and he looked away. At the other babies, at the efficient nurses working on the technology surrounding those babies. It was, simply, too much.

"Oh, excuse me," a young woman smiled up at him. In her rapture with her own crying baby, held up for her by a smiling nurse, she had backed into Ethan standing there frozen and misty-eyed.

He turned to her and acknowledged her apology with a smile. She was so young; too young, surely? But no, Elizabeth had looked just the same – flushed, happy and yet cautious – when they had stood admiring their own tiny creation. And so young. Their wedding portrait looked to him now like a pair of children dressed up as a bride and groom. Yet they too had been 'old enough' to produce Matthew. They had picked out the name already...for Ethan's father and for its biblical meaning of "gift from God." No "Baby Boy Stone" for them.

Ethan stood motionless until the young woman touched his arm.

"They're calling you," she said softly. "Which one did you want to see? Which baby's yours?" She smiled up at him, and let her own happiness spill over to share his own. Compare, perhaps, or share compliments. But his frozen teal eyes of sorrow made her step back.

"Oh, thank you," Ethan forced out the words. Trained, by background and profession, to be cordial, it was habit that carried him into action and he successfully turned his head to face the glass. His hands, still in his pockets, were sweating fists. There was no help anywhere and the smiling nurse was asking the same question with her raised eyebrows: which baby did he want to see? She was ready to show him the selected baby; to lift it from its small plastic cradle to meet him face to face. If he would only say.

Finally, after what could have been seconds or minutes he took his hand out of hiding and opened it, out toward the smallest, pinkest bundle, the one without a name, "Baby Girl Chace." And answered the nurse with what he meant to be a smile. The nurse expertly picked the baby up and brought it up close to the glass, holding her almost upright so that he could see the startled milky blue eyes

249

open, the tiny rosebud mouth work in silent effort. The baby's translucent skin reddened with a fussy cry, then paled again as the shining eyes dropped back into sleep. One tiny arm escaped the tightly wrapped blanket and hung relaxed, its ID bracelet huge and pristine around the frail wrist. The nurse shrugged, as if to apologize that the baby didn't want to perform right then, and Ethan's head dipped in the slightest nod of thanks. The nurse installed her back in the plastic box and went on to the waiting couple behind him.

He was glad the nurse was gone, relieved the baby was asleep again; couldn't bear to see the tiny eyes open again, filled to brimming with the milky blue of heaven. He would have swooned to see the perfect rosebud mouth work for nothing another instant. Sleeping, she was safe. With the dedicated strangers all dressed in blue she was safe. Whatever sorrows lurked about stopped at the brightly lit world behind the smooth, pristine glass.

"Baby," he whispered through the hard, cold glass and into her sleeping infant soul. And heard her sweet sigh even as he smelled the milky, baby scent of her wafting magically through the impervious glass. He let his stare slide slowly sideways and rest, fluttering, on every baby. They were all wrapped tightly as a papoose, their tiny tadpole bodies too small in relation to their heads that lolled weakly atop the tight blankets wrapped around them. He remembered the curve of Matthew's head, soft and pink and pulsing with warmth, like the inside of a new bunny's ear, and how it felt nestled against the palm of his own hand. So fragile. Lord, so fragile. Then he slid his sad eyes back to the one bundle that called to him. A moment where his soul felt the heartbreak.

All five of Ethan's fingers touched the glass as he now whispered to the sweet new soul of his infant daughter. His fingers, trembling with emotion, steadied him against swaying or even fainting, as he leaned toward the fragile perfection within and sent it his own life and will. At first leaden as he remembered his own tiny Matthew, he warmed and swelled into a steady beat again, and finally lifted up to soar with the possibilities before him.

"I didn't know about you, Baby," he whispered. "Didn't know you were coming into the world." Ethan heard the clichéd words in this new light. This baby was in this world. The same world he lived in. His baby.

But no, not as simple as that. This baby's mother had not even wanted him to know about her. Only Davy had been moved, finally, by the gravity of Teresa's condition, the peril of the baby with no name, to call him.

"Pastor Stone," he had said, no mention, no intimation that he had ever been anything else. "You need to help us." The unmistakable quiver and strain of

Davy's voice had been like a stone on his heart. To hear it again, after so many months. After so many things... And such an odd choice of words. Not a request so much as a summation of fact.

"Teresa is dying. She's in the hospital; she's just delivered a baby girl. You may remember about her heart condition; the doctors had recommended that she never have a baby." Because Davy left all the conclusions to Ethan, it had taken some moments to realize.

"David?" he had stopped him.

"Yes?"

"Teresa just had a baby?"

"Yes.

"Mine?"

"Yes."

"The baby is alright?"

"Yes."

"But Teresa is dying?"

"Yes." Their staccato dialogue had sounded like confirmation of a telegram. "I flew in when our friends called, but she was already in surgery when I got here. The doctors are doing some kind of procedure on her heart now, but they gave me no real hope." His voice was cut short by spasms of palsy or grief or both.

"I see." His own heart had rolled in sympathy. No hope. Why hadn't she told him about the baby? He groaned aloud at the dizzying reconstruction of events. Nine months ago. September. His baby.

"Teresa thought it was best if you didn't know," Davy had said simply, as if reading his thoughts.

"Yes."

"But now, in view of everything," Davy had stopped, overcome either by his own grief or the spastic betrayal of his own throat muscles.

"Yes?"

"I am trying to think of what is best for the baby."

"Yes."

"And I wanted you to pray. For Teresa."

Well yes, he thought, staring into the bright nursery. Babies change everything. His fingers still touched the glass as if rooting him to the spot. The nurses had said Teresa was still in surgery. Their looks told him how bad the situation was. He would stand here and wait with her baby then, wait and pray with her baby girl. Like he had with others, like he did all the time at the hospital with his flock and their families and heartaches. He would wait and pray. And try to forget that it was his baby too.

Inside the nursery there was a fresh flurry of activity; new doctors, carts rolling in and out, a janitor to mop the floor. Ethan watched the janitor squeezing the murky water of the mop bucket, making sloppy strokes there in the pristine blue world that seemed dirty, contaminated. No matter how safe and pure the environment, there is always filth. Even babies can be contaminated. Even in their perfect, fragile luminosity, there was nothing to keep them safe. Even if you took them from their pure blue world and kept them safe at home, still evil would lurk or tempt or grow unnoticed in the far corners. Anything could happen in this world. As it had for his young Matthew.

"And if your mother does die, baby," he whispered. "What then?" The tiny fists worked the air a moment in futile answer.

Ethan had told Elizabeth everything. But he had not known about this.

"Elizabeth," he would begin, softly, breathless.

"Oh Ethan!" she would cry when she saw the baby. He knew she would. "How sweet!" And she would reach her arms out to take her from him.

And they would sit very close and he would tell her the rest, the part he hadn't known.

"I didn't know how you might...." he faltered in his fantasy. "If you would want to see her," he would say. Yes, like that.

"Oh, Ethan," Elizabeth would sigh.

"After all we've been through," he would hang back, let her make the move, decide for herself how it would be.

"Ethan," she would say softly. "She's just a baby... her mommy is gone. Her father...well..."

Ethan felt saddened. And he bowed his head and prayed for Teresa, their baby, and for his own much-needed forgiveness. He prayed for the Lord's best for them all.

The people in the cooing little group inched away from the tall, brooding man standing so close to the glass that his reflection faced him nearly nose to nose. Maybe there was something wrong with his baby, they speculated softly, seeing his tears. They moved away discreetly, to leave him in the silent dignity of his sorrow, managing to celebrate their own joy and hope without intruding on his grief. Ethan stood stock still and oblivious to their quiet concern.

"I love you, baby," he whispered into her soul with his own. Loved her with a fierceness that made his heart thump harder in his chest and his breath go shallow as everything went dim and unsteady. He had loved his wife and son with the kind of love he learned from watching other fathers – his own father, friends' fathers, fathers in movies. And he had loved Teresa in a healing way – against all will, against all judgment, against all probability. Something in him had softened then; his passion for Teresa, his sin, his guilt, all led him through a narrow place he would never have gone. Back to his first love, the God he had not forgiven for his own tragedy. Even this pain, this stone over his heart as he watched the innocent bundle before him, was love. His pastor's heart had spoken the Bible verse "God IS love" to so many healing souls. Now he felt it in his own broken one.

"Pastor." Davy touched Ethan's arm lightly.

"David." He flinched a bit, then turned and held his right hand out to greet Davy. The left hand slowly abandoned the glass and wiped away the dampness on his own cheeks.

"Teresa?"

"She's still critical. No news." The straining economy of Davy's words was more noticeable than usual.

Ethan only bowed his head in answer; then reached out and held Davy's arm.

"Did you see the baby?" Davy asked.

"Yes." Turning back to the window, then ever so slowly back to Davy, he spoke the words on the card: "Baby Girl Chace, June 21, 5 pounds, 3 ounces, 18 inches long."

Davy turned in towards the window and rested on his crutches; he seemed small and exhausted next to Ethan. "She's asleep."

"Yes. They look like little footballs, don't they, all wrapped up like that."

They stood there several minutes in silent prayer; for both the new life before them and the one that might be lost to them. Then Ethan spread his fingers once again in a mute salutation to the tiny sleeping baby. The other watchers moved around them, their speculations stepped up dramatically by the addition of this pale newcomer to the mystery already growing around Ethan and the baby.

"David Hurt, please. Mr. Hurt." The nurse's crisp voice broke their peace as it boomed out into the hallway full of possible candidates. Ethan stepped in behind Davy's lurching rush to the white oracle.

"You are David Hurt?" The nurse registered surprise and then quickly tried to cover it with a brisk review of the chart in her left arm.

"Yes."

253

"Dr. Hinojosa is looking for you." She turned her smile up to include Ethan, standing just behind Davy.

"Teresa?" He and Ethan both froze.

"The doctor said to tell you that it was touch and go, but she is stable right now. I'll tell you the truth; I thought we'd lost her. But they were able to drain the pericardial sac. Well, I'll let him explain. We'd better get you back up there to intensive care." She looked at Ethan and back to Davy for some indication of their intentions, then, seeing Davy's grimace, futilely trying to hold back the tears, she busied herself once more with the chart.

Davy turned back to Ethan and leaned into him with one great jerking sob of relief. Ethan reached out to Davy's shoulder, silent but gentle, lifting his face and other hand up to Heaven in gratitude. Their eyes met and both whispered with relief: "Praise God."

"Yes." Davy was gathering his muscular impulses up into the energy necessary to go down the hallway with the nurse, back to Teresa.

Ethan's hands gripped Davy's shoulders and their eyes met in a moment of grace and understanding. "She mustn't know I'm here, David."

"No."

"I'm so grateful that you called me. Thank you."

"Yes."

"Please call me if you need anything, anything at all."

"Yes."

Ethan's hands held him there a second longer, then dropped. He could tell they understood each other and it was Davy's blessing and his loss.

"God bless you." And he turned back to the window and began to walk away. David would need his privacy to pull himself together and start the long walk back to Teresa. Ethan wanted to see the baby once more, as he knew he would never see her again. He could hear the creaking rattle that marked David's progress, then it stopped and the writhing effort of Davy's voice floated back to him.

"Her name is Pearl."

Ethan turned to him, a question on his face.

"The baby. Teresa named her Pearl."

"Pearl." Ethan repeated it to him.

"Yes." And he resumed his rattling, lurching journey in the wake of the nurse.

Ethan lifted his hand out toward Davy's retreating back. "Thank you."

Then turned back to the window, his heart loping now with his daughter's name dancing unfettered in his mouth. Pearl. Yes, and what great price. It made him smile. It was so like life. So like Teresa. So very much like God. The tiny perfection in the window was Pearl. An object of such fragile, delicate luminosity that he could barely stand to look at her, but tough and durable and full of the unbearable beauty and grace of God.

The nurses were starting to roll the bassinets with their famous celebrity occupants back into their work area. Ethan stepped up to the window just as one nurse closed the blinds, but, seeing him there so desperate, she opened them and signaled him with an open pinch of her fingers that she would give him another minute.

Another minute. To sort out the facts, the possibilities. To say what he needed to say to the tiny soul before him. The Pearl of great price. A huge breath filled his lungs, sobbing quickly beneath his loosening diaphragm to fill them beyond even that, stretch them into accepting the extra capacity of air. A tiny stretch and shudder from the baby echoed his own, and charmed him anew with the precious mysteries of life.

He thought of Teresa and the trail of her sorrow searching for a mother she could barely remember, hoping for something she would never know, her heart broken afresh at the dissolute reality she found.

"Pearl," he whispered, alone now in the bright hallway. He touched his fingers to the glass once more. "Your mother is going to be all right."

When you get to the center, he thought, there is always sorrow. The chewy nougat center of life. Hard, disappointing, yet somehow sweeter than you'd think.

"You be brave, little Pearl." His voice was a whisper, and a prayer. "Always know that you are God's own baby. Our flesh failed us, your mother and I, and we are not what we would have been. But there is grace in the world, baby Pearl, and I lift you up into it." Ethan's hand turned palm-upward and in his mind, in his soul, he held his baby there and lifted her into the love and good will of the Lord and the unseen angels. The thinnest gossamer web separated him from his young, laughing Matthew and this new tiny Pearl, and they were all – --his boy, this baby, himself, Teresa, Elizabeth, Davy– --suspended in it forever.

Never mind that he must leave her there. In his own soul he knew, with certainty that a perfect love, for Pearl, for her mother, would leave her without the sullied presence of the father she need never know. That, except for David's phone call, even he would not have known. Unbearable sorrow to leave her. Unbearable joy to know.

Already the plans were made for him and Elizabeth to move back east. Ethan would be a chaplain in a large hospital there, a "spiritual doctor." He would sit with people in their pain and sorrow, even as they left this world. And it would be his penance and it would be his healing. God's justice would also be his mercy. He would see to it that baby Pearl never lacked for anything; there were ways to accomplish that for her. And he would wait. Someday, maybe....

No. He would not let himself even think of it. It was all up to Teresa and the merciful Lord who had spared her life. He, for his part, would go where God had already called him and the work for which God was preparing his heart. And, if God were so gracious, perhaps he and Elizabeth would be blessed with another child of their own someday. Or they would adopt. This baby now in front of him would be a secret gem – a pearl in fact – tucked away beneath the surface of his new life.

The nurse tapped on the window to indicate she would be closing the blinds, visiting hours were over.

"Goodbye, Pearl," he whispered as he waved. He memorized her simple beauty, the sacred scene, putting her into his heart. There he could love her as he wished.

The nurse was satisfied when the tall, enigmatic man finally waved. She dipped her head to him and took away the yawning bundle, thinking the man could see her again tomorrow, shutting the blinds on his last desperate gaze.

And the angel that talked with me came again, and waked me, as a man that is wakened out of his sleep. Zechariah 4:1

35

Einstein's general theory of relativity implied that the universe must have a beginning and, possibly, an end.
Stephen Hawking

Teresa could see herself lying there on the white bed like a sleeping princess. The dark hair and skin now paler than ever, pale as death; she might be Snow White in innocent sleep, waiting only for a kiss. Darkness lay on her face like a pillow that would not let her breathe.

"*Duermete, duermete,*" voices came to comfort her. Sleep, sleep. "*Duermete, mi hija.* Sleep my daughter. *Ay, ay, ay,*" they cried, rocking her past the whispers.

Te vas a caer, mamacita. You are going to fall.

Ay, ay, ay.

And she did fall; fell away into the darkness.

She was a confused fledgling in her nest. Strangers, remarkable in their kindness, saved her. They may have even loved her; who could tell?

Who are you?

Who were you afraid you were?

Child of God. Child of God. Child of God.

No. Reject. Misfit. Miss Lonelyhearts.

No. Child of God.

"Live," she protested to the darkness, the memories.

Then the crushing certainty that she did not deserve to. Never a doctor or a lawyer. Or butcher or baker or candlestick maker. Not even anyone the world would call "artist." What did she matter to the world?

Barely, by sheer force of will, she opened her swollen eyes, squinted them against the bright lights, shining like the sun. The world was too real to live in; she could see only a crooked metal cross. Or was it a crutch?

She dropped back into the world of dreams, all indigo and umber, where her lover beckoned to her from the shadows. She strained to see his face, could see a red rose he held out to her, or the petals of a red rose, falling from his hand, like blood. There was a heavy hum, like a huge piece of machinery hidden far away, then she felt herself lifted as if in a huge electromagnetic field, silent but powerful; like levitating.

She slid down the rough sheet of the hospital bed until her toes touched the cold vinyl floor; her heart faltered and the pain swelled. "Touch me," she gasped, and touched her own chest with the fingers of her right hand. But her lover's lambent glow made him faceless and he did not move toward her.

Crying, she tried to contort herself into someone who could be loved, tried to imagine what was required of her.

"I'll do anything you want. The only thing I ever wanted was to be loved. To go to a safe place where I am loved…" tears drowned her voice.

Her lover – or was it an angel? – shimmered, then pulsed in a beat of radiance that raised the hair on Teresa's head. Then led her to another world shining on the horizon just outside the hospital window, outside the mirrors of this world. The air there was like Van Gogh's – visible, curling around her in great churning swirls and eddies. Every object was outlined in dark lines of certitude. She reached for her angel-lover, afraid she could not breathe this other air.

"I am afraid."

"I love you," the radiant being answered.

Then the heat of the sun burned the mist away, drying everything around her and sending it up into plumes of dust. It settled about her, huge dunes of sand like finely ground glass, pure and dazzling. She was alone in a strange land, small and lost and far from home.

"There is so much sorrow."

"Yes."

"There is nothing here; nothing to offer you. I do not even know where I am."

"I love you," it answered again, turning to her.

Why?

Does Love need a reason?

What is love?

This is love.

Is love whose face I see when I close my eyes? Or when I open them?

Yes.

Her own will was swallowed up into the will of the power that bore her. Teresa could feel the knotted bands that bound her to her sorrow, then the greater power of the stranger's love. His invisible hand pulled away the loveless past and she could hear it snapping like bands of heavy cord, or the deep roots of tenacious weeds pulled in a great grunting sweat from the earth that clutched them.

A moment of floating uncertainty and then she was free. Gone the ceaseless anxiety of searching for the one right answer to every question. Free in grace larger than that. The God of Yes. The God of love.

His hand reached around behind the free will He had promised to never usurp and brought mercy. Ethan had tried to tell her. Davy lived it out before her every day. Her own child's heart had stayed small waiting for it.

Freedom. She knew she could never take another step in the same old way. She was lifted out of the old life and into a new one, opened her eyes into a world so still and perfect it took her breath away before she realized she did not need to breathe. There, in front of her, was a beautiful girl... no, a woman... her breasts ripe and her countenance radiant. And with a sweetness, and tenderness that was so exquisite it brought tears to her eyes. And she saw tears slip from the lovely woman-child's closed eyes. She sighed with pleasure as if in a dream, turned a bit to loosen her gorgeous raven hair from her floating robes of light, and settled back into her dream. Who was this stranger... this celestial beauty sleeping in this strange world? This beautiful dreamer?

Teresa reached to touch the perfect cheek, unblemished and soft as a new petal on a rose. And the stranger lifted her own languid arm to match her.

A mirror. The perfect beauty was in a mirror.

Teresa began to smile and the mirror's echo was resplendent with the joy of it. She lifted her hands to her own tangled hair and saw the beauty do the same. This was no stranger, then. Then was she herself, Teresa, made perfect in this other world.

When she looked again there was a table in the wilderness. A banquet was laid out for the crowd that came and went. An old man with silver hair and laser beams for eyes separated himself from the crowd and came toward her. His hands opened up toward her, palms up, and then he blessed her. Said with her the prayer from childhood, to her Guardian Angel: *Angel benignisimo de mi guarda, tutor mio. Maestro, guia, ayo, defensor...* And a benediction that gave her to understand its own blessing: *bene*=well, *dictio*=speaking. A benediction speaks well of another.

"You are my beloved granddaughter. *Mi hijita.*"

And then she knew him.

"*Papi*," she whispered in delight. Not frail and thin like she remembered him in the mist, but like him in every way that mattered. He led her toward the crowd at the long table, pausing only to show her a placid pool of water, like a mirror, where yellow and white ducks floated in serenity. And when she stumbled he put out his strong hand and steadied her, whispered directly into her soul: "*Duermete, mi hija.*" The love that whispered her to sleep all her life was *Papi's*. Her own laughter echoed like rippling water in that distant world.

Pulling her into the crowd he covered her shoulders with a robe of light and she was as they all were. Wordless. Content. And warm for the first time in days. Papi stood behind her, holding her shoulders, and turned her to face a mirror of crystalline perfection. She too was a being of light, white and pure and new. Herself, only reborn as a princess of light in this new world.

Music filled the air instead of voices. There were words between the guests, but not spoken ones; words fulfilled somehow in the will of one toward another. To speak them was not necessary. No nuance or language or inflection to spoil the intent.

And there was Mrs. Matrisciano, barely recognizable; young, relaxed, laughing. She had no rules to enforce, she was a guest. She turned and lit up with pleasure to see Teresa.

"I always wished you were my little girl." Her eyes shone with it and Teresa knew that it was true.

Rose was there, too, young and robust, innocent as a lamb. The deacons from church too, conferring in tight little circles, and Ethan, and Ethan's lovely Elizabeth, moving among them with little cakes and encouragement. And *Papi*, her grandfather, lost in the mist for so long, his eyes blazing with the love that was just as she remembered it, just as she left it, even after her memory would no longer hold his face. She was always his "*querida Teresa.*"

A radiant hostess glided among the crowd, serving platters of steaming food, filling glasses. When she turned to them Teresa cried out to see her old roommate from the dark days in Dallas:

"Martha Ann!"

Her hands, beautiful flying doves, small, perfectly shaped, were everywhere laying out comfort like fairy dust. Her eyes shone with a burning brilliance that had replaced the deep pools of sorrow. *"I will take care of you,"* she said. And she did.

She could see her friends from the home: Chaya and Robert and Luis and La Dona Carmen, resplendent in jewels and robes of white light. It meant nothing whether they were living or dead, everyone her heart had ever known was there, though, like Peter Pan, she sometimes did not recognize them. The doctors were there, satisfied with the papers they trailed, the nurses, the old couple she held the door for in Dallas. Old Mrs. Kincaid, even.

"There are no dead," she cried out.

No, her lover agreed.

The long wooden table was covered in white linen and napkins of white linen settled everywhere like sleepy doves. There were great silver platters of food. And fruit pies, still bubbling through slits in their golden crusts. And baskets of fresh breads, yeasty smelling, their crusts gleaming. People were seated, dining. The sound was muffled like in a great carpeted hall, busy but subdued, silverware tinkling off in the distance like bells.

The elegant old man led Teresa to a place prepared for her and the others served her there – rich soup, steaming and creamy. Her host, standing at the head of the table, rose and extended the loaves of bread, his joyful smile dimming the others with its brightness.

"Davy?" Her breath would not come for a long moment. Was it her own Davy? Tall and whole; gone the crutches, gone the glasses his earnest blue eyes swam behind. Gone the lurching misappropriated intention of every movement. Here was a young man, tall and muscular and sure of himself and his every movement and sure of what he intended for her and his guests at the table.

"Teresa." When he spoke her name with that soft reverence, she knew it was him. She rose and stood before him, touched his face, moved into his arms. He laughed, deep and resonant, picked her up as effortlessly as if she were a little child, and held her. Her own laughter melted into his and the other guests fell away from them in a circle.

"You smell like flowers," he told her, smiling.

The thought came to her to open herself up to whatever she had been afraid of for so long. She had always loved him, always known he loved her. But his brokenness, like her own, had made her afraid. How could they meet each other's needs around their wounds? Yet their love for each other was always there.

They returned to the table and drank a cool drink and passed the basket of bread, each breaking off a serving for another until all were satisfied. They came and went, each at their own pleasure. Teresa ate until filled and then took a piece of cherry pie, hot and dripping in red juice, served tenderly by Rose, who knew it was her favorite.

Full now, it was her pleasure to rise and serve others, newcomers who continued to trickle in and find their places, even babies. All were served and satisfied. She passed often by the chair where her Davy sat handing fresh warm loaves to the new guests. She touched his hair, coarser and longer now, caressed the fabric of blue linen over his broad shoulders, brushed the full, happy curve of his lips, parted to smile at her. Her Davy; how could it be?

As they gathered, all dressed in fine linen, she looked up and out at the distant horizon, glowing like a sea of glass. Then a glorious cloud rose up out of it. At the center, a huge crowned figure of light rose up and spread its arms. Small figures emanated, glowing in colored lights, then separating and swirling in and out closer to her group. All smiled and nodded and raised their hands to them, gathering some of them to their own hearts, then opening their arms over to Teresa, then up towards the distant figure that turned back to them, eyes blazing with fire. Pure love. They all knew.

They swirled over to Teresa and encircled her. She could feel the perfect love emanating as she reached out, and knew, in her heart and soul, it was the baby she had so regretted aborting. Her tears came, yet the angelic presence touched her and swept them to itself. The love and forgiveness was unmistakable. "God is love," the whispers in her soul said… and the others coming and going about them, sang the most beautiful music Teresa had ever heard. "We never knew anything else but love. Our sorrows are for those who knew the sorrows. We will surround them with our love when they are here, broken by their sorrow and regret."

Then they all swirled away in a cloud with their beautiful music surrounding them. As Teresa sat back, overwhelmed with joy and awe, Davy rose and brought a newborn baby to her and laid it in her arms. It was beautiful and perfect, glowing as a pearl. Davy reached his powerful hand to stroke the baby's velvet skull, then kissed her tenderly on the cheek.

"Isn't she beautiful?"

Her love was a tight knot around them both.

"Perfect," Teresa whispered.

Davy's warm breath brushed her face like a kiss.

The beauty of the infant Pearl broke her heart, then filled it. She was weak and helpless and yet pulling love toward herself with all the power of the universe. Davy enveloped them both in safety and peace. Gone the days of loneliness. Gone the evil whispers.

"Davy, I always loved you." A tiny bloom of regret pressed her heart, sorrow that she had not been free to love him before.

"I know."

"I could not give what I did not have."

"No."

"I am ashamed to ask you to love me now."

"I love you."

Then her arms were empty again.

Teresa turned back to the hospital room, ever so small and dim now on the darker horizon on the other side of the dark glass. Almost she could see into the desperate little room. Almost she could feel the anxious tempo of the hallways full of rushing people. Almost she could see into the brightly lit nursery where little Pearl cried and waved her tiny fists at the loneliness, the white plastic ID bracelet loose on her tiny wrist. Almost she could see into the heart of the nurse who would carry little Pearl to her mother if her mother were only stronger, if her mother would only heal.

Teresa caught her breath and turned to the happy throng. "I have to go back."

Yes, they answered, smiling. It was all as it should be. She did not have to search for God's plan, the meaning of her life. She herself was God's plan. She was who He wanted where He wanted her just when He wanted her to be there. Just so.

She turned back to the hospital. There was Deacon Carpenter and Mrs. Carpenter with him, holding a gift for the baby. Teresa could see how those good souls would be like family to her and her baby.

And Mrs. M., prim and officious again, waiting in the lobby to see Teresa and hoping to see the baby. Professor Stout, stern in his pardon. And even Lencha, Carmen's daughter, crocheting a blanket in the most shocking, electric pink she had ever seen, with yarn she bought with the last of Carmen's egg money. The consolation of these and the others – Dad Morgan, Chaya, Jackie, her Davy – lay scattered at her feet like treasure.

And she could see beyond the dim hospital with its clanging misery, out into the world with its ubiquitous suffering. Martha Ann, stooped and shamed, healing from or going toward disaster. "Don't be ashamed," she called to her. Martha Ann's eyes stared blankly, bovine, then dropped in shame. "I love you." And Martha Ann's tiny ivy, now full and luxuriant in the kitchen window, arms open to the light.

It was, she knew now, no small thing to be loved. The thing her art could only hint at, that the endless attachments were only a shadow of. Love. Someone to tell us we're good, not bad. Protected, not abandoned. Safe, not in everlasting peril. Even in its pale disappointments in this life, it was no small thing to be loved. It was glory enough to be able to live in this world with the dream of the other. Strangers, pilgrims, like the Hispanics and Anglos of the Valley, neither sure whose home was borrowed, their will and identity divided but intertwined. Shining still, like Chaya's candle burning in the safe harbor of the *Avila Children's Home.*

No, it was no small thing.

"I must go."

Yes, Davy agreed.

"I do not know how I came here."

"The one who brought you will take you home."

"I don't want to leave you."

No.

Pearl's tiny little cries were louder now; louder than the peculiar music that filled the air. Louder than her heartbeat. She realized her arms were empty.

She turned to Davy. "I must go."

He leaned down and kissed her with a warmth and loving assurance she had only ever imagined. And then stepped back away from her, his guests with him. "Don't look at the light," he told her, his finger lifted in admonition and good-bye. The ring of endless light pulsed brighter, as if to keep her.

"Pearl," she cried out into the dim distance.

Teresa felt her weakness and pain return, like a leaden cloak she must wear. "I am so weak," she told her lover-angel.

"Yes," whispered her lover. "I love you." And he carried her. She heard a sound like thudding wings.

"I might be like this always, until the day I die." She looked down at her hand, its small whiteness, impossibly frail, held aloft only by the power of the stranger. It was Martha Ann's hand. Then she understood.

"I will take care of you."

Yes. Laughter like bells.

Coming back was the hardest thing she had ever done, a long, wearying trudge through iron layers of gravity pressing in on her until she wanted only to be light again. Coming back was a tunnel that grew darker instead of lighter. Dying, like oil painting, worked from dark to light; coming back was like her beloved watercolors, requiring a painstaking working from light to dark. The light – dancing, numinous – was at first a blaze of white, then shone like streaks of new paints newly laid out on her palette: Indian Yellow, Rose Madder, Viridian, Cobalt Violet. It became cold again and air whistled in her ears like arctic wind. Then crimson faded into rich plums and umber. The shadows were gray and bled into sepia, and indigo, then black.

Her heart was a bruised stone, unwilling and full of uncertainty and pain. But still she came back. Hope shone more radiant than memory. And as she trudged through the emptiness, suffered the black free-fall, she wondered why. Why come back at all? She had only her will to give. And chose to give her will to God.

And she remembered. The baby. Pearl. Her baby. Her chance to be what she had never had: *Mama*. Not even God got over losing a child, Emma had said. And Teresa smiled to remember her screaming Pearl. She would give Pearl what she herself had never had, and, in its passing, partake of it somehow.

Falling, falling.

The free fall again.

She reached out to the angel. This time it took her in its arms and held her. She closed her eyes against the pain and darkness, felt the solid body quivering, as a dove held a moment against its will, warm and feathered. She could feel herself drawn to the place behind its arms. The place that said it loved her.

This is who I am and only this, she murmured to herself, lest she forget.

This is who I am and only this. Remember the dream.

The shuddering angel sighed and held her closer, warmed her against its own silky breast.

The pain was so crushing for a moment she didn't think she could draw a breath. But she had to go to her baby, her Pearl of great price. That loss was the guarantor of love. That there was only a fragile, crystalline bridge between the living and the dead and only love could cross it.

She knew now what it was like to love someone so much that you would die for them.

"Touch me," she whispered. The brightness of the lovely dream world pulsed slower and dimmer until the room she lay in, on her crisp white hospital bed, became brighter and solid once again.

The angel touched her.

"Hold me." The angel pulled her closer, held her in warm, quivering certainty.

"Say my name a hundred times." She could feel the angel fluttering, pulsing, pressing its own warmth into her cold body.

"Teresa."

Her eyes flew open and she realized that Davy held her, his muscles roiling and writhing in determination to meet her need at any cost, his thick dark hair, slightly longer than she remembered it, brushing her own cheek.

"Teresa," he forced his unruly voice to whisper into her ear.

"Davy," she whispered, surprised that he could be in both worlds.

"Davy... I know who you are..." She tried to hold onto the memory, wrap her sleepy mind around the split reality. She wanted to share the dream with Davy.

"Yes," he whispered, having known her all along.

And slowly she realized she could not remember what the dream had been. Only that she was not an orphan, not a slut. Martha Ann wasn't a mental patient, Davy wasn't disabled, Lieserl wasn't Einstein's abandoned daughter. Only that they were all God's children and that they could never out-sin His grace. She remembered only that someone said she was good, not bad. Only the primal satisfaction and the feel of Davy's strong, steady shoulders under blue linen. Only that she was loved. Had always been loved, even before she was wounded. That she could give her wounded, imperfect love and it would be redeemed. It would be enough. That the world would dress you up and call you anything, but only God knows your true name.

"Davy," she whispered, pulling his warmth into her frozen body. She had always loved him. But lost love was the only one she ever understood; doomed love. Now, in the new bravery of the other world, it came to her that love might mean pain, but that she could hurt and live. It wouldn't kill her.

"I did not think you could forgive this, Davy. A baby, on top of everything else. It is too much..."

"You have the unfair advantage here, Teresa," he said, eyes lowered. "I have never loved anyone but you."

"I want to explain..."

"There is no need."

"What I wanted from Ethan was impossible: his identity, my lost baby back... to be more important to him than God.'

"I love you," he whispered, barely breathing. Love made the air between them sustain her. Love would have made it into water if she had been a fish and into fire if she were the sun.

She nodded and could feel his tears against her neck.

"I tell you the truth, Davy," she whispered, stroking his hair. "We are who we say we are. Child of God. Artist. Friend of man. I say we are a family, Davy. I say we are."

Again his hair nodded against her cheek.

She held him to herself fiercely, willing her own heart, stronger now, to fill him with her strength.

"Davy?"

He pulled back from her to search her face.

"Kiss me," she whispered.

"Are you asking?" he smiled, holding her face in his hands.

"Yes." Her arms tightened around him.

And it was as if she had never been kissed before. Everything she needed and wanted was in his love and now she could receive it. The purity of his love would keep them all safe. She didn't even need to ask about his love for the infant Pearl.

"Now I know what love is," she whispered, smiling.

"The baby needs us." Yes, Pearl needed them. Needed the two broken people who loved her, who were willing to create perfection for her out of their own broken pieces.

Yes, Davy's steady blue gaze answered, hungry for more of life than he had ever dared imagine.

"I feel so much stronger. Go see if the nurse will bring her to us."

Yes.

"We can do this, Davy." Teresa, with her strengthened soul, Davy with his resolute body. They could now offer the infant Pearl what neither of them ever had. Offer it to her clean, to love her, to save themselves. To cement the world.

How? his eyes asked, frantic for a moment.

"We're a family," she assured him.

His blue gaze wavered.

"Because of this love. Because… we say we are."

Yes. The confidence that had shone there for an instant suddenly returned and lit up his countenance. Davy made his rattling, determined trip across the corridor to scoop up their tiny Pearl.

Find out more about Kathy Egbert and the other books she has written at www.kathy-egbert.com.

www.ingramcontent.com/pod-product-compliance
Lightning Source LLC
Chambersburg PA
CBHW022152170626
46807CB00005B/2178